Loving Chloe

Also by Jo-Ann Mapson

Shadow Ranch
Blue Rodeo
Hank & Chloe
Fault Line (stories)

Loving Chloe

A Novel

Jo-Ann Mapson

FlamingoBooks
An Imprint of HarperCollinsPublishers

Grateful acknowledgment is made to Margot Liberty for the use of her poem "Epitaph," copyright © 1994 by Margot Liberty, previously published by Gibbs Smith in *Graining the Mare: The Poetry of Ranchwomen*, Peregrine Smith, 1994, edited by Teresa Jordan.

HarperCollins books may be purchased for educational, business, or sales promotional use. For information please write: Special Markets Department, HarperCollins Publishers, Inc., 10 East 53rd Street, New York, NY 10022.

FIRST EDITION

Designed by Elina D. Nudelman

Library of Congress Cataloging-in-Publication Data

Mapson, Jo-Ann.
    Loving Chloe : a novel / by Jo-Ann Mapson. — 1st ed.
      p. cm.
    ISBN 0-06-017217-7
    I. Title.
PS3563.A62A82   1998
813'.54—dc21   97-20578

98 99 00 01 02 ❖/RRD 10 9 8 7 6 5 4 3 2 1

To Deborah Schneider, my agent and friend,
whose courage in matters of the heart
is both enviable and inspiring

She never shook the stars from their appointed courses,
but she loved good men,
and she rode good horses.

—MARGOT LIBERTY, "Epitaph"

Acknowledgments

The writing of this book was greatly enriched by the friendship, support, and expertise of Stewart Allison; Jack Mapson Allison; Walter Lee Bennett; Susan Blandlin; Gil Carrillo; Sara Davidson; Earlene Fowler; Cynthia Gregory; Dennis Hallford; Lois Kennedy, M.F.C.C.; C. J. Mapson; John Mapson; Maria Elvira Nava; Martin Nava; Jennifer "Polo" Olds; my "adopted" father, Don K. Pierstorff; Nancy B. Scheetz; Floyd Skloot; Alexis Taylor; and Daisy Tint, M.D. The privilege of working with Sue Llewellyn, my copy editor, and Terry Karten, my editor, is a writer's dream come true. They are patient and wise women, always cheerful, always available when I need them most, and are cherished beyond words. My theatrical agent, Sam Gelfman, made a simple request that provided the gift of a "map," allowing me to envision the story's structure and its inevitable destination—thank you, Sam. Last but hardly least, I am indebted to the animal kingdom, particularly the redwing blackbirds who squabble at the feeder outside my window and the hawk who shakes them up every afternoon. When I look up from these pages and witness that world, I am humbly reminded of the transitory nature of my life. Also to those special creatures who honor me with their unconditional and sustaining love (three of the finest dogs ever to set paw on this planet): Señor Max, Echo Louise Dashwood and Koshare Verbena, and to my horse, Tonto's Sun Dancer, now enjoying his thirty-third year, much love and gratitude. To everyone mentioned here, and to anyone I may inadvertently have omitted, allow me to heap blessings on you all for enduring me.

Loving Chloe

Part 1
Cameron, Arizona

1

"Ow, dammit!" For one lengthy, inarticulate minute, Hank Oliver wondered if he might be hallucinating. As was his habit, left over from a scholarly life lived with great deliberation, he gathered evidence before committing himself to any one belief.

His thumb throbbed from accidentally striking it with the claw hammer he'd been using to drive the last few nails into the corral fence. There were black-and-yellow California plates on the old pickup and horse trailer pulling to a halt out back of his cabin. It appeared startlingly out of place, like one perfectly assembled establishing shot from a period movie. Hank stood at the edge of the handmade corral, listening to the drone of the old truck's steady engine. To his left stood the small, newly roofed cabin, and above, the blue-black Arizona sky was rapidly changing into night. On this remote stretch of country road there were no other houses, no porch lamps or streetlights, nothing to illuminate Chloe Morgan's expression and deliver him a clue as to what she was feeling. All he'd managed was her brief profile in the headlights, her face pale and startled, her eyes as fixed as a jackrabbit's.

Three tries and he finally managed to hang the hammer on the fence rail and to begin to believe she was here, that Chloe had indeed, as he'd so often wished, come to him from California. She opened her driver's-side door and the white shepherd dog leaped over her and out of the cab, running off to mark her territory in the scrub. Chloe slid out of the truck right after Hannah, but instead of coming to him directly, which was typical of her horse-woman's style, she hung back in the glow of the headlights. Turning her body sideways, she placed her right hand flush against her ribcage, just below her breasts.

Did she have heartburn from eating junk food while crossing the desert?

It wasn't until she turned her head and gave him a tentative smile that he recognized the posture for what it revealed. From the *Mona Lisa* on down to women he held the door for in the super-market aisles, he understood: Chloe was pregnant. And considering their history together, that meant he, Hank Oliver, was pregnant, too.

From the raw-cedar fence posts to her truck lay ten feet of red dirt and sandstone. How long should it take a grown man to cover such a distance—five strides, four? To Hank each step erased their three months of separation. As soon as he took her into his arms, he felt the assertive little speed bump of her belly against his own, announcing itself. It was mid-August, the kind of flawless northern Arizona weather that went down as easily as lemonade—and now felt like it might come right back up. The cabin was only partially insulated. The pipes needed wrapping if anyone was going to attempt winter here. Since June he'd been behaving like the proverbial grasshopper, living each day loosely, avoiding the hard look he needed to take at his frac-tured, jobless life. But with the arrival of the truck, all that fooling around had come to a halt. Nearby he heard the dog barking and the horse in the trailer bang an impatient hoof against metal. He took hold of the woman he loved and buried his tear-streaked face in her hair. Late this year or early the next, Hank Oliver was going to claim his first breathing tax deduction.

"Happy birthday," he remembered to say.

"Look here," she answered, patting her belly and laughing in that whiskey-barrel voice that never failed to make his blood run hot. "Look what you already gave me." Then she grinned and stuck out her tongue, and after that Hank was good for nothing.

After they'd unloaded the horse, walked him around the property, and let him sniff all the edges of the new corral, Hank shut him inside the fencing. He tossed the colt a flake of hay from the trailer while Chloe dragged a trash can over and filled it with water.

"You want to come inside?" Hank asked.

"No, I thought we could stand out here all night."

Nervously Hank led her to the cabin his grandmother had left him. Chloe might only be passing through, using him as a rest stop on her way to a new life elsewhere—and who could blame her, after last year? Since their lives had intersected the previous winter, Chloe'd lost a great deal. Her beloved old horse had died an ungraceful death, she'd been arrested for slugging a cop in that ridiculous land development debacle, and Hank's own jealousy hadn't helped. Now there was the complication of a baby. A million options existed, and each sat like a separate stone in his stomach.

From the old Germantown blanket he had hanging on the wall to the secondhand rocker he'd in a fit of whimsy painted robin's egg blue, Chloe sighed her approval. "Whoa," she said softly as she kicked off her Tony Lamas onto the wood floor. "If this was my place, you couldn't pry me out with a crowbar."

He thought of saying, *It is yours, if you want it*. Or nailing the door shut to keep her to himself, like some well-intentioned feudal overlord willing to sacrifice whole countries in the name of love. But if in the last eight months Hank had learned anything at all about this woman, it was that turning locks and demanding covenants were the quickest way to spook her. He stood dumbly by, watching her inspect his quarters, which all at once seemed so like her own digs back in the California canyon that he felt certain in his heart she'd stay. He showed her the three-legged metal horse he'd found in the cabin wall when he replaced some dry-rotted boards. He drew back the curtains to reveal the spectacle of the Arizona night sky. With no city lights to compete against, so many stars pierced the canvas it still took his breath away.

"I can't tell you how small it makes me feel when I look at that every night," he said.

She took hold of his hand and cupped it beneath her breast, swollen by the pregnancy. "I know what you mean."

Her ways were always this direct. Her anthem could have been "Let's Cut to the Chase." To Hank's surprise they made it all the way to the bed.

By a stroke of divine luck, he'd changed the dirty sheets that morning, replacing them with a worn-to-softness set bought at the thrift store. The smooth cotton was chilled to crispness against their bodies. At night the temperature dropped swiftly, five and ten degrees an hour. Chloe shivered and said, "It's colder than I thought it would be."

Hank pulled an old Pendleton blanket over her shoulders. "Two months from now, everyone tells me 'cold' takes on an entirely different meaning. Think you're up to it?"

It was a large, multifaceted question, one he regretted asking the moment the words left his mouth. "Oh, I can hang pretty tough," she said, pulling him on top of herself, so ready for making love that the moment their clothes were out of the way she drew him inside without any pretense at foreplay. To Hank it felt as if somebody had built a strong, engaging little fire between her legs. Doing without her had disciplined him, made him thoughtful and sober regarding much of his life, but that kind of governance ended here. Sliding inside her slickness felt like resuming the long, slow arc of an extraordinary dance, one he was an old hand at performing and had missed acutely. Here, in their embrace, all things became one body, one wild, howling song. No time had passed, no hurtful words had sunk their stony arrowheads into the heart's tender flesh. Everything was as soft and familiar as the sheets, and they fell headlong into themselves, giving up, no grace or pretense whatsoever.

An hour later, when they stopped to rest, they could hear Thunder whinnying from the corral.

"Maybe he wants more hay," Hank suggested.

"Always, but the little beggar doesn't need it or he's going to end up on Richard Simmons." She kissed Hank's nose and muttered, "All this wide-open space is probably freaking him out. I just hope the bonehead doesn't try to jump the fence."

"If he did, somebody would catch him and bring him back. That's the kind of people they are around here. Old-fashioned. Decent."

"Sounds like you're trying to push real estate."

"Only to you." Hank ran his fingers across her belly, above the line of her pubic hair, tangled and damp. He felt all over the definite round of baby riding high on her abdomen, its hardness tucked deep inside like a well-kept secret.

"You mind?" Chloe said, pulling on his pillow.

"Take it," he said, settling flat on the mattress while he thought of the myths he'd studied involving motherhood, the primitive cultural notions that, back in graduate school, fixed to paper, seemed so fascinating. Chukchi female shamans believed in the fertility of sacred stones. The female tree-embracers maintained that hanging umbilical cords from branches and caressing bark was how to make a baby. Early myths dismissed the idea that men played any part in this admittedly magical event. They indicated that fatherhood had been revealed to men only by the women, those careful keepers of the cosmic calendar, those true centers of the tribe, and was probably done with regret. He recalled a text on Ethiopian culture he'd read in graduate school that at first glance had sounded so profoundly simple: *A man may spend a single night by a woman, and then rise up to leave her, but a woman carries the fruit of their coupling nine months, directly under her heart. That child can never be dismissed from her heart entirely, not even when grown into a man, not even when she, or the child, is no longer living.* The Indian children who sometimes rode their ponies across his land offered a similar piece of wisdom. *You got to mind your grandmothers else they put you up on Spider Rock.*

Chloe brushed his hand away from her belly. "Stop inspecting me."

"Why?"

"For one thing, it tickles." She sat up in his bed and began braiding her hair by the candlelight. "You have such a funny look on your face, Hank. What in hell are you worrying about? I haven't even been here three hours and already you're brooding."

"I'm not brooding. I'm thinking about babies."

"For God's sake, what about them?"

He smiled. "The fact that we made one seems rather spectacular to me."

"I think they call that biology," she said, her fingers reaching the end of her blond braid.

"There might be a rubber band on the dresser," Hank told her, but Chloe let it fall loose and immediately started in braiding all over again. Her skin seemed to glow, as warm and lightly scented as the burning beeswax candle in a saucer atop his dresser. Pregnancy had darkened her nipples to a dusky plum, enhanced all the aspects of her he'd previously found irresistible.

"I need you to tell me something, and I need you to mean it," she said soberly, fingers working furiously now, this new braid tight and stiff.

He propped himself up, his weight balanced on one hand and elbow. "I'm listening."

"Say something happens, you meet somebody else, or I fall off a horse and get paralyzed—"

His smile sobered. "Jesus, speaking of borrowing trouble. You're not riding horses until long after this baby arrives. Don't even talk like that. That's inviting bad luck."

"No, it's planning for the future. If something happens, you have to promise me you won't turn your back on this kid."

"What makes you think I'd turn my back on our child? I'm so damn happy to see you I can't think straight. I love you, heart, soul, horse, and dog. The dog can sleep on the bed. *In* the bed, if that's what you want. That doesn't sound like father material to you?"

She traced her fingers over the faded pattern in the sheets. "I just don't want it on my conscience, Hank, bringing an unwanted child into the world. I know what it feels like not to belong."

"This baby already belongs, Chloe, just like you belong here with me. I'll keep you both safe."

For awhile she was quiet. "I wonder what your mother is going to say about that."

He could stand it no longer. He took hold of her wrists and pulled her down to him, kissing odd places that he'd overlooked in their hurry—her elbows, the indentation at the small of her back, the curving sides of her belly, her weak ankle that gave her the slight limp he found as intriguing as it was distressing. It was his fault she'd cut the cast off before the leg was properly healed. Chloe limped because he had pushed her to commit to something she was not ready to give.

"Iris a grandmother? She'll be overjoyed. Take up knitting."

"And old Henry senior?"

"The hell with him."

Chloe smiled shyly, as if she wanted to believe him. They began seriously to investigate each other, figuring out how their bodies—his summer-toughened and stronger from all the work he'd put in on the cabin, hers shaped so differently that it required some adjustments—would fit now that the initial blast of passion had cooled.

"This feels so right," he said, laying his cheek against the inside of her thigh.

She reached down and gave his nose a tweak. "Not there. At least not yet. I want you back inside me," she said. "Hurry up. But pace yourself, Professor Oliver, because I'm telling you right here and now, I expect you to make me happy all night."

As he balanced himself on his elbows and moved to do what she asked, Hank couldn't help feeling himself hold back, just a little, out of concern for the baby.

24 August

Dearest Mom,

I trust you're well and that Dad is out there on the
course, perfecting his chip shots and replacing his divots.
The days here are warm, clean, and much too short to
get all my work done. You wouldn't recognize the cabin.
The roof went on snug and held watertight in the last
storm. Chloe and I found a great little used wood stove at
the Big Tree Swap Meet in Flagstaff to replace Nana's
drafty old Franklin, which I sold to an antique dealer
(made $5!). All it needed was new glass in the doors, and
on a trial run, the kitchen got so hot we had to crank
open the windows. Great little stove, well-constructed.
With care it could last twenty years.

This is my roundabout way of informing you and Dad
that Chloe's with me again, forever, I hope. The day after
she got here I asked her to marry me, but she said——
wisely, I think—what was the rush, and given the situation, shouldn't we take things slow and ask each other
the big questions after we've weathered the winter
together. So, I guess in some ways my future is still up in
the air. However, there's one thing we both know for certain that I'd like to share with you. We're having a baby.
We think it's due in February, and I'm extremely happy
at the prospect of becoming a father. I had sort of given
up hope of things ever panning out in that particular
area. Believe me, I'm smiling as I write this. So, anyway,
we're planning to stick around here, a fresh start for both
of us. Northern Arizona University could only offer me
adjunct classes, so I'm interviewing at Ganado
Elementary up in Tuba City. Teaching third grade is not
what I expected to be doing at this time of my life, but
somehow big changes feel right, so wish me luck in your
old stomping grounds.

Now that Asa's reconciled with Claire, that leaves my

Irvine condo empty, so I've arranged for a small property
management firm to take over renting it until it can be
sold. You don't need to fret details in that regard. Mom,
I'm optimistic you and Dad will wish Chloe and me well,
and be excited for us about the baby. Take care of yourself, and write when you can.

Your loving son,
Henry

Hank signed his name to the letter, sealed the flap, and finished
addressing the envelope alone at the kitchen table, the glow of an
oil lamp casting flickering light across his hands. Chloe had gone to
bed two hours earlier, blaming the clean air, saying smog with-
drawal was making her sick, but Hank knew the pregnancy
claimed priority on her body, and that adjusting to the altitude
wasn't helping matters. He was fine here alone.

He blew out the lamp and stood at the window, holding the curtain away from the glass. Far across the sky, he could see momentary jags of lightning flicker out toward the Grand Canyon. Exactly
how far away it was, he couldn't tell. Out here the miles stretched
endless and uncharitable, playing tricks on the eye. He opened the
back door and stood in the doorway, chilly but content to watch
the storm roll in across the prairie.

2

"How far along do you think you are?" Dr. Lois Carrywater asked as she scanned the medical history Chloe had labored over in the clinic waiting room.

An embarrassing number of spaces had had to be left blank. Chloe eyed the woman who was going to deliver her baby. Not much older than herself, she wore blue jeans and an orange T-shirt beneath her lab coat, and she was FBI: full-blooded Indian. Chloe'd heard her say something in Navajo to the patient she'd crossed paths with in the narrow hallway. Forget the smile; this broad had access to cupboards full of nasty instruments with sharp points. "Five months, maybe? I've never had regular periods."

"Does that kind of cycle run in your family?"

Chloe rustled the stiff paper gown and gave her a flinty laugh. "Really couldn't tell you since Mama gave me up for adoption when I was two."

Dr. Carrywater set her file down on the exam room's short wooden countertop and snapped her strong-looking hands into latex gloves. "Sorry. I always have to ask."

She began the examination by listening to Chloe's heart and lungs. As she opened the gown, she fingered the scar on Chloe's back, unable to disguise her alarm at the makeshift stitching job from the old jumping accident. "Tell me, was the quack who sewed up your shoulder drunk *and* blind?"

"Neither, but Lord, is he handsome. Veterinarian buddy of mine. He did the best he could. I figured since it didn't cost anything, I was ahead of the game. I mean, it's not like I spend much time looking at my back."

The doctor made her perform some arm rotations to check the range of motion. "You're lucky the tendon wasn't affected." Then she discovered the scar above her right nipple. "The shape of this scarring almost looks like a human bite."

Chloe met her eyes evenly. "Oh?"

The silence in the exam room built as each woman refused to back down. "Well, then," Dr. Carrywater said and moved on to measuring Chloe's belly. The completion of each task brought closer the moment when she would ask her to lie down and she would lift the speculum from the instrument tray. Chloe steeled herself, tensing until she was nearly bowed above the exam table. The doctor placed a gloved palm against Chloe's clenched fingers. "Don't be nervous."

"I understand why you have to do it, but this poking around inside stuff's never set well with me."

Dr. Carrywater smiled sympathetically. "It's true, sometimes it can be unpleasant. I'll try to be gentle and quick."

Every step of the way she explained what she was doing and asked if Chloe was all right. Mostly she was, but not until she felt the release of the instruments and heard them clatter onto the tray did she relax. Mental pictures and echoes of another exam she didn't like to think about crowded her. Once encouraged, bad memories liked nothing better than to run away with the reins in their teeth.

"You like this job? Looking inside ladies' boxes all day?"

"Sure. I get to help bring new life into the world. Find me another career with those kind of perks."

"I'll bet you have to have a strong stomach."

"Sometimes that comes in handy." Dr. Carrywater drew a test tube of blood and handed it to the same woman who'd given Chloe the forms to fill out. Chloe held onto the cotton ball in the crook of her elbow and tried to reach for her clothes, but the doctor stopped her.

"You waited so long to seek prenatal care. Here people have reasons. But California? There's a clinic on every street corner."

"Maybe I wasn't sure what I was going to do about it."

"And now you're sure?"

Commitment to the baby held the power to blot out all her worldly mistakes. "Yeah, of course. Hank wants this baby."

"Hank isn't the one carrying it. Tell me how you feel."

The bleeding had stopped. Chloe pitched the cotton ball into the trash can. "About being pregnant? It's not my first choice to bloat up and cry over every little thing. But I want it. I'll do whatever it takes to help him get born healthy."

"Good." Dr. Carrywater began assembling a bag of vitamins and literature for her to take home. "You know, we don't have access to sonogram equipment out here. I'd like to send you into Flagstaff for that."

"Do I have to have one?"

"It would provide me with more accurate information about the baby's gestational age."

Chloe crossed her legs. "Here's the way I look at it, Doctor. The less medical stuff the better, okay?"

The doctor considered her words. "All right. I'm giving you a tentative due date of February second. Understand, without the sonogram, I might be off by as much as a month. And you must agree to come back in two weeks instead of four."

"Sounds like a deal I can live with."

Dr. Carrywater paused at the hollow-core door with its poster of the third trimester rendered in inhuman pinks and mauves, outside which real babies cried over vaccinations and patients waited while the unanswered phone rang on and on, begging for attention. "Any questions?"

"Yeah." Chloe presented her case logically and calmly. "I used to be a horse trainer in California. Been riding all my life. I've brought this colt out here I'm trying to gentle. It's okay to work him, isn't it? Hank's all paranoid. He said I had to ask."

"If you're talking about walking him by hand, and he minds his manners, I have no objections for the next few weeks."

"But a little riding's not going to hurt anything, right?"

"Riding?" The doctor laughed. "You're done with that for the remainder of the pregnancy."

"But I rode every single day back in California. Even with a broken ankle."

"This is Arizona. I'm a medical doctor, not a veterinarian. And last time I checked, ankles weren't babies. Maybe you need me to provide some more graphic examples."

"No thanks." Chloe made a face and went to the outer office to discuss the payment schedule with the pale-skinned girl who sat smiling behind the desk in her Peter Pan collar.

"We arrange payment on a sliding scale," she happily told Chloe as she pressed more literature into her hands. "Do you have regular employment?"

I used to, Chloe wanted to tell her. *I had a waitress job that paid great tips. I had riding students waiting on line, and kept close to current on whatever I owed. Maybe they weren't the best shots, but I called them, and my life worked pretty damn well.* She shook her head no. "My boyfriend's paying."

"Could you fill out his name and address on this form, please?"

"Sure." Chloe wrote Hank's name down, then put ditto marks on the address section. "It's all the same," she said, handing the paper back. "Everything except for our names."

"I see."

The town of Tuba City, which wasn't really a town at all but an administrative and trade center for the western Navajo tribe, seemed to be pretty evenly divided between the two camps, Mormon and Navajo. The high-buttoned blouse, the sensible blond haircut, and the smile that didn't quit even when her moral stance

was obviously offended pretty much indicated this one's camp was
the former.

"If you could just have a seat for one second while I answer this
phone, I'll set up your appointment schedule."

Chloe chose a plastic chair next to five other pregnant women,
four of whom looked just about ready to deliver. They were all
Indian, speaking their own language. The magazines on the beat-
up coffee table featured Mormon life, Mormon literature, and no
doubt some really pithy Mormon prenatal issues. The free literature on birth control and STDs in the wall pockets looked too
intimidating to consider. There was an urn with free coffee substitute set on a card table, but Chloe wasn't feeling that desperate.
She hadn't seen a gynecologist in maybe six or seven years and
imagine that, in all that time the process hadn't gotten any more
pleasant. The whole waiting-room thing was giving her a major
headache. "Tell you what, I'll give you a call," she said to the recep-
tionist and blew out the front door without waiting for an answer.

Five miles west of Tuba City on U.S. 160, about midway between
the junction and U.S. 89, she pulled the truck over from the highway into the dirt shoulder. The stretch of road was unfamiliar. The
sight of this wide-open prairie sent her heart scudding around
inside her chest like the organ had torn loose from its mooring.
Who could ever imagine sky this blue, this empty, unbroken by
neon or power lines? The land before her stretched emptily to the
north and west as if it had all day to get wherever it was going.
Where were the thrown-together housing developments, the fast-
food restaurants, the cheesy strip malls? Back in California, that's
where. The baby fluttered inside her, and despite the red rocks' gra-
dient splendor, she felt lonesome for all she'd left—near-gridlock
traffic, working two jobs, never having quite enough money to pay
her bills, Kit Wedler's endless teenage questions, something predictable on which she could hang her hat.

When Hank had come back from Flagstaff in his good jacket bearing bad news from the university, she half expected him to say, *Let's pack up and go home*. Home—California. But she could tell he wanted to stay here, that his grandmother's cabin meant something to him the way horses meant the world to her. *Screw those university eggheads*, she'd told him. *They don't know what they're missing*. That night they'd lain on their sides in bed facing each other, making love with as much enthusiasm as two people could scrounge from thrift shop sheets and a dwindling bank account. Between them the bulk of pregnancy had never felt more present, so life-altering, so damned *expensive*. Try as she might, Chloe couldn't lose herself in the spirit of their loving. A part of her felt reined-in and responsible. When Hank came, hollering his gratitude into her bare shoulder, she didn't miss the close-to-tears catch in his voice. She rubbed his back and planted kisses up and down his neck. Told him that he was her best lover—so far. That made him laugh and fall asleep smiling.

But he had found a job after all, and now Hank said he wouldn't allow her to work. *You'll rest until the baby is born. I'll take care of you.* When she opened her mouth to complain, he laid a finger across her lips. *Think of these last couple of months like a long-overdue vacation*, he'd said. If only someone could tell her how to do that. She wasn't a TV kind of person, not that they had one, and taking long walks with the dog had its moments, such as finding pottery shards, spotting the jack-in-the-box prairie dogs and picking the occasional wildflower. But it sure wasn't a reason to jump out of bed in the morning.

Just ahead on her side of the highway stood some of those roadside stands featuring bright Indian blanket roofs. She shut off the engine and hiked over to give them a look.

On the road to the Grand Canyon, which they hadn't gotten around to seeing yet, Chief Yellowhorse's hand-painted billboards and directionals abounded. *Friendly Indians here! We take 'em MasterCards! Stop! Turn back now or miss deal of lifetime!* The Indians manning these booths barely nodded a polite hello to her. She walked along looking at the jewelry and trinkets, then at the last stall, picked up a horse blanket.

"Eight-dollar special today only," the man in the dark recess of the booth said, then added softly, "That's a fair price."

"I agree." Chloe reached into her pocket to count her roll of dollar bills. She laid the money down. "This red and gray will look great on my horse when he's gentle enough to ride. He's chestnut, with a white—"

"Got bridles," the man interrupted, motioning to a cardboard box on the ground next to his booth. Chloe bent down to check them out. The hardware was good for nothing except decorating the homes of yuppies passionate for Western motif. Most of it was old cowboy paraphernalia, gag bits designed to choke a horse into submission, gimmicks to force him to spin faster or perform demeaning tricks under the threat of pain. Underneath the tangle of junk, though, she found a gray-and-white braided horsehair halter. "How much for this?"

"Forty," the man said.

Back home at El Toro Feed and Tack, a length of *pelo de caballo* not even half this finely crafted cost seventy-five dollars. She put more money down, her fingers resting atop the wrinkled twenties. *Be practical. You have no job. Doctor visits cost money. Hank won't let you ride.* But imagining the pleasure of seeing the halter on the colt's ungainly head, practicality took a flying leap. It wasn't denial to buy the tack. Denial was when Gabe Hubbard grinned after she asked him what he thought the funny twitchings in her belly could be. The veterinarian had howled with laughter, as if any woman who'd quit menstruating and couldn't recognize the advancing symptoms of pregnancy was beyond his scope. "You make this?" she asked the Indian.

"My brother Ned got all shot up in the war. Don't get out much. Sits and braids in his wheelchair."

"Well, tell Ned I'll put his handiwork to good use."

The Indian flattened her twenties into his cash box, then looked away vacantly, as if he heard such claims all day long.

Chloe felt compelled to make conversation, to establish the truth of what she was saying, to connect. "Such a big, empty chunk of nothing out there, isn't it? Sometimes it scares the crap out of me."

His raisin-black eyes seemed to look right through her. "Earth's our grandmother. Plant some squash, take a walk. No call to be afraid."

She gave him a half smile. "Yeah. Maybe it's the people who come walking into view we got to watch out for." She thought of Iris Oliver and wished she hadn't. Hank's mother's letters were bad enough; an actual visit might blow the house down.

A group of tourists began to inspect the Indian's wares and Chloe stepped back to give them room. He gave them his full, if luke-warm attention. She walked back to her truck and sat inside.

Not particularly hungry, she took a few bites of an apple, think-ing how happy her eating fruit would make Hank. Apples weren't broccoli, but they were close friends, and Hank was heavily press-ing the food groups. She stared northwest until her tiredness made those funny little heat shimmers before her eyes: A band of wild horses moving toward her, an Appaloosa and a gray, a buckskin, one remarkable pinto. They were unbridled, trotting, kicking up red dust, led by a horse so black and shining she knew at once that here was her Absalom, come back from horse heaven, equipped with perfect legs in this life, rightfully crowned leader. Her eyes watered from concentrating to visualize the ermine spots on his pastern. The pain of losing her horse still cut deep. The prairie's silence beat in her blood like drums, like the four-beat gait of hooves striking the tarmac running alongside the arena at her old stables. She longed to be where those horses were, but it was no place to be found on a map. Sometimes, back home in the canyon, when she was exhausted or worried about one of the lesson horses, her mind played tricks, went to strange places, heard peo-ple talking in Spanish, calling out to her. *Mija, lo siento, hasta la mañana*, they said, as if they knew her. Whatever it meant was beyond her scope. She set the half-eaten apple on the dashboard. It tasted so grainy she spit the last mouthful out the truck's window.

You waited so long to seek prenatal care. Clinics in California on every corner . . . the last time she'd been anywhere near a hospital was when Fats Valentine died. What was there to recommend a place that couldn't save the life of the first man she'd loved? And years before that she'd been raped, and had only gone to the emergency room because she knew enough about wounds to recognize that she needed at least eight stitches in her right breast or she might lose the nipple. Another pleasant medical interlude. Yes or No boxes didn't afford room for that kind of medical history.

She looked out the truck's windshield, past the dusty reddish film that clouded the glass. Afternoon sun glared in her eyes, and she knew there was no escaping once the trigger had been squeezed. Sooner or later the memories would deliver her a sleepless night. The Arizona summer sun streamed in her truck's windows, and Chloe was amazed all over again that even sixteen years removed physically, the rape kept at her, teaching her lessons. While it was going on, she thought it was the worst thing that could happen to a girl. But it wasn't. There was more—stuff nobody knew, not even Hank.

Today he was in some kind of meeting with the principal of the elementary school where, next week, owing less to his credentials and more to their desperate need, he'd begin teaching third grade. At night she could hear him sighing in his sleep, grateful down to his dreams. Compared to the breadth of knowledge he carried around, what he required seemed so childlike. He was a true puzzle. In her thirty-four years, there had been three humans to whom she'd uttered the words "I love you": a boy in high school whose name she couldn't remember. Ben Gilpin, her last, best foster parent. And Fats Valentine, who never once, not even when he lay in his hospital bed dying, said it back.

Chloe had said those words every time they made love, which was infrequent and, it seemed, always at her instigation. He'd be lying on the couch watching the races on television, drinking his gin, and she'd climb on, kiss his whiskered neck, run her hands down his pants until she had something to work with. Chugging along on top of the always-tired horseman, sensing how ridiculous that probably looked, she didn't care, she needed so badly to feel connected. Gabe Hubbard, DVM, had known exactly where to touch to make her respond. With Gabe screwing was so automatic that it wasn't even fun. With Hank, somehow, every time they turned to each other sex was brand-new. One time it might be fierce, each of them pulling so hard to get what they needed that they were slick with sweat and gasping for air. Another time, like a kiss on the cheek that grew into an embrace, things evolved slowly, transforming passion into something larger and kinder than she felt she deserved. After those times, Hank whispered in her ear, "You know, people aren't really allowed to feel this happy," he'd say, his breath raising the tiny hairs on her neck. "This happy, you're supposed to have a license."

He meant marriage. Chloe understood just how overdue she was to say those three words to him. They were only words. She'd fix him supper and sneak up behind him and kiss his neck and just come right out with it. Maybe. She fingered the horsehair halter, the heavy silence broken only by the occasional passing of RVs headed to Lake Powell or, depending which way they turned, the Four Corners.

One reason I'm excited about this job, Hank had said, *is insurance bene-fits.* The birth wouldn't be covered because it fell under the category of pre-existing conditions, but the baby would be, covered the minute he was born. In the bright sunlight and perfect eighty-degree weather, Chloe Morgan felt her unborn child stir inside her. *Stay put,* she mentally sent to the baby. *Nobody here is in any kind of rush.*

Ganado Elementary was linked by common buildings. Painted blue doors led to individual classrooms. The playground featured two basketball hoops and four-square lines newly painted onto the uneven blacktop. Across the way a few individual trailers served as offices. The school itself was set below a grassy yellowed hillside where most of the vegetation had been trampled down to earth by children's footsteps. Chloe followed the pathway around the back of the main building until she came to a barn with stalls.

In the fall air there was a definite equine scent. Cottonwood leaves blew across the makeshift corral, which was littered with aging, straw-laden droppings. If horses lived here—and the few pieces of equipment seemed to indicate they did—they were out to pasture for the day. She inspected the fence, constructed of tree limbs and baling wire. Maybe it looked like a joke, but against her hands it held, surprisingly sturdy, the way her own shack back in the canyon in California had added up to a larger sum than any of its individual parts. She wondered who had moved into it after she left, and if to that person, as it had to her, the four walls felt like a safe haven. Behind the corral the hillside rose gently. Chloe climbed all the way to the top, grateful to feel the pull of muscle in the back of her legs as she lengthened her stride. Near the top, a hundred yards away, five horses lazily grazed the scant forage near an old stock tank. Chloe shaded her eyes and studied them: An Appaloosa, one old gray so thick and stocky he had to be half draft horse. A buckskin, too, and one paint mare with conformation that, from where Chloe stood, seemed too good to be true. Chloe idly ran down the list of what the drawbacks could be—blindness, bad legs, a truly evil temper? Aside from the paint, the horses looked as if they'd served their usefulness and had landed at the school for tax purposes only. Well, that still beat Purina.

She sat down on the ground to wait. Below her, Hank was inside one of those buildings, being so nice and helpful that by the end of the first week of teaching he'd have made friends, earned his students' adoration, and have all those new stories to tell her at night while they ate dinner. What would she have to show, besides another inch to her midsection?

Every now and then the horses looked her way, unimpressed, then continued to dine on their scant surroundings. Slowly, in no particular hurry, they were coming her way. Four horses, like those she'd imagined while sitting in her truck on the side of the highway. All present and accounted for, except for one, their leader, the black gelding with three ermine spots and the wide, wide heart, who should have been there, leading everyone home.

3

Nine girls and eleven boys stared up at their new teacher. Dark eyes, black hair, little moon-shaped brown faces, each one expectant, curious, and empty of judgment. Hank's heart thudded inside his pressed shirt and his underarms grew damp. He wished Chloe were here beside him. She never got the jitters, whether squaring off with cops or confronting wild horses. That morning, she'd sleepily kissed him good-bye and said, "You won over Kit Wedler, I think you'll survive third-graders," and rolled over, snuggling deeper in the covers. The second he was out the door, he knew Hannah would weasel into his side of the bed, press her furry back against Chloe's pale, scarred one, and the pair of them, looking for all the world like the animal and human halves of one mythological self, would sleep hard another hour. Sleep was good for the baby. He'd recommended she take naps, too, until she pointed a finger at him and he knew he was close to crossing a line.

"I thought today we'd spend some time getting to know each other." Aside from a few quick grins, the faces remained blank. "My name is Mr. Oliver," he said quickly. "Before I moved to

Arizona, I lived in California." He pulled down an outdated wall map and pointed out the state. "Six hundred miles from where our classroom stands is where I lived. Right here. In a town called Irvine."

He traced the jagged coastline of his home state, remembering how easy it had been to teach at the community college. On the first day of classes, he passed out his course syllabus, briefly discussed which textbooks they would be using, mentioned the research paper that was mandatory to passing his course, and to prove he wasn't all business, attempted a few jokes. Then he assigned fifteen pages of reading and cut them loose. By the next class, three or four had always dropped out, stunned by the fact that he expected them to do some actual work.

Finally a hand shot up. Hank smiled, inwardly sagging with relief. A gold star for this kid. "Walter Johnson, isn't it?"

The children broke out in laughter, and Walter pursed his lips, pointing them at the others. "*Gé!*" he ordered, and jumped up from his seat, but the children didn't stop giggling until another child spoke up.

"Nobody be calling him *Wal-tah*," the girl said.

Hank checked his seating chart. His name informant was Belva Small. "Thank you for pointing that out to me, Belva. Tell me what they do call you, Mr. Johnson."

The boy sat down. "Dog."

"Short Dog!" another child hollered. "On account of he's not so tall, *enit?*"

This part wasn't in the guidelines Mr. Genoways had handed him. This part was strictly seat-of-the-pants. "Dog, then," Hank said calmly, ignoring Belva's laughter. "Back there on my desk there's an aquarium that needs setting up. Maybe later on you'd like to help me with it."

Dog Johnson nodded shyly, resting his embarrassed cheek against his fist. The other children stopped their teasing and wriggled in their seats, ticked off that the butt of their jokes had gotten the aquarium assignment.

"Since I'm new to the school, I wonder if anybody has any questions for me."

He expected all hands to wave, children to leap to their feet, things to get a little out of hand. But the children were quiet again, looking slightly self-conscious, and Hank pondered what tribal *faux pas* he'd committed ten minutes into what looked to be a very long day. He sighed, remembering Principal Genoways telling him that direct questioning was considered bad manners in the *Dinéh* culture, particularly with strangers. Well, he'd have to remedy his stranger status, and turn questions into discussions. Hank called on Chuey Alberto, the tallest boy in the class.

"Chuey," he said, running his finger along the coastline of California, where the map changed from desert brown to coastal green to an impossible blue he'd never witnessed in the water. "I used to live near the Pacific Ocean, close enough to drive to in my car."

"Must be good fishing," Chuey commented. "Big old trout in deep water."

Hank smiled. "Too salty for trout. But lots of clams, some tuna. I'm not that great a fisherman, truthfully. Maybe you can give me some pointers about the lakes around here."

Chuey nodded, the epitome of cool, an eight-year-old professional angler, and Hank got the feeling he'd made his first friend in room nine. "I know some of you have never seen the ocean. Let me tell you a little bit about it. The ocean makes a wonderful, rushing noise all the time because of the waves," he went on. "Dolphins and whales live there. Every winter they swim down the coast on their way to Mexico, where it's warmer." They had no idea what he was talking about. "I can get us a book from the library about whales, or maybe a film. If you'd like that."

A movie! They grinned, and he began to relax. "I want you to know something. Here in room nine, our classroom," he said, "it's okay to ask questions. In fact it's considered exceptionally good manners. So if anyone ever feels like asking me something, just raise your hand and I'll try to answer. If I don't have the answer, we'll look it up together."

Rain Desbar held out both her hands and wagged them furiously. "Can I touch your beard?"

Hank fingered it self-consciously, wondering if such a thing were permitted within the school boundaries. For the most part, the *Dinéh* men did not wear beards, lacking the profuse facial hair of whites. Hank envied them that each morning when he stood in front of the mirror deciding whether or not to shave off his summer's folly. "I don't see why not."

The children came to the front of the classroom, where they began to crowd one another to get to him. "One at a time," he said. "We're going to be together all school year."

Philberta Johnson and Nelbert Begay touched his forearms and squealed. "Ooh, he got hair on there, too."

"You swim in that ocean? Next to them whales?"

Juanita Littlebird wanted to know on average just how many fish he'd caught and what he used for bait. Waterdogs?

"You married?" Anna Ortiz and Tanya Blackwater asked in unison.

"Don't be asking him stupid marrying questions," Chuey Alberto warned the giggling girls. "Mr. Hank, you got a son helping you chop wood? I am one good wood chopper, anybody here can tell you that."

Hank had lost most of the previous night's sleep fretting. An hour before the bell, he'd printed MR. OLIVER, WELCOME TO THIRD GRADE, on the blackboard, then looked at the words from a few paces back, certain they looked bogus as he felt. But here they were, swarming over him, patting his face, offering to chop his firewood, curious and friendly.

He managed to pass out the art supplies and help them make namecards for their desks, half of them decorated with blue whales, before the first recess. They squabbled over who got to hold onto his hands as he walked them out to the playground into the bright Arizona fall weather.

"I'll show you around," Mickey Spottedhorse insisted. "I already been in third grade. I know way more than these *awéé'* baby guys."

*   *   *

Hank was torn between eating his lunch in the sun and watching his students play, or retreating to the teachers' lounge and enjoying forty minutes of peace and quiet. He supposed he needed to be social with someone over three feet tall if he was ever going to become a part of the whole at this school.

The lower-grade teachers and the principal made room for him at the Formica table in the teachers' "lounge." After lunch ended, the room was transformed back into its original status: waiting area for parents, ersatz nurse's office, and supply room. The fourth- and fifth-grade instructors, a man and a woman, sat by themselves on the couch next to a film projector. Like Hank, they were also white, but older, while the two women who taught first and second grade looked Indian and barely into middle age. Everyone said hello politely, scooted aside their chairs. Hank sat down, unscrewed the lid of his Thermos, and poured himself a cup of peppermint tea, the grassy color reminding him of Chloe's blatant distaste for anything green. *Except money. That I'll take with an open hand,* she often told him. The truth was, she didn't eat enough fruit or vegetables, and vitamins alone couldn't perform miracles. He kept up the threats. *You want our child born with rickets?*

"Hank Oliver, third grade," he said to the group, and after they said that's nice, where you from, what did you do before this, they went back to reading old magazines or finishing their private discussions. Hank ate his carrot sticks in silence, dreaming about the baby, imagining as he often did that it would be a girl. He envisioned her barreling into the world the same dramatic way her mother had entered his life, uncivilizing every neatly swept corner. He heard his daughter's first strong cries as she hollered out loud, declaring her presence. She would possess such an even disposition that the whole event would persuade Chloe that marriage was a part of the natural evolution of their procreation. There would be a small ceremony, during which he would slip a plain gold band onto her ring finger. She would kiss him and feed her bouquet to the ravenous colt. Then the three of them would put their shoulders to the wheel, work hard, and live long, productive, rewarding lives on the red rock his grandmother had left him.

Of course he understood that babies were unique, their little personalities shaped *in utero* by the union of each parent's DNA (which, there were studies, *could* be warped by diet), and God alone knew what other kinds of mysterious alchemy occurred in the womb. Simply to underscore her independence, Chloe might not agree to marriage. *Walk with a light step there*, he told himself. *She's here, and that's what matters. Love doesn't come easily to women like her, but maybe when the baby's born....* In the meantime he was throwing as much money as he had into remodeling the cabin. One thing Hank knew for certain would transpire when this baby was born: For the first time since he'd met Chloe Morgan, tendered her his heart, the weary organ would be divided in affections.

"So, how are you finding your first day, Hank?" Mr. Genoways asked, as he made his way toward the trailer's door. "Everything going okay for you? You need anything?"

"I'm fine," Hank answered. "They're great kids. Very enthusiastic. I've got high hopes for them."

The principal nodded and tightened his necktie. "Just the words I like to hear to settle my lunch," he said and shut the door behind him.

Hank folded his sandwich wrappings into his lunch sack. He had time for another cup of tea, more daydreaming, too, and was looking forward to both events. All the teachers were staring at him, but only Mrs. Chee, second grade, and Ms. Redwing, who taught first, were smiling. "Excuse me?" he said. "Is there a problem?"

Mr. Walker, who taught the fourth/fifth combination class, directed his comments to Mrs. MacNeal. "Let me get this straight. He's been here four hours and he still has hope."

Mrs. MacNeal laughed, picked at her greasy fried chicken bones, and the primary teachers looked away, annoyed.

"Permit me an admonition, Mr. Oliver," Mr. Walker said. "Set your expectations low. Half of these children are here only to take advantage of the free lunch program. They can't be expected to excel at anything academic, certainly not to master much above the basics."

"Oh, really? And why is that?"

Walker smiled. "Quite simply put, the very nature of the beast."

Hank looked down at his empty cup. A large part of him was so uncertain of his ability to do this job justice that he wanted to walk straight out of this room and keep going, not stop until he tasted his troutless, familiar ocean. But a larger part, he was discovering, intended to stay. Hank crumpled his lunch sack and assembled his Thermos. He rose and pushed his chair in to the table. "I'd love to continue this riveting intellectual debate, but I need to get to the library before the bell."

Mrs. Chee stood up. "Let me tag along with you, Hank. I'll show you where it is."

"Thanks." Muffled laughter echoed behind him as they crossed the tiny schoolyard.

"Betsy Redwing and I should have warned you," Mrs. Chee said, her small strides alongside his forcing him to slow down. "Ken Walker drove our last third-grade teacher out two weeks before the Christmas break. Poor girl swore she'd sell shoes at minimum wage down in Phoenix rather than teach again. It's not so bad here, honest. Just different. But his kind of bitterness is a real burden for the school."

"Then why on earth does he stay?"

"Three more years until he gets his full retirement benefits. You couldn't move him with a crane."

"And the children suffer? Is that school policy, Mrs. Chee?"

She slipped her keys from her skirt pocket. "Change takes time. Try not to let it interfere with what you can do. And call me Audrey," she said. "Betsy, Louise, and I are glad to have you on staff."

"Louise?"

"Our roving aide. Soon as things get settled, she'll give you one afternoon a week. That's all anybody gets. She's a volunteer."

Mr. Walker and his merry band of educational recidivists were probably yukking it up but good, Hank thought, as he discovered that the school library consisted of a converted closet holding possibly fifty ancient books. Many were missing pages and a goodly portion of those lining the tiny bookshelf were Flagstaff Public library rejects, too shopworn to engender a love of reading or tell a complete story. "This is the library?"

Audrey nodded. "Ganado could use a miracle where the books are concerned. Most of us trade back and forth, pool our lesson plans for copying."

"Can you ask around if anybody has a book on whales?"

"Sure. Well, I've got to get back to my classroom."

"Thanks."

After Audrey left, Hank stared at the ratty collection. How many times had he blown out an impatient sigh at the rotting community-college classroom carpet? Taken for granted such classrooms would be there for him to enter the next day and the next, or that his mail slot in the administration building would once a month deliver his paycheck? Made cracks about the college's obsolete library, all three thickly stocked floors? Room nine was perhaps twenty by twenty-five feet, a collection of recycled, out-of-date desks, the kind with heavy lids that needed to be opened and shut carefully, so they didn't crush a child's finger. That was okay; secondhand he could work with. True, his paycheck was much smaller than before, and still a month off, but until it arrived they'd survive. Even with these undeniable shortcomings, every face in room nine was filled with promise, and every one deserved a chance. He shut the door on the pathetic books and looked away. Showing his students the Pacific Ocean was six hundred miles beyond his grasp, today anyway.

On his way across the campus, he stared down at the ground. The red dirt appeared rocky and untenable, good for nothing. He stooped to pick up a piece of native sandstone and brushed the dirt from its surface. Flat chunks of it lay everywhere. He felt the slight weight of the rock settle in his palm. Flicking a thumbnail against the surface, he saw the mark he'd made remain behind. He could volunteer for playground duty. Or hide out alone in his classroom watching mud puppies traverse the secondhand aquarium instead of living out their intended lives as five-for-a-dollar bait fish in some redneck's Styrofoam cooler. There was no law against solitude. Audrey Chee offered friendship, and allies were important, but the idea that Ken Walker lay in wait for his students the following school year was a bitter pill he could not bring himself to swallow.

He wanted to do something about those books, but the truth was, the plumbing bill had gone several hundred dollars higher than he'd expected, and with the payments on the still-unrented condo, by the time the baby arrived, they could be scraping soup bones. The hospital bill had to be paid, and things might get even tighter if the transmission on the Honda didn't magically heal itself. Maybe he could spare a few dollars from his paycheck once a month. It wasn't that he minded perusing the secondhand bookshops, but used books weren't much of an improvement over the so-called library. He pocketed the stone and made his way back to room nine.

The children had sneaked in and sat in their chairs, quietly waiting for him. He supposed he should have reminded them to follow his orders to line up outside and wait until he arrived. But the afternoon sun shone in the windows and one of the kids—he knew better than to ask who—had set one of the free lunch apples on his desk.

"This looks like a very tasty apple," Hank said, picking it up and polishing it on his shirt. "How do you say apple in Navajo?"

"*Bilasáana!*" they hollered.

He repeated the word and they giggled at his accent. "What a treat for me to enjoy tonight, with my supper. Thanks to whoever was thinking of me. Now, it's a long ways until supper, and I believe we've got an aquarium to get going. But first I could use some help with naming these fish. Whoever would like to help me record the nominations for names, please raise your hand."

"Me!"

"No, me!"

"Don't be thinking no stupid *at'ééké* girl names," Chuey called out.

Hank called on Malinda Pasqual and Arthur Yazzie. After Dog Johnson helped him sink the pondweed's adventitious root bundle into the gravel, every child would have had a turn today at something. He slid his hand into his pants pocket and fingered the sandstone's jagged edge. It was just an ordinary chunk of Arizona rock, one among thousands. Only the scratch from his thumbnail personalized it. He might carry it with him every day.

4

After awhile, all it took was one *almost*-accidental flick of her finger and the envelope opened, revealing two familiar monogrammed folded sheets of stationery:

September 18

Dearest Henry,

Summer weather persists. Your father only needs a light sweater in the early hours when he begins his morning round of golf. My lab counts are due back sometime today. I expect they'll be just fine. Siobhan O'Keefe, bless her soul, passed away this week. I ran into her daughter Jaime when I went out to retrieve the mail this afternoon, hoping there'd be a letter from you. What a lovely girl, Henry. Divorced, a darling little boy named Trevor. She urged me not to mourn, said that Siobhan wouldn't have wanted any crying. The poor dear went in her sleep, which is, I suppose, the most blessed way,

particularly for such an active person. Jaime's thinking
about adopting a dog from the shelter for her father.
There are documented studies concerning pets helping
seniors live longer and more productive lives. These same
studies also indicate that the responsibility of caring for a
pet helps one avoid depression. Last month's *Modern
Maturity*, from which you might recall I used to frequently
clip articles I thought you'd find of interest, had quite a
spread on it. The August issue, with the handsome couple
hiking in the redwoods on the front cover, just in case you
want to read it yourself. Oh—have they built a library in
Cameron yet, or is the community still serviced by that
bookmobile with the secondhand novels?

Henry, sweetheart, your father and I are trying our best
to understand. It's not easy to believe this sudden change
in your behavior is at your instigation alone. Everyone
here at World of Freedom agrees, forty-three is entirely
too young for a midlife crisis. Here you were doing so
well at the college. I know your position being eliminated
was a setback, but there are five other community col-
leges in the county. Surely one of them would have
jumped at the chance to employ someone with your level
of experience. When I think of your lovely condominium
filled with renters it just makes me want to cry. The
beautiful curtains we picked out together, the Berber
carpet you took such good care of. It's this girl at the
heart of things, isn't it?

Dear, I've tried to see things from your perspective. A
man your age has certain needs. You get lonely. But the
world is full of deserving women, lovely, cultured single
ladies who would be honored to take your name and
make a home for you. You need a companion to attend
cultural functions with you and who will afterwards be
able to engage in lively discussion. Must it be this particular
girl? A criminal record, barely educated, limited social

skills—you hardly know her, let alone from what kind of stock she came. Considering her childhood circumstances, what is the likelihood of ever finding out?

Now she's pregnant. Has a physician verified this? You say you love her and intend to raise this baby. Loyalty is a noble trait and one of your best features, but try to remember, Henry, it cannot serve as a Band-Aid for life's insurmountable dilemmas. Sometimes even well-meaning individuals resort to chicanery when faced with situations beyond their grasp.

How I wish you could make me understand what is so terribly vital to your independence about cohabiting without benefit of clergy, living below one's means in the middle of an Indian reservation when there is a perfectly good life waiting for you right here in California.

Dr. just phoned with my test results. He says my platelets could be a "little more encouraging," and he wants me to come back on Monday to repeat the CBC. Probably just a mix-up in the laboratory. With the kind of turnover in office help these days, these things happen. Your father has a tournament Monday, so he really needs the car. I can get a ride on the O.C.T.D. senior bus. It drops off just one block up a very short hill from the medical center. Mrs. O'Keefe and I used to ride there together. "Safety in numbers," she always used to say. I guess I'll have to get used to going by myself now. If I can't get a seat on the bus I can always telephone for a taxi.

You are in my prayers, dearest.
Love, Mother

"You and all those fortunate few deserving of Iris Oliver's prayers." Chloe sighed, tucking the sheets of scented stationery back into the envelope she had so carefully pried open. She

inhaled deeply, craving a cigarette she wasn't allowed to have.
"She might be making that up about the blood tests, Hannah," she
said aloud to her dog, who had ridden along in the truck for company while Chloe retrieved their mail. "Iris Oliver, master guilt
queen of southern California, with special privileges in northern
Arizona as well. And it is her queenly duty to pry this low-class
barnacle and developing issue loose of her precious son even if she
has to resort to medical blackmail, girl." She bit her lip and studied
the horizon, where a band of gray-blue sky hinted that summer's
days were numbered. "Then again, she could be out of remission,"
she said, knowing if that were true, it would destroy Hank. There
was no rule that said Iris had to like her, but Chloe had kind of
hoped that by now they might be flirting with acceptance.

Hannah cocked her head as if studying her mistress's mood. Her
wet brown eyes looked deep into Chloe's. She took hold of the dog's
muzzle and gave it a good-natured shake. "We'll have to make a
special dinner for Hank tonight, won't we?" she said. "And sprinkle
it liberally with mother-guilt antivenin. Sounds like fried chicken to
me. Deep-fried greasy served alongside hot biscuits with honey.
What do you think, Bones Jones? Should we make chicken?"

The white shepherd woofed her huge bark, then laid her head
down on her paws. Chloe licked her fingertip and ran it across the
inside flap of the envelope, where traces of the original glue
remained. She held it fast for a few moments, then checked the
seal. Satisfied, she wedged the letter in the middle of their bills and
advertising flyers, giving them all a little crumple for good measure. Hank's habit was to slit envelopes on the side—he had a
major fear of paper cuts—though if it were up to her, she'd get out
of the truck right then, rip it to pieces, and scatter them to the
wind, let the prairie dogs use it for bedding.

Iris's letters came weekly, little pinpricks of guilt, yanks on one
very old umbilical. Hank *was* a good man. At least his mother had
the guts to admit that. He *was* honest and loyal, hardworking as
they came, handsome, too. Much handsomer after four months in
Cameron, Arizona, than his old, soft California self. Chloe had

been here with him a month and seven days, a world record considering her past relationships. Since Fats's death, she'd sworn off men, and then this professor had come along, lent her his shirt, which Hannah had logically shredded, and all that had led to the baby she carried. Some mornings she woke up to the dry northern Arizona air amazed at the facts.

But Iris's gut punches chewed on the edges of their happiness. *Well-meaning individuals.* Jesus H! Like she'd spent the last five months hawking her body on streetcorners and the baby was a sloppy tip, courtesy of a stranger. Some grandmother Iris was going to make. Forget the free baby-sitting. As for marriage, why anybody who disapproved that much of his girlfriend wanted her son married to her was truly confounding. Saying "I will" in front of a judge was none of that old busybody's beeswax. They'd get around to that part just as soon as the idea didn't make Chloe fall over in a dead faint. A husband who couldn't be bothered to drive his wife to the oncologist because it might affect his handicap—now *there* was a convincing argument for wedlock.

Chloe felt her heart tighten down a notch, the organ hold captive a thousand words she wanted to use to defend herself. But up against Iris, fighting wouldn't do any good. What she really needed was to stop at the market, buy that chicken. Grab a box of Bisquick and try to find some vegetable she could stomach that would also please Hank who, these days, seemed to be an expert on the nutritional aspects of plant matter as pertaining to health of knocked-up cowgirls.

After she collected Hank, Chloe'd get dinner started, cover the chicken in foil, let everything simmer. Then she imagined taking Hank by the hand, leading Iris's bad boy to their bed, where she would—there was no other way to put this—do her unladylike best to fuck his lights out. *That* was the kind of letter her Hank deserved, not just on a Friday night after teaching third grade all week and voluntarily staying late three nights to help the slow students, but always, every single day of his life, for putting up with such a stinky mother.

She fired up the Chevy Apache and signaled for a left onto Highway 89, toward Tuba City.

Dear Mrs. Oliver, she mentally composed, a letter she would never mail, let alone set to paper:

Women like me have known all our lives we could try from now until Judgment Day and never fit in with people like you. Hank and me have made a life here in your mother's old cabin. Probably not much of one in your eyes: We shop secondhand stores, eat off unmatched dishes, refinish furniture, drive down to the Big Tree swap meet in Flagstaff every Sunday. Pretty low-class stuff. A half-grown colt munches alfalfa in the corral your son built by hand, like some equine ark, maybe believing if he did it right, it'd call out to me all the way in California and I'd come to him. We're sending down roots, Iris, strong arms into the red rock and the dirt roads that run up to the cabin's front door.

Chloe'd never told him so, but early on, when she first met Hank and found out his parents were alive, she'd had this guarded dream she and Iris might one day become friends. Not mother-daughter close, but kick-off-your-boots friendly. How great that would have been—two women who loved the same man, sitting and talking. Under that beautiful silver hair and the fancy outfits, Chloe sensed Iris's tough core. The woman had lost her daughter. Loss was loss, and Chloe knew how it was to live your life constantly making room for sorrow. In addition to Hank, they had that in common. They should have gotten along. But Iris's letters made it clear that had never been her fantasy. Well, she could light candles, engineer dates for Hank with cultured divorcées, write letters that made her son go so quiet the silence raised Hannah's hackles, and none of it would make any difference. Hate never worked. Despite having lost a daughter and developed cancer in her lifetime, Iris still hadn't figured that one out.

Once, when Chloe was eight years old, one of her foster fathers had come into her bedroom at night. *He's going to tuck the blanket in,* she thought. *He likes me. Wonder if this might be the family that decides to adopt me for good.* In the semi-dark, she turned her face eagerly to his and learned just what hate could make a person capable of.

Since that night she'd spent far too many of the last twenty-six years glimpsing that same vacant look in far too many faces. Maybe some people couldn't help it. They'd been hurt so bad what they really needed was to be shown there was another way to get rid of the pain besides sticking their fingers inside little girls or judging grown-up sons by the women they fell in love with. Something large stood in the way of clear vision. All Chloe knew was that every time shadowy memories like that one crept up on her, she had to turn to face them blazing all the light she could muster. Good existed in everyone, even Iris Oliver, and Chloe tried to remain convinced there were reasonable explanations for the bad. She didn't hold stock in vengeful gods, no matter how many stories Hank could tell about people who did. She'd been hurt and lonesome a lot of her life, starting from her own mother giving her away when she was just a baby on down to what happened last spring with the cops coming onto Hugh Nichols's land and arresting her, but she didn't really hate anybody. Hate kept you separate from people. Separate was a terrible way to live your life, even if it sometimes looked easier on the surface.

Here in Arizona all she needed to do was glance up at the San Francisco peaks to the south to understand how small she really was in the grand scheme of things. Those stone giants stood, goodhearted and patient. The volcanic activity was peaceful today, but three thousand square miles of cinder cones and lava flows underfoot were a reminder that maybe they weren't finished. The Indians understood that; to them land was sacred. The Hopi believed the kachinas made the mountains their wintertime home, and that deep within the range lay the source of all rain clouds. According to the Navajo, Hank had told her, the peaks were one of the prime directions. Chloe thought maybe she could get behind religion that included mountains. Let Iris say whatever she damn well pleased. The baby spoke for them all. *We're Hank's future, Iris. Me and this baby. We're making a home here. Try to live with it. However you can manage it, make your peace.*

*   *   *

KTNN-AM 660 out of Window Rock, the Voice of the Navajo Nation, was playing doo-wop when Chloe drove into Ganado Elementary School's parking lot. It was a Friday afternoon; most of the students had already gone home, anxious for a weekend of playing. Only three teenage boys remained, shooting hoops on the playground, whooping congratulations at each other whenever one managed to throw the ball into the raggedy net. Chloe let Hannah out of the truck and brushed white dog hairs from the seat. The letters tumbled to the middle of the seat, Iris's stink bomb among them, just waiting to punch a hole in Hank's mood. *Summer sure as hell does persist,* Chloe thought, looping a halter and lead rope over her shoulder as she turned her face to feel the last of the day's sun warm her face. She laid her hand across her widening belly and tried to feel the baby under all those layers. He moved all the time now, as if her hands traveling over her skin represented sound; he was all ears to what she might be saying. She was getting used to the crawly feeling of him moving inside her, but not the idea of him someday coming out of her body for good. Being pregnant wasn't all that bad. She got tired easily but her breasts, damn, were beautiful. Everywhere she went men smiled at her. Maybe she'd stay pregnant forever.

She always arrived early, in order to stop and say hello to the horses, who'd been moved to the barn now that school was back in session. Poor old barn—the building had seen better days. Six falling-down stalls opened onto a piecemeal, common arena. It was the students' responsibility to keep it mucked and to feed the horses every morning and evening. With no piped-in water, the water had to be hauled, and mostly the kids remembered, but Chloe always made a point to check the trough. The quality of hay Ganado Elementary could afford wasn't the best, but Arizona horses were tough. They didn't know what to do with treats until Chloe arrived and started giving them lessons. She went from stall to stall, snapping chilly supermarket carrots in half, chatting to each interested muzzle that bent forward to meet her.

"Donatello," she whispered. "How are your legs today, old man?

Take advantage of this sunshine. Soak it up, winter's coming." She guessed the arthritic gray gelding was an Appaloosa/Percheron cross. Like Elmer, her old lesson horse in California, he looked like glue on hooves, but one couldn't ask for a better horse to teach tiny tots. She scratched his broad neck while he nosed her jacket for more carrots, and the smell of grateful horse caused her to fantasize about starting up her own riding school here in Tuba City. It would have to be nonprofit, or lessons for barter, because nobody here had much money. Hank would go ballistic if she tried to do such physical work while she was pregnant. He didn't like that she came down here. Christ, he wouldn't even hear talk about her waitressing until after the baby came, even though there were plenty of part-time possibilities in that area, and they could sure use the money.

She moved down the row, distributing the contents of her forty-nine-cent bag of carrots fairly. It was weird to wake up when she felt like it, and maybe do nothing more ambitious all day long than wash the dishes. She'd painted the kitchen walls, insulated the bedroom, and tacked up cedar paneling. She was about to start work on the bathroom until Hank decided that laying tile might be hazardous to the baby's health.

Inside the last stall stood the paint horse, at least sixteen hands of Overo Medicine Hat, chocolate-and-white mare, unreasonably sweet-natured, given her gender. Chloe fed her some sugar cubes and the mare nickered, and after they were gone, continued gently scrubbing her tongue over the outstretched palm.

So things had gone for weeks now. A bag of carrots and table sugar for this one horse who now trusted the woman who came by five times a week. Chloe held out the halter so the mare could sniff it, connecting the straps and buckle with her sugar fix. She slid it around the mare's neck, waited a minute, then moved it up against her nose. The mare blew out a nervous breath, settled, and Chloe fastened the buckles. The mare allowed herself to be led out of the stall into the arena. Chloe tied her to the fence and began brushing her shabby, well-marked coat. With regular grooming, vitamins,

daily exercise, this horse could be something. She had conformation, willingness, a kind eye. The Indian kids took the other horses
out on the school grounds, ran them into a lather, tried to learn to
rope off them, but the mare they left idle.

Today all that was going to change. Chloe threw a folded blanket
across the mare's back, pushed a hackamore bridle over the halter,
and hitched herself up. Before the mare could think about protest-
ing, Chloe cued her to walk and began to circle her around the
arena in figure eights. It was growing dusky, the Arizona sky
readying itself for another sunset, the paint box spilling its contents
onto the horizon. The basketball players stopped throwing the ball
and came her way.

"Hey, why you riding Sally?" one of them asked.

"Her name's Sally?"

"*Enit*. Sally Ride, like the astronaut."

"Well, Sally's a pretty nice horse. I think somebody ought to be
riding her."

The boy who'd spoken handed the ball to his friend and reached
out to pet the mare. "Yeah. But nobody does in case they might
accidentally wreck her." He pushed back his shock of hair, so black
it looked wet. "She belongs to Junior Whitebear."

"So?"

"Someday he'll come back, and if she's wrecked, Junior'll be
pissed and come looking for you."

"Let him. She won't be wrecked, she'll be in shape." Chloe
legged the mare into a trot. The horse made the transition easily,
her head bent, listening to Chloe's body with her own. "How long's
this Junior fellow been gone?"

The basketball players looked at one another and tried to
remember, counting on fingers. "Must be eight years now."

"That's an awful long time to let a good horse sit wasted. Some
people might call that abuse. I'm riding her."

The boy frowned. "What you gonna do when Junior shows up
and asks why you rode his horse without permission?"

Chloe smiled. "First I'll ask him if he wants to make something of it. Then maybe I'll kick his butt clear to Kingman."

They laughed, hit each other with the ball a few times, the way boys will at that age, Chloe thought, remembering the juvenile offenders she'd worked with, basically decent boys with rotten homes that failed to keep them out of trouble. These boys walking away from the arena fence were a year or two yet from cigarettes and baggy jeans, trying to convince girls to let them feel up their breasts. False bravado and stupid choices; that would be their rehearsal for entrance into the world of men. In Indian country all that was tempered a little by close family ties. Maybe postponed was better than nothing.

Chloe dismounted, checked the mare's feet for stones, gave her a quick brushing, and put her back in her stall. She whistled for Hannah and hurried off to find Hank. She hummed "Ride, Sally, Ride" and smiled to herself at the slight muscular ache tingling in her thighs. Thunder was too much of a baby to work yet. He wasn't gelded. If Hank wouldn't let her tile the bathroom, the mare would do as a substitute activity.

"Short Dog Johnson's turning out to be quite the artist," Hank said. "Today I read them the story of Daedalus and Icarus. Later, during art, kid draws a set of wings, Chloe. He has the architecture down fairly accurately, and he detailed each individual feather. He tells me, 'Mr. Oliver, if Icarus had been wearing this kind of flying wing he wouldn't have falled.' Falled. If there was a library worth spit in this town I would have bet money he'd read a book on avian anatomy."

"Maybe you're just one hell of a storyteller."

Hank smiled. "Thanks. I just wish the other kids weren't always giving him the business."

"The cooties thing, huh?"

Hank nodded. "Poor little guy. No dad in the picture, his mother working all the time. He's got no friends except for his sketch-book."

"Kids can be brutal. Second thoughts about the job?"

"No. Third grade isn't that bad, especially if we get sunsets like this one every night. Though I must admit I'm experiencing a philosophical conflict over having to assign a 'slow readers' group when half these guys aren't even on speaking terms with the alphabet."

"Sounds like typical school bullshit to me."

Hank leafed through the mail, his fingers stopping at his mother's letter. He set the envelope down on his lap, unopened.

"Aren't you going to read it?"

"Later on," he said, leaning over to kiss her.

Outside, the highway peeled away behind them. They passed the roadside stands, empty now, in the shadow of a billboard for a drilling company. "Red Power" was neatly spray-painted over the advertisement, obscuring the company's intentions, more like an insistent claim than any graffiti announcing gang boundaries. Hannah sat up between them as Chloe drove the winding road to the cabin, whining when she recognized they were nearing home. Hank tapped the letter on his thigh, and in Chloe's mind, the song was singing itself deep into her cells: *Ride, Sally, ride.*

5

Saturday, November 28

Dear Kit,

It's been raining like a bitch for weeks, then about a
half hour ago, everything suddenly went so quiet and
creepy I looked out the window and what do you know,
my first Arizona snowstorm. So I run out there and hold
up my hands like a three-year-old, watching the flakes
land on my skin and melt. If anybody saw they'd no
doubt think, "Typical Californian."

Hank's off in search of a cord of wood that won't cost us
a fortune. Money's tight, but he'd never say so out loud.
Getting pretty good at this man-against-the-wilderness
routine, our Hank. Braving the supermarket, too. Mark
my words, after that, he'll stop off at some used bookstore.
He'll go without shaving cream and wear socks with holes
in the toes, but when it comes to books he shakes the wallet clean. Ain't that just like an educated man, spending his
last few dimes on books for the classroom? Something to

remember when you start liking boys. Meanwhile,
Hannah and me are snug indoors by the stove, looking out
the windows. Where there was bare red earth and rocks
now it's starting to make little drifts against the barn, real
pretty, kind of like those old-time Christmas cards with the
sprinkled-on glitter. Only sun-baked California babes like
you and me can get a kick out of such weather.

You asked what it's like being pregnant. Truthfully, I feel
like a pot-belly stove, hot down there all the time.
Everybody's wearing thermals and here I sit, barefoot. You
should see my breasts—big as grapefruit! I take off my shirt
and Hank gets this really stupid grin, like he hit the tit jackpot. My bad ankle swells a little, especially after I ride. I
swear, Hank about freaks every time I get within ten feet of
a horse. Like I haven't ridden every single day of my life
save for the one I was in jail. The doctor at the clinic gets all
riled about it, but the way I see things, if I have to give up
cigarettes and coffee, I get to keep riding. That's only fair.

Lots of color horses on the reservation. The big-mouthed
cowboys tell endless jokes about them, like wearing big
hats and sucking a cheekful of Copenhagen makes them
experts on anything besides stained teeth. I've been kind
of looking after the school horses while Hank teaches.
There's a pretty decent paint mare who belongs to this
jeweler dude who everyone says got world-famous and
moved off the reservation to someplace yuppie. The Navs
go on about him like he's their own personal long-lost
Hollywood Square. I wonder if he trained her. She has one
of those rocking-horse canters you'd just die for.

Hank's happy enough. I watch him with the Indian kids.
It's just elementary school, making their letters and sounding out words, poster painting, but he comes home so
excited you'd think the teaching part beat the paycheck.
Summer wasn't so bad, when there was stuff to do, like
work on fixing up this place, go exploring, but I miss stink-

ing of horse sweat, aching in every muscle, serving breakfasts and filling up my pockets with tips. These days it's mostly my bladder that gets sore thanks to Junior riding it all day. Feels like a million years ago I had my own school, lesson horses, riding students. When Diane took over did she keep offering the group lesson on Saturdays?

God, I miss California. The view of the Painted Desert from Third Mesa, those tiny horsehair baskets they sell at the Cameron Trading Post, the big charge Hannah gets when she dumps over the trash cans Hank thinks he's booby-trapped—it's all right, but it isn't home yet.

Hey, ask your dad if you can come visit for spring break. Tell Rich Wedler his last best waitress said he should cut the moths loose from his wallet and fly you to Flagstaff. If he won't spring for the shuttle from Phoenix, I'll drive down and get you. Mention that we have three museums and the Grand Canyon'd make a great science project. Tell him you need cross-cultural experiences. Tell him Hank said that part.

And speaking of foreign lands, in a couple more months I guess I'll be somebody's mother. Hard to picture. This baby has got to be a boy because I sure don't have a clue how to raise a girl, unless she's just like you, all attitude and pretty red hair. Speaking of hair, are you still dyeing yours Down There?

Write soon. Send pictures. Here's one of Hank just before he fell off the barn roof. He only bruised his shoulder a little. I slathered it with Bigel oil. Hope you guys had a great Thanksgiving and your father didn't feed you diner chow. Say hey to Lita for me. Tell her to keep chopping the vegetables on a slant. I know how much that rankles your dad.

Big hugs from the big mama,
Chloe

P.S. Thunder just laid down in the snow and made a horse angel!

                              *   *   *

Chloe set down the ballpoint pen and stretched her cramped fingers, examining her winter-chapped hands. As she stamped and
licked the envelope for the letter to her old boss's daughter, she ran
her toes over the back of the sleeping dog beneath the desk, digging deep into her thick, white fur. Hannah sighed and, without
opening her eyes, continued napping. When the weather started
turning bad, thunder and lightning, tennis-ball-size hail, the shepherd ran away, down their dirt road toward Flagstaff proper. One
time she'd been gone a week. Chloe finally discovered her hanging
out with the bikers at the Silver Saddle Saloon off Highway
89—*forty* goddamn miles away. The bikers made remarks about
how a mother-to-be who couldn't keep her dog at home wasn't
likely to fare better with a child, and Chloe was afraid to flip them
off, this being their territory, not hers. Bottom line, until spring
Hannah stayed tethered to a lead or indoors where Chloe could
keep an eye on her.

She sniffed at her cup of tea and gave a little shudder: cold,
green, and definitely good for you. If only there were some
Hershey's cocoa in the house. She pictured that old-fashioned,
sturdy brown-and-silver tin with the pry-off top—universal kid
medicine. Chocolate helped. Strong black coffee would be better,
but if Hank smelled coffee on her breath, he'd be on the phone to
Dr. Carrywater in the time it took her to spit it out. *If I was meant to
eat grass I'd have been born a cow*, she tried to tell him. But then he'd
kiss her neck and gently press his hand to her belly, saying, *Do you
have any idea how sexy pregnancy looks on you? I get hard just looking at
you. Drink half the tea, do it for the baby.* Mostly she did, but their
spiky cactus plants on the kitchen windowsill didn't seem to fare
too badly on herbal supplements.

As she watched her colt try to make sense of the snow, she imagined holding a Wedler's Café mug of steaming chocolate. Atop the
surface puffy white marshmallows bumped each other like chunks
of melting iceberg. It would be a Thursday afternoon in Kit's dad's

restaurant, Chloe's last break before filling ketchup bottles and salt shakers, wiping down the Naugahyde booths, collecting Kit, and heading out to the stables. Some old geezer in the corner would be snoring over his newspaper, and Chloe would just let him nap there until she finished her cocoa. She'd hear the sound of silverware clattering into dishwater, smell whatever soup was simmering for tomorrow's special, almost taste the undercurrent of Comet and disinfectant floor cleaner, and all that familiarity would make her feel safe.

Maybe in the crowded supermarket aisles of Flagstaff's Food4Less Hank would right this minute pick up her thoughts and pull down a package of chocolate from the shelf. Not likely. Hank didn't veer off the shopping list the way she did, instinctively understanding that fat yellow potatoes or homemade tacos could go a long way toward soothing the melancholy from aimless winter days. Particularly not an ex-college professor now teaching elementary school to Indian children for less than half his usual salary.

She'd come to him with nine grand and pocket change—her settlement from that developer-engineered bust on Hugh Nichols's land, where the police had broken her ankle and charged her with assault when what they were really angling for was a way onto Hugh's property. If Hank's lawyer hadn't fought so hard, she might still be sitting in that jail cell, her skin crawling with shame. He'd stood by her, and continued to do so, even though she could tell his parents considered her pure trailer trash. That kind of loyalty made it as much his money as hers. They'd put it to good use building the barn, wrapping the summer cabin's water pipes in heat tape, double-glazing the windows, buying new tires for her truck, and rebuilding his Honda's transmission. The biggest drawback to having money was that it didn't last forever. Hank had the condo in California up for sale, but the real estate market there was "soft" or some damn thing.

Sometimes it felt like they were just sort of dragging along with the program set by the baby, the by-product of their crazy-for-each-other desire. Well, worrying was one sure way to get wrinkles. As if he sensed her fear, outside, the colt brayed in terror at the snow.

She sighed, dribbled tea on the cacti, poured the excess down the granite sink, slipped on Hank's sweat pants and jacket, and toed her feet into her old Tony Lamas. She twisted her thick blond hair back into a bun and anchored the ballpoint pen through it. Grabbing an afghan from the couch, she wrapped it around herself, hitched the leggings over her belly and opened the back door. She'd learned not to trust those bright blue skies. Arizona winters played practical jokes. The air was so bitter that each cold breath felt as if it could freeze her lungs. To the northeast the sky was crowded with pewter-colored snow clouds, moving along toward Colorado and New Mexico. She stopped a moment in the yard, getting her bearings, fighting the solitary panic that sometimes came over her way out here with neighbors and a real town so far away. The idea of a winter's worth of snow on the way was a little blinding. The bigness of sky felt all-encompassing, as if the swirling white dust were the result of some massive bird fluttering his wings. *I don't belong here*, she thought, the scar on her shoulderblade itching as it always did when she was feeling without purpose and eager to hit the road. As if to concur, the baby kicked hard at her ribs, twice.

When Dr. Lois pressed the stethoscope to her skin and chatted about growth charts and gestational age, Chloe smiled vaguely, imagining the pregnancy was happening to someone else. After those exams she rewarded herself with a ride on the jeweler's mare. In the shadow of the cottonwoods, along those bare dirt roads, she gulped in the fragrance of fall turning to winter hungrily, the fresh, dry, earthy smell scrubbing her clean, simplifying everything, erasing these unspeakable thoughts. Astride the mare at the canter, she imagined the baby clinging to her ribs and her unspoken warning: *Any child of mine better learn to hang on*.

From the barn she took careful steps along the fenceline through the snow toward the squealing horse. Beneath her boots she could feel ice crunching. It would be a mistake to hurry. She could fall;

the baby could get hurt. Too many nights she woke perched on the cliff edge of dread that he might have something wrong with him already. The months had passed so quickly; she hadn't seen the doctor until she was five months gone. She'd never heard of a pre-natal vitamin until the tall, dark Indian physician tucked a bottle of them into her hand, insisting she not skip a day until she delivered. But this baby grew and thrived no matter what she fed it. Corn chips or chili, or that one day last week she put away a whole Halloween bag of Reese's Peanut Butter Cups. Whoever he was, chowing down inside her, she was growing one tough little pony.

Low in her throat, she made nickering noises and stretched out a hand to the colt. Inside her palm rested the last handful of grain, mouse-nibbled and meager. Wild-eyed, Thunder sniffed the snowy air, catching the scent. The idea of food began to work its sedative magic. He came her way, inch by inch, placing each hoof down carefully, checking to be certain that the snow would hold him. Chloe waited, her body still, snow falling on her shoulders, sprin-kling the afghan's loose purple weave. If there was one thing Chloe Morgan knew how to do, it was be patient with animals. Waiting was step one in an animal's coming to trust you. Patience helped one make difficult decisions, too, like having her old horse Absalom put to sleep when her mind knew he was beyond saving yet her heart wasn't so convinced. She missed that horse as much today as she had the day Gabe Hubbard slipped the needle into his jugular. Thunder was company; Absalom was like standing in the presence of a mute angel. Waiting, she imagined, would eventually convince her if what was in her heart amounted to real love or whether it was just some extended case of midlife lust. For the mil-lionth time since her periods had stopped coming, she wondered: Would she wait to love the baby like that once he was born? Could a motherless woman like herself even hope to learn the art?

Other women wanted babies in such a direct, certain way. They didn't have these continuous, nagging doubts. Some spilled over with maternal instinct so thick they ran ads in newspapers. These same ladies didn't care to sift through older children offered up for adoption and never chosen, like Chloe had been. They didn't wonder who their real mothers were or *where* they were; they were grandmothers-in-waiting, links in a common, unbreakable female chain. In the classified section of the paper there were always a few of those please-have-a-baby-for-us ads tucked between people wanting to get rid of satellite dishes and jet skis, high-dollar items that had failed to heal bad marriages. They promised to pay for all the medical expenses, maybe buy you a new car if you gave them your baby. Not a puppy from an oversize litter or a horse you'd outgrown—your own flesh and blood. Christ, what made a woman go through nine months if she wasn't going to keep it?

"Here, now, you idiot," she soothed to the horse, reaching over the fence to stroke his neck while he ate the oats. "It's only snow. If I can hack it, you can, too."

She had turned thirty-four on August 13, standing in this very spot, alongside the fence of this corral Hank had just finished building to hold the horse he'd bought from Asa Carver and arranged to have given to her. The gift meant more to her than any stupid diamond ring. If the truth be known, his faith had driven her past the California/Arizona state line and the opaque, greenish Colorado River. She'd crossed over the state border and stopped wanting to turn back. It was the first time in her life since Fats died that she felt herself moving with purpose toward something.

But saying that out loud was impossible. She cooked dinner, folded the laundry; in bed she kissed Hank for all she was worth, and lately had *thought* about adding a muffled "I love you" to her sexual repertoire. But when Hank made love to her, it was as if he was constantly pushing for more. No matter how many places she hid herself, he poked at every one. What he wanted she did not know how to deliver. Nevertheless, every morning it came as a profound surprise that here, three months later, the baby almost ready to be born, she still felt the hesitation. Not that Hank wasn't worth loving, because if any man was, one who paid your bail, hired a lawyer, and abandoned his old comfortable life for you surely was. It had to do with her history. She had buried Fats

Valentine vowing to never again let love infect her soul. Maybe perseverance was another name for love.

The colt greedily finished the oats and ran his rough pink tongue across Chloe's palm, making her shiver and grin and feel maybe just a little bit sexy. *It's* Hank's *baby you're having*, she reminded herself. *Not just your own, his. Iris is full of shit.* There might even be a dotted line dividing the baby's body where his features and genes made up a smart, thriving kid headed for college, while her half with its mysterious history—that shade tree of who-knew-what genetics—scowled and waited to be assigned to permanent detention.

She turned her head at the familiar sound of the pickup, gears grinding to make it up the gravel driveway. Hank was back home, safe again. He got out of the truck holding two bags of groceries. From the top of the bag clutched in his left arm she spotted the tin of cocoa peeking out, the light glinting off the silver metal. Her throat tightened, and she willed the tears back into her ducts. This was a good life, a real one. She turned away from the horse and walked as fast as was safe to the father of her unborn baby.

6

"Goddamn son-of-a-bitch cheap-shit pot holder!" Chloe flung the useless square of terry cloth into the sink, dropping the saucepan in the process. Boiled red potatoes jumped in their skins, rolling across the floor in the scalding water. Hank bent down to pick them up with a dishtowel.

"Go put your feet up and read a magazine. Let me finish supper like I wanted to in the first place."

She ran cold tap water over her hand. It was only a steam burn, but it was aggravated by a solid week of cabin fever. "You're the one who works all week," she snapped. "The least I can do is rustle your dinner."

Hank turned off the tap and inspected her palm. "Which you do all week and I deeply appreciate. Last time I checked, this was the weekend, which is my turn to cook. Besides, I make better mashed potatoes than you do. Let me get you some ice."

"I don't need ice!" She sat down hard on the couch.

As if canned stew and bread on weekdays constituted the royal treatment. Chloe hugged a throw pillow while he mashed leftover cloves of baked garlic in with the potatoes, adding a generous dollop of sour cream, as if she were a prize cow he was fattening up for the county fair. He rolled the chicken pieces she was planning to fry in cracker crumbs, then set them under the broiler. He steamed broccoli, then made a sauce of lemon and butter to pour over it in an effort to disguise the fact that like herb tea, it was green and healthy. Her hand throbbed, and her skin felt stretched to the breaking point. There weren't any magazines in the cabin she hadn't read three times over. The weather was driving her crazy. Snow fell, then melted away in the bright sun only to sleet and fall again. The climate was so dismal that if they'd had a TV the reception would be for shit. She took deep breaths and tried to calm herself down, scrub away the claustrophobia. She imagined the paint mare underneath her, the two of them moving effortlessly through the woods. When Hank called her to the table, she'd eat the damn vegetables and smile.

Hank whistled as he set down plates. He'd spent the day splitting wood and courting frostbite. All that work they'd had done on the plumbing, and then the damp spot appeared on the floor. Despite it all, his glass was set permanently at the half-full mark. Iris was right; there were women in the world who deserved such a great guy. Too bad Hank hadn't knocked up any of them.

Twenty minutes later, she sat at the table and humbly lifted her fork. "Some feast. Thanks."

"There's enough for seconds, if you want it."

Undoubtedly thirds on the broccoli. "Let's just see how far I get with this."

They ate supper with the curtains open, watching the snow continue its descent. The radio weather report had sounded ominous. A foot on the ground and two more on the way. Nobody dared say the word blizzard. The snow looked like it was going to stick. Build up into drifts that would last until spring. Hank refilled her mug with cocoa and apologized again for the lack of marshmallows.

"It's okay," she told him. "But next time, buy a giant bag. Those suckers are so full of preservatives they'll last until the year 2000."

"You know, with the baby, you really shouldn't have preservatives."

Her face burned. "Yeah, you're right. Plain cocoa's fine."

He smiled. "I want you to get used to this. Me making dinner, you just resting."

Hank wanted what his mother didn't, and all she wanted was something to do and a few lousy marshmallows. After they'd finished supper, he cleared the dishes and set them in the basin. When Chloe saw him starting to reach for the dish soap and sponge, she said softly, "Hank?"

He turned to look at her. The changes in the California professor whose life she'd run her train into only eleven months ago continued to transform him. The day they first met she was elbow-deep in mare's blood, helping Dr. Gabe Hubbard yank a colt from its dead mother. The pale and slight man who had unwittingly tendered her his shirt was no longer nose-deep in student papers and community college politics; he was a ruddy-skinned, windburned Arizonan. He had calluses and muscles, the emblems of a working man. He wore flannel shirts open three buttons down his chest and Sears catalogue long underwear beneath. The pectoral definition beneath his shirt pockets had the power to make her stomach tighten, her juices flow, to make her yearn to do all the things to him that had led up to the pregnancy that now bound them to each other.

Chloe stroked Hannah's head. "Dishes will still be dirty in a half hour."

Hank came to the rocking chair where she sat and knelt down. "What's the matter? Is your back aching again? Do you need a massage?"

"For God's sake, Hank. What were you, a servant in a former life?"

He laughed. "Who knows? One of the unfortunate drawbacks to reincarnation is never being privy to what went on before. All I know for certain is I'm a grateful man in this one." He lifted her sweatshirt and kissed her hot, round belly, the place he always kissed first.

She thought about his words as she held him close, felt his lips move in a silent language, his face nestled close to the source of her deeper aching, the longing that never seemed to get satisfied. He wore his desire as openly as a tattoo, and the frankness of it got her all excited. The baby seemed to kick the both of them at once, to say, *Enough of that already. Get to the practical issues: Agree on my name.* There was time for all that later. She took Hank's hand and led him down the hall to the bedroom.

December 3
Le Butt End of Hell

Dear Chloe,

Whereas junior high school bit the occasional weenie, high school sucks decomposing donkey. My classes are as boring as they were in September:

Algebra I, too dumb to discuss. I am getting a C.

World History, like if the Crusades isn't a fancy name for rape and pillage, then what is? I'm getting a B because the teacher likes it when I argue with him. I guess it proves one of us isn't dead.

Check this out: For Physical Science my dad had to sign a permission slip so I could learn about doing *It*, like the walls in our apartment aren't so thin and him and Lita so mega-horny I can't hear them every night. *Oh, Rich, my wild knight! Enter my kingdom!* I'm getting an A in there. I'm a little tired of hearing about zygotes and unwed mother statistics, I'm sure! Don't they have any unwed father statistics?

Art, at which I completely, totally without question fail. Kit Wedler, the reason they invented paint-by-numbers!

English, which is all about stupid stories, verb tenses and semicolons. Way major duh; how did I manage to communicate without them?

Which brings us to my old favorite, P.E. Well, at least here no one monitors the showers. It's pass/fail and even the geeks pass.

You have snow? Real, actual snow? Not trucked in by Century 21 realtors so kids can sled for an hour and destroy the park grass? We had Santa Ana winds all this week. It's eighty. I'm still wearing shorts and T-shirts and flip-flops and gobs of sunscreen. I wish I could come see you right now. Mr. Gaytan, my English teacher, is reading us "The Lottery," and no, it isn't anything to do with this week's jackpot, it's some dopey story about stoning a poor lady to death. Probably he wrote it since no one I asked ever heard of it.

Well, keep your fingers crossed Lita can convince my dad to buy me a plane ticket for Christmas. I can't wait to see your boobs! Thanks to Science I now know what you do with a condom—roll it over a banana! I can definitely help fruit avoid getting pregnant in the future. This morning Lita looks at me and goes, "Honey, you are growing into a woman," and gets all misty over her shredded wheat. I mean, really, gag me!

So why haven't you and Hank got married? Afraid he'll make you wear aprons and bake cookies? Hank makes way better cookies than you ever could. You know, if you got married, I could be your bridesmaid. We could wear matching dresses and carry those bitchen blue roses. I'm baby-sitting all the time now, so I could take care of the Joey for you if you want to get a job. I wouldn't charge you very much if it meant I could leave this god-forsaken pit of a school and all the backpack-toting Doc Marten zombie clones.

Hey, do you guys have a computer? Lita bought us one and I have E-mail now. My address is GrlNxDr@cms.com. It is *so* cool surfing the Net. I have a friend in Portugal and this one guy in London thinks I am on that show

Friends! So E me if you do. I can forward you a list of the coolest websites.

Time for lovely P.E. We are doing soccer, which you will not be surprised to learn sucks just as much as basketball. If by some miracle the ball comes my way, I plan to kick it straight over the fence.

Love from your once again redheaded in all areas, including Down There, friend,
Kit

P.S. Here's some cool boys' names I picked out for you during the interminable (Oh, God, I'm actually using a vocabulary word!) "Lottery" reading: Keanu, Corey, Rory, Ocean, Nathan, Colin, Clark, and Sam. My vote's for Ocean, but Sam's a good name, too. Basic and easy to spell. The baby Edmund and Maria are adopting on All My Children's *name is Sam. Edmund is a* fox among foxes.

Chloe refolded Kit's letter into her jacket pocket and pulled up the flaps of her collar before she made her way back to the truck with their bills and advertising circulars. The Cameron Post Office was about the size of a rich lady's walk-in closet. Their box was #879, zip code 86020. On the bulletin board above the lick-your-stamps counter hung a pest-control announcement regarding the hantavirus. It sported a line drawing of two innocent-looking deer mice/vectors. Chloe'd heard the news bulletins, but not of any actual person who'd caught the virus. The usual navy recruitment poster offered a way out of poverty if you could believe all that job-training horseshit. The Navajo Tribal Authority Purification Report inferred that "total coliform presence in the water supply was within acceptable limits," translating to: Find shit in your water supply, it's your own damn problem. She tried not to look at the missing children posters, but that little girl from New York State was still up there. In her photo, smiling big for the camera, Mona

H. was five. Next to that picture there was a computer-generated likeness of her at age ten. Most of the time the notices said "custodial dispute," which meant that the missing tot was probably safe with one parent when a judge had decreed she was supposed to be with the other, but this little girl was a stranger abduction. Five years was a long time to beat those kinds of odds. Heartache didn't come close to describing how the mother of that little girl must have endured the years. Chloe pushed open the snow doors and walked back outside.

The Trading Post stood like a picture postcard of the old West—brown sandstone walls, tiny white Christmas lights illuminating the frost-rimed store windows, a smoking chimney inviting hardy winter tourists into relative comfort so they could load up on unique, authentic, Native American Christmas gifts. The Laundromat and a small grocery attached to the Trading Post each had a separate entrance. The market was pricey compared with Flagstaff, but sometimes that beat having to drive an hour in the snow to pick up a quart of milk. Behind the gift shop, the restaurant with the pressed-tin ceiling offered ordinary coffee and decent Arizona fare, not to mention authentic fry bread, deep-fried pillows of mouth-watering dough. The massive sandstone fireplace was no doubt blazing, making for the perfect place to sit and chat away a cold afternoon, but not a drop of alcohol would contribute to the ambience in reservation territory.

In California somebody would have torn the place down, modernized it to contemporary blandness, but one of the reasons the Trading Post stood intact was its historic significance. It had been built in 1916, named after Ralph Cameron, Hank had informed her, Arizona's last delegate before the territory declared statehood. Hank knew things like that; Chloe could go her entire lifetime unaware.

There was a newly built, pseudo-adobe two-story motel between the museum gallery and living quarters, usually occupied by the now-absent owner, and a multitiered old rose garden, the bushes pruned back for winter. Hank said they shot commercials for art magazines in the museum, taking advantage of the saguaro-rib ceilings and turn-of-the-century antique Navajo blankets. Across the parking lot from the house/museum stood their tiny post office and the gas pumps. The Honda tended to get stuck in the snow, so they usually took the truck and drove slowly. Given a bad enough winter storm, even emergency vehicles had difficulty getting through. Chloe got in the Chevy truck while Hank filled up the gas tank.

He was eyeing a brand-new four-wheel-drive Jeep Cherokee some tourist had pulled into the service bay. Chrome accents and tall ribbed tires, stereo blasting—men drooled over that crap. Hank had never seemed the type, but Chloe sensed his palpable envy at the go-anywhere transmission, the lure of a new car that didn't require babying. Ever practical, he coveted it about as long as it took to fill the tank and check the oil.

He got in the driver's side and turned the key in the ignition. "You mind going in the Trading Post so I can talk to Dog Johnson's mother for a moment?"

"Might as well. My big ass'll fall asleep sitting out here in the truck."

He gave her that look that meant, *Say "butt." "Butt" is such a cute word; "ass" is bowling alley talk.*

She grinned. Pregnancy hadn't crippled her ability to needle his upper-class upbringing out here in the bush. They drove fifty feet and parked, zipped up jackets, and got out. Around them the winter winds keened eerily. They were near the lip of the Little Colorado River Canyon, where the wind gusted constantly over the red rock formations sounding for all the world like the faint whistle of an ancient somebody looking for his lost dog. Hannah was locked up safe at home. Snow seemed to relieve the animal of what little brains she had left. On her fifty-foot tether, she raced the fenceline, deviling Thunder. Maybe, Chloe thought, winter had caused the white shepherd to enter a canine second childhood.

Hank held the Trading Post door open for her. Wonderful, woodsmoke-smelling heat blasted Chloe in the face. Just inside the door she asked, "Hank, ever wish you'd knocked up some girl who at least had a college education?"

A pair of elderly tourists shot her disparaging looks.

He squeezed her hand and whispered, "There's book-smart and there's heart-smart. Given the opportunity, I'll knock you up again."

The shocked tourists paid for their gewgaws and left in a huff. Maybe they didn't have sex anymore. All that belly-slapping, sweaty play was part of their history, like Ralph Cameron and Arizona's territorial status, so they bought expensive statues and tooled silver, desperate to fill up the empty places. She thought of Kit's letter in her pocket and prayed Rich would let her come for spring break. Chloe could last until spring if she knew Kit was coming. Kit Wedler—a high school freshman—aside from a dead horse she couldn't revive and a man she'd once loved who drank himself to death, there wasn't anybody else alive Chloe wanted to see.

Hank went to speak with Corrine Johnson. Corrine ran the shop in the owner's absence. At ninety pounds, the last five made up of squash-blossom necklace, her appearance could deceive, but only once. Her son Dog had a gift with paints and colored pencils. Hank spent extra time with the boy all the other children lived to bully, and urged Corrine to encourage him in the arts, hoping to boost the boy's self-esteem. Corrine's response was consistent: *Whatever gifts Dog's got will last past childhood. They'll keep while he learns his numbers and letters same as anybody else.*

While the two of them butted heads over educational approach, Chloe wandered the store aisles, admiring the riches, saving the pawn jewelry she adored for last. On the right side of the show-room, mass-produced tourist items like mold-cast storyteller dolls and imitation San Ildefonso pottery bowls hardly stayed on the shelves a week. Icky dyed turquoise adjustable rings hung from a turning tabletop rack on one side. From the other flashed copper bracelets that might not do much for arthritis but would for sure relieve you of five bucks. The tourists ate it up. There were color posters of the Grand Canyon, all purples and peaches that made the natural wonder look like an airbrushed Disneyland sunset. All

Chloe'd done so far was peer over the south rim while Hank explained that it wasn't merely a canyon, it was a "geological clock," and that every color variation in the rock represented a different era, replete with different inhabitants. All that history! If the span and depth of the canyon alone hadn't made her dizzy, his words drilled the point into her marrow. She tried to imagine what it looked like from the inside looking up. Arizona, with its big sky and rocky monuments, its wide-open reservations and crazy cowtown redneck inhabitants, made her feel as tiny as the egg that had tumbled down her fallopian tube and turned into their baby.

The Trading Post bookshelves were thick with hiking guides and fly-fishing advice. Below that umbrella stands held those corny bow-and-arrow sets made of rubber and plastic. Corrine kept a steady stream of R. Carlos Nakai flute music going in the background. Sometimes she lit incense, and the place went otherworldly and dreamy. There were ample kid diversion kits, ranging from coloring books Dog Johnson would turn up his nose at to Travel Yahtzee. Chloe studied it all, trying to imagine a life with children. Every weekend she told Hank she'd check out the Thrift Shop with him, take a look at those cribs and baby strollers, but nearly always found some excuse not to go. She was afraid to tell him that she felt superstitious, that if they got too "ready," something was certain to go wrong. Besides, babies could sleep anywhere, in a pinch, inside a dresser drawer or a laundry basket. All they really needed was diapers. Right next door they sold diapers. Under the long skeins of dyed wool hanging from the ceiling just above the customers' heads, materials the weavers sometimes took in trade for their wares, which sold in the blanket room, diapers, lotions, and cans of baby formula abounded.

She passed by the designer concho belts with their three-thousand-dollar price tags and the special displays of featured artists in the center of the store. Polaroids of Hollywood stars were thumbtacked to the walls. Ann-Margret and Morgan Fairchild decked out in southwestern jewelry. Once Corrine made a special point of showing them a belt and earrings of spiny oyster and coral pieces custom-designed for Elizabeth Taylor. Tiny Corrine pinned the heavy earrings to her lobes and modeled. Her brother, Oscar, took one look and said, "Now all you need is a construction worker and a prenuptial."

That new jewelry was too much like a modern-art-museum exhibit, some of it so outlandish it seemed like a waste of precious metal. At the pawn case Chloe's heart beat a little more in tune with the silver. The old pieces spoke her language. Worn thin and dull, little nicks and scratches reminding her of old school-horse tack, the silver was lovingly buffed from its original shine to absolute ownership. She understood the desire to wear the ungodly huge stones set into buckles and cuff bracelets. It made sense, if you only got to own one beautiful thing in your life, if the rest of your life was about scraping the barrel. She appreciated the painstaking labor involved, but more than that, how it must have felt to give it up when times got hard.

Some of more simply crafted items were marked as low as twenty dollars. Oscar might be able to cut her a deal on one of those bracelets. Come April, Rich willing, she'd haul Kit up here and let her pick out something for a belated Christmas present. Kit would adore one of those stamped bangles. Polish it up like Oscar said, with Ivory dish detergent, the original shine would come back. Through the glass Chloe mentally inventoried all the ticketed items and let her gaze come to rest on her favorite piece, an oblong, odd blue stone set in an unremarkable silver band.

The egg-size stone was the blue of jay's wings. Unique in the sea of vivid turquoise, it was a brighter blue than slate, but deeply flecked with gray, as if far down in the heart of the rock there lay another, more complicated history. Whoever set it into the band had chattered the silver's edge to mirror those serrated gray flecks. A stone to dream on, make wishes on, she thought to herself, knowing if she said so aloud, Hank would probably tell her to lie down and make her drink something green.

Corrine's brother, Oscar, came over and opened the locked case with his heavy ring of keys.

"That's okay, Oscar. I'm just looking."

"You come visit this ring a lot, Chloe," he said, lifting it from the case and setting it atop the counter on a square of presentation velvet. "Maybe this here stone's talking to you, you know, telling you something important."

Unable to resist, she picked the ring up and slid it to the knuckle of her left ring finger. It would have easily gone further, but she didn't want to find out it fit and then have to give it back. She squinted up at the Indian man who was slowly becoming her friend. "Oscar, you're not talking to a tourist, so stop yanking my chain. Or are you trying out some kind of new-age sales technique?"

He laughed, exposing the whitest teeth against his dark skin. "Hell, no. That's Lander blue. From Battle Mountain, Nevada. Vein's been mined dry. In this whole store we got only maybe two, three chunks of actual Lander. You must love it a lot to come visit it all the time."

"Yeah, I guess I do."

Oscar did repair work for the Trading Post customers and when the need arose, reluctantly stepped in as a part-time salesman. He wore thick-lensed black-framed glasses and had skin the rich brown shade of her old Hermès saddle, the one she'd left behind in California for Wes McNelly to sell. In his gray Polartec pullover, Oscar looked gentle and friendly, the antithesis of Corrine. Except for times she saw the whole Johnson family gathered together at Indian functions, it was hard to believe they were brother and sister. "This ring says something to me, all right. It says 'Hey, guess what? I cost three hundred and seventy-five dollars.'"

Oscar laughed and she handed it back.

"Damn, that's a lot of money. Think anyone will ever buy it?"

"Somebody should." He held the ring up in the light a moment before sliding it back on the velvet cone with the others. "I know for a fact this ring used to belong to old Molly Manygoats' grandfather, Ben. That was way before your time or mine. If some jeweler worth his tools was to come and take a good look, like say Junior

Whitebear, he'd be able to tell, you know? Probably buy the ring just to set the stone free."

"Are we talking the same Whitebear who owns that mare down at Ganado El?"

"Yeah. Sally's his horse."

"So what's the big deal about him anyway? Nobody can mention his name without sounding like he's a holy man."

Oscar looked away and Chloe could tell she'd touched a nerve. "When a Skin makes good, people sit up and take notice. Then they start lookin' for reasons to resent him. That's Junior all over the place. But it really is that good of a piece, that ring. Junior's in New York, I bet, someplace with central heat and Wonderbra models. Probably has better stones than this old ring falling out of his pockets. Probably never even thinks about what he left behind. Tell you what. Get Hank to buy it for you if you love it so much. Corrine likes to give him the business, but she's fond of Hank, you know? All that being nice to Dog gets to her. Yeah, doing for her kid is the best way to get a favor out of my sister. Corrine'd work out a real good layaway. Why don't you ask for this ring for Christmas?"

For a moment Chloe's heart soared. In their old world, where paychecks came for each of them weekly and Hank had a pension plan he hadn't borrowed against, such an undertaking might have been possible. Extravagant, but within the realm of possibility. How could she ask for a turquoise ring on the merit of its prettiness alone when the ring Hank *wanted* to give her was a wedding band? She patted her belly. "Oscar, see this blimp in the hanger? This here's what Hank and me are giving each other for Christmas."

Oscar winked and pulled a tooled silver baby rattle out of the display case. He rolled it across the velvet and inside, small pieces of metal rattled, making a faint baby music. Taking full advantage of the salesman's opportunity set before him he said, "Then ask for this."

A horsetrader's smile turned up the corners of Chloe's mouth. "You're getting good," she said. "Not quite as cutthroat as Corrine, but you almost had me."

"Don't be so quick to walk away." He pressed the rattle into her open palm. The silver was warm from his fingers and as light as a bird's bone. "This here is one of Whitebear's early pieces. Look at the work, you'll understand why everyone thinks he's so hot."

How could she not look? Incised into the rattle's swooping barbell ends were wavy lines for water, miniature segmented horsetails growing at the water's edge, and a simply rendered but unmistakable fawn, its head bent to take a drink. On the rattle's handle a small humpbacked bear was stamped alongside the initials JR and the word "Sterling."

"How much?"

Oscar made a grim face. "Well, say Corrine knew this piece had come in and that it was Junior's, you know? It'd already be on its way to Tucson to this *bilagáana* collector who's got a standing purchase order for any of Whitebear's early stuff. But hell, just because Corrine's acting like a manager don't mean she has to know everything goes on around here. Anybody else's rattle I'd say twenty bucks. Can you go twenty?"

Chloe shoved her hands into her pockets and curled her fingers around her wallet. She felt the baby inside mapping her abdomen wall from the inside with his little empty hands. Everyone deserved one special treasure from childhood. All she had was that beat-to-shit photo of herself on a photographer's pony. She unfolded a pair of tens from the wallet and set them on the counter. Her cheeks flushed. "I must be insane. Oscar? Don't tell Hank."

He smiled. "Don't tell Corrine neither."

"Deal." She tucked the rattle into her pocket and ran her thumb and forefingers over the smooth metal. "Have swell holidays, Oscar."

"Hey, you guys come for dinner on Winter Solstice. I make a killer venison stew."

"Sure, we'd love to."

"*Hahgo lá ne'awéé' neínílí?*" he said as Chloe looked across the room to see where Hank had gone.

Because they had been having this same back-and-forth conversation since August, she knew the literal translation: *When is this baby coming?* But like so much of the Navajo culture, there was a second meaning, an inherent humor so embedded and subtle that sometimes even Hank missed it. In this case it was a cautionary. *Are you taking care so this baby will be born at the proper time?*

"*Inesddin,*" Chloe responded. *I'm still getting used to things.*

7

December 9

Dearest Henry,

The last time we were apart for the Thanksgiving holiday was when your father and I took that trip to Ireland. I remember the brochure made everything look so quaint and festive and being extremely thankful for my lined rain-coat! We decided against getting a whole turkey this year. I bought one of those precooked breasts so we wouldn't be up to our eyeballs in leftovers. Your father didn't care much for it, claiming it was overseasoned. He's probably right, but to tell you the truth, this new medication makes everything taste somewhat bland, and I find I'm rarely hungry enough to finish an entire meal. The Jacksons came by and we played some truly horrific bridge hands. But all that's beside the point, which is, dearest boy, that I hope you enjoyed a decent holiday so far from home. Did you have a potluck supper with some of your fellow teachers?

Hmm. No mention of Hank's "offbeat love affair" and how it was ruining his life. Also pointedly absent was Iris's persistent bickering about the question of paternity. Nevertheless the undercurrent of guilt was present, and as always, running at high tide. With a glue stick she'd bought expressly for the purpose, Chloe resealed the envelope and jammed it back in the PO box. Why finish reading what could only get worse? Cranky old bitch had way too much time on her hands. Salty turkey tits, for Christ's sake. You could say grace over hot dogs or caviar; the whole idea was to be grateful you had food on the table to eat. If this is the way they treat you, Chloe decided, I'm lucky not to have a mother.

While Hank read *Merry Keshmish* to the third grade, a hundred yards away in the school barn behind the classrooms, Sally's whiskered muzzle quivered in interest. Other people came into the barn, but they made nasty, quick movements, scaring the small band of horses. Chloe was different. In her pockets she carried bruised apples, molasses-coated oats, carrots she'd snap in half below a horse's nose so that the scent exploded through the snowy air like a promise of spring. While the other horses dozed and twitched, the chosen paint mare stood patiently as Chloe cinched a bareback pad over her broad back.

"Sally," Chloe told her as she drew the mare closer to the gate. "I dreamed that Junior Whitebear came back and tried to steal you away from me. I'm so nuts about you I tried to give him my baby in trade. It was a girl, and all she did was cry. Of course, I'd never give the baby away, you know that. She's—*he's*—a part of us, me and Hank. Just like you're a part of me. Let's go for a short ride through the woods, Sally. Let's fly. In case by some miracle Mr. Whitebear does come back."

The mare nosed the rope loop from the top of the pasture gate and placed her broad body between the fence and the open pasture. *Stay back*, she was signaling to the other horses. Sally Ride was intelligent. She'd been trained with patience and love, and her first inclination was to trust. A maiden in her ninth year, the cups of her young teeth were beginning to disappear from grinding away at the hay on which she lived. "Dental stars" were visible on the front of her incisors. In a few years, it would be impossible to judge her age without a degree in veterinary science or a horse-woman's instinctive eye. Sally could have babies or live out the rest of her days bored in this barn, waiting for somebody to ride her again on a regular basis. Today she anticipated trotting along the dirt road down by the fairgrounds where the cottonwoods grew thick and tall by the creekbed.

Chloe hoisted her heavy body using the fence rails. She gripped her calves around the horse's barrel and legged her toward the few trees, bare-branched and stark against the blue winter sky. In December the country appeared desolate, the land overworked and untillable. Yet only fifteen miles southeast, in Coal Mine Canyon, there was fuel for the taking, and to the northeast, twenty miles or so, near Red Lake, the distinctive sandstone buttes of Elephant's Feet stood waiting for someone to appreciate their bizarre natural beauty.

The mare wasn't properly shod for winter riding. Who on the reservation could afford snow tires, let alone winter shoes? Had Sally been properly equipped, Chloe would have pulled up her collar and headed out. They couldn't go far and not be discovered. At the trot Chloe held herself in a two-point stance, hovering safely above the mare's spine. The seasoned muscles in her powerful thighs worked to keep a center of gravity that balanced the bulk of baby without exerting too much pressure on her lower back.

The brisk winter air tasted like a clean bite of heaven. "What are you waiting for?" she whispered into the mare's pricked, alert ears, asking Sally to extend the trot as fast as she was able. The eager horse transitioned into a collected canter, just a few hoofbeats short of a full gallop.

Hank was on playground duty when Chloe returned, her cheeks high with color. All around him third graders bundled up warm in jackets were throwing balls, racing and shrieking, squeezing every last bit of fun from the recess. The smile he gave her turned guarded the closer she came. She kissed him on the mouth, and he broke away, saying, "You smell like horses."

"I smell like horses because they're in my blood. Get a clue, Professor."

He placed his hands on her belly, as if checking to make certain the baby was still there.

"Relax, I haven't given him away yet. Tell me all the things your kids did today. Show me what brilliant masterpiece Short Dog painted. Then let's knock off early, go home, and heat up that stew. I'm starving."

Hank gave her another appraising look. "Today's the day I work with my slow readers. And don't you have a clinic appointment?"

She sighed. "You're right. I forgot. But it's not for awhile yet. Maybe I'll go back and visit the horses."

His eyes said it all: *Maybe I can't prove anything, but I'd lay down money you've been astride a horse.* He suspected all that, and somehow he still wanted to marry her.

She guessed that later she'd have to give him a back rub, since she was too pregnant to offer him comfort with her body anymore. She didn't mind taking him in her mouth or rubbing the hard, hot length of him between her breasts until he groaned and spilled across her skin. As far as she was concerned, his groan of gratitude was pleasure enough. But lately when she touched him sexually, Hank got all fussy and distracted, as if her thinking about fucking at this stage of pregnancy wasn't ladylike or motherly behavior.

"Or I could always go sit in the staff lounge and write a letter to Kit," she said.

His whole face brightened. He threw a ball that had landed near them back into the crowd of children. "Good idea. It's warm in there. My Thermos is half full—you could have a cup of tea. Be sure and tell Kit I said hello."

*   *   *

"I hope these numbers mean I need a new sphygmomanometer."

"A what?"

Lois Carrywater, M.D., unstrapped the blood-pressure cuff from Chloe's left arm and rolled the black fabric onto her right. She squeezed and listened again with her stethoscope. "What have you been doing? Mountain biking?"

"Nothing out of the ordinary, honest."

"*Chloe.*"

"Dr. Lois, what's it like being an Indian woman doctor around all those townies? Besides lonely, I mean."

Dr. Carrywater frowned and pressed her fingers to Chloe's wrist, counting the beats. "They don't ask me to play golf. Don't think you're fooling me, by the way, trying to change the subject." She lifted the tips of her stethoscope from her ears and plucked a chocolate brown mane hair from Chloe's long-sleeved T-shirt and held it up for inspection.

Chloe breathed deep and relaxed all her muscles, trying to slow her heartbeat and urge those numbers down into a safer range. If she had high blood pressure it was news to her. Maybe she felt a little lightheaded at times, got a headache now and again, but at nearly eight thousand feet and so butt-freezing cold out here, wasn't that a way of life?

Dr. Carrywater penciled notes in Chloe's file chart and spoke without looking up. "We're assuming your due date's February second."

"So you keep saying."

"You understand first babies sometimes arrive early?"

Chloe nodded.

"And so you're starting to get things ready?"

Chloe thought of the silver rattle, tucked far inside her underwear drawer. They'd go crib shopping this weekend for sure. "What do I really need besides diapers?"

Dr. Carrywater sighed, looking weary beyond her years of schooling. "Do you *read* the pamphlets I give you? Let's see. A baby thermometer—they're not the same as adults.' Diapers, yes, and pins and salve and talc and baby soap. Soft towels, sleepers, blankets, booties, bottles, because even if you're planning to nurse you still need one or two for sterile water, backup formula, electrolytes in case the baby develops a bowel condition. Some couples like a camera—"

Chloe held up a hand. "Okay, okay. So we'll go shopping."

"*This* weekend." Dr. Lois delivered one of her rare smiles. The thirty-year-old woman behind her medical persona rose to the forefront, and Chloe saw that in her own determined, quiet way, Dr. Lois could be as pushy and manipulative as Hank.

"Tell you what," she said. "I'm going to step out of the room a moment so you can undress and pull this sheet over your legs. It's a month earlier than I like to do a pelvic, but I want to anyway. I have a hunch your little bandit might stage an early appearance."

"Early?" Chloe said. "How early are we talking? Not before Christmas?"

"Let's hope not." The doctor put her hands on her hips and gave her that no-bullshit, wide-open stare. "Nothing's for sure until you stop riding that mare."

In the teachers' lounge/supply room, a beat-up plaid sofa, a Formica table, four molded plastic chairs, and a pile of magazines allowed instructors a place for time-out and Chloe a few moments out of the cold while she waited for Hank to finish up. Nobody else was there. Probably everyone was home soaking beans for supper or scraping frost from their windshields trying to see clearly where they were going. She sat down, her insides still feeling strangely invaded from the internal exam.

December 14
Tuba City, Eight whole degrees out

Dear Kit,
    Think about it. You name a kid Ocean anywhere but
California, people assume right off you're a tree hugger

or a space cadet. They already call us prunes, which I
guess is some deep and crushing California slur. Sam's a
good name for a dog, but we already have Hannah.
When I showed Hank your list he said he wanted to
name her Annie, after his sister that died. I go, So what's
he going to do when all the kids beat the shit out of him
for having a girl's name? Most of the boys around here
are named Clint or Buck. Sounds like grades of hay. In
Garth Brooks territory, names with more than one syllable seem to be frowned on.

About sex, Kit. Don't go trusting that condoms rule out
pregnancy one hundred percent of the time. Sex is dangerous. I'm walking proof of that particular fable. Stick to
horses. That's all the advice I feel safe in dumping on
you.

And why are they making you read depressing shit
about stoning people to death in English? Hasn't your
teacher ever heard of Marguerite Henry? Anna Sewell?
Even Dick Francis? My lady doctor over at the clinic told
me I had an "irritable" uterus today. How about that? For
once my insides match my outside. She isn't very popular
since she's not a white guy from town, but I like her all
right. We get the lectures over with fairly quick. A great
ride on Sally today. Saw two elk down by the creekbed.
I'm going back tomorrow.

Chloe had flinched at the probing, drawn her knees up and said,
Stop it, and had meant it. *You be sure to let me know if you pass the
mucus plug before your next appointment,* Dr. Lois insisted. *Watch for it.*
What a dreadful-sounding term. Quit poking around and there
won't be anything to look for, she'd told her. The assortment of
McCall's and *Family Circle*s on the tabletop were well-thumbed, all
the hamburger recipes torn out. Chloe scanned a flyer for last summer's Indian oil-painting competition, and wondered who had
won. There was a pile of entry forms on a bulletin board announc-

ing the spring Coconino Center for the Arts mixed media show, including a children's division. Hank would urge all his pupils to enter, and if Corrine allowed it, Dog Johnson might win a ribbon. From the pile of papers she unearthed an old catalog for several Indian jewelers.

The heavy cover stock was decorated with their names in a fancy typeface and embossed Indian symbols—a Kokopelli playing flute, a stylized sunburst with slits for eyes, and the rounded outline of a bear with what looked like a lightning bolt inside it that Oscar Johnson told her was called the heartline. The catalog pages featured black-and-white photos of five-feather Yei pendants, China mountain earrings, and inlaid squash-blossom necklaces much simpler than those Corrine favored. The fat silver storyteller bracelets fronted an out-of-date price list. On the back of the circular there were pictures of the artists. Ray Tracey in his buckstitched leather, looking so handsome he could be a Hollywood movie actor; a chunky-faced guy whose name was obscured by a coffee spill; and in profile, lean, with craggy high cheekbones and a shock of dark hair shaggily cut, falling into his face and over his broad shoulders, Junior Whitebear. Hardly more than a boy, really, but the picture could have been old. He aimed his cocky grin toward the person holding the camera, reminding Chloe of the puffed-up bravado of the juvenile offenders from the Carlson Ranch in California, those bad boys she'd tried to teach horsemanship in an effort to deflect their more criminal urges. Handsome, but handsome was often the same as dangerous.

"What are you looking at so intently?" Hank said as he came up behind her, his arms full of newspapers.

Chloe tapped the photograph. "He doesn't look Navajo," she said. "Maybe that sounds prejudiced, but his face is shaped differently, and his skin's so much lighter."

Out of teacherly habit, Hank neatened the magazines after he set down the stack of papers in the recycling box. "He's probably not full blood. I think Corrine told me that once."

"Why were you asking Corrine about Junior Whitebear?"

"I don't remember. Maybe she brought him up. How was your appointment?"

"I gained a pound. Corrine's full of stories."

"Indeed she is. Did you hear the baby's heartbeat?"

"I forgot to ask for the stethoscope." Chloe studied the jeweler's face once more. Maybe half Navajo. Maybe—if she squinted and needed glasses and had never met a Mexican. He looked Mexican, plain and simple, like her buddy Francisco back in California, or any of the other horse people she knew who called themselves Mexican or Chicano or Salvadoran. She tucked the catalog under her half-finished letter to Kit. "Think anybody'd mind if I take this?"

"Any particular reason?"

"Just to look at. That's all."

Hank smiled. "Fine with me. Now let's go. Leftovers await. Nothing but the best for my baby."

She laughed, wondering which baby he meant.

December 19
Chez Wedler's, where today's special is Pumpkin Soup,
AKA the Golden Hurl

Dear Chloe,

Really sad news. Hugh Nichols had a stroke! He can't talk or anything. Edith moved back in to take care of him. Me and Diane drove by and checked their horses. They're fine, but that crazy Palomino broke through the fence and Francisco went off about the price of wire versus what he called the "shotgun solution," but I think he was just trying to make a joke, everybody's so tense. Edith said to tell you she reads Hugh your letters and he gets all choked up so to please keep on writing even if he can't answer you back, okay?

Now, finally for some good news. Guess who arrives December 26 with her sleeping bag and fifty bucks' baby-sitting money? I peeked at my presents and one of them's a plane ticket. I know, I know, like, grow up already, but California's pretty lame when you're almost fifteen and live five hundred miles from interesting things like actual snow and real live Indians. I can't wait to see you (and your boobs)! Hank looks so buff in that picture you sent. My dad said maybe he was replaced by an alien life form, like that movie we watched on HBO, but I think Hank is cute. You should marry him. Anyway, ask him to pretty please make some of his chocolate chip cookies on Christmas day and don't you go eating all of them since I've been dreaming about those cookies since before he left. I'll call the minute I get there. I have a really great surprise I'm saving for you. It is *so* amazing!!!

Happy Jesus's birthday as the all the born-agains go around saying. I'm like, Does that mean forget the presents and you'll pray all day? As expected, I got no answer. Eight more days!

Love,
Kit

Chloe smiled at the childlike handwriting, the little hearts Kit drew to dot her *i*'s. Next to her, leaning against the post office table beneath the bulletin board, Hank's expression was sober as he read his mother's latest letter.

"Your mom doing okay?" she asked.

He rubbed his chin and sighed. "She was in the hospital for a few days. Tests."

"What kind of tests?"

"She didn't really go into detail."

"Your dad could have called or something."

"Or I could have called them."

Chloe looked up at the flyer of the lost girl from New York. In her bones she could feel the girl's mother's dread at another holiday season approaching with no daughter to hold in her arms, make cookies for, no stocking to stuff. "Maybe you ought to go see her, Hank. For Christmas."

He looked out the glass snow doors for a few moments, then turned back to her. "It's our first real holiday together."

She touched his arm. "I know. But if you think about it, really it's just another day. People get all excited over it because of advertising hype. Go to California if you need to. We can celebrate Christmas when you get back."

Hank rubbed her back.

"Oh, that feels good. Don't stop, whatever you do."

He rubbed in wide circles. "Look, it means a lot to me that you'd sacrifice it. But the truth is, we can't afford the plane fare. I've got a line on a part-time job during vacation."

"Doing what?"

"Helping unload trucks at Purina in Flagstaff."

The baby executed one of his trout spins in her belly, and Chloe laid a hand there to quiet him, feeling once again, in this partnership, just how much she wasn't pulling her weight.

"No elk today," Chloe said to the mare as they trotted through the woods toward the main road. "Guess we just got lucky that one time. Well, I don't know about you, Sally, but I'm glad. If we saw elk, we'd likely hear hunters, and then I'd probably have to dismount and perform some elk CPR." She patted the horse's neck. A part of her heart was falling in love with this mare. She felt a momentary pang of guilt that maybe she was forgetting Absalom. Before them sun had melted a stretch of maybe fifty yards of snow. Red earth shone through, and Chloe couldn't resist the invitation. She sat back, asked the mare for a canter. Beneath her, Sally changed gaits with a bolt. God, how free running felt, as if she were once again a single unit, responsible only for her own life. Cottonwood branches rushed by her. Winter air took sharp nips at her face. The bare patch began to diminish quickly, and Chloe sat back, cuing the mare for a transition to a posting trot. Instead of a fluid rhythm rising up to meet her, she felt a distinct pull, something hot inside, the feeling of flesh tearing loose. She halted the horse immediately, dismounted, and stood there a half mile from anywhere, breathing in short panicked gasps, afraid to look down, the reins shaking in her gloved hand.

December 21—Winter Solstice
Second Mesa

Dear Kit,

We're in the village of Shungopovi on the Hopi reservation. We came to see the dances, but they haven't started yet. This place is like walking through a history book, all sandstone and mud huts. Everything's leaning and threatening to fall and here sit all these Indians on top of the roof. Hank's all excited. He loves watching the kachinas, even though he wouldn't dance himself if you held a gun to his head.

Kit, all day I'm thinking how on earth could Willie leave you? You're pretty and funny, real good with animals. Generous and smart, too, so smart I'd be damned lucky to get one like you, I'd be thanking stars the rest of my life. I'm thinking Dr. Lois and her pamphlets are a load of manure. She keeps trying to scare me with graphs and crap, like a spooked mother would be better than a calm one. There's a lot I'd like to say to Willie, wherever the hell she is. Probably just as well I can't, since now I supposedly have high blood pressure and I'm supposed to "make an effort to stay calm."

Compared with the Navajo reservation, this place looks pretty much like a desert. No trees whatsoever. Hank says they get only about twelve inches' rain a year, but they still manage to grow corn and beans, and raise sheep. They must collect the dew in their hats. We had to park about a quarter mile down the road and hike the rest of the way in along with thirty or so other people. Hank said this dance was not to be missed, which must mean high culture or something I won't know how to appreciate. At least there's a bunch of other white people standing around looking as out of place as I feel. We have to wait here, away from the kiva, on the main road which curls around their village. After this, we're invited to the Johnsons' for dinner.

*You'll like Oscar and Dog. Corrine takes some getting used to. Jesus, Kit, my
back is just killing me. I wonder if I've slept on it wrong or—*

In her head Chloe frantically composed her letter to Kit as she
wove between bystanders facing the narrow sandstone-and-mud
houses. The rich smells of simmering stews and bread frying in hot
grease laid their paws on her, coiling around her perpetually hungry stomach. Cries of excited children frayed her edges. Skinny
yellow stray dogs threaded their way through the crowd, looking
for handouts, and she wanted to feed them before she fed herself.
She walked purposefully, mentally composing that letter, trying
the only way she knew to shake off the ache periodically clenching
its fist into the small of her back. She retraced every moment of the
previous day's ride, reliving the moment when the error of assuming her prepregnancy muscles were a match for thirty extra
pounds and a nearly full-term baby had proved otherwise.

They had only cantered for a few moments. Maybe she'd come
down wrong. That sharp pull inside her, and later on, when she
peed, it was a funny color, not bloody, no "mucus plug," whatever
the hell that looked like, just wrong. She'd walked the mare back
to the pasture, stepping gingerly, expecting something dramatic,
like a bona-fide labor pain, to strike her belly. But it didn't happen.
She even went so far as to wander over to the clinic, hoping some
doctor might be around seeing to an emergency, but everybody
had gone home, and those people worked long enough hours as it
was without bothering them with what was probably nothing.
When, an hour later, the pain disappeared, she saw no reason to
mention it to Hank. Hank worried enough, and with his mother in
such bad shape he didn't need any extra problems.

At home she'd let him tuck her in bed early, finished a mug of
horrible green soup, and sneaked a Milky Way when he was busy
working on the leaky kitchen faucet. Fear tired her out. For an
hour she lay in unbroken sleep. Then she'd awakened with a variation of her losing-the-baby nightmare. This time she'd left it in
the woods in order to enter a cross-country horse event. She was

riding Absalom. Together they took fences at record speed. When she remembered that Absalom was dead and the baby might be trampled, attacked by wild animals, crying all alone out there in the woods, she woke drenched in sweat, her heart racing. Hank was asleep next to her, his right hand beneath her pillow. She hadn't the heart to wake him.

This morning she'd felt fine, had almost erased the pain from her memory. Then the walk from the truck brought the shadow of the pain back, a little yanking pull that refused to be ignored.

She placed a hand on her back, took deep breaths, and felt much better. In her mind's eye she pictured the rattle made by Junior Whitebear. February 2 was thirty-three days off. Plenty of time to get the stuff Dr. Carrywater said they needed. A clown kachina suddenly appeared from behind one of the ladders leaning against the old building. His black-and-white stripes blurring in front of her eyes, he leaped straight at her, shaking his watermelon rattle, puffing out his belly in a parody of her condition, making everybody laugh. Chloe stood rooted to the spot, afraid to move. The dancer smelled of the rich black-and-white oxides with which his face and midriff were painted, and down deep, a masculine scent as strong as a horse's. Again he shook the rattle, his oversize lips and paint-dotted cheeks so close to her own he seemed frustrated she didn't understand what he wanted. Then Hank was at her arm, gently backing her away.

"He's warning you to move aside, Chloe. Watch now. Right where you were standing, that's where the next dancers will come from."

And they did. They seemed to rise out of the earth itself, scores of them appearing from empty spaces, transforming the drab brown buildings and gray winter sky to a festival of colors. Big-eyed Buffalo Dancers carrying bows and arrows, Rainbow Dancers with muffs of white fur and massive headpieces, the heavy-winged Eagle kachina with his yellow wooden beak. It was otherworldly, the singing and rattles focused on celebrating the shortest day of the year with a dance to bless their people. A sun-faced kachina in his red-yellow-and-blue circle face shuffled by, turning to face the non-Indian onlookers. His slit eyes and inverted triangle mouth appeared mocking. Hank seemed entranced, but the painted stare made Chloe understand how distinctly out of place they were. Here, they were watchers, not members of a tribe three times attacked by the Spanish. The Hopi had had the Catholic religion foisted on them; had been ordered to surrender a good portion of their crops to that same church, responsible for beating their warriors and for burning some of them alive. Until that moment they hadn't been a fighting culture. In desperation they'd thrown a couple of priests off the cliff, and since 1680 no Catholic church had bothered them. This was deep spiritual calling being enacted before her. They had no business gawking at it like some Hollywood movie. She glanced over at Hank, witnessing the yearning in his eyes. He ached to know all cultures inside out. Maybe he wanted his white skin and fractured life to fit into the sea of brown faces and their ancient family ways now that his family was so far from him. Iris's letters all sang the same refrain: *Henry, your father and I simply have to believe you've taken leave of your senses. . . .*

Chloe stepped aside to let a kid dressed in so much winter wool that only his eyes and nose were bare find a spot between adults to stay warm. The wind stung her face and blessedly, once again, the baby inside her seemed quiet.

The Johnsons' house was close to home. Hank had a beginner's technique book on acrylic painting for Short Dog, one of his used-bookstore finds. Chloe could always say she was too tired, could they drop off the book and go home instead? Oscar's award-winning venison could be packed for the road. *It's the best*, he'd said, *a rib-sticking meal, you know? Come eat with us. I promise you guys an evening you'll never forget.*

She looked up at the dull sky and knew it would be rude to turn the Johnsons' supper invitation down. I'll ask Hank to rub my back, she thought to herself. It's just a pulled muscle. I won't ride anymore. Everything will be okay. In front of her, the dancers stepped in their ancient knowing rhythms.

Part 2
Tuba City

8

It was into a true Phoenix rainstorm that Junior Whitebear deplaned from the United 747 and began the long, slow trek across Sky Harbor Terminal. From his window seat he'd noted the runway blackened with rain as the plane landed, imagined the hiss as landing gear met wet tarmac. Now visible through the splattered airport windows was the wintry worst southern Arizona had to offer: a gray December rain, just verging on sleet. Back in the Bay State, where he lived, weather like this suggested an optional raincoat and an excuse to sit inside and have a drink until it passed. Here people drove into one another's cars, sandbagged their non-native landscaping, called up the television stations as if hassling the weathermen might do something about it.

In one hand Junior held a zippered leather duffel carry-on, in the other one of those trashy lawyer-turned-thriller novels with the embossed gold title. Once inside the terminal, he set it down on the first empty seat he came across. Stupid book had cost him almost seven bucks at an airport newsstand. They weren't known for being repositories for great literature, but by the end of chapter one, Junior'd decided he'd rather read the magazines in his seat pocket instead. Nevertheless, for that kind of *béeso* the least he could do was recycle it.

All around him travelers walked purposefully in every direction, squinting at dim terminal screens, trying like hell to get the numbers squared up with the gates. Junior had spent most of the five-hour flight anticipating how he'd feel once he reached Arizona. Only subtle differences were discernible. His breathing seemed slower, aligning itself with the pace of eight years previous, when he'd charged out of the state into a larger world he was convinced would bring him satisfaction. He checked his watch; he'd have to hustle to claim the old man's remains before the mortuary closed. Maybe he should hold a memorial service, dump Jimmy's ashes in an old Gallo bottle, let the drinking buddies stop by and tip one last swallow in memory of Jimmy Whitebear. One thing drunks always had plenty of was buddies. They possessed a unique logic, which at its most fundamental layer insisted there was no reason they could not imbibe the fruit of the vine for fifty years and emerge unscathed. Jimmy was no different than anyone else in that particular tribe, except that now he was dead, but there was company to be found in the afterlife, too. Nobody in Arizona would miss one more dead Indian.

After dispensing of the earthly remains, Junior would be alone in the world, with no immediate relatives connected to him whatsoever. There were a few distant aunties and a cousin or two, but he hadn't seen them in over a decade. He had the feeling this change diminished the jewelry he'd made, the money he'd earned, the miles traveled in his thirty-eight years—his worldly résumé disintegrating while he flew over the country, back into his old life. Well, to be honest, that worry had lurked in the back of his mind all the time before Jimmy died anyhow. Lately he pretty much started over every single day, beginning with waking up and discovering with whom he'd fallen asleep.

He got in line at the America West ticketing counter behind a young couple trying to manage six pieces of luggage and their little boy. About four years old and wound up with energy, he was wearing hearing aids that plugged into a radio-size battery pack. His mother, a tall, tough-looking blond with hair shorter than her husband's, was signing to him the same offhanded way she might have spoken if the kid could hear. Junior didn't know sign language, but its translation was fairly universal: *Settle down, young man, or there will be memorable consequences.* The line moved ridiculously slow, and the boy kept on trying to run off. Finally the father scooped the rambunctious young one up in his arms. The boy hugged him fiercely, jabbering to himself and driving a toy car across his father's shoulders. The look of complete acceptance that came over the man's face made Junior want to take up Jimmy's profession, professional wine tasting.

"Ticket to Flagstaff," Junior said when he made it to the ticketing counter.

"This must be your lucky day," the America West clerk said. "Last seat on the last shuttle going out tonight. Weather's coming in."

"Looks to me like it's already here." Junior leaned the arm of his deerskin jacket on the countertop so that the beaded fringe hung downward as he signed the credit card receipt. His black hair was bound into two plaits that hung down his back nearly to his waist, heavy as a second set of arms. He had bound them himself early this morning, in another time zone, in the false light of a hotel bathroom. This woman ticket seller had the look: She wanted to undo the bindings, rake her fingers clear down to his scalp. She was just inches away from reaching across the counter to give them a tug. When women did that he fought the urge to tweak their nipples, ask them how they liked their own space being violated. Thanks to Kevin Costner and the Hollywood movie studios, Indians were sex symbols, dark skin and long hair a source of enviable intrigue, not emblems of poverty and injustice. He chided himself. She just wanted a little flirting, that's all. "Should I expect a lot of turbulence?"

"Not necessarily."

The bruised-plum smile the counter girl shot him seemed to cast her teeth in a shade of blue that reminded him of the inside of mussel shells. The lipstick starkened her already white cheeks to an unhealthy pallor, similar to what he'd seen on too many sick boys in the seaside art colony where he'd been living for the last couple of years. These nineties ladies and their Elvira makeup—they looked like they had chalk running through their veins. Did they think all men were latent necrophiliacs?

"You could always stay at a hotel here in town. Wait and see what the skies are like in the morning."

"Yeah, I could do that." He raised one eyebrow and she stared at him, fingers poised over the ticket. Any man approaching forty appreciated a pass, but Junior got the feeling the wild bareback ride in fancy sheets she was offering came with a hidden price tag. In the morning she'd squint and ask him what kind of Indian he was, claim some distant relative of hers was Cherokee; they frequently said Cherokee. Despite all outward appearances, she could be carrying the virus he'd watched decimate the population of his little town on the tip of the Massachusetts coast. These days you wrapped the rascal and said your prayers. Was one night and another debit on his credit card worth the worrying? He leaned closer to let her know he was flattered. "Sugar, you're making it awful hard"—he paused to let the double-entendre perform its trick—"for me to walk away. Maybe we can do something another time. I got to get on up to the res tonight."

"The reservation?" Her eager smile withdrew. She didn't look like she'd heard of anyone actually *living* on a reservation. "I guess somebody there's expecting you."

He adjusted his inlaid bracelets along his wide brown wrist and thought of the old man, his fists seemingly made of bone, the cutting remarks that slipped so easily from his father's tongue just before he started hitting his wife or his son. Imagine, all that pain reduced to what fit in a casket, a crematorium fire, a mortician's ash box. "No, ma'am, not a soul. Just have to settle up one old debt and be on my way back east."

"Too bad. Here's your ticket, sir."

Sir. Adios. Sexual tension ebbed, and her smile geared up for the next customer as she waved good-bye.

He was hungry, but on board United Junior'd accepted one of those awful hot bread sandwiches, and now his gums felt purely lacerated. Coffee, he thought, a little jump start, if there was a decent cup to be found that didn't cost five bills now that, thanks to Seattle, coffee had been elevated to near religion. Airport terminals all smelled the same: Dirty carpet, recycled air, the sweat of nervous travelers rushing to planes, their poky souls unable to keep up, left stranded and fretting in the cavernous building. Terminals were spooky to begin with, homes to heavy machinery passengers depended on to lift them from here to there without a second thought of all the underpaid, pissed-off help at the controls. Junior watched out the window of many a plane while luggage flew from hand to asphalt and the guys in the yellow jumpsuits enjoyed the perks of the job. He never traveled with any more than he could stuff under the seat in front of him. Like the storm clouds gathering upstate, he could feel the presence of all those travelers' confused spirits, their leftover expectation for a vacation they missed and the childlike ability to huddle together in corners where nobody swept. It was such a lonely, lost-dog feeling that it made him tally up all his regrets of the last nine years.

Women used to top his do-over list. Simple girls who broke him in that he'd outgrown and abandoned. Their needs had never entered into the equation. Somehow, they had led a skinny half-breed to these long-legged beauties who got hot for him the moment they saw his jewelry. Despite their bony appearance, these women could be ungodly strong. They'd wrestle him into bed and ride him until he lay drained at their long, elegant feet. Next they talked him out of earrings or a bracelet, dumped him, and went on to the next guy. He guessed he'd become immune to women. His regrets weren't about the female sex anymore. Things went a little deeper than that. He was going home to settle his conscience, deal with the guilt of having done well in the off-reservation world once and for all. Nothing but physical confronta-

tion could remedy that particular illness. Not the money his jewelry was bringing in, not those big-city galleries that hosted his
shows, not the parties people threw for him that he always ended
up sneaking out of when he could no longer pretend to be enjoying himself. It was time, and Jimmy's death gave him the prod
he'd needed.

Hoisting his duffel, he made his way to the gate. This was
Arizona, all right. Weavings draped down the cinderblock walls in
the escalator area. A group of tourists pored over the jewelry case
in one of the airport gift shops. They were buying turquoise earrings and liquid silver necklaces, spending large. It was maybe the
last hour of vacation and they wanted a memorable purchase to
make up for whatever had been disappointing. For every tourist
woman walking into the gift shop, a minimum of seventy-five dollars fell on the credit card. Double that, if it was a trading post,
which was one reason he still let them sell his work up at
Cameron.

He bought some mocha java from a college-age Indian kid, and
the boy smiled at him as he handed over the cup. "How's it going,
brother?"

"Good enough so I can't complain. And you?"

"I'm in out of the rain."

"A good place to be." Junior stuffed a buck in the kid's tip jar and
walked on. There was a time he would have felt at the peak of success to have mass-produced pieces of his work on consignment in
one of these gift shops. Such ambition was considered high for
reservation life, but after a year or two away, he knew how low it
placed in the larger world. His success had exceeded his ambition.
Sami Gee, his agent, said he was now considered "collectible," a
word that sometimes made him feel good, like an Anasazi petro-
glyph turned up unexpectedly on a canyon wall when hiking a difficult trail that led to someplace beautiful. Junior could lay down
cash for fine things. The Nogales custom bootmaker Paul Bond had
plaster casts of his feet. All he had to do was punch up their telephone number and tell Ernesto what kind of skins he fancied, and

select a style for the tooling on the shaft. The trappings of success didn't measure much on a person. Their actions spoke the larger truth. In Tuba City his French jeans would draw smirks and comments of selling out. The old guys who'd taught him silver would look at his work and give that half nod that meant, *Sure, this is flashy stuff. What are you doing to make a difference, here, among your people?*

A question he knew better than to try to answer. Three hundred odd miles up the mountain, providing the snow held off, then in the dusk he would see his old stomping grounds. Along the way, the bonus of a Flagstaff sunset. Somebody might take pity on his old skin, offer him a tasty meal of squash stew, want to listen to his stories. He thought of Corrine Johnson, his first love, and wondered if she still lived in the same old house of her mother's, or if she'd moved on to the city, like she always threatened she'd do.

Junior stared out the windows at the arriving and departing jets, waiting for his flight to be called. Kids from the adjacent gate raced back and forth, thick into the business of play. Every so often their parents set down their newspapers and made feeble attempts at hushing them, but he could tell they were hoping they'd wear themselves out and sleep on the plane. Junior loved children. They were tiny aliens inspecting the planet. Especially infants. On planes they gave adult passengers the once-over and an opportunity; all they wanted in return was a genuine smile and some respect. Give them any bullshit, they'd reward you with crying the flight's duration. If he was lucky enough to make eye contact, Junior always made certain to give babies a respectful nod.

He watched the little rockets of energy, brown eyes wide with possibility, their small hands clutching toy planes as busy mouths generated sound effects. The dreams they fashioned as they ran along the rows of seats spilled into his own sorrowful lot, perking him up momentarily. He wondered how and why it was adult imagination got tired. You were born with such abundance. If you didn't get it beat out of you by a drunk father, if some *bilagáana* teacher took an interest in you instead of cuffing your ears for speaking the wrong language, a tended imagination was capable of producing magic. But that was no guarantee the gift would stay faithful. One day you could look up from the silver and find it gone, your special talent rendered ordinary. Oh, maybe not so any-body really noticed except yourself. There just wasn't anything fresh to say, no news for the waiting metal in your hands. It became as much a job as selling shoes.

His eyes grew weary, unfocused and in the translucent airport glass he could see his own face staring back at him. Was he jaded from too much praise? The brown eyes looked permanently startled, as if flash cameras illuminated his universe. Maybe he was like Jimmy after all, drunk on all that attention. But no one could claim his was a happy face. The high cheekbones and dark skin sought something or some-one—to Junior that much was clear—that it hadn't been able to find out there. Yes, he wore a hopeful mask sewn onto a thirty-eight-year-old body, and he was stuck with all of it.

Unlike the Skywest shuttle for Delta—his other option—the turbo-prop whose every seat was both a window and an aisle—the America West Dash–8 was pressurized, seated thirty and came with a pretty stewardess bearing a fruit basket and canned alcoholic drinks for sale. When they were all buckled in, she made her speech. "Welcome to America West's shuttle service from Phoenix to Flagstaff, Arizona, gateway to the Grand Canyon. Normally this is a thirty-minute flight; however, this afternoon we're anticipating some minor delays due to the weather in the area. Flagstaff ground control reports two feet of snow on the ground and expects twice that by midnight. Because passenger safety is foremost with America West, we'll be taking the best route we can and hope to sidestep the nasty stuff."

"Which means another damned delay," said a tired young woman in a business skirt and blazer with the W. L. Gore emblem on her briefcase. From surgical heart patches to dental floss, Gore was Flagstaff's most prestigious company store. Around it in Flag stood the university, Purina, and a slew of cut-rate motels. The abundance of leftover hippies and beer-swilling rednecks about filled things up. Junior watched the businesswoman reluctantly stow her laptop computer. No solace in the keyboard until after takeoff. They taxied down the runway, gained speed, and he felt the familiar jolt of liftoff, always a hopeful if slightly terrifying feeling.

Once they were airborne, the stewardess served canned Bloody Marys to three old white ladies looking desperate for anesthesia. Tomato juice and vodka coupled with a rough flight was not the best idea, in his estimation. Every passenger's thirst slaked, the stewardess strapped herself into her seat and opened a paperback Tony Hillerman. The passengers sat quiet, those of them lucky enough to have window seats anxiously glancing out the portholes into the late afternoon air.

"*Ya hey*," Junior said to the guy sitting next to him. "Any chance you heading up to Tuba City?"

"Nah, I live in Flag," the man answered. "Only need to keep my government house six months longer, then I can sell her. Heading down Nogales way. Better weather, for sure. Got me a cousin working those new minicattles in Patagonia."

"Miniature cows?"

"*Enit*, brother, it's the latest thing. Take up less open range. Like them yuppie vegetables you see in the market. Baby squash, potatoes no bigger than your thumb, all costing double and people can't wait to buy it."

Tiny cattle foraging in the desert—Junior couldn't make it come together in his mind.

"So," the cattle enthusiast went on, "Tuba City. You must be coming for the Solstice dances. Hate to say it, but you're gonna be late."

"Oh yeah, the dances. Actually, I have a little business back home. A long time ago I lived here. I'm coming back."

The man looked down at the floor of the plane. "Awful damn

nice boots for winter on the res. Guess your people don't keep sheep."

Junior held out his arms, showing the intricate tooling and inlay detail on his bracelets and watchband. *"Béésh łigaiitsidii;* I work silver. Right now I'm sort of taking a breather."

"Nice if you can afford to," his seatmate said. "Good-looking bracelet."

"Thanks."

The plane swooped low, hitting a pocket of troubled air, and conversation abruptly ended. The only sound in the cabin was the occasional gasp of the frightened old white women sucking in their Bloody Mary breath, every now and then breaking into Catholic prayers. *Hold that plane up, Mary!* Junior eyed the stewardess, rapt in her pages. When the help panicked, it was time to worry.

They circled the Flagstaff airport for a good twenty minutes before the pilot switched on his microphone. "Folks, I'll be frank. I can't see a damn thing out there, and since this is a VFR outfit, we're going to head north and see if the Grand Canyon airport looks any better."

Grumblings broke out in the tiny plane, most notably from the businesswoman. Hot-tempered little firecracker like that Junior wouldn't have minded spending a night with, but all she saw was the numbers on her spreadsheet and the next bonus check headed her way.

The pilot broke in again after a few minutes. "Looks good down there. We'll be on the ground shortly. Our cabin attendant will provide you with information on bus service back to Flagstaff."

Landing at the Grand Canyon. The Quonset-hut airport with its cement floors was definitely nothing special. Outside of the massive stone fireplace, it served mostly as one giant poster board for sightseeing planes, helicopters, and blister-raising mule rides. A stroke of luck for me, putting me closer to Tuba City, Junior thought. The old man could wait until morning to be picked up. He wondered who he could call for a ride into town. Did Oscar Johnson still live there? Would he speak to Junior, considering the circumstances of his leaving? Junior thought of Corrine's angry face and decided, well, taking the bus as far as the highway he'd be almost close enough to walk home, though first he'd have to get out of these showy boots and into his hiking shoes.

He rode the bus as far as the Cameron turnoff. At the confluence of the highways the driver graciously agreed to open the door. Chill wind blew in and Junior stepped out. The bus continued south, and he began walking north. It was only a quarter mile.

The Trading Post exterior had been remodeled, but under its new fittings he recognized the skeleton. He took a deep drink of the dry winter air and made his way across the parking lot. A bank of pay phones lined the outside wall. Inside, aisles of jewelry, the stone fireplace roaring with warmth, real restaurant coffee, none of the fancy flavors or prices. He let himself in.

The glass countertop was scratched. Countless trays and coins had slid across the display case's surface. Junior Whitebear stood, hands in the pockets of his leather jacket, peering in at a presentation of his own bracelets and the catalog for his work open to his full-page studio portrait. Jesus, I'm wearing more makeup than Tammy Faye Bakker, he thought. A bony, determined-looking woman came to stand on the business side of the counter and he looked up, surprised to see it was Corrine Johnson, his old Corrie, twice as pissed off as the last time he'd seen her. "Hey, Corrine," he said, smiling. "It's been a long time. How are you doing? How's your brother?"

Corrine looked stricken and said nothing. She never was in any particular hurry to make him happy. She swished her tiny butt off in another direction to wait on a few tourists checking out story-teller dolls before she acknowledged his presence. Junior wondered where the hell Shane Myers was. Cameron was Shane's place, had been for twenty years. Was he in rehab, dead, or what? Corrine standing there acting like she ran the place.

"Let me just wrap this fellow up for you in tissue paper," she said

to the tourists who had bought a mudhead storyteller and a graduated set of pale green Papago baskets. "Then he'll be nice and safe
on the plane. Where do you live? Iowa? Now, that's a real nice
state. Good for growing corn."

Junior supposed in almost nine years a person could change her
ways, but this Iowa-tissue-paper talk was way over the top for
Corrine Johnson. What Corrine was about was storms and gale
winds, animal passion. This kindness to tourists was an act, staged
for his benefit. As soon as she felt he'd stood there embarrassed the
proper length of time, she'd click out her claws and reduce him to
the size of the ribbons decorating her blouse. Hell, he deserved no
better. He'd left her the way he had because there was no other
way to leave such a woman. Their last encounter had taken place
on top a Chief's North Phase blanket in the bed of Oscar's old
pickup on a dirt road out by the fairgrounds. Underneath a fat yellow moon that was spilling its influence over everybody, Corrine
straddled him, her back arched in ecstasy. He knew she believed
that giving herself to him connected them for life. He'd always felt
kind of bad about leaving her that way. Corrie needed someone
dependable, a man who could ride herd on his own wildness. An
arrogant silversmith willing to risk failure in order to sell to the
larger world hardly fit the bill. If he'd taken a job at the utilities
company like she wanted, he knew he would have ended up bitter,
leaving her eventually.

But she had loved making love almost more than he did. She
was one of those multiply orgasmic women, completely without
inhibitions about showing off her talent. Under her Junior had his
bags packed and change of address already filed. He was just waiting for her to finish like any gentleman, then while she slept he
would steal away into the night. Oscar knew his plans and didn't
approve. *Don't do it, man. It's a bad idea. Stay here and we'll open a shop
together. We might not get famous but we'll have regular work.*

Corrine slammed the register drawer shut and turned to him,
her pretty face dwarfed under all that anger, like a separate person
still lived inside in a far-off corner. It almost looked as if some

drunken sculptor had done a sloppy job on her, leaving her with a sneer instead of a smile. He hoped she hadn't developed diabetes, like her mother and auntie who'd both died from it. The diabetes that ran in the Johnson family was a one-way ticket.

"You here looking for a check, Whitebear? I can write you a check. You want to pull all your merchandise so you can put it in some fancy-ass gallery? I'd be more than happy to help you pack it up. Say it's something like that, Junior. Something we can take care of real quick and tidy up forever because I'm a working mother and it's closing time." She folded her arms under her slight breasts, and the flower ends of a tarnished squash-blossom neck-lace clattered against each other.

"None of the above, Corrine. I came home to bury the old man."

She softened. "Yeah, I heard Jimmy died. I'm sorry. He was a sweet old guy."

Sweet as the wine he'd guzzled. "Yeah, well, you know how it was. Jimmy'd been trying to drown himself for as long as anybody knew him. He's at the mortuary downtown if you and Oscar want to pay your respects. Maybe we could have coffee and catch up. Oscar still around?"

Corrine seemed to stop and consider the option for a moment. Junior thought playing the sympathy card that way, she might ease up. Jimmy'd loved Corrine. Corrine excused Jimmy all his drunken escapades, even made excuses when the man beat Junior to a pulp. "Yeah, he is. We'll come by—for Jimmy. When are you leaving?"

Whoa, that was quick. "I'd planned on tomorrow, but the weather's for shit and I'm not in any hurry. Maybe I'll stick around awhile. I don't know—Christmas."

"You're staying?" She sputtered, then looked quickly away in the direction of her staff, who appeared to be unobtrusively dust-ing pottery but were listening hard. They moved to the rear of the store where the blanket collection was housed and the acoustics were vastly superior. "Where, Junior? You buying a government house? Planning to set up a tipi on the prairie?"

"Corrine, it's snowing out. I just wandered in here looking for a ride to a motel."

"Did you hear I'm raising a son now?"

"No, I didn't know that. Congratulations. Who's the lucky guy who captured your heart?"

She set her hands on the edge of the glass counter and studied its contents. His own bracelets, fine inlay work, storytellers, twisted rope, wristwatches .... Junior looked at objects Corrine was studying, pretty sure they weren't seeing the same things at all. When she looked up, she was smiling this little smile that made his blood go thin and watery, like any moment what was in him, his essence, might run down his pant leg and puddle inside his boot.

"Nobody. My heart's my own. When you left—or likely some-where in the three months before that when you couldn't seem to get enough of fucking me every night—you and me made a baby, Junior. You've got a son now, Mr. New York Hotel Life, and about eight years of back child support."

"We had a kid together?"

"Dog!" she hollered, and the eight-year-old came peeking out from the Trading Post restaurant, his dark brown hair cut in an attempt at a popular style, as spiky on top as it would go. He clutched a sketch pad under his arm and pinched a charcoal stub between his thumb and index finger. He hid the charcoal behind his back and studied Junior blankly. "Did I do something bad?"

Corrine signaled him over, close to her. She placed her hands on his shoulders and gave him a little push forward. "No," she said. "You been asking me about this since you learned to flap your jaws, so take a good, long look. This man's your father."

"Mom, that's Junior Whitebear."

"So it is. Why don't you take him in the kitchen until I'm done closing the registers. Find out where the hell he's been your whole life and after you do, be sure and ask him if it was worth missing you growing up. Then get him to buy you some new shoes."

The boy's face went from confused to sober. "Kitchen's back here," he said to Junior, pointing.

"Yeah, I remember where it is," Junior told him. "They still make that cherry pie?"

Dog nodded. "It's my favorite."

Junior smiled. "Mine, too. I like it heated up, with two scoops of ice cream melting all over it. Maybe we could get some, if it won't spoil your dinner."

"I'm pretty much always hungry," the boy said.

Junior patted his ribcage. "Looking pretty skinny there for an always-hungry boy. You got a tapeworm for a pet, yeah?"

Dog giggled, and Corrine dug a pencil out of her skirt pocket and began tallying up numbers on a clipboard. Junior motioned the boy on to the restaurant and reached for Corrine's arm.

"Dog? Jesus, Corrine, what's up with that? Some kind of horrible nickname?"

"A skinny brown stray dog was the first thing I saw when I woke up from having him. It made me remember how you sneaked off. Since then, everyone calls him Short Dog. He's in the lower percentile on the growth charts. His real name is Walter, the same as yours."

"Listen, Corrine. Think you can ease up on me a little? How was I supposed to know you were pregnant? You think I would have stayed away if I knew we were having a baby?"

She bit her pencil impassively. "Yep."

Junior put his hands in his jacket pocket. "Damn, Corrie, I'd've come right back if I had known."

She crumpled the paper on her clipboard. "It's easy to say that now, after you've ridden the good, long ride, isn't it. Maybe it's better this way."

"I miss eight years of his life and you call that better? How do you figure?"

"I've been keeping track, Whitebear. Since I came to work here full time, I've learned percentages, commissions, and I understand what goes into profit. You went out there in the white man's world a broke Skin. Now you come back wearing custom boots, fancy beaded jacket, looking pretty Hollywood. I'm guessing your pockets are full enough you can start paying for the privilege of father-hood. A college fund. Nice clothes, like the other kids wear. Regular doctor visits. I got a list as long as Highway 89."

Junior wiped his face with his hand. He had broken out in a cold sweat from the moment she said the words "single mother." Walter waited for him at the table. His *son*. Under his hands Corrine had once felt as sleek, hot, and unpredictable as lightning. She had given birth to the boy. "Whatever seems fair," he said. "I want to do my part."

Corrine had tears in her eyes. "Just remember. Your part and mine, Junior. They're always going to be separate parts."

He pressed his lips together and tried to make sense of what Corrine was saying. "I walk in here, feel like I landed on another planet. You think I'm going to try to take him from you? Relax. You're his mother."

"That's right. And you're the sperm bank."

"Fine, Corrine. Whatever you want to call it."

Disgusted, he walked to the rear of the store to sit down at the table Dog—what kind of nickname was that for a child—had chosen for them. The boy was nervously wiping charcoal smudges off his fore-arms with a napkin. He hunched over the sketch pad, dying to show it off, embarrassed that it might not meet with approval. He laid his napkin across his lap, then jumped up when Junior got to the table, which sent the paper fluttering to the floor and him to the verge of humiliation. Junior reached down and plucked it from the carpet.

"Here you go, Walter. I can never keep them on my lap either."

"Nobody calls me Walter."

"I do." In those eight years away from the res, Junior had come to understand that one of the best things about Indian kids was that they weren't shy, constipated about displaying affection. Anglo kids stiffly shook hands, afraid to hug, already emulating adults. This boy was equal parts eager and uncertain. Corrine had brought him up proper, respecting his elders, even when they showed up unannounced after eight years and suddenly turned out to be his father.

"I ordered you some pie," Dog said. "And coffee. But if you don't like coffee, there's Coke and other stuff. I mean, I could drink the coffee."

"I like coffee. Why don't you come on over here and let me look at you?" Junior said. "Eight years old. Imagine, all this time my heart was missing something, and it turned out to be you. Damn. I'm your dad, Walter."

The boy fitted his slim shoulder under Junior's, causing the beads on his jacket fringe to rattle. He looked up at him, eyes shining with Corrine's same fire.

"You don't have to say anything. We'll get to know each other. See what happens." Junior let the boy set the boundaries. He kept his desire to swoop this child up in his arms and dance all through the restaurant in careful check. He'd learned a lot in that other world the past eight years. But smelling that boy, feeling his warmth, knowing his flesh was here, he knew he'd missed a great deal more.

9

"Get in and try not to piss me off," Corrine said, indicating the passenger door of the truck.

Junior looked around the old Chevy short-bed, seeing the broken radio knobs, the hairpipe necklace hanging from the rearview mirror, candy wrappers, and Coke cans littering the floor. "Jeez, Corrine, I never knew you were so sentimental. This is the same truck, *enit*?"

"Used to be Uncle Oscar's," Dog said. "He gave it to Mom."

Junior remembered his and Corrine's last night together, their bodies slick with sweat. In the bed of this truck, they had made a baby, Walter, perhaps on that last night.

"It runs, and it's a reliable vehicle," Corrine answered. "That's all there is to it. Everybody buckle up. We got to get home for dinner. There's people coming."

"Oscar's making deer-meat stew," Dog said. "He invited my teacher. I want you to meet him."

"I'd like to. Better ask your mom, though."

Stretching his fingers across the bench seat, Dog measured out the space between his parents. Junior smiled, already thinking of Arizona summers, when the weather was bright as sterling, and they could practice roping cattle, play basketball, ride horses through the hills, go exploring. Or rent a houseboat on Lake Powell, do a little fishing, camp out. Maybe, if Corrine was feeling generous, he could take the boy back to Massachusetts and show him the Atlantic. "How's my mare doing?" he asked.

Corrine snorted. "Nine years later, he bothers to ask about his horse."

"Eight. I send money for her care. All I was asking for was a report."

"This white lady been riding her," Dog piped up. "She lives with my teacher, Mr. Oliver. Mr. Oliver likes my drawings. He says I make great pictures. She's horse crazy, and she's going to have a baby."

"Horse crazy, huh?"

Dog nodded. "She's real good with horses. She don't spoil 'em or hit 'em, and still they mind her."

"*Doesn't* spoil them," Corrine corrected. "Which is lucky for you, Whitebear." She switched on the wipers and chuckled. "White girl looking after the old horse thief's mare. That's amusing."

Junior put his arm around Dog. The hell with what Corrine thought about that. They rode in silence the fifteen miles up Highway 89 to the 160, the road that led to Tuba City. Eventually, if you turned right, it went by Second Mesa, Kearns Canyon, and Fort Defiance. Then it forked off to the left into 191 and Canyon de Chelly. At the Main Street light in town, they took another left, passing the Chat 'n' Chew burger palace, the independent gas station, and several stores that had been built during his absence. The Navajo-owned Chevrolet dealer was advertising great deals on used cars, secondhand trucks, and four-wheel-drive Jeeps. *How about that?* Junior thought. *Here, in this one small corner of the world, people still possessed the morals to call a used car used instead of "preowned."* The Quality Inn came into view, and Junior looked over at Corrine. "Right here's fine."

She clicked on her turn signal indicator, braked, and Dog shifted
in his seat. "Mom?"

She smoothed her boy's hair. "What?"

"Oscar could drive him back," he said. "After dinner."

Corrine hesitated. A car passed them, then another. She clicked
the blinker off and continued down the street. Junior kept silent.
He knew better than to say a word.

He left the Johnsons at the doorway of their frame house, assuring
his son that he only wanted to say hello to his mare before dinner,
that he could walk the short distance down to the school by himself, he knew the way. The horse wasn't going anywhere; he
wanted to give Corrine and Dog some space, as well as think about
being a father himself. Hearth smells came at him from various
doorways as he made his way down the side road past parked pick-
ups, junked-out cars, woodpiles, and stacks of old tires. The frozen
ruts in the dirt toward the old school were deep and familiar. At
the tail end of his elementary schooling, Junior had gone here.
Jimmy'd stayed sober long enough to march him into the office
and enroll him. The white kids called him "brown shit" or the
more eloquent "timber nigger." The Indian kids whispered stories
about his white mother. Though it was culturally taboo to speak of
the dead, their childlike fascination with such matters often over-
powered the ban, and face it, his mother's story was as dramatic as
her pale skin color had been. Veronica Whitebear had hanged herself from a cottonwood tree out by the fairgrounds, a grocery store
sack thoughtfully pulled over her face to spare whoever found her
the more gruesome aspects of her chosen method of earthly exit.
Her fingernails were newly manicured in a vivid shade of pink that
to this day Junior could not bear. Below her bare feet, new patent-
leather high heels lay on their sides in the dirt. Every last grisly
detail was passed around the school. What the teasing white kids
didn't understand was that Junior felt grateful to be lumped in
with the Indians. He'd choose to be a bona-fide goat roper any day

over mixed blood. What the Indian kids didn't understand was that his father had driven his mother to that noose, practically given her lessons on how to tie good, strong knots on a nightly basis. For years, in order to keep her from the cottonwood tree and the length of rope, Junior'd had to make himself very quiet, very still. But eventually the noise got to be too much to bear, and Veronica embraced the tree.

The classroom exteriors were painted a sandstone color that made the demarcation between dirt and building indefinite. The school boasted a new sign with those pin-on letters, like every other school in America announcing basketball season. There was a game this weekend, Tuba vs. Cameron. He thought he might ask Dog to go, maybe Oscar too, if Oscar didn't punch him out on sight. In the past Oscar had always appreciated a good game of ball.

At the school barn entrance, Junior noticed a white woman bent low over the horses' watering trough. She braced herself, one gloved hand clutching the tank's metal edge. With the other she was hammering hard at the icy surface. She was breathing hard, her blond hair falling into her face, winter jacket unzipped to reveal an advanced case of pregnancy. Everywhere he looked today the world seemed to be full of mothers. He leaned against the weatherbeaten wooden doorframe, hands in his pockets, watching the woman pound away at the ice. Behind her, horses nosed over their stalls interestedly, but he didn't see Sally. Well, goddamn, a defrosting iron only cost around fifty bucks. Maybe he'd buy one for the school, donate some time to work on fixing up this ratty old barn. He walked forward a few paces, and then from the recessed stalls, Sally looked up from her flake of hay, her white muzzle tinted green, her comma-shaped nostrils quivering as she took in his smell, cataloged the memories, decided whether or not she knew him. She let out an inquisitive whinny, and Junior's heart just about broke in two. He fell in love the same way he had all those years back when she was a damp little filly peeking around her mama's flank. *Hey, Beautiful*, he thought, *you're growing up. Pretty soon, we'll go for a ride again, talk things over, just you and me and the earth underneath us.*

The noise stopped as the pregnant woman let the claw hammer fall to the dirt. She placed both her hands on her lower back but made no sound. Junior watched her suck in her breath, grit her teeth for several long minutes, so long that he straightened up, thinking he was going to have to go over to her in a minute more, maybe pound her on the back or something to get her started breathing regular again. He remembered the children playing at the gate at Sky Harbor airport, and tried to picture Dog as an infant. Corrine would have held him every minute, sung him through fevers, celebrated every time he turned his head. Then when he started in with the crayons and the sketchbook, she had to have begun worrying. Damn, he wished he had been there. The pregnant woman squatted down to retrieve the hammer and apparently thought better of her actions.

"Dammit, dammit, damn, damn, damn!" Her voice rose in fury almost one entire octave.

Seemed pretty clear to Junior that breaking through the ice was only a matter of time; she was unhappy being in labor. So why wasn't she tucked in a hospital bed, surrounded by nurses and monitors and all that expensive *bilagáana* medical equipment? He couldn't imagine what she was doing in a reservation school barn. "Ma'am?" he said softly, trying not to alarm her.

She turned to look at him, her mouth slightly open, a chipped front tooth visible. Her eyes startled like a skittish colt's; then, as if she was ashamed to be caught here, she let him have it. "Who the hell do you think you are, spying on me like that?"

He kept his voice casual, conversational. "I'm Junior Whitebear. That's my mare, Sally. You need a hand there with the ice?"

"I don't need a hand with anything." She grimaced. "Why'd you have to come back?"

There didn't seem to be a reason that would please anyone. From the guy on the plane on down to Corrine, every time he tried answering that particular question he came up short. "Well . . ." He didn't bother explaining any further because right then the woman's water broke. He'd seen this happen before, with animals, as well as in his brief and ill-fated year of premedical study at U. of A. The gushing fluid darkened her sweat pants. She let out an embarrassed "Oh," splaying her legs like a horse, and clutched at her belly.

He went to her. "Let's get you inside somewhere warm." He bent and scooped her up in his arms.

She struggled in his grip. "Put me down, goddammit. I can walk wherever I'm going."

A tough one, and a mouth on her. "You planning on doing a Mary-and-Joseph in the dirty straw and horse buns here? Giving birth you need a clean, warm place. We can go right up the road here to my friend's house."

She screwed up her face. "I'm not 'giving birth,' here or any-where. Put me down."

"When the bag of waters breaks, you're supposed to lie down and have the baby. Getting up can give you an infection." He started to walk, looking at her belly, that taut basketball shape pok-ing at her thermal shirt. "Surely your doctor told you that by now."

"My doctor said I've got thirty days to go."

He laughed, continuing to walk back toward the Johnsons' house. Another contraction seized her, and she cried out. "You got maybe a couple hours."

"No! Don't say that!"

In his arms, she felt like maybe 150, not so much to carry back to the Johnsons'—the equivalent of two Western saddles and a sack of grain. As the contractions came and went, she rounded her back, burying her face in his neck. "It's okay to yell," he said, his laboring breath coming in visible silver wisps in the evening air. "Scream if it helps. That's supposed to move things along."

"How the hell do you know?"

"I went to college."

"Bully for you." Her heart was no longer in fighting him. Junior held her close and reserved his strength for carrying her, for breathing, taking a brief time-out every fifteen feet or so to rest before moving on. She reined it in the entire way back to the Johnsons', and for some reason he felt amused by that and oddly paternal, as if somebody upstairs had decided winter solstice was the perfect occasion to send Junior Whitebear as many lessons as could be stuffed into one day.

"You'll be all right," he said, huffing steamy breath out into the cold night. "We can lay you down in the front seat of Oscar's truck and drive you to the hospital in Flag. There's time."

"Oscar?" she said.

"Yeah, my friend."

"Oscar's *my* friend." She curled up in another contraction, stifled the yowl, and, counting back from the last one, Junior decided, *Well, no, maybe there wasn't time. This baby was going to be born soon, probably in the Johnson home, wherever they could clear space.* "Better tell me your name," he said. "I always like to know the names of the women riding my horse."

"Chloe Morgan." Her voice sounded small and controlled for the large event taking place inside her.

"Chloe," he repeated. "Tell me, you always tend horses when you feel labor coming on?"

"We're having dinner at the Johnsons'. I went to see to the school horses' water. They can go without hay, but not water. On the weekends the tank sometimes freezes—" She stopped in the middle of her sentence, and Junior could tell that this new pain thumbed its nose at the previous contractions.

"Like today?" he said, trying to distract her.

"Can't you hurry?"

"It's not much further." Her face was close enough to his that he could see her chipped front tooth up close and the lack of makeup, a plain girl, not what he was used to, pretty enough, but a hard kind of pretty.

The contraction passed, and she took a breath, squeezing his arm. "I think we should stop."

"Out here in the road?"

"Yeah."

"Why's that?"

"Because I'm nowhere near ready to have a baby. We don't have a crib or anything."

Junior laughed. "It's not like it's the end of the world. Women say it hurts wicked bad during, but after, you have the present of a sweet-smelling new little baby to keep."

"Some present. Jesus. It really hurts."

Humming a little, he said, "A baby's the best kind of present I can imagine. Even if it comes to you through pain."

"Like you'd know anything about that."

He winked. "I might surprise you."

She smelled like the Atlantic, fishy and raw, elemental, like some watery creature making a difficult transition to land. Standing outside his rented cottage in P-town, he had smelled the ocean hundreds of times over, taken the bracing scent for granted. Now he knew he'd never inhale it again without remembering holding this woman in his arms. Years of working the grinding wheel had erased his fingerprints, rendered his identity to a name in a gallery catalog. He was the sum of his work, nothing more. But here he stood, flesh and blood, holding on to a woman about to give birth, a woman who wielded a hammer like a journeyman carpenter.

On the Johnsons' porch, he turned Chloe sideways in his arms and kicked at the doorframe with his bootheel. When Dog opened the door, Junior shouldered his way inside. "Found her in the barn," he said. "Somebody better call her doctor."

"Dad?" Dog said, trying out the word. "That's the horse lady I was telling you about."

"Hank." Chloe stretched her hands out to the pissed-off-looking white man standing behind Oscar. "I'm sorry."

Junior laid Chloe down on the living-room floor. He stripped off his jacket, rolled it up, and placed it beneath her head for a pillow. The TV was on *Wheel of Fortune*, somebody's grandmother getting all excited about buying an E. "Corrie?" he called. "Got a blanket?"

Behind him he heard the clatter of silverware.

"Oh, my God, is that Chloe? What did you do to her, Junior?"

"Nothing except give her a lift. Her baby's coming."

"I think we can see that."

"Who are you?" the white guy demanded, and Junior stepped between him and the woman in labor.

"Listen," he said. "She doesn't need a bunch of questions, she needs some clean towels and the doctor. Quit acting like a jackass and get on the phone. Her water broke down in the barn."

The man's face blanched until he looked like he was going into labor himself. "She's in labor?"

"Buddy, I'm telling you, she's *really* in labor," Junior said. "This baby's coming *now*."

"Hank?" Chloe asked, then let loose with a string of words Junior couldn't quite catch. It sounded like Spanish.

Hank sobered up in a hurry. "Call the paramedics. Oh, my God, Oscar. Do you guys have paramedics?"

Oscar said, "We got great volunteer firemen."

Junior surveyed the commotion taking place in the Johnson living room. Every corner was taken up by somebody posturing and complaining and paying no attention to Chloe. He looked around the room for Walter, and found him standing by the telephone in the kitchen. They made eye contact, and Junior tried to let his son know everything was going to be fine.

Corrine grabbed the old Chief's blanket from the couch, knelt down next to Chloe, tucking the blanket beneath her knees so her legs were bent. "You doing okay?"

Chloe smiled. "Oh, sure, Corrine. I peed all over myself, my favorite thing to do. And by the way, this really fucking hurts. Way more than that stinking doctor said it would."

Corrine looked up at Junior. "It's supposed to. Otherwise, people'd do nothing but make babies day and night. And that wasn't urine, Chloe, it was birth waters. There'll be more where that came from."

"More good news."

"Dog, run and get sheets out of the cupboard. Those old soft pink ones. You," she pointed to Oscar. "Call Dr. Lois and tell her we're having a home birth."

"But it's too early. She needs to be in the hospital," Hank repeated, trying to push his way past Junior, who feinted this way and that, like a boxer, keeping the space between them clear and distinct. "Look," he said, "it's my baby."

"Then act like it," Junior said.

"We girls need a lot of things we don't always get," Corrine soothed, rubbing a washcloth over Chloe's belly where the skin stretched tight. "Besides, it's too late for wishes, Mr. Oliver. Your baby's coming, early or not. Junior, remember when we used to yank calves for the McNellys? Remember Future Farmers classes?"

"Sure, I guess so."

"Good. Because I've got a rash on my hands from silver cleaner. I don't want to risk touching inside her. Somebody has to and you have the most experience. Go wash your hands and hurry back."

"Nobody touches anything," Hank insisted, "until I call the hospital." He yanked the wall phone from Dog's hands, punching numbers crazily, getting them so mixed up he had to hang up and start all over again.

"Mr. Oliver?" Dog said. "Say the number. I can dial for you."

Junior washed his hands at the kitchen sink, removing his rings and scrubbing hard with the dishwashing soap and scrub brush until the skin felt starched. He breathed slow and easy from his diaphragm, trying to steady his nerves. He kept waiting for the woman to cry out, thinking if she would just give in, the baby would come easily, and he wouldn't have to do this.

Corrine stroked Chloe's arm gently. "It's going to be fine," she kept reassuring her, and every time Corrine said that, Chloe shook her head no, believing not so much as one word.

Junior looked away when Corrine removed Chloe's sweat pants and underwear, bunching them on the floor and covering her with a clean sheet, running a wet washcloth over her crotch and thighs. Corrine brought out the cloth stained with blood, wrung it dry over a bowl, and then made eye contact with Junior in a determined way. She held up a corner of the sheet, nodded her head, and Junior glanced down, seeing a smooth, ivory thigh with a trickle of blood staining it like a line on a topographical map. Between her legs, Chloe was swollen and damp with the birth process.

He whispered, "I think she's already tearing a little. Corrine, college was a long time ago. So was pulling cows. Give me some silver, I can make her baby a bracelet. What I can't do is work a miracle."

"It's exactly the same as it was with calves," Corrine said. "Ease a couple fingers inside, get a feel, tell me what's going on. I'll talk you through it."

At the wall phone, Hank was yelling that having a baby was too an emergency, and Dog was calmly observing his teacher's antics. Oscar brought the last of the towels from the closet and a ball of unwrapped kite string left over from springtime. Chloe pressed her chin to her chest, grunted, and Corrine reached up, grabbing her arms.

"You concentrate on lying quiet. Don't push."

"But I have to—"

"Fight it."

Gingerly, aware that he could not be more intrusive, Junior steadied his fore and middle fingers and fitted them inside her. Vaguely, he remembered the school films, the book diagrams he always found more engaging than the text alongside them. Animals did just fine on their own most of the time. People had problems. He sought the lip of the cervix, and found none to speak of. If she was that stretched, the birth was imminent. He felt for the dome of head that by now should have been palpable in the birth canal.

"Tell me," Corrine urged.

Behind the bulge of fluid-filled membrane, he could detect a round shape, but it was not the baby's head, it was the butt end. A girl, he decided, noting the absence of male equipment. In horses they called difficult deliveries dystocia. Roughly it translated to,

Wish it was another way. He eased his fingers back out. "Feels like a breech," he said softly. "I don't feel legs or knees, just bottom."

Corrine sighed, and Hank stretched the telephone cord as far from the wall as it would go. "Hey! What do you think you're doing?"

Oscar held him back.

Junior dried his hands on the towel as he answered. "I'm trying to stay calm and help, which is a little more than I can say for you, buddy. Oscar, can't you get this guy a cup of coffee or something?"

"Come on, Hank. Corrine knows what she's doing. Her and Junior there, they both yanked calves for the McNellys the whole time they were growing up. It'll be okay."

"Chloe's not a cow," he said, and Oscar took the phone out of his hands, made space for him, let him kneel by Chloe's head so that he could be a part of what was happening.

Junior watched as Hank cradled Chloe's face gently. He reached down to clasp her right hand in his, pressed his cheek to hers. She looked up at him, panic in her eyes. There was love there, too, but it was more definite on his part than hers.

"Why didn't you tell me you were having contractions?"

She turned her face to the side, bit her lip. "I wasn't sure that I was."

Junior wondered how she broke her front tooth, if some asshole had hit her or if she'd gone off a horse. Her brown eyes were full of tears, but she'd be damned before she let them spill over. With how much this had to hurt, her stoic demeanor intrigued him. White women generally went into hysterics over a chipped fingernail. Not this one. She acted like she was Indian.

"All I knew was it hurt, and I thought it was because I rode the horse when you made me promise not to. I'm sorry, Hank. *Lo siento. A lo hecho, pecho.* . . ."

Hank looked up. "What is she trying to tell me?"

Corrine elbowed him back. "She's out of it. Quit asking her questions she can't answer."

At the kitchen sink Junior scrubbed his hands for a second time, thinking hard. He checked his fingernails, then rolled his sleeves back and removed his watch and bracelets, scrubbing to his elbows. Dog handed him a towel and looked up into his father's face, worried.

"You give your mom this much trouble, Walter?"

The boy grinned. "I forget."

"Later, when this is over, let's ask her. I want to know everything I missed, *enit*?"

"You think the horse lady's going to be all right?"

"Yeah, she looks pretty tough. But we could use some help. Think you could round up some other women who've had babies? The older ones?"

Dog nodded. "Sure. I can get Ivana Yellowhair's mom. And Robynn Cameron's. They're both grandmothers."

"Great. Run and find them. Bundle up. It's cold out there."

Oscar repeated the instructions of the voice on the other end of the connection. "They want to know can you see the head?"

Junior returned to Chloe, shoved the sheet back and quit acting polite. This was just another mare in trouble, a cow who needed a hand—and that hand happened to be his own. "Tell them it's ass first. And," he looked up over her knees to see Chloe press her chin to her chest involuntarily. "Tell them she's pushing, and that it's coming right now."

The second bag of waters broke over his hands, the smell thick, sweet, oceanic. No turning back now. Mentally Junior reviewed the facts: Baby a month yet from term. Labor rocketing along. When his fingers slid inside her, she'd felt dilated to the span of his palm, which, given the size of a newborn's butt, ought to be wide enough. And the bottom was coming now. He felt it lightly graze his hands, move forward, the little bluish body coming toward him, pinkening in the air.

"Here we go," Corrine said.

Junior readied himself to catch her, to turn the little body to either side to deliver her arms safely, so neither would catch behind her head, cutting off circulation either to a limb or the cord.

Through clenched teeth Chloe cried out, and the tiny body nearly slid through his palms, a slippery little reed of a girl. The head was still inside. Hank sighed, and Junior wanted to. Hank figured the hard part was over, but Corrine, who knew better, was still holding her breath. "You see the cord yet, Junior? The head's coming?"

"Yeah, the head's coming right now," he said, and it was, the tiny wrinkled face and the cord pressing above her button nose. He tucked it away with his fingertip, and then he was holding an infant in his formerly useless silversmith's hands, looking down at this underweight creation, still connected by a rippled cord of striped flesh to what had fed her the last eight months.

"Take a look at your daughter," he said to Hank, who lifted Chloe's shoulders up to see.

"Look, Chloe. It's a girl after all. Oh, my God. She's beautiful. She's looking at us. Her eyes. Like whale's eyes."

Chloe tried to raise her head from the jacket. She tried her best to smile, return the good wishes everyone was beaming her way, to say thanks. The baby began to make soft mewing noises, and Chloe's smile drained of color. "Hank?"

"She's fine. It's all over. We're doing fine here. You're a mother."

Now Corrine sighed. Junior wrapped the baby in a towel and handed her to Corrine. He wiped away blood.

"Tie off the cord and deliver the placenta," she whispered.

He finished knotting the string. "Nothing's moving."

"Come on, Chloe," Corrine called out. "We need one more good push out of you."

Eyes closed, she lay back against Hank's hands, her tired breathing slowing. "I'm gone."

"Chloe?" Hank said. "Open your eyes and look at me."

Corrine shushed him. "If she won't push, then you got to give it a little tug. Clamp it off and let's get it out of her. Her color looks bad."

Hank kept talking, shaking Chloe's shoulders, but she only woke

up enough to give them a half smile. Corrine held the baby close.
"Do it, Junior."

Reluctantly Junior gave the cord the tiniest of tugs. The placenta
delivered, the deflated basketball-size mass of tissue tumbling out
intact. He thought, *Thank you. Now maybe I can take a breath here.*
Then the blood started coming, not gushing, but steady, and more
than there should be, soaking the towel.

"Corrine," he said. "What have I done?"

Then the grandmothers were at the door, and the voice on the
phone abandoned on the rug was calling out, asking what was
happening now: Was the baby there? Behind the grandmothers
Dog led the volunteer firemen in, suited up as if they were expecting a house on fire, not a tiny, troublesome black-haired baby.

10

Like an old Kodak slide forgotten in the projector, the blurry memory was cast in amber light, darkened at the edges as if the faces on film were overexposed. *No seas payaso, buki. Out from under that table, ahora mismo! Mija, don't you make me come after you like last time!*

But she wasn't coming out. She planned to make herself so small she could slip into the cracks in the floor. *I'll ride away on my horse's back, into the sky, hide behind the moon. . . .*

From crest to hooves, Chloe ached. I'll bet this is what dying's like, she imagined, you see yourself someplace you're not and more than anything—being held in Hank's arms one more time, training Thunder to do everything Absalom could, seeing the baby—you just want to go where it doesn't hurt. The nurse at her bedside finished checking her vitals and switched off the light. Dream-memory reached up and took hold of her again, the equivalent of her family album.

The kitchen was her favorite room. The walls were yellow and shiny, same as the tablecloth it was okay to spill on. Under the table rust peeled off in interesting jigsaw shapes. The cupboard didn't close all the way. She saw the Cheerios box peeking at her, and the C&H sugar cubes. When nobody was looking, she climbed up on the counter, took one, and sucked on it. Pretty soon she was going to be two, with a cake and presents. She was *big*. And she was wearing her good nightgown—with the real ribbon on the front. It was for summer only, but she wasn't either catching another cold. Uh-oh. Somebody wasn't careful with scissors. See the gashes in the floor? You don't want *that*. They cost money to repair. She hid her pennies in there. She'd need a lot of money later when it was time to run away. Everyone ran away sometimes. Her daddy had. He'd be hungry when he came back. She would share her Cheerios with him. She was good at sharing.

Even in her small history she understood that flight was essential. Sometimes when she rushed to hide under the table, her small toes caught in the buckled linoleum. If there was blood she might cry, but only softly and to herself. Worse than blood, the uneven terrain had kept her toy horse from proceeding at a smooth gallop to the pantry door. Now his leg was broke. If a horse broke his leg, he disappeared. In the pantry, among cans of tuna and vegetables, empty cardboard packing boxes, there was sanctuary. In the middle of raised voices and swinging fists, an almost-two-year-old sometimes forgot to be careful.

The smells of the kitchen varied. The blue haze of tobacco smoke rising upward in dishwater steam. Bacon. Inches of yeasty stale beer forgotten in amber bottles. Burnt toast crumbs. Coffee nobody drank left too long on the stove, percolating into bitterness. Underneath all that a faint, comforting perfume persisted, so indistinct it might have been bath powder or a hint of bar soap clinging to skin. Chloe'd come to recognize the scent as the sum of her mother's parts: that faceless humming figure standing at the sink. Over thirty-four years, this vision had focused down to a single, precious hand. Sometimes fingers patted her head when she accidentally got a bump, but if she got too near the stove—too near, period—the palm might deliver a swat that sent her to her knees, breath knocked clean out of her. It was all she had of her mother, that Jekyll-and-Hyde hand. But once upon a time, it had held a baby, freshly delivered from the depths of her own body, the same way she ought to be holding her own baby right now. She couldn't hurt so badly down there without having given birth. So where was the baby?

Half awake now, she lay in the hospital bed with her eyes closed. In the dark, when the pain had been overwhelming, a nurse came to replace the IV bag. Other than ask if Chloe needed another shot, she hadn't said much. Was the baby all right? She tried to remember if it had cried, but of the birth in the Johnsons' living room she recalled only bits and pieces: Corrine's soothing voice, her hand on Chloe's calf, the television on some game show, Hank's face pressed close to her own, as she struggled to push out of her body what felt like a full-grown horse. That Indian with his hands between her legs—the one who owned the mare—Sally. Oh, God. Had she maybe lost the baby?

She squinted. It was definitely day, bright lights and the resolute disinfectant smell purging whatever might have gotten soiled in the night. Nearby she heard trays clattering and smelled breakfast.

"I know I'm in the hospital," Chloe said to whoever was turning back her sheets and lifting tape from her belly. "Only question is, Which one and how did I get here?"

"Flagstaff Medical Center. Ambulance. There. Now you're all cleaned up. You want to try a little Cream of Wheat for breakfast? Think you can hold that down?"

Chloe licked her dry lips. "I don't get coffee? Here I've been good almost nine months, they promised coffee, and they were lying the whole time?"

The voice broke into a familiar chuckle. "Can't talk you into decaf?"

Chloe made a face and opened her eyes. "Dr. Lois?"

"Sorry to have missed the main event. Sounded pretty dramatic."

"The baby's okay?"

"Tiny, but a trooper." Dr. Carrywater's expression remained cheer-

ful. Freshwater pearl earrings graced her ears, and she had her long
dark hair twisted into a bun at the nape of her neck. Maybe this was
her go-to-town look. She held out a plastic tumbler with a straw.
"How about starting out on water?"

Chloe leaned forward and cried out from the pain of using her
stomach muscles.

"You're ready for your next shot. I'll call the nurse."

"No." Chloe swallowed the water, which tasted tart and clean, as
if snowmelt had just sluiced down the mountain. "It doesn't hurt
so killing bad I need my head messed up as a bonus."

"You might not want it now, but in the next half hour you will.
You had some emergency surgery last night."

"Surgery? I thought I had a baby."

"Well, you did that too, but you were hemorrhaging when they
brought you in. We removed your uterus to stop the bleeding."

"Hemorrhaging? What are you talking about? Where's my baby?"

"Lower your voice, Chloe. There are new mothers here, trying to
sleep. Rest, and I'll stop by again later." She turned to go.

"Wait," Chloe whispered. "Please, Dr. Lois. You can't just tell me
you cut my womb out and then leave. What about my baby?"

"She's here. Down the hallway."

"She?"

"Yes, a little girl. Remember?"

A minute went by, during which Chloe racked her brain for
details, coming up short. "Well, do I ever get to see her?"

The doctor's pager beeped and she glanced at it momentarily.
"They'll bring her around when it's time to feed her. For now I
really think you should just rest."

"Oh, no. I'd better see her. Right now. So I can tell for myself
what's going on."

"Chloe, your baby's sleeping, and you should be, too. You've
been through a rough time."

It came to her then, that picture of the birth waters spilling down
her legs in the school barn, Junior Whitebear carrying her to the
Johnsons', Hank screaming into the telephone. "I wake up here

alone, my guts on fire, no baby, you tell me I had surgery, so please hear me when I say I need to see her. Hank'll remember the details. Soon as he gets here, he'll help me get it all straight in my head. Where's there a pay phone so I can call him?"

"Hank's your husband, right?"

It sounded so cheap to say boyfriend. Kit was right: She should have married him.

"You might as well bring me the baby. I'm not going to believe she's all right until I see her for myself."

"Chloe, I counted all her fingers and toes myself. Same as you did when she was born. You've been through major surgery. The anesthetic confuses some people. You just don't remember."

Chloe's cheeks burned. She'd been a mother less than twenty-four hours and already failed. Raising her chin, she said, "There a telephone around here so I can get some answers?"

"Here, on your bedside table. You need a phone book?"

"I *live* there," Chloe said. "I think I remember the number."

Dr. Carrywater pressed the call button and spoke into the wall speaker, ordering Chloe's breakfast. "I'll stop by this afternoon. We'll talk more then."

Chloe couldn't look at her. She nodded, concentrating on dialing their number, but the hospital operator came on the line and began explaining how long-distance calls needed to be billed to a personal phone card, and suddenly the whole effort seemed more complicated than it was worth pursuing. She hung up. Screw it. Hank would show up soon. This was his baby too. A girl, like he wanted. A daughter. Unless the baby was not okay, and her secret horseback rides on the mare were responsible, in which case she'd be lucky ever to see him again.

A nurse set down a breakfast tray, uncovered a bowl of whitish, lumpy gruel, and handed over a spoon. "Enjoy."

"You're kidding, right?" When she left, Chloe squeezed the tears crowding her eyes back into the ducts. She hungrily spooned warm cereal into her mouth and then immediately looked for somewhere to spit it out. Syrup, brown sugar, even raisins would have helped. She set the spoon down on the tray and tentatively explored the bandage spanning her abdomen. Things down there were beginning to ache with purpose, building up speed. No uterus. That meant all her cards lay flat on the table. This baby girl was a one-shot deal.

She pressed her call button, and a voice issued forth from the wall speaker. "Yes, Mrs. Morgan?"

She didn't bother to correct her. "Can I change my mind about the pain shot?"

The nurse returned swiftly, her shoes moving noiselessly across the hospital tiles. It hurt so badly now that Chloe couldn't help softly whimpering. The bed tray cranked over her abdomen prevented her from finding a comfortable position. The sheet against her body seemed to be the weight of ten wool blankets.

"This will help you rest. When you wake up, call for Yvonne. One way or another, I'll get you down to NICU."

"NICU?"

"Neonatal Intensive Care. Try not to worry. All the preemies go in there. It doesn't necessarily mean anything bad."

That seemed fair, inevitable, but not convincing in the least. "I'll try to believe that."

"Good, because it's true." The nurse injected a full syringe into the clear IV tubing, and as Chloe watched it empty, her limbs began to fill with the cottony thickness of sedative. *I must be pretty bad off,* she guessed, *them pumping me full of dope every time I open my eyes. Well, here I go.* The toy horse reappeared in her small hand under the kitchen table. *El no tiene madre? Que verguenza!* someone was saying. And then, *Here is your locker. You can put your things here.* A Breyer Little Bits chestnut gelding, four white socks and a blaze the color of the moon. She'd mended its leg with a Band-Aid. It had fit just so into the palm of her hand, tucked safely under her pillow when she slept. She'd been afraid to name it because once named things became so precious it was agony to lose them. They had loads of boys' names picked out for this baby, from Kit's teen heartthrob Hollywood list to Chloe's personal favorite, Chase, but not one single girl's name except Annie, after Hank's sister. Seemed like bad luck to name a premature baby after one who'd died. Where had the toy horse ended up? Did they send it along with her to the children's home, or had it gotten lost in that gouge in the flooring with her secret stash of coins? Chloe trailed her fingers over her belly and fingered the thick wad of bandages. Pain was a touchstone, a place to come back to. Sleep laid its hand over her face, blocking out her worries. She stood alone in the yellow kitchen again, calling out for someone, anyone. The toy horse melted into her hand like dark pigment.

Late-afternoon sun shone through the bank of hospital windows. The ringing of nearby telephones, the soapy-clean smell of showers and hard-edged laughter finally woke her. Still giddy from the pain shots, she smiled, hearing what sounded like an echo of Kit's giggling. Kit found humor in every corner of the universe. Across the room a teenage girl was swigging from a two-liter bottle of Dr Pepper and talking on the hospital phone.

"I'm naming him Montana Estes Park San Francisco Peaks Watson," she announced. "Who says a baby can't have all the names of my favorite places?" Then she lit a cigarette. "I'll call him Monty, Mother. It is *so* a perfectly normal name." She hung up the phone, said, "Bitch," took a few quick puffs on her cigarette and stubbed it out in her WAY TO GO, RHONDA! floral arrangement. "Freakin' hospital rules," she said, when Chloe raised up on her elbow to investigate. "Don't give me any crap, okay? I put it out."

The room had four beds, and each was filled. Yellow gingham curtains were pulled around the other two. Smart roommates, Chloe decided, sleeping it off, and wondered whether she could possibly find the strength to pull her own drape. She lay back pondering the problem until the nurse who'd promised her a visit to the baby came into the room pushing an empty wheelchair. She stopped, sniffed the air and shook her finger at Rhonda. "Girl, I swear I catch you puffing one more time, I'll . . ."

Rhonda, on the phone again, held her palm over the receiver. "You'll what? Kick my poor, defenseless premature baby and me out in the snow? Go empty a bedpan."

"Premature, my foot. That baby's tiny because she smoked two packs a day all nine months she was carrying him," the nurse muttered under her breath as she locked the wheelchair next to Chloe's bed. "Come on, let's get you in the limo and go see your daughter." Arm at her elbow, she helped Chloe battle the dizziness of standing up for the first time, and hooked her IV bottle to her chair.

"Why can't I walk?"

"Like to see you try," the nurse answered. "You forget you just had a hysterectomy?"

"No. But I've been wondering who said they could do that."

"It's in your chart that your doctor stopped by and talked to you about this."

"Yeah, I heard the story. What I don't know is why they had to take it out."

"To save your life, I imagine." The nurse patted her shoulder and handed her a folded slip of paper. "Your boyfriend left this about a half hour ago. You were sleeping so hard he didn't want to wake you."

"Wish he had."

"Bad dreams, honey?"

"The worst." Chloe unfolded the pink While You Were Out. It was indeed Hank's handwriting, artistic and even, not one word misspelled.

> Thank you from the bottom of my heart. She is as
> beautiful as her mother. Rest, and heal quickly. I'll see
> you tonight. In the meantime, think of names and
> remember how much I love you, which is infinite.
>
> Hank

Chloe folded the note between her fingers and scrubbed the tears dripping down her cheeks. "Damn, I don't know what's gotten into me," she said, sobs beginning to break forth, crying like she hadn't done for anyone since her old horse, Absalom, had to be put to sleep.

The nurse handed her a tissue. "Baby blues," she said. "They're inescapable. Soon as your estrogen kicks in, they'll go away. I've seen it a thousand times. You cry so hard you think you're empty. Then they put that little baby in your arms, and love floods the empty places, and you're never alone again."

Maybe we should name her Kit, Chloe thought, wiping her cheeks, trying to quell the tears, flowing mindlessly now, in perpetual motion, like the Pacific Ocean back home in California. *A baby could do worse than be called after a red-headed ball of teenage flame.*

NICU had only two occupants on December 22, Rhonda's multi-monikered, smoke-stunted son and the tiny black-haired girl whose ID bracelet read "Girl Morgan." The nurse helped Chloe slide her arms inside a paper gown and put on a surgical mask. She supervised Chloe's hand washing at the sink, then she wheeled mother over to meet daughter, opened the isolette, and placed Chloe's hand under the tiny capped skull of her baby. Together they lifted her out of the blankets, and for the first time Chloe held what had all those months been growing inside. She looked down into her daughter's face and saw a miniature mouth curl up in one corner the same way Hank's did when he was sleeping. She marveled at the black hair—where had that come from? Whatever of herself had she given to this baby? But there was something besides bone and muscle. The baby yawned. She looked fragile but bullheaded, possessed of a tough, survivor's spirit—that was Chloe's contribution to this baby.

"No one told me it would feel like this. No one said."

The nurse tucked the hair falling into Chloe's face behind her ear. "How's that, honey?"

Chloe rubbed her thumb across the unbelievably soft skin, the fingers with nails so infinitesimal they might be flecks of mica in the side of a rocky canyon. "That you automatically love them. That it peels your soul raw to look at her."

The nurse smiled. "I've heard that happens."

"I mean, the whole time I was pregnant I had these feelings that maybe I wasn't fit to be a mother, like maybe the best thing I could do was give her away to somebody who could do a better job."

"And now?"

"How could I take my next breath without her?"

"Nature's plan exactly," the nurse said, and sat down and began reading a *People* magazine.

While the nurse scanned the latest dirt on the Hollywood stars, Chloe held onto her own cosmic chunk of creation. Her infant daughter made puppy noises in her slumber. Her limbs were no bigger around than a doll's. She watched the rise and fall of the baby's chest, her not-quite-finished body performing all the magic people took for granted every time they lit a cigarette or yelled, "Fuck you!" just for the hell of using bad words. How could she have thought riding a horse was worth jeopardizing this? She could hardly imagine riding a horse again. She would be far too busy holding this nameless girl tightly, keeping her safe from harm.

She remembered how Fats Valentine used to sing sometimes, like when they were spending the night in an unfamiliar barn, preparing to show horses the following day. Fats had a Burl Ives kind of voice. He made goofy old songs, that nobody but him knew the words to, mean something special. He recited old cowboy poetry, like Curley Fletcher's "The Strawberry Roan," a sixteen-stanza saga recited in such exacting rhythms it might as well have been set to music. "King of the Road," "Dang Me," "An Itty-Bitty Tear Let Me Down." She wished Fats were here right now. He'd know what to sing to the baby. All she could think of was the Mexican folk songs Francisco used to whistle while he mucked stalls at her old California stables. Could you whistle to a baby? Tentatively, she bent her head to press her mask-covered mouth to the baby's forehead.

"*A la rro, rro, niña, a la rro, rro, rro. Duermase mi niña, duermase me ya,*" she half-whispered, half-sang. She seemed to have known that old Spanish lullaby forever. When a horse looked to be considering colicking, or one was coming out of a bad time, and it became her job to walk him through the night and keep him among the living, these same words were the ones she always sang. "*Señora Santa Ana por que llora la niña? Por una mansana que se le perdido. . . .*"

"That's pretty," the nurse commented. "Isn't that off the new Linda Ronstadt CD?"

11

Over his bouquet of yellow roses, Hank smiled broadly, as he always did when he was worried sick. Chloe had to bless the man's heart for trying; counting the bunch Francisco had brought her sixteen years ago for high school graduation, this was the second time in her life any man had brought her flowers. The florist had tucked baby's breath into the arrangement. It was amazing they got anything to bloom in December.

Kit Wedler was with him. Chloe tried to sit up, but the effort hurt so damn much she gave up, rested against her pillows, and waited for them to come to her. Kit was still on her diet. The carrot-haired teenager was decked out in a hot-pink parka that looked like it had just had the price tags ripped off it. She toted a small pink teddy bear and a large McDonald's bag.

"Can you believe it?" she squealed. "My dad acting cool for the first time in his life? Changed my plane ticket the minute Hank called and didn't even go ballistic over paying the extra fare. Thanks to Lita the terminally optimistic, Rich Wedler is born again. Chloe, she buys him tiger-striped bikini underwear, and he even *wears* them! God, Chloe, hate to say it, but you look thrashed. So where's the baby? I can't wait to hold her. Here you were all certain it was a boy. What are you going to name her? Promise me you won't give her a stupid Christmas name, like Angel or Winter, or something New Agey like calling her after a kind of crystal. Promise. She'll hate you for it, I swear."

Kit rattled on. Chloe met Hank's eyes with her own and pressed her lips together tightly, forcing a smile. He set the roses down on her bedside table next to the telephone and bent close to give her a kiss. His carefulness she could understand. Hank'd had practice at being careful, dealing with his mother's illness. She wasn't the only one hospitals spooked.

"It's so great to see you." Chloe let Kit fold her into a hug. "Listen, I can't wait a minute longer for you to meet her," she said. "Go down the hallway and turn right. She's in the nursery at the very end. They won't let you go in, but you can look through the glass. You can't miss her. There's only one other kid, this poor little boy saddled with so many names they had to use two cards to get them all on there."

Kit twirled the teddy bear around by one of his stubby arms. "You know, it's not like I'm dense. Way *duh*, leave the new parents alone." She sighed and set down the bag of hamburgers. "But no one eats these until I come back, okay? All they served on the plane ride was rat bait."

"Rat bait?" Hank echoed.

"Those stale old oatmeal airline cookies. It's what you get when you fly budget." She took off her jacket, draped it over a chair and marched out the door. Then they were alone.

Hank sat down on the bed and Chloe felt the staples in her belly pull. "I've never had anybody bring me roses."

"I wanted to say thank you."

"Okay. I guess you're welcome." She knew he meant for going through with the pregnancy. For eating a few green things when he'd badgered her to. For not riding the mare any more than she had.

He shook his head as if to clear it. "What an ordeal. If things ever settle down, I'll bet I could sleep for a week. Did this really happen only twenty-four hours ago?"

"They let me hold her this afternoon, Hank. Not interested in my groceries, but to have her in my arms was really something."

"Still, it's good that you tried."

She gave his arm a small pinch. "You think I wasn't planning on feeding her? Jesus. Why don't you get over here in bed next to me and hug me like you mean it?"

"Chloe, there are other people here. You just had surgery—"

She kept her face calm and passive. "I know all about it. I'll feel guilty until I cash in my chips for riding that mare."

"Dr. Carrywater said it might not have been the horse, Chloe. The placenta tearing away from the uterus like that and you bleeding. They had to remove your womb, or you could have died. You're lucky you didn't."

"So I heard."

"It happens to some women."

To *some* women. But it wasn't a thing that happened to responsible women who put the baby first. The price she'd paid was permanent. She turned her head to glance over at the roses, the forced, lemon-colored, perfectly shaped but unscented blossoms more like an idea of roses than the real thing. "Now there won't be any more babies. I know you, Hank Oliver. You'd have a houseful."

He blew out a breath. "So maybe that's a good enough reason to keep teaching elementary school."

"Or maybe someday you'll meet some other woman, one who's got all her equipment. Smarter, too."

All at once the weariness in his face seemed to catch up with his words. He was quiet for several long moments. "When will you give that old song and dance a rest? We have the most beautiful daughter in the world. Let's just count our blessings. And settle on a name while we're at it. Every time I walk past the nurse at the desk, she waves papers in my face."

Across the ward the other mothers were visiting with their husbands. Siblings were discovering how to get acquainted with the newest member of the family. Rhonda had finished her jug of Dr Pepper and was well into a plastic drum of red licorice twists as she penned out baby announcements. She was on the phone, too, but as far as Chloe could tell, she hadn't had a visitor or an incoming call. "Maybe her middle name could be Silverado Canyon," she said, laughing as much as her torn-up belly would allow.

"Excuse me?"

"Nothing. A joke," she said. "Did you call your parents?"

"First thing this morning."

"Is all forgiven, or have I given birth to the devil's spawn?"

"I said, 'Good morning, Grandmother,' and Iris started to cry. That was about as far as we got. Then my father took the phone and suggested it would be a good idea for me to come for a visit now instead of after Christmas. Apparently my mother's not doing as well as I thought."

Chloe felt guilt rise up to choke her. All those letters of Iris's she'd pried open—her narrow heart would land her in hell. "He's right, Hank. You'd better go."

"In awhile. After everything here settles down."

"It's your *family*, Hank. You don't have to wait around for me."

He took hold of her ringless hands and studied them. "Yes, I do. You and the baby are my family. My first priority."

"All I meant was, I think I can manage to nurse a baby. Corrine and Oscar are close by. And now that Kit's here she can help me out. It's Christmas break, the perfect time. You wouldn't even have to miss any work. Book a flight. You'd hate yourself if you waited and then—"

Kit came scowling back into the room, Junior Whitebear at her side. The Indian who'd delivered the baby held a black cowboy hat in his hands. He was wearing that fancy beaded leather jacket lined with fleece, the one Chloe had used as a pillow. Kit cocked a thumb at him and said, "I found this guy looking through the glass at *our* baby. Either he's one hell of a baby-furniture salesman or he's telling the truth. Somebody set me straight so I can start being nice to him or kick his ass."

"I'd cast my vote for being nice." Hank stood up and shook Junior's hand. "I never got a chance to thank you."

Junior nodded to him. "Just glad I was able to help, man. You got some tough women in your corner, Hank. Didn't think Red here was going to let me live." He looked over at Chloe and smiled. "So. How's Mama doing?"

"Mama's hanging in there." His smile was one of those Sugar-I-know-where-you-live grins, the kind Chloe tried her damnedest to avoid. It traveled all the way down to where his hand had been and lodged there, taking its sweet time poking around. Chloe pulled at the flimsy hospital gown, her swollen breasts straining against the fabric. Imagine, that same hand shaking Hank's had been inside her, had delivered the baby. She felt hot and shaky and wondered if she was developing some postpartum fever. She pulled the covers up to her neck.

"Had to come make sure the wee one was doing okay," Junior said. "Damn pretty baby. That black hair is something. Wonder where she comes by it."

Hank said, "She takes after her mother, who is long on mystery."

"*Enit?*" Junior said.

Kit gave him a puzzled look. "In what?"

"*Enit,*" Hank translated. "That's Indian for agreeing with somebody. It's similar to saying 'Oh yeah, sure, you betcha.' However, in this case, it's intended as a question."

"Well, pardon me," Kit said. "I only got here a few hours ago."

Junior was impressed. "You don't miss much for a California transplant, Hank."

"It's the kids in my class at Ganado. Some days I wonder who's teaching who."

"My boy Walter thinks highly of you."

"Dog Johnson's your son?"

Junior set his hat down on top of Kit's parka in the bedside chair no one had claimed. He smiled broadly, and Chloe thought, *Now, there's a set of lips that could make a whole county of women turn permanently stupid.*

"Yeah, he is."

"Dog's a great kid. Sure loves to draw."

Kit said, "Pardon me, but who in their right mind would name a kid Dog?"

Junior looked at Kit and smiled. "I agree. It's a long story, and Corrine tells it with enthusiasm, so be sure and ask her yourself. Now Hank, being surrounded by a tribe of wild women here, you probably understand exactly where I'm coming from on that score. This fetching redhead speaking her mind here seems like she takes after the mother, too. Any relation?"

Kit blushed, her freckles disappearing under the rush of blood to her cheeks. "Chloe and me *are* kind of like sisters."

"Is that so?"

Chloe said, "Yeah. It appears we have the exact same lack of manners."

"Hey, you won't hear me minding when people are honest," Junior said. "World could do with more of it, that's for sure."

"*Enit*," Kit said, and the Indian man broke out laughing.

Junior Whitebear laughed from deep in his gut, the same way Fats Valentine used to, Chloe noticed. If laughter had a texture and a color, Junior's was the silvery old wood good barns were built of, solid lumber slapped at by wind, but standing up proud in the elements.

He slid his hand into his jacket pocket. A glint of bracelets peeked out from his right sleeve. Chloe wished she had the nerve to call him to her bedside, push that sleeve up, and study his jewelry, see how it compared to the rattle she'd splurged on and secreted away. Now that they'd talked about the baby, everyone stood awkward and quiet. Hank looked at Junior in a way that made Chloe remember the time he had taken a swing at Gabe Hubbard and in the process, earned himself a shiner.

Junior said, "You've got yourselves one skinny little reed of a baby. My recommendation is to wean her directly onto frybread. That'll put some weight to her."

While Hank laughed politely, Chloe felt recognition strike her like lightning, travel inside her as deeply as the place where her womb had been cut away. "Reed," she said. "Hank, don't you think that's the perfect name for her?"

"I always thought it was a boy's name."

"Oh, nobody goes by that old standard anymore," Kit said. "In my history class there's one girl named Michael and two named Taylor. And in case you never noticed, Kit swings both ways, as in Kit Carson, King of the Pathfinders, Comanche killer. Whoops. Junior, I didn't mean anything by that. It's just the crap they teach us in school. Are you mad?"

"No offense taken, Kit. Think of that stuff as academic comic-book adventures. Your education doesn't end with school." He retrieved a small silver cup from his deep jacket pocket and held it in his dark-skinned palm. His hand was so wide that the cup, resting there, resembled a jumbo thimble, something that might fit a giant's thumb. The silver was hammered all over in minuscule indentations, the curved handle inlaid with stripes of turquoise, spiny oyster shell, and chevrons of blood-red coral. "Reed's first present," he said, tipping it into Chloe's hands. "If that's what you decide to call her." Briefly, they touched, his skin so warm and familiar she felt slightly alarmed.

Chloe said, "Reed is exactly what I want to call her. And this is beautiful. Thanks."

"Let me see it." Kit held out her hand, and Chloe reluctantly let the cup go. "Did you make this? Oh my God, it's bitchen."

Junior grinned. "Glad you approve. I'll be keeping Sally exercised now that I'm back in town, but when you're well enough, maybe we can talk about you riding her. Kit, you enjoy northern Arizona. Let me know when you want the nontourist's tour. Us savages know secret places guidebooks don't." He winked. "I better move it along. Got to see a man about a horse."

Junior picked up his hat and set it on his inky hair. He turned to walk away, and it seemed as if every person in the ward forgot about babies long enough to watch him go. He reached the door, and Chloe burst out laughing. Kit stared openmouthed. "Oh, my

God, Chloe. He looks like that actor in *Thunderheart*. Remember the fox cop who was always outsmarting Val Kilmer? How'd you meet him?"

Chloe stifled her laughter. "Total accident. He surprised me in the school barn and yanked out my baby."

"Still. I mean . . . and the cup . . ." Kit had that look on her face, turning wistful over something she had yet to experience but could no longer live without. Gaga.

At this rate, Chloe thought, she'd forget about the hamburgers altogether. "Listen, isn't anybody besides me hungry?"

Hank was fairly bristling. "I'd like to know what's so damn funny about that guy needing to take a leak."

Chloe placed her hands over her belly so it wouldn't hurt while she laughed. "Nothing. It's not funny at all." She laughed again.

"Wait," Kit said, shaking her red hair, curls flying. "I feel like I missed *All My Children* for a month. Somebody start at the beginning, and tell me what's gone on since I left." She pulled a chair away from Rhonda's bedside, where the girl-mother was now doing her makeup, thickly caking mascara onto her lashes. "I ask you," Kit whispered. "When's the last time anyone in America voluntarily used *blue* eyeliner?" She retrieved the hamburgers she'd bought on the way to the hospital, handing one to Hank, one to Chloe, saving the McLean Deluxe for herself. "Way major tacky. We're talking *way*."

I'm beginning to feel like a mother now, Chloe thought. *Like a good girl, my youngest is sleeping, while my troublesome middle child's busy issuing fashion tickets. My oldest is looking for the quickest way to rumble with an Indian jeweler who's—poor guy—only off trying to find somewhere he can water his snake.*

"Three days at most," Hank insisted. "I'll be back before New Year's. We'll bring Reed home and celebrate."

Chloe didn't let on, but she had her doubts. She'd strived to be a star patient, doing everything the nurses told her in order to get released sooner, and she acted her bravest around Hank. Deep down, though, she had the feeling Iris was getting ready to check out. How long something like that could take was anybody's guess. Hank was Iris's only living child. He needed to be there. Chloe could be generous, even if Iris didn't think her capable. They had the rest of their lives to be with Reed. Corrine and Oscar would take turns driving her to the medical center. A few days, even a week, however long it took wouldn't hurt anything.

In the Flagstaff airport, Oscar Johnson stood by the rock fireplace while Chloe kissed Hank good-bye. A pine fire was crackling in the grate, and enough snow had piled up outside that it sure enough looked like a traditional Christmas Eve. Kit was relating the endless plot of some movie she'd seen, and good-hearted Oscar was nodding every now and then, acting interested. Hank backed away from her toward his plane, nearly bumping into the exit door. Then he waved one last time, the expression on his face so uncertain that Chloe felt like someone had ripped another major organ from within her, just leaving her there bleeding all over the terminal.

Oscar gently took hold of her arm. "We need to get going. Them roads look nasty, and you got to rest."

Chloe nodded blindly. She wanted to stay and watch the plane take off, make sure it got and stayed airborne until it was out of her sight and in the hands of the pilot. She understood the basic principles of aerodynamics but doubted them. How else was she supposed to feel, since she'd never been on a plane? Kit opened doors for her and helped her into the Honda. Oscar's Blazer was too tall for her to climb into, so he'd left it at the cabin and was driving Hank's Honda. They pulled into the stream of traffic. Downtown Flagstaff glittered like one massive advertisement for the holidays. Christmas lights and neon motel signs cheerfully offered lodging. Last-minute shoppers rushed red-faced from the cold, hurrying from one store to another, lugging packages.

"Thought maybe we'd grab some takeout for the drive home, you know?" Oscar said. "What are you craving, Chloe? Mexican?

Hippie vegetable-arian? Or should we swing by the medical center for some more of that real tasty hospital chow?"

Kit laughed. "Vegetarian, ha. Order her a burger that's still mooing and extra large fries soaked in beef tallow. Me, I get to be on a diet for the rest of my life. Chloe never gets fat unless she's pregnant."

"I have been there and I have done that, thank you very much." Chloe leaned her chin into her palm and looked out the car window. The Pony Soldier motel offered steam heat and free cable TV. She wished she had the kind of bucks to park there and take cabs to the hospital. She didn't like the idea of being so far from Reed that it took an hour of someone else's driving to get to her any more than she relished pumping her breast milk into bottles. "Whatever you guys want is fine with me, so long as it's nothing green."

"Not even a pickle?" Oscar asked.

"Nope. Not even."

Oscar made a left, pulled to the curb, and left the motor running outside Martan's Mexican Food. Chloe shut her eyes and listened to Kit hum along with the radio until Oscar returned with loaf-size burritos.

"There's the bar Hannah loves to run off to," Chloe pointed out as they began to leave Flagstaff behind. "The Silver Saddle Saloon. For a while there, she was getting to be a regular. I hope she's behaving herself and staying home. Since we hooked up, I've never missed Christmas with Hannah."

"Hannah's a smart dog. She'll hang by the woodstove until spring," Oscar promised. "Then maybe you can get her one of them tracking collars like they put on the wolves over to Yellowstone."

"I remember this one Christmas with Willie, that's my mom, Oscar," Kit piped up. "We were living on the commune in Big Sur. In tipis, no less. It rained all the time, and instead of presents and turkey, everyone was fasting and chanting all this rama-lama bullshit I never understood. There was about ten of us kids altogether, and we kind of wandered around feeling useless and hungry. Then all these people showed up with Taco Bell food and bang, total pig fest. So it's understandable that I have an issue with food. Anyway, that's what Lita calls it, 'your issue with food.'"

Oscar laughed. "Then I got me an issue, too. A good meal's about as close to religion as you can get."

Kit folded the foil around her burrito and stuck it back in the bag. "Totally, Oscar. I just wish worshipping at the altar didn't make me fat."

Chloe studied the snow-dusted pine trees and closed-up bait shops, this stretch of highway always feeling so lonely. About the time they reached Cameron, Hank's plane would land safely on the ground in Orange County. He'd shed a few layers of clothing, rent a car, drive to see his parents, go to bed in their house, and wake up in the morning without her. Here it was, their first Christmas as parents, and they had neither each other nor a baby to celebrate it with. Well, she could do worse than spend holidays with good friends. Hank would call. Kit was here and she'd see Reed tomorrow. Friends had gotten her through the bulk of her life. She nodded off, so exhausted that she didn't wake until the car hit that one rut in their road that not even a deep pocket of snow could smooth out.

Oscar checked the woodpile and gave Kit a lecture about keeping the stove burning properly. Chloe reunited with Hannah on the couch. Her dog planted her front paws on the cushions, sniffing her mistress all over, trying to decide what the hospital smells meant. "Relax, girl," Chloe soothed. "I'm fine. Hank's not here. You can come sit up on the couch beside me." But Hannah had never been much for on-the-furniture unless it was a bed. She turned a circle on the floor, then settled herself within reach of Chloe's hands.

"So, Kit," Oscar said as he was putting his jacket back on. "You know how to drive a car, yeah?"

"Nope, not yet."

He jingled the Honda keys. "Driving in the snow's a skill you can always use."

"Oscar," Chloe warned. "She's fourteen years old. They don't even let you get a learner's permit until you're fifteen and a half."

"That so? Man, you Californians come up with some dumb rules. I was driving good by the time I was twelve."

"I'll be fifteen pretty soon."

Oscar zipped his jacket. "Never know, you might need her to drive in case of emergency."

Kit straightened up, trying to paste a logical face over sheer excitement. "That's a really good point, Chloe."

"I thought that was what we had Oscar and Corrine for. To drive until Hank gets back or the doctor gives me clearance."

"It is, it is! But what if a storm downed the phone lines or—"

"All right already," Chloe said. "Just don't you get any wild hairs that a few lessons in Hooterville entitle you to drive back home. And don't tell your dad."

"Like I would." Kit gave Oscar a kiss on the cheek that made him grin. "Can we go right now?"

"Tomorrow."

"I can't believe how cool you are. Are all Indians this cool?"

"Nah, it's my personal burden. Well, better go see to the horse and get on home. Merry Keshmish, ladies." Oscar let himself out.

Kit sat on the floor stringing popcorn, eating as much as she was threading. "Why is it I can supposedly eat as much of this stuff as I want, according to my diet, but without butter it tastes like crap?"

Chloe lay on the couch under an afghan, wide awake from her nap in the car. "You could try that fake butter. I've seen it in the store."

"Gross. I'd rather starve. You want the other half of your burrito?"

"Tomorrow, maybe."

"How about a Coke or something?"

Kit was acting so nervous Chloe figured she'd better give her a task. "I don't think we have any. Know what I'd really like?"

Kit strung three more kernels and grinned wickedly. "Junior Whitebear in a loincloth?"

"No, horn brain, I'd like a cup of tea. Not that green crap of Hank's, regular old tea steeped long enough it'll stain my teeth. Would you mind making me a cup?"

Kit got up and began filling the kettle with water. She craned her head around the stove to talk. "I love this cabin, Chloe. It reminds me of your old place in Hughville, you know, like if it grew up."

Chloe tried to picture the small room through Kit's eyes—the romance of a one-bedroom cabin went a long way when you weren't overdue on the bills, trying to stay warm, and about to move a baby in. "Yep, it grew a bathroom and running water. On which I find myself becoming completely dependent. Can't hardly imagine going back to the other way."

"But this is the coolest room of all, don't you think? Ever since I got here I've been sleeping in front of the stove in my sleeping bag. With the wind roaring outside, me all snuggled in, it's just way romantic, don't you think?"

"Way. Keeping warm is definitely romantic. And Reed will certainly appreciate it."

"Reed. That is the greatest name." The kettle began to steam, and Kit turned off the burner. "It's funny that she doesn't look like Hank."

"She looks like a tiny little monkey who got born way too early."

"Who's getting bigger every day," Kit protested. "The nurses all say so."

Chloe cupped her swollen breasts. "I wish I was nursing her for every feeding."

"Really? Bottles seem so much neater."

Despite the nurse's assurances that the pain would pass, Chloe felt the aches travel hotly through her breasts. It wasn't so much the physical act of not being able to feed the baby every meal that was disappointing. She pumped out milk, and they gave her bottles whenever she cried. It wasn't even the relief that passed through her body when Reed nursed. Two years ago Kit was walking right past the lingerie department on her way to the toys. This was a kind of need and longing Chloe couldn't explain to her. "Hank really wants me to nurse her. He says it's better for the baby."

Kit shuddered. "I don't think I could let a baby do that to me. It creeps me out."

"It's not so bad after a while."

Kit handed her a blue mug, from which fragrant steam rose. "I have the totally bitchenest Christmas present for you. Do I really have to wait until tomorrow morning to give it to you?"

Chloe's heart softened—hormone surge—she thought, wondering when the estrogen pills would begin to level her out, make her feel like her old crabby self. "I don't have anything for you to open. I was planning on taking you to the Trading Post so you could pick something out yourself."

"It's okay. We can do that when you feel better. So can I give you my present now or what?"

"Sure, Kit. If that's what you want."

"Okay. Be right back." She rushed down the hallway, and Chloe sipped the hot tea, enjoying its warmth traveling down her throat. Why was it that the simplest home fare tasted so satisfyingly real compared to hospital food? She tried to imagine what trendy trinket Kit was about to lay on her—a twin to that crystal necklace she was wearing, the "kind all the girls on Melrose Place wear"? When Absalom died, Kit had braided some of his tail hair into a keepsake bracelet Chloe couldn't quite bring herself to wear. Nevertheless, the gift was one of her most treasured possessions.

Kit returned holding a large brown envelope in her hands. "We got this computer disk in the mail. Ten free hours on the Internet. I went way over ten hours, but after I told Lita how much homework I could do on it my dad subscribed."

"What's the Internet?"

"It's hard to explain without a computer to show you. Basically it's all these different places you can go and talk to people, look for information. In cyberspace."

Chloe laughed. "This is exactly why you need to get good grades and stay in school. I have no clue at all what you're talking about."

"Well, anyway, through Keyword and Search and the World Wide Web Crawler, I found this list of places. Severed Strings, Birth Quest, Finders Keepers. You remember that report I did on you last year?"

"I remember." The interview was supposed to be on an influential female role model. Kit's probing had taken her back to uncomfortable memories of foster-care days. The tea tasted dull on her tongue, and she set the mug down next to Hannah, who sniffed it and decided she wasn't interested. "Why don't I like the sound of this?"

"Relax. It's nothing terrible. I mean, all I did was take some of the stuff you told me and scan your baby picture in and download it and put your name and birthday in like I was you and I was looking for, you know, your mother."

"Jesus, Kit!"

"Please don't be mad, Chloe."

"I'm not mad, I'm stunned."

Kit held out a letter that had been inside the brown envelope. "Thing is, I got this back, Chloe. I think maybe I found her."

Chloe could not bring herself to take the envelope. She looked at the return address, handwritten in ordinary blue ballpoint. *Hacienda de Tres Hermanas*. Rural Route 36, Box 11897, Patagonia, Arizona. It was postmarked Tucson.

"I didn't open it."

I would have, Chloe thought. *Read it, then likely burned it in the flames of good sense.* "And I'm not going to, either. Put it away, Kit."

A long moment of silence ensued, then Kit folded the envelope into her jeans pocket. "God, Chloe, say something! I'll throw it away if you don't want to read it. But please, please, don't be mad." Kit started to cry.

The air in the room was close with the odors of woodsmoke, popcorn, and Kit's bubble-gum-sweet perfume. Aside from a shocky, hot feeling flooding her belly and face, Chloe felt dead calm, as if what lay inside the envelope frightened her so fundamentally there was nothing left over in her to spend on fear. It could have been a bill, one of Iris's mean lectures, or even Rhonda's baby announcement, the assortment of favorite place-names falling off the allotted line into the margin.

"You're pissed."

"Well, gee, Kit, it's not like you put my name in for a contest to win a free gym membership. This is heavy stuff. Why the hell didn't you ask before you did that?"

"I don't know. It seemed so one-in-a-million that anything would come of it. And I had ten free hours! I didn't think it could hurt just to look."

Chloe sighed.

"It could always turn out to be the wrong lady," Kit said, scrambling hopefully. "It's almost Christmas. I'll make us a pot of cocoa with zillions of marshmallows, and we can listen to country radio all night, talk about horses, just the two of us, go back to the way things were. Right?"

"Sure," Chloe said, to comfort the girl. But assurances didn't stop the spiraling changes. What Kit had done changed everything. Chloe wanted to say, We can forget about the baby in the preemie unit, and Iris dying in California, and me here without my uterus, and how I feel every time that goddamn Indian jeweler looks at me. We can take a handful of happy pills and play Let's Pretend for the rest of our lives. But she knew the road she'd lived in fear of crossing all her life had opened before her. She had no choice but to put one foot in front of the other and start walking.

12

Before breakfast the temperature hit eighty degrees. Henry senior opened the traditional Christmas bottle of Lancers red and poured out three glasses. Hank and his parents gathered on the matching sofas around the miniature potted Norfolk pine atop the coffee table. Aside from a single strand of silver garland and the paper star, which, when unfolded, became their insurance agent's Christmas card, the boughs were bare and green. When he turned his head to the left, Hank could just glimpse the flip side of the star, where lay a year's worth of months, during which, payments provided, insurance coverage might keep one financially secure.

"What happened to all your ornaments?" Hank asked his mother, who wore an emerald green robe and matching slippers, and ignored the wine, sipping herb tea.

"Nothing *happened* to them. They're still in their boxes."

"You're falling down on the job, Mother," he teased her. "I remember when you used to start decorating the day after Halloween."

"You know how it is," Iris said. "It's not as if we entertain all that often. All the dusting and so forth. I can't manage it."

Dad could do it, Hank thought, and immediately chastised himself for posing such a pointless solution. He watched as his father poured himself a second glass of wine. "They say red wine is good for the ticker," Henry announced, patting his chest for emphasis.

"In moderation," Hank commented, remembering his Christmas morning grape juice when he was a child; then, as a teenager, the day his father secretly made the switch to wine, laughing so hard at Hank's bewildered expression.

"It's Christmas," his father said, his mouth tight against the rim of the glass.

Iris got up from the couch and gathered up napkins and coasters. "If you two gentlemen will excuse me."

That was her traditional exit line as she departed for the kitchen to make the spinach-and-mushroom omelets that were also a sanctioned element of Oliver holidays. After they attended a non-denominational church service, opened gifts, and ate turkey, they would have checked every step off the Christmas to-do list. In the seven months since he'd seen his mother, her skin had lost much of its color and elasticity; her carefully applied makeup only emphasized the long downhill slide. Last night as he lay on the sofa bed trying to get comfortable, all he could think of was her face as she greeted him at the door. Sunken in against the bones, it resembled a skull. And her hands—her rings sliding up and down her fingers. Just to the left of the coffeepot, in vials of that amber plastic, such an ominous hue, so many prescription medicines lined the kitchen counter. She hadn't been taking this many pills when he left for Arizona. Had her going out of remission been a direct result of him not coming home?

His father switched on the television, and Hank fought the urge to put his foot through the screen. "Come on, Dad," he kidded. "What could be on? The Yuletide Golf Tournament?"

His father gave him an uncertain smile and switched the set off. He cleaned his fingernails with a paper clip, then picked up a magazine from the coffee table and began leafing through it.

The clatter of eggs being whisked into a copper bowl sounded much more alluring than trying to engage the old man. Hank got up to see if he could help in the kitchen.

"Go visit with your father," Iris said. She had pulled a stool up next to the stove and sat there chopping fresh spinach leaves. "I can manage."

"He's reading *Time*. Let me make the toast. White or wheat?"

"Wheat." Iris began to assemble ingredients for the omelets. "You know, Sweetheart, cancer doesn't render one incapable of preparing a meal."

Here was a little of her old spirit, then. Saying the word aloud meant she was still in there fighting. Hank kissed the top of her gray braid, wound around her head and secured with a silver and turquoise hairpin Oscar Johnson would have been able to place within a year of its origin, as well as name the mine from which the stone came. "Nobody said you weren't. Just tell me he helps out once in a while."

She set down the whisk and sponged up a spill. "Henry, please. Don't have flown all this way just to start an argument."

Hank dropped two slices of low-calorie whole wheat into the toaster. "You know, Mom, even in world wars soldiers call a truce for major holidays. Direct me to the DMZ, and I'll gladly do my part."

"Be the bigger man," Iris urged, turning the edges of the omelet. "Extend your hand first."

Hank handed her a Spode plate. "Hasn't that been the prime directive of my life?" Her mouth was set, her face focused on folding the eggs evenly. He thought of Chloe's approach to breakfast, which involved throwing eggshells toward the sink and, considering Hannah's catching abilities, a 50 percent success rate. If the yolks broke, the eggs got scrambled. Chloe did things once and rarely fretted the small stuff. How many breakfasts had he wolfed down, never realizing what it had meant to his mother to serve them as turned out as prep school boys? Chloe said, *Butter your own toast,* and she meant it. Before she'd gotten so heavy with the baby, she'd sat on his lap and they'd eaten off the same fork. She had, in a manner of speaking, unbuttoned his top buttons. Insisted a little red meat wasn't going to kill him, and it hadn't. He had looked forward to beginning their own set of holiday rituals, hanging the baby's tiny stocking in anticipation, marking a place for her. Reed was here now. Gowned and gloved, his face masked, Hank had held her exactly twice. At four pounds she felt as light in his arms as a Christmas package. All those monitors and IV lines connected her to the hospital, keeping him from feeling she was totally his, that he would ever be allowed to take her home. He glanced at his mother, wondering how it came to be that a couple who couldn't wait to make love before they were married ended up so far apart.

"Maybe I'll give Chloe a call."

"I think you should wait," Iris said. "She'll be tired, just out of the hospital. When the baby comes home, she'll get little enough rest. Let her sleep in."

For the second time that morning, Hank reached for the Polaroid in his shirt pocket. Shot through the plastic housing of the isolette, the image was grainy and indistinct. His daughter lay squinty-eyed and naked except for an oversize diaper. She was wired to various machines whose proper names he did not know. When Reed was born, Junior Whitebear had wrapped her in a clean, folded sheet and handed her to Corrine. From Corrine, Reed had gone to the ambulance attendant. Junior's had been the first hands to touch her.

Hank sensed his mother next to him before her hand reached up. Iris smoothed her fingers over the tiny face in the photo and her expression softened.

"Well?" he asked, wanting her to fawn and dote, pronounce the baby perfect, acknowledge her presence as a good omen for everyone's future. But Iris only handed it back to him, returning to easing the spatula under the last omelet.

"Your father always says, 'All babies look like Winston Churchill.' He thinks that's such a funny remark."

"Surely your firstborn granddaughter doesn't fall into that category?"

For a moment his mother seemed about to say something of

importance. Her brow furrowed, and she bit her lower lip the way she often did when her opinion, differing from Henry's just this once, mattered. "You know I tend to go along with whatever your father says."

"But not why."

"Let's just say it's easier and leave it at that."

"And God knows, easiest is best." Hank turned the picture toward his heart and slid it into his pocket. Fine. Let them both wear brooms up their asses. He'd call the airlines and see if he could catch the late flight to Phoenix, ride a damn bus up the mountain.

They sat down to a silent breakfast. His father brought the Lancer's bottle to the table, and Hank inwardly fumed every time he looked at it. Drink had always been a tall order in the man's vocabulary, but this A.M. tilting toward excess was new. Iris cleared her throat, which was Hank's cue to say the blessing. Before he did, Hank took out the photo of Reed and propped it against the wine bottle. He looked at each of his parents, understanding that this might very well be the last year they three would sit at this table as a family, torn by the complex feelings that notion caused to flood through him.

"I never knew what bounty meant until I saw my own daughter come into the world. Between Reed and Chloe, I find there's no end to my blessings." And then he gave them the generic "Blessed, oh Lord, are these thy gifts," a prayer he'd recited since childhood. He unfolded his napkin, passed the salt to his father, and swallowed his precision omelet, concentrating on his women waiting for him, seven hundred miles away.

"Dad, take a walk with me," Hank said when he'd finished the supper dishes and Iris was resting on the couch, eyes shut, listening to the Pavarotti concert on PBS.

"I'm tired."

"A short turn around the park won't kill you."

Henry senior collected a golf sweater from the rack by the door.

They walked outside into the approaching dusk of California winter: Coral-and-violet birds of paradise bloomed, fountains sprayed crystalline water, the well-trimmed grounds of World of Freedom proclaimed their eternal anthem of spring to the elderly.

"What is it? Do you need money?"

"No, Dad. I have enough money. I want to know what the doctor says."

Henry senior made his don't-worry face. "Oh, you know. Things could always be better. You try the community college over there in Flagstaff? Sometimes lateral moves can provide the most secure routes."

"Dad, I have a job I like. Has the doctor given you any idea as to how long Mother will be able to fend for herself?"

"She made a great meal tonight."

"That she did. But she's failing. I can see it."

"Your mother is doing just fine."

Hank sighed. "If that's so, then why the message that I should hurry home?"

Henry senior inspected a blue hibiscus, some spindly new variation that coordinated perfectly with the landscaping. "Blue flowers. What will they come up with next?"

"Dad."

"Hank, it's Christmas. We can talk about it later."

"No, Dad, we can't. Christmas is over. I have a family back there waiting for me now. I left them on our first holiday together because you made it sound like Mom was at death's door. I find her preparing meals, shooing me out of the kitchen, but there're ten different bottles of pills on the counter and she takes three naps a day. We need to talk about this now. We need to make plans."

Henry senior put his hands in his pockets and walked to a low brick planter spilling out blood-red bougainvillea. Unseen birds chattered to one another. An Anna's hummingbird darted in and out of the blossoms, its iridescent breast flashing in the waning sunlight as gaudily as sequins. He looked out toward the empty clubhouse. "I don't see the hurry."

"Are you trying to protect me? Isn't that kind of pointless?"

His father wouldn't meet his eyes. "He said that it's moving throughout her intestines. They can't cut anything else out, just give her pills to control the pain. It has to, you know, run its course."

"Did he give you a timetable?"

"Three months. With luck, as long as six."

Hank felt sweat trickle down his spine. Somewhere inside he'd known, but hearing his father voice the words was a terrible confirmation. He remained standing despite the loosening feeling in his knees. All his life his father had been remote, and not even his wife's death was going to change that about him. Earlier, in church, surrounded by many other residents of the retirement community, his father's face had gone vacant when he made the sign of peace and shook hands with the man seated next to him. Knock all you want, nobody got inside Henry Oliver. Sure, the minister was up against presents and family recipes, a tough combination, but even Hank felt affected by the ceremony, the familiar carols and the Christ child's story, a reminder that birth, any birth, was a miracle of the most enormous order. Reed had tipped him over into sentimentality this year, but that feeling always enveloped him at Christmas. Just never his father. After the service they got in the car and drove home. His father poured brandy into his coffee, switched on the television, and didn't budge until Iris called them to dinner.

"Would you like me to give the doctor a call? Would that make things easier?"

"She doesn't want to go to the hospital," Henry said firmly. "She wants it to happen in her own bed at home. I've promised her that much."

"You can't do everything by yourself."

"You'll help me."

Hank pinched the bridge of his nose. "You know I'll come as often as I can. There are questions of practicality and distance involved, Dad. Maybe we can hire a nurse or contact a hospice. I've heard those services can provide real comfort."

Henry looked up at him, startled. It was as if he were making actual contact for the first time since Hank had arrived. "What the hell do you know about saying good-bye to your partner of almost fifty years? Somebody who ironed your shirts, bore your children, stayed with you every step of the way, even when you didn't deserve it? You aren't married. Shacking up with a tart who trapped you the oldest way in the book. I saw that picture. The baby doesn't even look like you."

The shock Hank felt was piercing. The fist that tightened at his side immediately went slack, leaving his heart scraped hollow. He understood that this nasty crack had more to do with Iris losing her battle than anything about Chloe. "Trashing the woman I love and the mother of my daughter is not a place you want to go to. I'll stay over long enough to speak to Mom's doctor, to help you assemble a game plan. Then I'm going home. When things get bad, I'll try to come back on weekends. I'm telling you, I'll *try*. Otherwise, since it's always worked for us before, let's keep our distance."

Henry senior cocked his head and looked up at his son as if he were speaking another language. He said nothing and Hank wasn't even sure that beneath all that alcohol, the man had heard him.

Hank walked away, tracing the perimeter of the parking lot, circling the clubhouse, studying the shallow lap pool nobody ever swam in, and the common lawn, so green and evenly trimmed his father could have practiced putting there if such a pleasure were within the rules. The California dusk was fragrant with flowers and newly watered grass. He heard Christmas music spilling forth from a few stereos, but everyone was indoors, occupied with friends or family. When he returned to the condo, Iris had already gone to bed. His father sat outside on the patio. Hank stood in the kitchen and watched him puff clouds of smoke into Iris's garden. After a few minutes he used the kitchen phone to call Chloe. Kit answered.

"Hank!" she said. "Merry, merry. It's snowing. The real thing. All white and beautiful and butt cold. I got to help Chloe nurse the baby. Well, not really *nurse* her, but I got to sit there and watch. Oscar is so cool, Hank. Him and Corrine brought us deer meat and squash stew for dinner. Sounds gross, and it was, I mean to look at, but oh my God, when you taste it? Heaven. Only problem is, I totally feel like I ate Bambi for dinner. Hey, you know about karma. I was trying to explain it to Oscar. Eating a deer, that's really bad karma, isn't it?"

"Kit, I think both you and your karma will survive one meal of venison. May I speak to Chloe?"

"Sure. Hang on."

Kit hollered so loudly he had to jerk the receiver away from his ear. When Chloe came on the line, she was breathless.

"Where are you? The airport?"

"I wish. I'll try to catch a flight home tomorrow. Miss you, baby."

"Me, too."

"I hope you're not overdoing it. Are you resting? Eating right?"

"Yes, I'm resting."

"Is Kit driving you crazy?"

"Mostly she's a big help. How's your mom doing?"

Hank detected a strange tension in her voice and felt responsible, leaving her dependent on neighbors they'd known only a few short months, not being there to make sure she followed the doctor's orders. "Not great. I'm going to speak to her doctor tomorrow, and then I'll try to catch a plane home. Forget all that. How's our baby?"

"Beautiful. And hungry. Reed has quite the temper when she's kept waiting. I keep expecting to get nipped but she loves my breasts."

"Me, too. Finally, a trace of her father surfaces." Hank tapped his foot against the shiny linoleum. "I can't wait to see her again, hold her in my arms."

"Hank?"

He heard that strain in her voice surface again. "Yes?"

"Are you sure you can't come home tonight?"

"You know I can't. Weather permitting, I'll be there tomorrow afternoon. I need to talk to Mother's doctor. As usual, my dad's not dealing with things. I'm the only child here."

There was a small pause before she answered. "Sure, I understand."

"I'll make this up to you," he promised, "even if I have to dig a moat and fill it with alligators myself. From now on, Christmas will be just us three, okay?"

The second night the couch hadn't gotten any more comfortable. Hank held on to his pillow and tried to entice sleep to come to him. When he was a kid, he had lined his gifts up on his dresser so that he might glance over at them in the night, be certain the new and coveted toys were real, the requisite sweaters and underwear to expand his wardrobe lesser in importance, but nevertheless part of the same package. This Christmas his mother had bought him a gray-and-white Woolrich sweater and thermals. They were still sealed in the catalog plastic. For Reed there was a hastily wrapped bit of history: His old battered pewter porringer, unearthed from some cupboard or other. Nothing for Chloe, not even a congratulatory card. Within their narrow moral framework, he knew his parents had stepped widely out of their usual path to do this much. John Wayne Airport had gift shops. He'd pick up something there for her, say it was from them. Little lies like that didn't count.

He wasn't the only "only" child here. He thought of the silver cup Junior Whitebear had given to Chloe in the hospital room. It was a work of art. The man had earned respect in a difficult profession. Giving Chloe that cup was almost like presenting someone with a savings bond that in the future could help a then-grown child afford college. But somehow when Whitebear looked at Chloe, none of that rationalizing sat right in Hank's stomach. Junior's expression told the real story. Hank knew: He looked at Chloe in exactly the same way.

Could a baby bind a couple together, strengthen their love? It hadn't accomplished that for his parents. Factor in his sister Annie's death, and these nearly fifty years Henry senior was touting as accomplishment made the union sound like a kind of endurance trial. Divorce wasn't a stigma, but neither was it an Oliver tradition. "Shacking up," as his father so endearingly put it—was it really so different from marriage? Marriage might not lash two hearts together to ride out the larger waves, but at the very least it forced you to file a joint tax return. Deductions—another good reason—he wasn't done working on Chloe yet.

He dreamed of Reed's birth. In his dream *he* delivered his daughter, and she arrived full term, growing instantly into a dark-eyed little girl who laughed and reached for him, saying "Here's my daddy," leaving no question as to her loyalties or her paternity.

In his office the doctor laid the facts out as plainly as possible. "At this stage the primal responsibility is to control your mother's level of discomfort, Mr. Oliver. With the efficacy of drugs available today, there's no reason for her to experience unmanaged pain."

That scared feeling, loosing the hinge pins holding his knees together, made Hank's entire body go cold. He accepted the hospice pamphlets from the man and nodded. He'd come here so that he wouldn't have to speak in code from his parents' telephone. He wanted to see the doctor's face. "I don't intend to sound callous, Doctor, but my father's attitude—"

The physician interrupted him. "This is a very difficult ordeal for everyone involved. Preparation is a wise avenue to take. It's good you came."

"My father says he wants to take care of everything."

"Understandable."

"Yet emotionally he's rather negligent. I'm living in Arizona now. I have a new baby. Just a few days old. And financially, well, I can't afford extended visits."

"Call the hospice people. Go back to your wife and child. When circumstances require your presence, you'll be notified."

Which sounded an awful lot like jury duty. "Thanks for your time, Doctor."

"You're welcome. And don't underestimate your mother, Mr. Oliver. Iris is a strong woman, strong enough to ask when she is in need."

*   *   *

Half an hour later, Hank hung up the pay phone outside the supermarket where he had stopped to buy a soda, having secured his
reservation for the flight home. He stood there for a few minutes,
watching the line of silver carts filled with groceries make their
way to various cars. A young mother fed quarters to a mechanical
pony, looking off into the distance as the kid indulged in his brief
ride. The sun was as bright as August, lulling everyone into a
sleepy, post-Christmas daze. The thick traffic on El Toro Boulevard
stank of exhaust. Somebody honked his horn and cars trickled
forth, hoping to make the green light. Hank gathered his courage,
found his rental car in the parking lot, and fired up the ignition,
staring at his old familiar landscape, astonished at how much it had
changed since he turned his back on it, and how little that mattered to him.

He sat with his mother on the small patio off the kitchen. Her ken-
tia palms were doing well, as were the few orchids. She had let the
African violets get leggy. His father's dirty ashtray sat on the glass
tabletop between them. Iris reached out and wiped it clean with a
tissue.

"Every morning at breakfast he informs me he's quitting smoking. Then, at night, I hear him outside, sneaking around."

"He's worried," Hank said. "Maybe smoking is his way of dealing
with it."

Iris looked at her son. A slow and deliberate smile spread across
her face. "It strikes me as odd that this is so much harder on you
both than it is on me."

"Is it?" Hank asked her.

"Absolutely. I feel myself giving in, a little bit here, a little more
there, each and every day. You both have to go on after I'm gone. I
confess that worries me—how on earth you two will ever manage
to communicate without my running interference."

"We'll hire a diplomat," Hank said, and his mother laughed. "I wish you'd come back with me and see the baby," Hank rushed on. "You know I'd have brought her with me if she weren't so small. Mom, she is gorgeous."

"Maybe I can see her this spring."

"Don't say that to be polite with me. Please, as hard as this is, let's try to be honest with each other." The tears took hold of him, and this time he didn't try to stop them from flowing down his cheeks.

She laid her hand across his forearm. "Oh, honey, I'm sorry. It's just that this is finally *my* life, Hank. Now, what little of it I have left. If I seem selfish, please don't hate me for it. Someday you'll understand."

He nodded. "Sure."

With a thumbnail she lopped off a shriveling cymbidium blossom and tossed it in the carpet of baby's tears that grew along the patio edge. "I was secretly hoping you'd name her Ann, you know."

"Chloe decided."

"As all mothers do. You should probably leave for the airport. Traffic can be brutal this time of day, plus you need to turn in the rental car."

Hank swiped his cheeks clean and got up from the table. "She gives Churchill a run for his money, Mother. I'll get a camera, send pictures, prove it to you."

Iris remained seated. "You do that, son."

13

Hours after the Johnsons left, this disappointing holiday was thankfully ended, and Kit had begun snoring in front of the woodstove, Chloe sat up, studying the firelight reflecting off the mica panels, playing through Kit's long, curly red hair. All through that long, quiet day neither had mentioned the letter. That night Chloe could think of little else. Kit's ability to set things aside amazed her. Imagine being so young and sure of yourself you could fall into sleep like that, as if it were a trustworthy embrace, God's arms right there to catch you, banish every bad dream. Insomnia had punched her ticket, so she made real coffee and poured herself a cup. *You're better off letting sleeping dogs lie*, she kept telling herself. *What you don't know can't hurt you*. Old sayings were about as useful as the pain pills the hospital had sent home with her, which left her dull and stupid and craving more. She sipped her coffee, petted her dog, and watched the sunrise. The furry white animal gazed up, sensitive to her mistress's mood. California winters Hannah could handle, but the northern Arizona cold crept into her bones. Sometimes she had trouble getting up onto the bed, and Chloe

wondered if she took her to the vet there might be some new miracle to stop the animals you loved from getting old seven times
faster than you.

She wasn't angry with Kit, not truly angry. The teenager's own
mother was lost to her, off living her life so selfishly that Chloe felt
reasonably certain Willie'd sacrifice Kit completely if it meant one
more Dead concert where she could flail her arms in a crowd and
pretend she was still twenty-nine years old. Lots of girls managed
the teenage years without a mother present, and Lita tried her
damnedest to fill the gap. But the toll all that exacted on Kit gave
rise to the girl's ˙determination to soften every hard edge she ran
into with dreams and romance. Which was the reason she'd gone
after finding Chloe's mother instead of her own. Kit was the one
desperate for a tear-jerking reunion. Wherever Chloe's mother
was, she'd bet the woman thought of the daughter she'd given
away as no more important than shoes that never quite broke in to
a comfortable fit.

Outside the wind howled, and she could hear rain spattering the
cabin's windows. Give it a few minutes, it would freeze and then
turn to snow. Snow on top of snow on top of snow. She pictured
Reed snug in her hospital bed, some nurse quietly feeding her a
bottle. This might not be just a letter from her mother, but Reed's
grandmother as well. *Ojos vemos, corazón no sabemos*—Francisco back
at the stables in California used to say that all the time—"The eyes
you can see, but it's hard to know what's in people's hearts." The
letter was just across the room in Kit's pocket.

Chloe thought of all the times she was bleary with exhaustion,
or half asleep, and Spanish echoed in her head. Songs, stories,
voices, and she'd wondered where on earth all that had come
from. Patagonia was near to Nogales, a border town. Did this
woman speak the language, too? It was only about a seven-hour
drive from Cameron. It could just as easily have been Minnesota,
North Carolina, or nowhere at all, but here they were, living in the
same state, within a day's drive of one another. Luck like this, Kit
ought to spend her lunch money on lottery tickets.

Chloe sipped her cold coffee and made a face. Even if she did a crazy thing like ask Oscar to drive her all that way, who would feed the baby?

"Never saw such a bunch of lazy women," Oscar said as he kicked snow from his boots in the back doorway. "I been up working since first light. Come on, throw some water on those pretty faces, get with the lipstick. Got horses to feed and a big after-Christmas sale going down at the Trading Post. Then we'll hear your excuses about bad dreams and too much eggnog."

Kit rolled over in her sleeping bag and yawned. "This is a free country, Oscar. I'm on vacation. It's not like me or Chloe has a job."

Oscar scoffed. "Maybe you two live in a free country, but I've yet to meet the Skin who does. Not even Mr. R. C. Gorman can afford to sleep this late. Got to get his red ass up and roll out lithos if he wants to keep his belly full. Wonder what a driver's got to do to get any coffee around here."

Chloe lifted her head from her arms. Sometime in the night she must have lain back on the couch and dozed off. Her belly was a little less sore than yesterday, but now she ached in a million places from sleeping in such a cramped position. "The one thing we've got in this kitchen is coffee. Pour yourself a cup and stop complaining."

"Pour me one, too," Kit said.

"You're too young to drink coffee," Oscar said. "Have a glass of milk."

"Oscar," Kit said, slowly dragging out the syllables in his name. "The only milk in this house is in Chloe's breasts. She's not exactly shopper of the year."

Oscar blushed and looked out the window. "Kitten, don't ever talk like that to a man who hasn't had his first jolt of morning java. I'm going to be off all day on account of what you just said."

"Well, it's true."

Chloe smiled as the Indian set a cup on the table. "Speaking of that particular subject. You're here to drive me to the hospital already?"

"Nah, Corrine'll be by to take you later. She needs to go into Flag, pick up a load of storyteller dolls from Coconino Center for the Arts. I really got to work on the repair orders today. I'm so far behind it'll take me until spring to catch up. Kit, you interested in earning some money? I could sure use somebody to straighten out my invoices. Five bucks an hour, and we don't got to clear one penny of it with Uncle Sam. Free lunch in the restaurant."

"Um, I really need to help Chloe," Kit said, a little nervously. "That's the only reason I'm here."

Kit was behaving as if the letter wedged between them, irrevocably altering their relationship. After the long, quiet Christmas, Chloe knew a break would do the girl good. "Take her along if she wants to go," she said to Oscar. "But don't work her all day. Let her have some fun. Lend her your snowshoes. Poor kid's so bored she's keeping track of my milk."

Kit rolled up her sleeping bag. "Thanks, Chloe."

Chloe smiled at her across the room. "Stay out of Corrine's way. And try to keep from getting frostbite. Your dad wants you back with all your toes."

"I think I can manage to keep my shoes on in the snow." Kit disappeared down the hall to the bathroom.

Oscar yanked at his shirt collar. "You two."

"What about us?"

"You're sure different than Navajo girls. All this talking about bosoms, what's inside 'em, sleeping late as dogs, snapping at each other. Where's the respect?"

"We *love* each other, Oscar. We don't have to bother with respect."

"You're both so—what's the English for it?"

"I don't know. Gorgeous? Sexy?"

"Cagey. Hard to outwit, harder to keep up with."

"And that just intrigues you to pieces, doesn't it?"

Oscar grinned. "Well, every man either of you comes into contact with ends up dancing. Junior Whitebear'll never be the same."

"Oh, stop it. A month goes by, some new girl discovers him, Junior will forget he ever laid his hand on my crotch."

"I kind of doubt that."

They could hear the shower running. "If Kit starts in washing her hair, you'll be here until dinnertime."

"Man, I got to get back to the Trading Post or Corrine'll kill me. Can't we do something to hurry her up?"

Chloe pointed to the kitchen tap. Oscar turned it on hot, full force, and a wail emanated from the bathroom. A few minutes later, Kit stomped out, fully dressed, her wet red hair tied back with a purple ribbon that caused Chloe's heart to spasm. She was such a baby. This trip to Arizona was supposed to be fun, but turned out to be baby-sitting infirm, cranky adults. "Now she deserves some coffee," Chloe said, and winked at Oscar as he poured out a second cup.

"Corrine'll be by in an hour or two. Maybe you can get some Coke down in Flag so this child will have something to drink."

"You know, Oscar," Kit said, icily. "In some countries girls are married and mothers by my age."

"Sounds like a blast," Chloe said, reaching for her wallet. "Here. Pick out something for yourself at the Trading Post. My treat, so long as it's under twenty-five dollars."

"I think we can make a pretty fair deal with that. See you around supper time," Oscar promised. "Kiss the little *awéé'* for me. Buy those groceries. Hey, make me a real supper."

"I might just get ambitious and do that."

"And then you'll be sorry," Kit said. "Lay on the couch all day or Hank will kill me."

They left. In the silence of the cabin, Chloe dressed herself, resting her sore body between tugging on layers of clothing. She slid her hiking boots on, became frustrated that she couldn't come up with some way to bend low enough to tie them, then sat waiting in the rocking chair for Corrine to arrive. Outside the colt stared back at her from the corral, snow piled up on the ridge of his spine. Each time he exhaled, small plumes of warm breath rose from his nostrils. He studied her, as fed up with winter as was Hannah. Hannah nested herself atop Kit's sleeping bag. No reason for a dog to get ambitious with snow on the ground. The rain was back, big, wet spatters hitting the windows. Chloe wondered what the weather was like in Patagonia. Winter, certainly, but a much warmer version. Was her mother staring at glittery Christmas ornaments, sorry another holiday had gone by, or was she glancing out at the mountains, thinking about the letter she'd written? The whole thing was a rat's nest, plain and simple.

An hour later a horn honked, and Chloe startled awake. Hannah investigated, barking as she nosed her way out the dog door. Usually Oscar parked around back, between the house and the barn. It was easier for Chloe to get to the car with less snow pack to wade through. Maybe Corrine thought parking behind someone's house was impolite. Pushing up off the arms of the rocker, Chloe got to her feet and started toward the front door they hardly ever used. Corrine's truck wasn't there, but a late-model red Jeep Cherokee was. No dog, however, and no driver.

"Hannah?" she called. Chloe turned and walked to the rear of the house. Someone stood at the corral fence, stroking her colt. She opened the back door and chill air blasted her face.

"Checking out your horse," Junior Whitebear announced. He scratched the colt's neck, swiped the snow from his back, and walked toward her. "Looks pretty decent. I was thinking maybe I might sneak him out and ride him all over hell and back without asking your permission."

"Go right ahead. He's not saddle-broke."

"That's not a very nice thing to say to someone first thing in the morning."

"Have me arrested."

Junior looked down at the ground. When he looked up again, he said, "I've got your number, you know. The only reason you talk so nasty to me is you can't stand how much you like me."

She laughed. "Weak line, chum, and I've heard them all. I'm disappointed."

Junior made his way through the snow toward the back door, Hannah at his side. Her dog had decided he was one of the good guys.

"I miss not having a dog."

"So why don't you get one?"

He shook his head. "I travel too much. Wouldn't be fair to the dog."

"Yeah, dogs have a way of making you put down roots."

He walked into the house. "So do babies."

Chloe held on to the arm of the rocker, supporting herself. "Where's Corrine?"

Junior smiled, showing a momentary flash of white, even teeth. "Pipe burst in the Trading Post john. She's waiting on the plumber who supposedly fixed it last month so she can chew him out. Opportunities like that don't come along often enough for Corrine. By the time he gets it fixed, poor guy'll be wishing he'd gone into brain surgery instead. I offered to drive you to Flagstaff and pick up those dolls at the art center."

"That was big of you."

"Big?" Junior let himself in the door, shut it behind him, and squatted down to tie her shoes. "Let me guess. It's okay to deliver your baby, but I can't be your taxi. Here I thought maybe you'd ask me to be Reed's godfather. Not to mention I was planning to let you be the first woman who gets a ride in my fine new set of wheels." He ruffled Hannah's fur and spoke into the dog's face. "Tell you what, dog. You can be first. Forget this other woman. She's too mean."

"That's your Jeep?"

Finished with her shoes, he stood up. "Bought it Christmas morning off the Chevy dealer's lot."

"It's not a Chevy."

"They're what you might call a multicultural dealer. It's got four-wheel drive and a heavy-duty heater. I don't need rhino bars and so forth. Army engineering will do me."

From the front-door vantage point, Chloe studied the car's aluminum rims. "Nice, if you're into that yuppie shit."

Junior laughed loudly. "Yuppie? Wow, I've been cussed before, but you really know how to wound a guy." He waved in the general direction of her truck, which she had about given up driving on the slick, snowy roads and parked alongside the barn. "Now that particular Chevy's what you might call a classic."

"Might, nothing. You're looking at the best truck America ever built."

"Classic doesn't count for much when you hit ice."

"Haven't hit ice I couldn't handle yet."

Junior folded his arms across his chest. The fringe on his jacket waved like strands of his hair might if it was ever set free from the tightly bound braids. She wondered if he did the braids himself, or if there was always a willing woman around in the mornings.

"You are one tough little mama, I grant you that. But one of these days you will hit ice, I guarantee it. Let's get you down to see the wee one. I'll go warm up the car."

Outside in the front yard, she stood watching while Junior got out of his car, returned her gaze, and never even once broke eye contact. His self-assuredness royally pissed her off. "What're we waiting for?"

"You to decide you can trust me before we get in the car, I think."

"Oh, for Christ's sake. What's not to trust? You already told me you have fucking four-wheel drive and you can see into the future. It's freezing. Move your ass so I can get in the car."

He cocked his head. "You're a different kind of new mother, you know that?"

"Well, if there's a mother mold, I'm sure I won't fit it. Can I bring my dog?"

"Sure, if she wants to go." He opened the driver's door and pointed. Hannah sniffed cautiously, then sat back down in the snow.

"It's okay, Hannah," Chloe said. "Load up."

The white shepherd trotted off to the corral and began playing tag with the colt.

"Just you and me, I guess," Junior said, loud enough for his voice to carry across the yard. "You want the dog on the lead?"

"If you wouldn't mind."

The drizzling rain began to turn to snow. Flakes hit Chloe's face, stinging where they landed. "Damn this endless winter," she muttered under her breath. Junior finished securing Hannah and returned, offering his arm for support while snow crunched companionably beneath their boots. Chloe studied the distance from the ground into the passenger seat. "I don't think I can manage that with stitches in my gut."

"No problem." Junior scooped her up into his arms and set her down on the passenger seat. Without breaking stride, he reached across her and snapped the shoulder harness around her belly, adjusting the strap so it wouldn't cut into her breasts. His breath was warm and sweet on her face, smelling of coffee and sage, like early summer mornings had, five months ago, when she had basked in the sunshine and felt peaceful. "Shoulder harnesses and air bags," he said. "This here is one safe harbor of a car, *asdzání*."

He was only calling her a woman; there wasn't anything personal in stating biological facts, but the way he said it, his voice lowering, the intimacy of another language, was disturbing. He shut her door and crossed to the driver's side. Chloe watched his braids lift slightly in the bitter wind, snow flecking his dark hair. His skin was the color of that expensive coffee drink, *latte*, which she tried once and liked in spite of its absurd price. Her full breasts throbbed. *Safe harbor, my ass. I am in deep here*, she thought. *All the way to Flagstaff I'll pretend to take a nap.*

Junior didn't say much on the way to the hospital. They drove down the highway at a moderate speed, passing farms gone soft and pretty as Christmas cards, past miles of green pines, branches drooping low and tipped with glittering ice. The normally wide-open sky felt pinned down to the earth, dense and gray, and Chloe wondered if Hank was flying home today, if planes would even take off in this kind of nonsense. The closed-up bait shops by the roadside looked as if they might crumble under the elements before the next fishing season came around. Every bar's parking lot was full. Before she'd left the hospital, Dr. Carrywater told her there was a medical term for this hopeless feeling, Seasonal Affective Disorder, or SAD, an apt acronym if ever there was one. She pretended to be even more tired than she felt.

At Horsemen's Lodge, one of Flagstaff's finer dining establishments, Junior slowed slightly and pointed. "I worked there two summers."

"Is that right? I used to be a waitress."

"So Oscar has informed me."

"Arizonans tip well?"

"Around here they don't much care for dark skin on the inside of restaurants. Waiter jobs go to pale-faced college boys. I took care of the horses, bucked hay, organized rentals for hunters."

"And then?"

He looked over at her, his proud face amused. "Got myself fired."

"What did you do? Bang the owner's daughter?"

"Worse. I refused to let this drunk hunter take out one of the few decent horses. She'd pulled up lame, really sore. This *nittáá* wanted to be riding a pinto when he killed his elk. Probably thought it would make for a better photograph or something. Wouldn't take no for an answer."

"Did you deck him?"

"Nope. I liberated the horse. Told the owner she must have run off. Lost my job over it."

"That's pretty shitty."

"Seemed like a fair trade at the time. The horse stayed safe. As a matter of fact, she was Sally's dam." He waved his hand. "Happened years ago. Not even sure why I thought of it. I've had a lot of jobs since then. Much higher shittiness index on a lot of them."

Chloe played with the shoulder harness, slipping her bare hand around the cold buckle. "You continually surprise me, Mr. Whitebear."

Junior was quiet for a long time, long enough to pass the gas station, Mary's Café, and most of downtown and to head up the road toward the hospital. At the sight of the building, Chloe's breasts began to tingle, and she pulled her jacket close, afraid they would leak before she could get to the baby.

He pulled into a parking space, cut the engine, and looked at her. "Is that a good thing, you suppose, to constantly surprise another human being?"

She thought it over. Her mother's letter was so fresh in her mind she was having trouble concentrating and keeping her guard up. "Sometimes surprises can be the only thing keeping us going."

"Until they turn to ice."

"There you go again, trying to freak me out."

"Just want to keep you on your toes." At the maternity ward floor, he checked his watch. "I'll come back in an hour. We'll get under way before the snow gets too heavy."

"In the safe mobile with the yuppie wheels."

He smiled. "You bet."

The nurses all watched him go. Chloe saw a candy-striper flash all ten fingers across the counter to her onlooking partner. The two young women laughed, then reluctantly resumed shuffling papers. The elevator doors shut, and the Indian man disappeared from view. So what if he was good-looking? Beauty was the thinnest layer of a person, light years away from the soul. She opened the door into the nursery, washed her hands with the antibacterial soap, and got ready to feed her daughter.

Reed had that funny, tan cast to her skin, the infant jaundice Dr. Lois had told Chloe to expect. The nurse explained that the baby needed to sleep under the bilirubin lights, and that she wanted Chloe to cut short the cuddling. "Get her fed and back under the lamps. Pump out your breasts afterward," she said matter-of-factly, as if it were as simple a procedure as wringing out a wet towel.

When she left the room, Chloe gently inspected her daughter.

Her face was smooth, her dark hair so fine and soft it felt like rabbit's fur. The instant Reed's tiny mouth clamped on her nipple she felt the milk begin to flow. It stung and she tensed, trying to get beyond the pain. Reed fussed, and then somehow they both traveled past the discomfort, and she felt she could endure the process. The nursing always made Chloe want to cry. With every pull of Reed's mouth, Chloe's belly ached, experiencing the phantom cramps that were supposed to help the womb that was no longer there return to its normal size. She ran her free hand over Reed's tiny head. Her daughter's thick, dark hair grew upward into a whorl at the top of her skull, glinting in the artificial light. She fed her for fifteen minutes on one side, then took a time-out as the nurse lifted her to change her diaper before switching to the other breast.

"I've got to go check my patients," the nurse said. "I'll be back in just a few minutes. Don't try to lift her yourself. We don't need adhesions, do we?"

Chloe gave her a look. The woman could think she was an idiot if she wanted to; there was no reason to encourage her by answering.

When the door next opened, Chloe didn't look up. She wasn't ready to let her daughter go back under the lights. She wanted to hold Reed, to bask in the way her tiny nose flared each time she breathed, to wait for her to open her eyes again. She heard the chair scoot out behind her, and felt the baby startle at the sudden noise.

"Sorry," Junior said softly.

The hair on the back of her neck lifted. Her breast was fully exposed, and he wasn't even trying to look politely the other way. "I'm not quite finished here."

"Take your time. The weather's turned to shit anyhow. We can't go anywhere until the snow lets up a little." He moved the chair so that he was facing her.

She turned her face to look at him, but he wasn't staring at her breasts, he was fixed on the baby. One dark hand reached out across the space between them and stroked the baby's tiny pink cheek. The movement caused a trickle of milk to leak out the side of the tiny rosebud of Reed's mouth.

"I think that baby's full."

"I'm not allowed to lift her up," Chloe snapped. "I have to wait for the nurse."

"Let me go wash my hands. I'll do it."

Junior placed his palms carefully around Reed's blanket. Chloe felt cool air hit her breast. She covered herself quickly and buttoned her shirt. Junior held the baby close and jiggled her gently in his arms. Very softly, he started to sing, one of those eerie chants similar to what Corrine played over the sound system at the Trading Post. His eyes were shut and he was elsewhere, unembarrassed. Somewhere in her deepest self, Reed's brain was recording this memory. She might not ever remember who'd sung to her, but there would come a day she'd hear a similar music and stop whatever she was doing for a moment and feel full and sleepy. Chloe watched, helpless to stop him, nervous at what it could mean. Then the nurse returned, holding her arms out to the baby.

"I think it's great when Daddy takes time out to be here for the feeding," she said, tucking Reed into her isolette under the healing lights.

Chloe looked up. Junior was smiling that crooked smile at her. He didn't bother to correct the nurse. "Mama, let's get a move on," he said, and extended his hand to help her to her feet.

14

The windshield of the Jeep grew thick with snow, each individual flake accumulating in a crust against the wipers. Junior peered through the tracks as he pulled to the curb on East Santa Fe. Traffic was chaotic, everyone trying to get home before the roads became impassable. "Let's kill some time in a restaurant," he said. "You got anything against Chinese?"

"I won't eat that raw fish crap."

He grinned. "Let's see, that fish crap they call sushi, or is there some other raw fish crap you find offensive?"

"Whatever it's called, I won't eat it."

"I'm curious. Have you tried it, or is this dislike innate?"

Chloe huddled into her jacket, staring back in the direction of the hospital. "Whitebear, leave me alone."

He thought of how she had stood in the school barn, loudly denying she was in labor. Now when she left the little one it was as if she'd cut off her arm. Every time he had to say good-bye to Dog, he felt the same painful fractures, not that it mattered to Corrine.

The Grand Canyon Café wasn't much for interior decor, but its adobe storefront possessed the look and feel of historic Flagstaff. Without asking where he wanted to sit, Chloe carefully slid into a window booth. Arizonans frequented this place when they were sick of the steak houses, so there were generally seats to spare. In downtown Flag, most necks ran to red, a color that had nothing whatsoever to do with Indians. Junior imagined things weren't that different from an Asian perspective. Holler melting pot all you wanted, in terms of tolerance, nothing monumental had changed around here. Christmas night he'd walked into the Museum Club to grab a beer and listen to the band. Within minutes there was some party drunk in his face calling him "Chief." He thought of all the abuse Dog must already have experienced in his short life and wished he'd been there to walk alongside his son.

Chloe didn't even pick up her menu. She stared out the window at the traffic, her face so sad Junior didn't bother asking what she wanted. He set about ordering his favorites.

"We'll start with potstickers. And an order of *hoong sien* bean curd, the *young chow* fried rice, and some of those pancakes with the plum sauce."

"*Sake?*"

"Green tea for me, thanks, but sure, bring some for the lady." Chloe was staring at him, her mouth slightly open in surprise. "I'm sorry. You don't drink?"

"I drink."

"Well, you're not driving, so it can't be that. You one of those girls who only eats salad? I can call the waiter back. Every restaurant's got lettuce."

She picked up the table decanter of soy sauce and inspected its list of ingredients, then gave it a sniff and wrinkled her nose. "You're quite the old hand, ordering for women, eating out in restaurants. I notice you didn't waste much time checking the price column."

He looked down at their menus, stacked one inside each other, snuggling like an old married couple. He thought of all the five-star places he'd dined in, compared them to this café, then sobered at the idea of Chloe considering that this meal represented a splurge. "My wallet can handle dinner in Flagstaff."

"A *lot* of food. You must be hungry."

"What we don't eat we can take back to the motel with us."

"Motel? Excuse me? You stood in my front yard bragging about four-wheel drive—"

He gestured toward the window, interrupting her. "You think four-wheel will keep idiots without it from running into us? Hank'd have my hide if I returned his woman injured."

That made her laugh. He focused on that chipped tooth, which just intrigued the hell out of him. Forget the Christmas decorations, damn if her smile didn't just about light up the whole room.

"Yeah, old Hank's been known to raise a fist. But he's in California, he won't know if we're driving in the snow. I could handle this powder in my truck, no problem."

"Too bad you're not driving, then, because I'm telling you, I know bad snow when I see it."

"The weather will perk up. I'd bet my horse on it."

Behind all this tough patter, Junior believed he recognized the presence of Jackrabbit, who was frequently mesmerized by headlights. The animal was generally so nervous he was willing to cross against traffic, an often-fatal guarantee he didn't have to remain in the all-too-terrifying present. A good therapist might say that Jackrabbit had a little control issue going. Where along the way, Junior wondered, had this woman become so suspicious of men? Hank seemed stand-up; Dog defended his teacher like the man was a superhero. Little stories floated around the reservation: Children who were lazy at home walked five miles to the Oliver place for the privilege of chopping wood. Old women fought over which days of the week they got to bake him loaves of bread. This was nine-yards kind of treatment, rarely afforded white guys, which meant he deserved it.

"I was thinking check in for a couple of hours so you could rest. Things clear a little out there, I'll wake you up and drive you right home."

She gave him a smirk.

Junior looked down at the worn tabletop and said, "Food, lodging, shelter from the elements. Where I come from that's called hospitality, Chloe."

She pressed her lips together tightly and went quiet. Damn, now their conversation would grind off-kilter the rest of the evening. Junior shot her his best smile, the one that sent photographers to snapping and his publicist into paroxysms of marketing joy. Sami Gee often remarked, *Whatever you do, my son, never lose that grin. It's ninety percent of the sale.* "More good news if you can stand it," Junior said. "Mr. Big Wallet will even spring for dessert."

"I have a question for you."

"Fire away."

"Just where exactly did you live before coming back to Arizona? Must have been someplace where men make all the decisions. Please tell me so I can make sure never to move there."

"Outermost tip of Massachusetts. Lots of artists live there, a regular colony. Lots of restaurants, too."

"And you tried them all."

"I'd rather spend my energy working on jewelry than cooking."

"And does the same hold true here?"

Cold and heavy, it came to him suddenly, the thought of bulk silver, how the stones and metal used to glitter and beckon to him in his dreams. How the ideas were there in his mind, anxious, begging to be housed in the metal. As shocking as a hard slap across the face, he had to acknowledge the loss. What did he tell her? That once art had flown out the door as merchandise and come back as checks? That now he wore talent around his neck like the proverbial albatross? It could have been the chipped tooth that touched him as much as her baby. He didn't want to shrug off what she said. This time, for no good reason, he wanted to answer from his heart. "Junior Whitebear is on hiatus," was what Sami Gee told anyone who asked. Then he went into his "artist refilling the pot" spiel. Galleries loved that, so long as they had back stock to sell along with the story.

"Awhile back something happened that kind of took the heart out of things for me."

"Some girl break your heart?"

He cracked his knuckles and watched her shudder at the sound. If he could blame his mother's suicide for some sort of latent break-down, the answer was yes. If it was the scores of young gay artists he had come to count as his friends one by one getting struck down with the HIV virus, then it wasn't a girl thing at all. "Listen, don't make me talk about it too much, or it'll spoil your appetite."

"So you're not working, but you still have the means to indulge your restaurant weakness. You got yourself a stock portfolio, Junior, something like that? If you're rich, how come you don't throw some money at your son's school? Hank says they've got a shoestring budget that's running out of room for knots."

"Jeepers, is your heart made out of cast iron? Having money changes a man. I indulge certain weaknesses and ignore others. I didn't know there was a problem at the school. If they need money, I'll give them whatever I can. Sit there and tell me there isn't some-thing you'd cater to if you had the bucks to make it happen."

He could tell he'd tapped the right vein. For a moment her brown eyes went far away, and she softened the way she did when little Reed was in her arms. Then she laid her hands flat on the table. Her cheeks were still a bit chubby from pregnancy, but even in the brief period between the birth and this snowy evening, the weight was beginning to drop from her frame. She was one of those women who burned her fuel, and she wasn't looking so plain to him after all, but fiery, which seemed far more interesting.

"I've got a new horse nobody's wrecked yet, a *classic* truck, and a dog whose major faults are hating men and running away when it thunders, both shortcomings perfectly understandable. I've got clothes enough I can go an entire week without washing them. I get laid frequently enough that I don't sport a sour attitude, and there's a few good friends I can count on when I'm broke who'll lend me money when I need it. Of course, these same friends tell me when I'm acting stupid, and often I need to be reminded of that. What the hell else can I possibly cater to?"

Junior smiled. That "getting laid" business went a long way toward disarming him. He had a feeling she knew it. He leaned in on his elbows, narrowing the table space down to a more intimate playing field. "You forgot being a pro at holding back. Wish I knew the reason why. Well, give me time, I'll figure it out."

"Good luck. 'Cause there ain't anything more to it."

"I think you're lying."

She didn't break eye contact until the waiter set down the tray of sizzling vegetable potstickers. Neither did he. They leaned back at the same time and regarded the food. Junior loaded a plate for her and unwrapped Chloe's chopsticks.

"Just get me a fork."

"No way, sister. This is the Grand Canyon Café. Years of tradition are at stake. You pick with sticks." He fitted the slender pieces of wood into her hand, demonstrated how they opened and shut, then guided her to a potsticker. Predictably, she tried to pull away, but he didn't let go until she'd closed her mouth around the doughy treat.

"Not bad for foreign," Chloe said.

"Which illustrates my point."

"What the hell point am I missing now?"

"That by eating in restaurants, one indulges. And it's not a bad thing, in fact, sometimes it can lead to interesting consequences."

She gave him the fisheye, kept on eating. More snow fell, creating drifts now, the flurries occasionally becoming so dense the windows whited out for brief moments. The other customers were evaluating the weather, too. The heater was turned up high. If you had to be stranded, this was a cozy place, with all the great cooking smells surrounding them, the booth comfortable enough to lean back and put your feet up on the opposite bench.

Chloe drank a sip of her *sake* and wrinkled her nose. "They forgot to put this wine on ice. Should I say something?"

"Hot drinks with hot food, cool drinks with cool. It's an Asian thing."

"Yeah? Since when are you Asian?"

"World travel."

"Don't tell me, okay?"

"If that's how you want it." He thought about how he'd deliberately sneaked up behind her in the hospital nursery. For a long moment before announcing himself, he had stood there just to watch the way she leaned her swollen breast into the hungry little girl's mouth. Chloe had lovely breasts, of a size that would spill out of his palms and tickle his fingers. And the baby, he couldn't get enough of Reed, that was true. But this wasn't about catching a peep of what wasn't his. Already he'd had his hand inside this woman, had witnessed her most intimate event. It was as if had he done anything else, his actions would have interrupted fate on a massive level. Jimmy died, and his closest surviving relative was supposed to claim his remains. Jimmy was still sitting in his urn on some particular shelf, waiting, while Junior followed this new and compelling trail. A familiar panic began to strike him, adrenaline rush prickling his skin, tapping into something larger, humming the way acupuncture needles hit meridian pathways. He set his chopsticks down in the porcelain holder and placed both hands around his warm teacup. He had that sinking feeling his *łłaajíéé dittidí* were leading him down a troublesome alley, and he let himself travel along behind those trousers, curious to see where they were going. He drifted, and in his mind's eye visualized red canyon walls, petroglyphs, felt a fine sheen of sand blowing in a chill wind. He smelled spring grasses, tasted cool water that was partially snowmelt, partially rising up from the earth, and he could hear the tinkling of sheep's bells among the barking of young dogs who were supposed to be working but were playing for as long as they could get away with it. Someplace in this scenario, Chloe was nearby, and there was a pair of horses who knew the canyon deep in their genetic coding. Sheepishly, he looked up at the woman across from him. She had a smear of plum sauce at the corner of her mouth. He reached over and with his thumb and wiped it away, then stuck his thumb in his mouth and sucked it clean. *She's going to be mine*, he knew. Not how or where or when or even why, but it was a gift from the universe, and he could walk away from it or ask it to unfold in his arms.

"Why did you do that?"

Reluctant to exit his daydream, he saw her face suffused with blood, passionate heart energy directed toward him. This was the farewell appearance of his good sense, he recognized that much. His sober reasoning, which had served him so well, was falling off the wagon, voluntarily, headfirst into the snow. Ambulatory but limping, it trotted off, eager to party on the ice patches, happy to fall down perfectly manageable hills, to break important and necessary bones and carry on yodeling. Belatedly he gave her his answer. "Because it needed doing."

She pointed at him with her chopsticks. "I've got a napkin, buddy. All you had to do was say something."

"Sorry."

"It's okay, but mind your manners. Now, this purple stuff that looks so terrible. What's it called again?"

He straddled the two plains of existence, desperate to hold on to the vision, savoring the taste on his tongue. "Plum sauce."

"Made with regular old tree plums?"

"I don't know. I can ask the waiter."

"Never mind. I don't want anybody telling me there's monkey brains in it. It tastes too wonderful."

"No brains so far as I know of." *Not even in me*, he thought, *but damned if I'm going to let you in on that.*

The wind blew and the snow thickened. Junior's motel plan, which he'd mentioned just to get her used to the idea, and to buy time, was looking downright necessary. No way they could drive back to Cameron. Spending the night with her appealed to him; spending it in a ditch did not. The Pony Soldier was as good a place as any. Horse nut like her might even appreciate the funky neon sign, all those horses running in a perpetual, sizzling trot.

"I know you won't believe this, but my room's flooded," Junior explained at Chloe's door. "A pipe burst."

"So get yourself another room."

"Believe me, I tried. The guy at the desk said they're full up, thanks to the snow. I told him to call me here as soon as they get the problem squared away."

"If this is some kind of cheap—"

Silently, Junior toed off his left boot and removed his sock, squeezing it for emphasis. Water dripped through his fingers and spotted the carpet. Chloe sighed. "Come in. I was about to call Kit."

From the queen bed nearest the door, Chloe dialed out. She listened a long time, then hung up. "Not home. Guess I'll try the Trading Post." She punched up those numbers and waited some more. "Oscar," she said with relief into the receiver. "I know, I know. It's a blizzard here, too. We're going to have to stay the night in Flag. If you've got a pencil I'll give you the number. By the way, heard from Hank?"

Barefooted, Junior got up and laid his socks across the heater vent. He stood at the window, pulling the heavy brocade curtains aside so he could look across the highway. The occasional optimist headed north, driving slowly in the dusk, headlights casting arcs of light across the white road. He remembered when the first hurricane warnings began to come over the radio in Provincetown, urging everyone who hadn't evacuated to batten down the windows and stay indoors. Most residents were so eager to hang on to their small stretch of coastline, to have it to come back to, that they had amply prepared and stuck it out. Every year in the west, fires burned through the forests, sometimes clearing whole groves of old growth, redefining the national parks and canyons, periodically reminding everyone to respect Mother Earth. Junior hadn't nailed one thing down during the hurricane. He blew town, took care of some business in Manhattan, saw whatever play was getting the raves that month, and got taken out to dinner by some fawning gallery owner who wanted to show off his connection to Native America. On his return, only one pane of his front window was lost, knocked neatly out to the edges, as if excised by a glazier's knife. A puddle marked the wood floor beneath the window. Walking the streets in the storm's aftermath, this undeserved luck convinced Junior it was time to stop hiding out on the East Coast. He took long walks on the beach, exercising dogs for his fellow artists, men who had gotten too sick to do it themselves. He continued to set stones in patterns so familiar he could have done them in his sleep, and there was never a problem unloading his silver. But after awhile he couldn't call this kind of activity art. He needed to be uncomfortable to get to the heart of things, and knew that if he hightailed his skinny half-blood butt back to where he'd grown up, laid his cheek against the cracked, red earth, eventually he would come face to face with the cottonwood tree where his mother had strung herself up like a gutted deer, and that was where he would discover what was missing. He'd known that even before he heard his father was dead, but Jimmy's death made going home that much easier. Now he was learning a lesson from another storm. For that, Hank Oliver might decide to punch him out. So be it; a night alone with Chloe might be worth a broken nose.

"Jesus H. Christ, Kit," Chloe was saying into the motel phone. "I'm a mother now. I think I can keep a governor on my hormones for one night. Trust me, okay? And make sure Hannah has fresh water. Eating snow makes her puke. When Hank gets in tonight, tell him to call here." She paused. "Well, I guess you can wake me up then."

She hung up the phone. "Teenage," she offered.

"Temporarily wiser than the Dalai Lama."

"Not to mention redheaded," Chloe answered back. "That kind of stubborn she'll never grow out of."

They sat on their respective beds and watched the television for a while. Junior could tell Chloe wasn't really interested in CNN. He switched it off with the remote and turned the small radio/alarm clock on the table separating their beds to the college jazz station. He checked on his socks and turned them over so they would dry on the other side. Chloe lay down on the bed, staring at her hiking boots.

"Want those off?"

"I need help with the laces."

He sat on the edge of her bed, untied the shoes, and pulled her feet free. Her wool socks were a tweedy blue, typical winter wool, but she hadn't learned to layer a pair of cotton ones underneath, so her toes were icy. He rubbed her feet through the heavy weave. "Get under the covers."

"I will in a minute. Need to do something first."

"Can I help?"

She laughed dryly. "Sure, if you've expressed milk from aching breasts, you're the man."

"I've milked cows."

"Well, that's about what it boils down to, but I think I can manage. If you'll excuse me."

He got up and stood between the beds as she passed. She walked into the bathroom and switched on the light, closing the door behind her. It wasn't a very well-constructed door. The molding had warped from the steamy heat of long showers travelers took when it wasn't their utility bill. The door touched the frame and bounced back open a few inches, a gap through which Junior could see Chloe's elbow lift as she raised her arms to unbutton her blouse. Her blond hair spilled forward as she leaned over the sink. She sighed, a painful exhalation to which Junior listened hard, the resonance of such pure, physical relief causing him to shudder. His thoughts explored side routes with determination: calving time on the ranches he'd worked; the bawling of cows that needed to be milked; his fingers closing around the warm, rubbery teats of a swollen udder; Chloe's fingers against her own nipples. The fact that he was standing only a few strides away, listening, did not help any. He looked down at the legs of his jeans, the left side riding slightly tighter now, and was ashamed of himself. He heard water run in the sink. Eventually she came back to her bed, buttoned up, grim faced.

"Didn't take you very long."

"Oh, I gave up," she said. "Nobody said there would be so much of it. Or that getting it out would be such a bitch. I'll try again later." She grimaced. "God, listen to me. Count yourself lucky that I can't bore you with the story of my labor. It's all just so damned *female*. Men hear women talk about it, they turn white or flee. Sight of blood used to send me running. But after delivering Reed—well, you were there."

"It doesn't send me running. I cherished every minute of it. In fact, I've been thinking how Reed sort of connects us for life."

Chloe laid her head down on the doubled-up hotel pillow. "You and Reed, maybe."

"It connects you and me, too."

"That kind of talk scares me, Junior."

"You've been scared since the day we met."

"Entirely possible."

"Why is that?"

Chloe tipped her head back to look at the painting hanging above her bed. In varying shades of pastel, a big-eyed Indian girl and her pet lamb looked up at a rainbow arcing across the sky. "Did you flood your room on purpose?"

"No. But I did want to be alone with you."

She sighed. "Come on, Whitebear. I live with someone. I just had a goddamn baby. My insides are all torn up. Even if I wanted to, which I don't, I couldn't sleep with you."

"That's what white guys are like, isn't it? Every time you're alone with a woman it has to mean sex. No wonder they all die so damn early."

She laughed. "I wouldn't classify it as a *white* thing, Junior. You boys all seem pretty equally infected with girl flu."

"Hey, now. I just want to get to know you, here, in private where we can talk. How dangerous can that be?"

"Dangerous as ice."

He turned the radio down. "Yeah, it's dangerous being an adult and having control over your emotions. Damn, you're pretty."

"Oh, for Christ's sake, I've never been pretty, and saying I am doesn't impress me."

"How about attractive? Can you be attractive?"

"No, goddammit. Now change the subject, or I will hitchhike home.".

"I love how you cuss like a hand. You've got a worse temper than I did at sixteen, and I was a handful."

"But that's okay because I'm *pretty*."

"Sally misses you. I come into the barn with a bucket of oats, she looks around behind me, disappointed you're not there."

"She likes cube sugar. Don't leave your horse alone for eight years and maybe she'll remember you next time."

"You don't get it, do you?"

"I don't want to."

He folded his hands. "I been with a lot of women, Chloe."

"Well, give yourself a badge!"

"I said that only to give you an example. Put all those women together on a list, and they don't add up to anything memorable. You, on the other hand—"

"Live with somebody."

"Who's not even here."

She sat upright. "Hank's mother has cancer, Junior. She's probably dying while we're sitting here, and you're trying to figure out how to make a pass at me. Can we fault her son for wanting to be there when she goes? Or does that sound old-fashioned to a guy like you? Maybe you'd leave your mother to die alone, but Hank sure wouldn't."

Junior rubbed his face before he answered. "I'm sorry to hear Hank's mom is sick."

"Mighty big of you to admit while you're sitting here about to deliver the come-fuck-me line."

"My mother killed herself when I was about Dog's age. Your mother's death is not something you really get over."

Chloe looked at him hard. "I'll be damned. You're not lying. She really killed herself?"

"Your daughter came into the world through more blood than I thought was inside anybody."

"I'm sorry—"

"Stop. You misunderstand what I'm trying to say. This past year I volunteered with the Project Angel Food people. It was just spending a couple hours a week with sick people, men mostly, artists I knew. Walking their dogs, changing the CDs on the stereo, reading to them."

"Sick people?"

He nodded. "HIV hit the gay community where I lived awful hard. I thought maybe helping out would make me feel less guilty about being healthy. But those boys just—" He stopped and searched his mind for the proper word. "Dried up. I'm telling you, Chloe, no more to them at the end than husk. After a while I had a hard time putting together jewelry at all. Everything piled up on me. I felt like a coward, but I had to stop doing it. Delivering Reed, all I meant to say was, you have no idea what a relief it is to be a part of what happens at the other end of the spectrum. Welcoming somebody who's just starting her life. Especially when Corrine decided to keep my son's birth from me. There's nothing logical about it, but I'm clinging to Reed's birth like a lifesaver."

Chloe swallowed hard. "I'm sorry about your friends dying. That must have been horrible."

"No, it wasn't. Just sad, the waste of it, being able to offer only temporary comfort when they were begging for a cure. With my mother, it was too late even for that. I found her strung up in this old cottonwood tree. Try as I might I couldn't get the knot loose. Had to leave her there. I was short, like Dog is. Had to go find somebody taller, you know, to cut her down. I picked up her shoes, ran like hell to the nearest house, clean out of my head, holding onto those stupid high-heel shoes. I've been mad about that for most of my life, you know? Project Angel Food helped. Those men allowing me to help them, one less thing for them to worry about." He inhaled deeply and began to unravel the suede binding on his left braid. "But your daughter is the first real healing medicine to happen to me in a long while."

"Me, too, Junior."

Junior was quiet. He heard the tremble in her voice. He wound the rawhide into a spiral on the table separating the beds, and sat there with one braid tight and the other hanging loose. "Does shit like this happen with every man you meet?"

"You were in the wrong place at the wrong time."

"You, too, then? You feel it?"

"Maybe I feel it. Which doesn't mean I have to act on it."

"But you can sense how badly I want you."

"Yes."

"I'm sitting here spilling my guts."

"Maybe that's typical behavior for a world traveler."

"Let me tell you, it's not. How about I just come on over to that bed and hold you?"

"No. You'll want to touch me and kiss me, and neither of those things'll be enough. That's not dangerous, it's just plain stupid."

"So what are you saying—we sit here and hold it in?"

She nodded. "It's the responsible thing to do."

"Even when you admit you feel it."

"Hank is the first decent man who ever loved me. God knows why, but he does. I haven't had that great a life until now. Bills, bad relationships, lost my apartment, for a while there I lived in my truck. Last year I hit this cop and got thrown in jail. You want to know who paid my bail, got me a lawyer, stuck it out with me? Hank. Here I can't even manage birth control, and it doesn't dawn on me the reason I'm not having periods has anything to do with a baby until it's too late for an abortion. How many men do you know who'd not even miss a beat, just outright propose when a woman shows up with news like that?"

"Me, for one."

"Hank." She gave Junior the finger, and he lay down on his bed facing her. They stared into each other's faces. Desire was so backed up inside him, Junior felt dizzy and congested. Chloe's smile had taken the long adios. Maybe it wouldn't ever come back. She stared into his eyes, then, after a long time, reached her hand out between the beds. Junior quickly slid his hand into hers, clasping her fingers. She pulled each digit loose, took hold of them one by one and studied them, touching the short, clipped nails, the dark, hardened calluses under his knuckles, his smooth fingertips. She examined his jewelry with care, and pushed her fingers under his watchband to where the skin of his wrist was thin, where the veins lay blue and full-to-bursting with his blood like individual rivers. As if the action was an afterthought, she kissed him there, just once, her eyes tearing up. He'd pushed her too far. Now he didn't know what to say, and damn sure didn't think he better do anything. She let go long enough to reach up and tuck her thumb under the first button of her blouse.

"You want me? Fine, then, here I am."

"Chloe, stop it."

But she didn't. Like a dog who'd eaten much too fast for his own good, Junior felt his gut twist into a figure eight, punishing him for his hunger. Chloe separated the two halves of the shirt and he could glimpse white bra, the left cup stained damp. She arched her back and undid the catch, pulled the bra away. Her nipples were as dark as the plum sauce in the corner of her mouth when they were in the Chinese restaurant. She cradled her breasts in her fingers, looking down at them, her hair obscuring her face. Junior knelt at the side of her bed.

"You don't have to prove anything to me."

He gave her his hand. Gently, she showed him how she used her thumb and forefingers to press the milk down and out of herself. Like he had demonstrated with the chopsticks, she closed her hand around his, and he saw bluish fluid begin to spill, to collect in his palm. Wordlessly he brought his palm to his mouth and took a taste. At that moment her brown eyes opened to him. He could have made out an itinerary for the furthest corner of the planet, and in this moment and no other, he knew she would travel with him willingly.

She shivered, pulling his face down to hers and murmured something into his ear so low he thought it must have been his own blood speaking, giving him instructions. He caught her lower lip in his teeth, then hungrily pressed his mouth to hers, his tongue

catching on the chipped tooth, lingering there, then moving decisively beyond.

Around two in the morning the message indicator light on the
phone began to pulse orange. There it was, the beacon back to the
world they'd effectively left behind. Junior reached a hand out and
placed the complimentary note pad over the light. Chloe slept next
to him, turned away, snuggled deep in the covers, her mouth as
bruised as his own. He didn't move in case she might wake up,
look outside, and see that hours earlier, the snow had stopped.

15

I guess it would be selfish of me to ask you to stay any longer, wouldn't it? Even one more day. You're busy. You have a life over there. . . .

His mother's power to instill guilt was peerless. Iris's last words rang in his ears the whole flight home and would—he felt certain—echo in his head for months, possibly years to come. After sitting fourteen hours in the Phoenix airport, the weather broke enough they finally started letting the shuttles take off. He'd caught a ride with Chuey Alberto's uncle at the Flagstaff airport, smiling inwardly at the idea of the weary traveler home from another battle, surprising Kit and Chloe. He hadn't expected to walk into his grandmother's cabin and find Junior Whitebear holding Reed in his arms, rocking the fussing infant as if she were his daughter, or that Chloe would be standing out in the snow screaming at one of the tribal policemen who'd finally appeared following her repeated calls about Kit being missing.

"It's your job to find her no matter how old she is, goddammit," Chloe was saying, getting right up in the man's face as if he didn't take her seriously next she might go for his gun.

The T-shirt he'd bought in the airport gift shop—featuring a silk-screened John Wayne on horseback—seemed superfluous when she explained that Kit had been missing since the previous evening. Chloe and Junior had driven to the hospital that morning after spending the night in Flagstaff. The news that everyone had been waiting for—Reed had gained the necessary weight to be released—allowed them to drive back to Cameron bearing precious cargo, only to discover that everyone believed Kit was with somebody else.

"Something happens to her, I'll skin and cook your balls myself," Chloe said, her voice shaking with rage.

From experience Hank knew that kind of anger hid massive, underlying terror. Only veterans of the Chloe wars were able to recognize it. "Jesus H. Christ, Hank, make this guy *do* something," she insisted. All this before hello.

He motioned to the policeman to wait a minute and led Chloe inside to the couch. "Lie down," he said. "Shut your eyes."

Hank invited the man into the kitchen. He threw his carry-on bag in a corner, saw that there was coffee in the pot, poured the man a cup, and asked how his animals were doing this winter.

The cop nodded at Hank. "Cattles're fine, never to worry. It's those damn horses about to break me." He shook his head. "Hate lettin' 'em go hungry, but the cost of grain, you know."

"Tell you what, Nelbert. We've got surplus grain. Let me make you a gift of a couple of sacks."

The cop smiled. "That'd be great."

"I'll just load them in your car, then."

As they walked out back, Chloe opened her mouth to say something, and Junior patted her hand, silencing her.

Methodically Hank slid the fifty-pound sacks into the trunk of the car. "You know, we could sure use some help on that missing girl."

Nelbert made a face. "Your wife say that girl near to fifteen. Plenty old enough to be goin' home with a boy. Give her few days."

"Nelbert, I hear where you're coming from. But this girl's young for her age. She's not a local. You know how that can be. Whatever you think we can do to help locate her, I'm open to hearing it."

The cop took a panoramic view of the property and then glanced back at Hank. "My grandmother knew your grandmother, Mr. Hank. Said she was pretty nice schoolteacher."

"Glad to hear she's still remembered. I aim to carry on the tradition."

Nelbert thought awhile. "Let me gather some guys together, see what we find."

"Appreciate it."

He drove off, and Hank stood alone in the razor-edged wind, shivering. He heard the barn siding soughing as the metal torqued in the swiftly moving current. He gazed across the snow-dusted prairie and wondered how he was supposed to handle the presence of Junior Whitebear in his house. Snatch the baby from his arms, chew him out, and tell him to hit the road? Or was he supposed to thank him once again for being there when he was not? Junior came out of the house and stopped a few feet in front of him.

"I'll find her, Hank. You don't hear from me, it only means I'm still looking."

Hank watched the Indian get into his fancy Jeep and drive off toward Tuba City. Maybe he would find Kit. He hoped he did. That was as far as he could allow his thoughts to travel at this moment.

"It's all my fault," Chloe said, her voice hoarse with worry and crying. "The snow got so bad we had to spend the night in Flagstaff. I called, she got kind of nervous about the idea of being alone." She bit her thumbnail. "Not that there was anything to worry about."

Hank understood all too well how Kit must have felt. There were times Chloe's past actions preceded her and this sounded like one of them. "Maybe she felt abandoned."

Chloe's face crumpled. "Hank, I *told* her we'd be home in a few hours; I checked with Oscar to make sure he knew what was happening. He and Corrine wouldn't let her stay alone overnight. She was supposed to call them. I don't know what went wrong."

"How long has your truck been missing?"

Chloe struggled upright, the facecloth falling to her lap. Reed whimpered from the playpen across the room. "She took my truck?"

Hank wondered just how preoccupied Chloe had to be to overlook the absence of her dearest possession. "Well, let's say you were a teenager cut loose in a strange place, and there were keys hanging on the rack. Don't you think it would at least cross your mind?"

Chloe picked up the facecloth and waved it like a flag of surrender. "What the hell can I do?"

"At this point, put your faith in the tribal police."

"You know how I feel about cops! And that asshole wasn't about to fart until you bribed him with our grain."

"Things are done differently here. It's not California—"

"California my ass! You opened the barn door and basically asked him to rob from you. Maybe Junior'll get lucky. He knows this place inside and out."

"Yeah, Junior's a lucky guy, isn't he?"

Chloe looked up at him, desperately wanting his words of reassurance. "That's not what I meant. It's just that if he doesn't—"

Hank turned his face away, biting back the words he wanted to speak.

Like a miniature queen, Reed lay tucked in a nest of blankets inside a secondhand playpen near the woodstove. Her father reached inside and carefully picked her up. Her brown eyes were open, taking in however much of this world a new baby could. He swore her dark hair had grown an inch in the few days he was away. She was wrapped up tight in layers, the intricate, swaddling way the Navajo mothers bundled their babies. Probably Junior's handiwork. Other than her decidedly more Anglo features, Reed could have passed for one of their tribe. Hank supposed that when Chloe had checked her out of the hospital, people would have mistaken Junior for Reed's father. He forced those thoughts from his mind and settled in the rocker, holding onto the slight weight of his daughter, basking in her radiance, trying to latch on to her calmness.

Chloe folded the washcloth and set it on the arm of the couch. "We're hip-deep in homemade bread. I think there's eggs. You want an apple, some of that herb tea?"

"Nothing. I ate on the plane."

The baby cried most of the night, and Hank stayed up with her, jiggling her gently in his lap, rubbing his hand over her tiny belly as it heaved with sobs. She didn't want to nurse, didn't want water. Her diapers were fresh, her bottom adequately powdered. He stoked the stove so she wouldn't be cold. After two hours of Reed's crying, Chloe flopped down on the floor, resting her head on Kit's sleeping bag. Nervously Hannah sidled in next to her, shying whenever Reed's cries reached the higher pitches. Chloe's voice was ragged, echoing her daughter's. "Christ in heaven, what does she want? A pound of flesh?"

"*Shh*," Hank said. "She's used to the hospital, that's all. Noise, lights, nurses coming and going. It's going to take her a while to understand this house and us."

"Another night like this? No way I can take that."

"She's a tiny baby, Chloe. Cut her some slack."

"I'm trying. Really I am."

Reed wailed again, and Hank had to admit, the sound was piercing. Hannah funneled her mouth into an O and howled along with the baby.

Chloe sighed. "Well, that's that. I'm tapped clean, Hank. I have to sleep."

Hank heard the defeat in her admission. "Sleep, then. I'm not stopping you."

She stood up and wrung her hands, glaring at him. "I don't know how to do this!"

"You think I'm an expert? It's our shitty luck that between us we don't have one decent mother we can call on for advice."

Chloe bit her lip and stared at him. "Why don't you ask one of those goddamn bread ladies to help out. They all think you hung the freaking moon."

"That's the first good idea to come out of your mouth. Maybe I will."

"Give her to me."

Hank handed the baby over. Reed's screaming hit an all-time high, and Chloe visibly winced. She yanked her shirt open and offered her breast, already leaking milk, which seemed to incite even angrier shrieks. Chloe handed the baby back to Hank and stood there looking for all the world like the Lady of Wild Creatures at Ephesus, contemplating slicing off the useless piece of flesh in order to improve her archery aim. "Fine, then." She pointed a finger at the screaming baby. "I'm going to the bedroom. Wake me up when she can talk and manage the goddamn toilet."

Hank sighed. The power of reason insisted that eventually, sometime, Reed had to tire of her efforts, and that once exhausted, she would sleep. In his heart he believed all that was about as possible as the tribal cop's horses coming through the winter fat, sassy and sprouting wings. He paced the floor while Chloe slept, Reed propped on his shoulder, making her discomfort known. Each time he tried the rocking chair, Hannah came to sit on his feet, her normally upright ears flattened in fear. He reached down and stroked her fur. "I can't rock if you keep on doing that," he cautioned the shepherd. She pinned her ears at the thin wailing and crept across the room to sleep up against Chloe, who had returned from the bedroom and sprawled on the floor.

The dog was incomplete without the woman, the woman limping along in search of the dog when she wasn't at her side. They catnapped; Reed cried. Hank wondered if Iris would have been able to quiet Reed—that is, had she cared to acknowledge the presence of her only grandchild long enough to soothe her. And the cherry on the top of this day was that Kit was still out there somewhere, having either abandoned the truck or crashed it. Forget questions of liability; who she was with and what she was doing—this teenager whose mother had spent most of her adult life in communes—that had him concerned.

At dawn Hank heard the Jeep pull up. Hannah wagged her tail. I am hereby betrayed on all fronts, Hank mused blearily. Junior knocked softly before letting himself in.

"Figured nobody was sleeping," he said. "Got a little news. Don't know if you want to hear it."

Hank pressed a finger to his lips, nodding toward Chloe, who lay on the floor hugging Kit's sleeping bag. "She tried to hang in. I'm glad she was able to fall asleep."

Junior looked at her. "Pretty wrecked. That surgery requires serious rest."

"Try telling her that."

"I have. Once." He took off his jacket and Hank heard the clack of beads, his bracelets striking each other. "Why don't you let me hold her? Get yourself a cup of Joe and shake out the kinks."

"Thanks, I was about to go begging." Reluctantly, Hank handed the baby over.

The minute he settled Reed in his arms, Junior's face lit up, and the man started singing. The chant was familiar, the repetitive *hey-a* soporific, relaxing to Hank's ears. Reed's staccato cries dwindled to whimpers. She quieted. Whether that particular miracle resulted from the man's voice or sheer exhaustion was a matter of argument in which Hank didn't care to engage. "What is that?" Hank asked. "Some kind of lullaby?"

Junior looked embarrassed and set the sleepy baby down in the playpen. "Actually, it's a sheepshearing song my aunties taught me. I don't know much else except Top Forty."

Chloe stirred in her sleep. Hannah, thrilled with the quiet, happily beat her tail against the floor.

"You're in love with her, aren't you?" Hank said.

Junior nodded, looking down at the baby. "I delivered her and she's beautiful. How could I not be?"

Hank set down the coffee cup and rubbed his eyes. "That's not who I meant."

"Yeah, I know."

"So. Don't you think we should talk about this?"

Junior shook his head no. "I think if we try that, the only talking we're likely to end up doing's gonna be with fists."

"Probably."

"Besides, I like you too much to break your nose."

"Well, my nose is grateful. It's the rest of me I can't speak for."

"That's the devil of things, isn't it, Hank? Us both fairly decent men, there being only one of her."

Hank handed Junior the cup of coffee he'd poured for himself and got himself a second mug from the cupboard. "Maybe you'll get over it."

"I'm trying."

"Good. So what's the story on Kit?"

Junior sipped his coffee. "Spotted the truck about three this morning. Talked to some of his neighbors at first light. She's with a twenty-year-old kid, I don't know his family. He rodeos, landed in the ribbons a couple of times. This one other guy who was there said she was hanging around downtown at the pool hall. Went with him willingly. Nobody thought anything of it until I asked. Big old dent in the driver's-side panel of Chloe's truck. What do you want to do about it?"

Hank swallowed his mouthful of coffee. He should have stuck to tea, he thought, and poured out half the coffee and refilled it with milk, hoping that might calm his stomach. "I guess wake Chloe up and give her the baby. Then what do you say we pool our efforts and break the son of a bitch's nose?"

Junior grinned. "Well, among a few other parts I can't wait to get my hands on, I'd say that pretty much covers my feelings on the subject as well."

Kit didn't say a word when they pounded open the door. Her red hair was wet as if she'd taken a shower. She was wearing all her clothes, and they seemed to be on straight. She didn't smell like wine or recent sex, and she wasn't hung over so far as Hank could tell. Mouth out to there in a pout, she handed Hank the keys and opened the passenger door herself.

"Hope whatever happened in there was worth it, Kit," he said. "I have to tell you, if you thought Rich ever came down hard on you, when Chloe gets her hands on you you'll think your dad is a diplomat."

Kit looked straight ahead through the windshield as if frozen prairie covered with junked-out cars, frozen tires, and scraggly cattle were a fascinating landscape on the Nature channel.

Junior came out of the house a minute later. He leaned in the passenger door, made a big show of wiping his hands on a handkerchief, the little bit of blood on his knuckles leaving a noticeable streak. He balled it up and stuck it in his pocket. "Girl," he said, "I wouldn't stand in your boots for any amount of money today. The shit is going to *fly* when you get home. And that's probably only the half of it, having to do with swiping the truck and that dent."

Hank looked at Kit and said, "You put a dent in the truck?"

Junior whistled. "And it's a good one. Five hundred in bodywork, by my guesstimate."

Hank suppressed a grin.

"Well, Hank, I got important stuff to do. You give a holler if you need help mopping up when Chloe's finished with Miss Grand Theft Auto here."

"Will do."

They drove home in silence. *Why do I have to like this guy?* Hank was thinking. *All I need is one substantial reason to kick him in the gut, and I've got three or four. But he's decent, and every time I hit somebody over Chloe, I end up making a fool out of myself.* He thought about asking for Kit's perspective, but it was probably better to let Kit stew on what was in store for her. Before he had the transmission in park, she hit the ground running.

Hank walked around back, stood by the fence, and the colt came over to him. He broke the tiny icicles off Thunder's velvety muzzle. The horse's sweet breath came at him in rich, warm, aromatic

steam. Like the first summer morning Hank had spent here, the
horse smelled like a pocket of calm, a time when Hank didn't know
he was about to become the father of the town crier, that his
mother was dying, that Junior Whitebear existed. The horse was
the only smart one of the bunch, standing here unencumbered.
Hank was cold and tired and longed for his bed, but he wanted to
give Chloe some privacy to speak her mind to Kit. He didn't relish
being called on to mediate the particulars or hand out punishment.
After a while it occurred to him he'd best get back in the truck and
drive to the feed store before it closed. He had to; they were completely out of grain. The guy who worked the counter was decent;
maybe he'd let him take it on credit.

A week later New Year's had come and gone. Nobody donned a
party hat, nobody mentioned champagne. They started a game of
Scrabble but neither Chloe nor Kit could spell worth a damn, and
Hank made excuses about needing to do some reading for school.
A letter from his mother sat on the dashboard of the Honda,
unopened, the envelope rippled from the dry cold, the ink fading
from constant exposure to the light. Kit and Chloe stomped around
the cabin passing each other in the hallway and sniping: "If it's not
too much to ask, would you please put the cap back on the goddamn shampoo after you're finished using it?" "Do you really
think I'd use shampoo that doesn't have a pH of at least 4.5? *Duh!*"
Women. What corner of his house was left untouched by them?
Everywhere he stepped there were diapers, hair scrunchies, breast
cream, magazines with articles on improving one's orgasm—and if
he so much as set down a book, Chloe was at his heels, sighing,
snapping it up, and shelving it out of sequence in the bookcase.

Reed delivered a few more nights of first-class inconsolable wailing. They were all so sleep-deprived it took Corrine to suggest that
maybe if they took her to the doctor they could put an end to the
agony. It turned out she needed more supplemental feedings and different vitamins. The iron in the standard baby issue, Dr. Carrywater

suspected, was the root of the trouble. Reed had a sensitive gut, just like her daddy. Nevertheless, once she started crying in earnest, the only sure-fire cure was Junior singing the sheepshearing chant.

I have no fucking pride left, Hank told himself one night when Reed was in full force and he'd driven all over town trying to find the man. *Junior, name your price, just teach me the song.*

Junior taught it to all of them—*hey-a, hey-a,* and the pitch and lilt of the notes wasn't so hard to remember. When he sang, Hank visualized fluffy white lambs by the dozen, willing them to soothe his daughter. The rhythm of the song, rising and falling like breath, was as easy as loving Chloe had once been. When Junior sang, Hank could imagine the small flocks being cajoled into pens, receiving a quick but thorough clip, the shearers sharpening their blades against stone, the first shiver of air against newly exposed skin, all the history of the Navajo people, the complex family lineage. They all sang, even Kit, a chorus of determined foot soldiers, but the little demon could tell when it was Junior singing to her and rarely tolerated impersonation. Chloe would look up at Hank with bloodshot eyes, and what else could Hank do but nod, *Go ahead, call him, sleep with him, hell, I don't care. Just find a way to get us some rest.*

The cabin walls seemed to close in. All those bodies inside, so few of them actually communicating. When school started, Hank threw himself into the task, thankful he had somewhere else to go.

16

Chloe made the call from the Trading Post pay phone rather than take a chance that from home Kit might overhear her lying to her father. She dropped the coins into the slot and dialed the number, easing her glove back on before her fingers froze. Rich answered, "Wedler Brothers Café. This better not be a salesman," and they resumed the argument they'd been having all week.

"Look, this surgery took more out of me than my lousy uterus. I need her here a while longer. You know as well as I do missing one week of high school won't kill anybody." She crossed her fingers. "Kit says all they do the week after Christmas break is show movies. I guess the transition back to real life's just as rough on the teachers."

Her old boss had a built-in bullshit detector. When she'd waitressed for him, he'd rarely fallen for her excuses when she tried to call in sick. The fact was, Rich Wedler knew her as well as a brother might. "I couldn't care diddly if she misses class, Chloe. I can, however, smell horse manure clear through this phone line. Since I know I'm a halfway decent fry cook, I doubt my end of the spatula is flipping the turds. Start telling the truth."

"I am—"

"Incapable, how well I know. Put Princess She-Ra on the phone, and let her try to lie to me. Better yet, let me talk to Hank."

Chloe stared out across the parking lot to the adjacent Chevron station, which appeared to be having a slow day. "Hank's at work, and Kit's in the shower."

Rich laughed. "*Guinness Book of World Records* showers she takes. However, instinct warns me other reasons than my daughter's hygiene are to blame for her not being able to come to the phone. Come on, spill."

The only vehicles parked between the painted lines in the Trading Post parking lot were Corrine's truck, her own Chevy Apache, and in the next row up a fancy rental van that had just finished unloading nine Asian tourists. Out toward the highway she saw the red Jeep Cherokee approaching. Its signal indicator flashed for a left turn. Dammit. Her heart beat a crazy rhythm, and despite all those stitches and missing parts, her groin felt instantly oiled, ready for a coupling she wasn't supposed to want and wasn't prepared to explain. "Okay, Rich. Here's the deal. Things are a little bit shitty right now. Kit's fine, I promise. It's Hank's mom. She's really sick. He flies to California every other weekend, I swear. I can't exactly go flying this premature baby all over hell and back. Also the Olivers, and I quote, 'question Reed's paternity.' Believe me, there's something wicked lonely about this country when it's just me and Reed by ourselves. I can't manage it yet. Call me selfish if that makes you feel better."

"You *are* selfish."

The Chevy Apache looked quaint, frost riming its windshield and the driver's side door slightly concave. One more week, then she was allowed to drive, but when had bullshit warnings like that stopped her from what needed to be done? She'd been motoring along on the sly for days now, and nothing had happened except she'd gotten a few quiet minutes to herself. "I'll send Kit back as soon as I get the go-ahead to have a real life. Driving, lifting, that sort of thing. You have my word."

Rich was quiet a minute, and in the background she could hear the familiar restaurant clatter, the tink of the order-up bell he used to hammer when she didn't move her butt fast enough to deliver the plates. Rich softly called out, "Lita, Sweetmeat, I believe these goddamn pancakes are growing mold."

Chloe smiled, homesick for her old life, its predictable hardships, which seemed manageable compared to this. Her convincing fibs had gotten her out of many a fix. If she told enough of them and waited him out, eventually Rich would see her side of things, cave in.

"All right," he finally said. "But you send me back a daughter in worse shape than I sent you, you pay with interest." He hung up the phone without saying good-bye.

Chloe watched the Cherokee hit the same dip in the asphalt that she always did when she came to collect the mail. A million empty parking spaces, and Junior pulled the Jeep up beside her truck. It was like some weird evolution: Corrine's short-bed, her own truck in the middle, Junior's yuppie sport utility vehicle at the tag end of things. She hung up the phone and walked on over. What good would it do to try to hide? Instinctively the man seemed to sense the moment she drove into town for a checkup, or that she'd be grocery shopping in the disposable diaper aisle the very minute he decided diaper bargains weighed heavily on his mind, too.

"Lord, I wish you'd quit spying on me," she said as he climbed out of the Jeep and shut the door. "I have enough troubles without being reminded what a faithless bitch I am every time I turn the corner."

Junior cupped his gloved hand against her cheek. "Hey, beautiful. Ever going to tell me how you chipped that tooth?"

"I already did. None of your fucking business." She took hold of his hand, intending to pull it away, but even gloved, his fingers felt warm, and it felt so nice to be touched that she let her own hand drop to her side. When, a long minute later, he removed his hand, her cheek felt the abrasive scrape of wind and nothing more.

"How's my Reed?"

"*My* Reed is working on sleep these days. A definite improvement on her previous hobby, screaming."

"Good. And how's our Kit?"

"Still giving me the guilt rays and the silent treatment. Every night she cries herself to sleep in front of the stove. This whole thing is giving Hannah colitis, I swear it is. Every morning I have to clean up one mess or another. And the sand's definitely running out of the hourglass, Junior. I can't hold her dad off much longer, and I don't dare send her home all fucked up when I don't know what's wrong. Damn, I wish she'd open up to me."

"Open up to her and she will."

She delivered him the look he deserved.

"You're getting to be famous in these parts for that mean expression. Corrine tries to copy it, but she can't even come close. Do it again. It gets me all stirred up, *na'nishhod at'ééd.*"

"Didn't your mother tell you it's not nice to make fun of girls who limp?"

"Whoa! Armed yourself with a conversational Navajo dictionary, yeah?"

"I memorize the words, and then I ask Oscar to translate."

"Oscar's a good friend, especially when you open up to him. Probably like you used to do with Kit."

"Dammit, Junior, like it's that easy. No wonder men are so confused. You think everything's about fairness, like I tell her a secret, she tells me what happened that night."

"I can see that you're both working pretty hard to make what's simple stay difficult."

Fine lines around his brown eyes crinkled in delight. So much for his East Coast complexion, she thought. No matter what your cultural background, Northern Arizona's dry winter sucked a person's skin dry. She woke up every morning wishing she owned stock in Nivea face cream. "Why's everything I say strike you so damn funny?"

"Because all the toughness in you is like old skin. So useless you're itching to shed it. You think you need to say all those cuss

words, but you don't. You let all that go for a night with me at the
Pony Soldier. Remember?" He placed his hand against her belly,
and suddenly it was as if she wasn't wearing thermal underwear
and a heavy jacket at all. "Fifty times a day I think about the things
you said, what we did."

Chloe did too, but she'd stop breathing before she'd admit it.
"Well, you're a big boy, and it was only a foolish couple of hours.
Get over it. Go make jewelry and be world famous." She saw the
hurt briefly visit his eyes, and was sorry she'd opened her big
mouth. "People say I shouldn't be allowed out in public."

He took her hands in his and stepped closer. "You are definitely
more interesting in private. Circumstances, Chloe. That's all that's
separating us. Soon as you get this thing with Kit cleared up, let's
go somewhere neutral, talk things over. Decide what to do. Take a
little trip. You ever been to Canyon de Chelly?"

Chloe squinted at the horizon, where the mesas stood waiting
for the light to paint them various pastel colors. "Why not? Maybe
Hank would spring for our gas money. Junior, wake up. The only
thing we should be doing besides pretending we don't know each
other is working at developing amnesia."

He looked to the north and the south, then drew her out of sight of
the Trading Post windows, behind the rented van. She could smell
the bite of exhaust a new car gave off. Her head ached with worry. He
was going to kiss her, and like little hussies, all her nerve endings
stood up on tiptoe. Inside, where her stitches were dissolving as they
healed, things pulled uncomfortably, her flesh trying to resist the call
of desire. "I don't want you to do that," she said, stammering the
words out, stopping only when his mouth closed over hers.

"You wanted it," Junior said softly, then kissed her again.

"Come help me down at the barn," Chloe announced to Kit the
minute she walked in the door. "We can't muck out properly, but
we can scrape up some of the fresh horseshit before it freezes. Put
your jacket on; it's cold out there."

Kit set the sleeping baby down on the blankets in the playpen and slowly began to get up and slip on her tennis shoes. "Boots," Chloe said and opened the back door, going on ahead.

Kit laughed dryly as Chloe confronted the shovel, frozen fast to the ground in three inches of ice. "What? You think this is funny? Here a tool *somebody* forgot to hang up's frozen to the ground, there's work to be done, and you find it *funny?*"

Kit crossed her arms and looked away. The smirk on her face made Chloe want to grab a horse crop and smack the sass out of her. But Kit wasn't the one who needed sense whacked into her. "Fine, then. Trot your butt up to the house and bring me a pan full of hot water."

She watched the girl step carefully across the path of stove ashes Hank spread across the snow each morning. He had given up trying to stop her from doing any work and settled for admonitions about being careful. Maybe he didn't know she was driving, but she could tell he suspected. Shit, he was probably checking the odometer, planning to hide her keys next. Her eyes teared up at the thought of all that caring. Every night he came in the door exhausted, took a wailing baby from her arms, and rocked her to sleep. Chloe was an inch away from packing it in, but Hank never once lost his cool. He was more adept at diapering than she could ever hope to be, continually pointing out some tidbit on child development he'd found time to read and mull over. He fell into bed and slept while she lay there worrying. On top of all that his mother was dying, and Chloe still hadn't located the guts to tell him about what Kit had done, about that letter from Tucson, which might be from her very-much-alive mother. She gulped cold air, trying to clear her head. Thunder pawed the ice, leaning his weight against the fence, feverish with winter confinement. *If I was home in the canyon,* Chloe mused, *by now I'd've hit the road. This is far too much shit for anyone like me to sort out. I'm selfish. I lie. I do all right with a dog because dogs won't hold you to a schedule. But a baby? What was I thinking? And Junior Whitebear—there goes the wrongest move I could possibly make.*

That was her old self talking, and she wasn't the only one regress-
ing. Seemed like for each pound Chloe'd taken off these last few
weeks, Kit had added one. Inside the barn, she broke the baling wire
on the second to last bale of hay. Oscar was supposed to deliver them
more this weekend. There was a little of her money left, but Hank
would pay the feed bill; he had the check all made out and sitting on
the kitchen table. Her breasts throbbed. She nursed the baby whenever she could, but Reed never seemed to empty her. Out loud, she
said, "Well, Thunder, I can't save the world, but I have enough milk
to feed six hungry orphans. Maybe I can sell it, what do you think?"
She threw the colt a quarter flake to settle his nerves. When she
turned around to wipe her hands, Kit was standing in the barn doorway with the saucepan of water, waiting for instruction.

"You were a Girl Scout," Chloe said. "Figure it out."

With little ceremony Kit upended the water over the shovel
blade. Just as Chloe expected, with a loud ping, a good-sized piece
of metal chipped off and the shovel toppled to the ground.
Thunder startled and ran around his hay into the barn.

Kit swore softly.

"You learn anything from that?"

"I guess I should have poured the water on the *ground*, not the
shovel. Do I have to pay for it?"

"No, you have to live with it. Every time you want to dig a hole
and can't get the shovel blade to cut in straight, you'll remember.
When bad things happen, these little lessons can be very consoling."

Kit looked up at her, annoyed. "Well, *déjà*-fucking-*vu*. You
sounded just like Lita for a second there. Did you take two of those
estrogen pills today by accident?"

Chloe handed her the shovel. "No, I took one, and so far I feel as
mean as I did when I still had all my parts." Thunder came out of
the barn, nosed them nervously, then lifted his tail and shit all over
the remains of the hay flake. "Guess what, Kit? Right behind you
there's a big steaming pile of work calling out your name."

Kit huffed and scraped the arena with her broken shovel. Chloe
stood along the fenceline, watching, pointing out a few places

where the ice was slushy and making her work those down to the dirt. Then she watched as the girl hung the shovel on its proper hook and picked up the saucepan. "Come on up to the house. I'll make us some cocoa."

"Let me make it," Kit said. "I'm supposed to be helping you. I've been such a b-i-t-c-h lately it's the least I can do."

Chloe nursed Reed while Kit worked in the kitchen. She listened to her daughter's noisy suckling and felt such relief at letting all that milk go. *Fill yourself up, skinny girl. Get chubby. Drink all afternoon; this bar is wide open.* Junior's face above hers in the parking lot at the Trading Post flashed through her mind, shaming her nearly to tears. It seemed like before he kissed anyone—Dog, Reed, herself—he always touched the tip of his tongue to his lips. Hank kissed like a boy just learning the art, eager to try something new every time. Junior's kisses she'd recognize blindfolded. They were professional. And effective. Since Reed, Hank kissed her with respect, but behind it, desire lurked. Like last night, him saying wasn't the six-week waiting period just about up? He'd done some reading—did he ever stop reading?—and thought six weeks after female surgery a woman was healed enough to make love to the man she loved. So which man would that be? Junior pressed his mouth to hers, and Chloe swore she tasted something sugary flowing between them, something as sweet as that night in the motel. Meanwhile, Hank waited patiently.

She was boxed in here, no visible outlet. She laid Reed across her lap and rubbed her back the way Dr. Carrywater showed her would relieve any gas. Her daughter stubbornly clung to things, necessary burps, the silver rattle, strands of Kit's long red hair. Reed didn't relish the idea of letting go any more than her mother did holding on.

Chloe cleared her throat. "Tell me what happened, Kit. You know it's not going to get manageable until you do."

Kit set the cocoa tin on the counter. "I don't know why you keep bugging me. I gave my cherry away. Big deal. Get over it, okay? I did."

"If it's such a little deal, then what's the harm in telling me?"

Kit sighed. "What in the hell could possibly change if you know the details?"

Chloe nodded. "You're right. Nothing will change except you might feel a little cleaner."

"I feel clean."

"Because you take three showers a day, Kit? What's up with that? You used to be fine with one."

Kit turned the wooden spoon she'd been using to stir the cocoa over in her hands. She didn't speak.

"Tell me. After, eventually, you can start having a life again. It won't ever be a regular life, but it does get tolerable. If you hold it inside, this thing will eat you from the inside out."

Kit looked straight into her eyes. "You hold it inside. You keep everything in. Sometimes I don't even know who you are."

"Maybe you're right. If so, I'm a walking example of what you don't want to become. I can't commit myself one hundred percent to anything, not even to Hank. I'm scared and angry all the time. I'm uneducated and good for nothing except horses. I love you, kiddo. Please do this another way."

"God, Chloe, let it go! I don't even think about it."

Chloe took a deep breath, damning Junior's advice that the only way to unlock Kit was to first use the key on herself. "Did I ever tell you about the job I had at the fairgrounds?"

"No. Why? Did you break a shovel there?"

"No, I broke this." Chloe grinned wide to expose her chipped front tooth. "Want to hear how it happened?"

Kit stirred the cocoa and stared glassily at the cacti on the windowsill. "Bet it wouldn't make any difference if I said no."

"That's right. Listen up, Kit. I'm only going to say this once. You tell anybody what I said, I'll call you a liar."

Kit set the wooden spoon down on the stove. "This is going to make me cry, isn't it?"

Chloe straightened out Reed's tiny clenched fist. "I don't know. Maybe it's supposed to. I was eighteen when it happened," she said. "I knew it all. Same as you, Kit, only you really are smarter than me. There was this traveling rodeo. Toured all the county fairs. The guy was handsome, headed for the PRCA, and he told me I was cute. Me, the girl who fed horses, mucked stalls, and got paid four bucks an hour to push around a wheelbarrow full of shit. Watching bullriders break their necks came free. So did being an idiot. 'Come watch me,' he said. 'I win my event, I'll buy you a cold one and a night you won't forget.'"

"If this is how you lost your cherry, I really don't care."

"Will you just shut up and listen?"

"God. Sor-*ry*."

"He missed the money by two points. His buddies were riding him about losing. I started to go back to work, but he said losing wasn't any reason not to celebrate. I remember him saying that as clear as I remember anything about that night. We went to a country-and-western bar. They never even asked for my ID. The whole thing felt weird, right from the start, you know, those icky vibes you get when you're in over your head? I asked him to please drive me back to the fairgrounds. He said, 'No problem, we'll go right now.' Then in the parking lot, he opened his door and I started to climb in, but he yanked me back and started kissing me. It wasn't what I had in mind, but I thought, *Fine, just kiss him. Afterwards you can go home and brush your teeth.* But the next thing I knew he shoved his hand in—" She gestured to the fly front of her jeans, across which Reed lay sleeping. "Here."

"Okay, Chloe. You can stop now. I get the picture."

Chloe thought about how she had been thinner then, all muscles and bone. Wiry enough so she regularly took horses over the jumps bareback. The cowboy shoved her down on the seat of this truck and with one hand yanked both her jeans and underwear down together. *I'm hobbled like a horse,* she remembered thinking; *even if I can get away, I can't go far.* Her ankles burned, chafing as he shoved her legs apart. On top of her, he was so heavy she couldn't find breath enough to scream.

"The buckle on his belt kept smacking me on my hip, but that was small-time compared to how awful it felt when he put his dick inside me."

Kit shut her eyes.

"There was this little rip in the headliner of his truck, up near the rearview mirror. From time to time, I could catch a glimpse of my own face looking back at me, like a separate person, the one I never listened to."

Kit refused to meet her eyes. Chloe was relieved. No matter what Junior thought, she couldn't tell Kit how just before he came, the cowboy had torn open her shirt, bent down, and bit her right breast so savagely that he'd lacerated the skin just above the nipple. Like some rabid animal, as if he wanted to tear it off. That whenever Reed started to nurse on that side there was this awkward and difficult moment when she remembered the cowboy's perfect teeth in the bloody grin, and how she felt both Reed and herself struggling to move past that barrier.

"The first chance I got, I hit him with my fist. Which was the biggest mistake I made."

Kit made a soft cry.

"Come on, Kit. The guy was twice as strong as I was. One of the times he hit me back, he chipped this tooth. A souvenir. I didn't even feel it, I was so grateful to hear him finish, to feel him climb off of me and shove me out the door into the parking lot. Then the truck started up. The sound of that engine told me two things: I was alive and that son of a bitch had hit the road."

Kit went to the kitchen sink and leaned over, gripping the sides. The sweet smell of scalding cocoa filled the air.

"Kit?"

"No."

"I was going to ask if you could take the baby. My legs are falling asleep. I still have trouble getting up from this position."

"I can take her." They changed places, and Chloe walked to the corner window and pulled the curtain aside. She twisted her hair into a ponytail, then let it drop across her shoulders. Kit leaned over Reed, talking baby talk, her wiry mass of red hair looking for all the world like sprung copper wiring. Chloe fought the urge to open the back door and run to her truck, to just get in and drive away. "Whatever happened to you that night also happened to me, Kit. You're under eighteen. They call it rape in the eyes of the law."

"Chloe, it wasn't like that."

"Does that mean sex was both your ideas?"

Kit tucked Reed's blanket under her feet. "Well, it kind of started out that way."

Chloe bit the inside of her cheek. She knelt down at Kit's chair and laid her head in the girl's lap, pressing her cheek against Reed's tiny sleeping face. She reached a finger up, hovering above the soft spot in Reed's skull.

"The fontanel," Kit whispered. "I learned that in Science."

Chloe lifted her face. "Don't chicken out on me, Kit."

Kit sighed. "Afterwards, all I could think was that someday some asshole was going to try to put his hands on Reed. It made me so goddamn angry! I'm glad Junior beat him up. No, I'm not. I mean, I sort of liked him until he stuck his thing in me. It hurt, and he wouldn't stop when I asked him to. He goes, 'It's already in, I have to finish,' like I was a video game he'd paid for. I wanted to like it. It seemed important. He sort of reminded me of Junior, and I love Junior, he's so nice. And handsome. But it was pretty much like you said it would be, nasty, and I wish I could go back and do it over."

"Did he use protection, Kit? A rubber, spermicide?"

Kit let out a nervous giggle, and Chloe could hear the sob building up behind it. "A green condom. Green! Never thought the first one I'd see in action would be that color."

"That's good."

"Don't say that, Chloe. None of it was any good. Here I've been waiting all my life for a boy to like me, and now I'll have to become a lesbian."

"I think there are a few more alternatives open to you."

"Well, I don't."

"Even if that happened, it wouldn't be the worst thing. Especially if you wore the same size shoes."

Kit smiled. "Right."

Chloe stroked Kit's hair, pulling damp strands away from her flushed cheeks. Rich's daughter wore her emotions like gaudy makeup. In the hospital, toting her bag of hamburgers and the teddy bear, Kit had seemed wide open and innocent. The last two weeks the only place she looked was inward.

"Chloe?"

"What?"

"Did you and Junior—you know—while you were in that motel?"

"Of course not. I just had surgery. And I'm with Hank."

"But you're not married. You said you couldn't make a commitment."

"People don't have to be married to keep promises. We slept on separate beds and waited out the snow. That's all."

Kit sighed. "I'm glad. Because if something happened to you and Hank, I'd just give up on the world, I swear I would."

"Nothing's going to happen."

Kit wrinkled her nose. "Whoa, all of a sudden Reed smells really funky. I think she needs her diapers changed."

Chloe patted Kit's shoulders. "Go take a long bath. I'll deal with Miss Stinky. Use up all my bubble bath. Promise me you'll cry. Then the three of us will go into town and buy something really good for dessert. You can even drive my dented truck."

Kit looked up at her in awe, the way she used to when Chloe had explained to her various secrets to riding horses. No way was Chloe going to jeopardize that by telling the truth.

At two A.M. she got up to feed Reed, surprised when the baby went back to sleep. Sitting alone in the rocker, Chloe was restless, fitful, the lies ricocheting around in her skull. Could she keep them all straight? Dinner had been fraught with jagged silences. Hank talked about his day; Chloe nodded in the appropriate places. They made hot fudge sundaes, but nobody finished eating them. Kit still avoided direct eye contact. Now she was asleep on the floor, but sooner or later, Chloe knew Kit would have her own two A.M. accounting to face down, and she couldn't help her with that. She wondered where Junior was. Asleep? Or deep in conversation at the Museum Club bar with some woman who was deciding whether or not she'd take him home. The best thing to do was take Kit to Dr. Carrywater tomorrow, get her checked over and outfitted with birth control. That wasn't overstepping boundaries, it was thinking smart. All those years ago, she wished there'd been some-one to do it for her.

Hospitals were bound by law to report such crimes, but laws hadn't convinced Chloe it was necessary to press charges. Her fos-ter parents had warned her about older men. Plus, she had beer on her breath, had gone with the cowboy willingly. The fair job ended, and she went back to working for Fats. The Mexican boys who loved to tease her and steal kisses quickly learned to take no for an answer. *La Rubia* is in a bad mood, they whispered behind her back, loud enough for Fats to hear. Under the tiny stitches in her breast, the tooth imprints turned black, then began to ooze yel-low with infection. She returned to the doctor. Chloe remembered standing in the privacy of an empty stall late one afternoon, her shirt unbuttoned, bra lying on a nearby bale of hay. The doctor said to finish all the antibiotics and change the dressing three times a day. Fats walked in, carrying three sacks of feed, which he dropped when he saw her. He groaned, a low, sorrowful, male noise she never wanted to hear again in her life. He high-stepped through the spilled sweet feed, saying, "Morgan, who's responsible for this? Better tell me now, otherwise I'm going to rip anyone who comes within five feet of you to shreds with my bullwhip."

She hadn't, but Fats didn't let her alone. He heaped on chores, forced her to exercise twice as many horses, bought her lunches she didn't want, and insisted she eat when simply the idea of any-thing entering her body made her throat close. He'd said, "You may hate me now, but together we'll make you forget about what happened."

Men always wanted to make things better, even when all they could possibly accomplish in doing so was make it worse. The really good ones had a complex that way. The blue-dark of the night was broken by Arizona's winter stars, and in a few hours the sky would begin to lighten at the edges. Hank would get up, shower in the dark so as not to wake anybody, eat his breakfast cereal alone, drive off to work. His life moved forward in a linear progression. Chloe was amazed that even sixteen years physically removed, the past kept tapping her on the shoulder. Fats had meant well. While rape seemed like the worst thing that could happen to a girl, it wasn't. A year later she'd turned up pregnant with Fats's baby, purely by accident. The sleep anesthetic cost more than she had in her savings. The doctor's job was to switch on the machine. It made a constant, whirring noise until the fetus was expelled, when it thumped distinctly, just that one time. He checked the contents of the canister, patted her knee, went on to his next patient. A half hour later, the nurse let her sit up and get dressed, made her drink a Dixie cup of pineapple juice. Dear God, she prayed, let that green condom have done its job. Do not let Kit be pregnant.

She must have nodded off in the rocker, because one minute she was feeling regretful about the abortion, and the next Hank was there, kissing her neck, placing Reed in her arms. "What a picture you two make," he whispered, quietly so he wouldn't wake Kit.

Chloe could feel Reed rooting around for her nipple. Hank stood there a moment, his briefcase in hand. "I love you," he said, as if he'd been up all night rehearsing for a part he knew he wasn't going to get. Then he shut the door quietly behind him.

17

"Because I think there's a little more to being a father than taking the boy to dinner on Saturday nights, Corrine." Junior presented his case, taking care to mention that Dog deserved *both* their
best efforts, but Corrine wasn't hearing it.

"He calls you on the phone every night."

"Sure, and I get to say 'Sweet dreams,' but that isn't the same as
telling him a bedtime story. There's no hug at the end, only a dial
tone. I can't speak for Walter, but that's not enough for me."

Corrine sipped her Coke, attending to the stacks of paperwork
covering her desk. Junior hovered in the doorway to her small
office, waiting. Would the winds shift his way? He'd been in town
over a month now—proof he took his son seriously. Things around
the Trading Post were tense. Over the next few days, magazine
people would shoot the yearly advertising layouts. Unhappily for
Corrine, who liked to run it all, this coincided with a Trading Post
trunk show of pawn bracelets. Tourists were due to descend. The
motel was already full up with reservations. When Shane Myers
ran the Post that kind of schedule was regular day-to-day business,

but Shane was a wild man. Corrine didn't look equal to the task. Not to mention it was January, the dead of winter. The best people could do was bow their heads and trudge out the long trek toward spring. Yet Junior sensed there was something else going on: Corrine's cheeks were puffy, and her coppery skin had the slightest yellow cast to it. Secret drinking, or just plain neglect? Junior watched her crumple her empty Coke can into the wastebasket, yank another off the six pack on her desk and pop the tab.

"You got a touch of flu going there, Corrine? Maybe you need to take a couple of days off instead of jacking yourself up on sugar and caffeine."

"I take one afternoon off, this place falls apart. What I need is a vacation."

"Take one. The Post will survive."

She tapped her pen against the Coke can. "Too much going on right now. I'll go just before spring, before things get really busy."

Junior knew she meant that about as much as he intended to pick up his father's ashes today. Corrine might send Dog on a trip. She might even tell Oscar to bag the repair work for a few days and go elk hunting, but she hadn't been kidding when she'd told him she was married to the job. He understood. Once he'd felt that same way about the silver.

She motioned Junior to step aside so she could sign a UPS receipt. The waiting driver grabbed the clipboard and scurried away.

"Come grab some late lunch with me, Corrine. We can't settle anything with all these interruptions. We need to finish this conversation concentrating on what's best for Walter."

In the Trading Post restaurant she ordered a bowl of mutton stew, then jumped up out of her chair to holler forgotten instructions to one of her clerks. While the cook assembled the meal, Junior stared out the plate-glass windows at the rocky outcroppings behind the restaurant. Drab by comparison to what lay a few miles to the west, eventually the stones gathered enough strength of conviction to fall off into the colorful maw of the Grand Canyon.

Long ago, before his mother got sad about everything and stayed indoors all the time, she had taken him hiking, entering the canyon via a secret trail, which only the Havasupi claimed to know about. *First People lived here over four thousand years ago*, she'd told him, and his child's mind tried hard to wrap itself around so large a number. To what could he compare it? Stars in the night sky? Grains of sand at the edge of Lake Powell? Hand in hand, they walked among the travertine pools, looking for evidence of his ancestors. His mother was a white woman, but she knew about the split-twig figures the people had left behind, examples of which he'd only seen in museums. She knew stories deep in her heart, and when she told them, his own heart listened. That was supposed to be Jimmy Whitebear's task, but Jimmy only knew one story and it came in a bottle. Junior's mother revered this canyon as much as she did the Navajo way of life. She prodded her boy to seek out arrowheads, which somehow she stumbled across by the score while her son had trouble spotting a single one. He understood now that what she intended did not concern the locating of arrowheads; this was her way of instructing him to develop an affinity with the natural world, a world in which solace existed. If as a child he learned to behold the natural beauty of the landscape, he might not be lured into town away from his tribe. He might believe the reservation was home, not a ghetto. *Paradise*, she had called it. But paradise hadn't been strong enough to keep her tethered to the land of the living. She'd hung from that tree like a broken bird. He wasn't tall enough to cut her down. He would never be that tall. The waitress brought his tea over, and he smiled, thanked her, and meant it.

Junior blew over the surface of the hot liquid. Outside the snow was thin, blown away by the incessant wind. Hardly more than a glittering dust now coated the rocks. He thought of Chloe's mouth under his a few days ago, when he'd kissed her in the parking lot and lightly touched his fingers to his lips. We have traveled miles beyond smitten, he said to himself. We are standing at the edge of the canyon, and all that plenty is within our reach. But it's a long ways down. We got no parachutes to help us make sure we land in one piece.

"So when is the memorial service for Jimmy?" Corrine asked when she returned to the table. "Or you planning to hand him over to the Catholic church?"

"Let them do the dirty work? I don't think so." Junior stirred his tea though he'd added nothing to it. "Jimmy's pretty comfortable up there on the undertaker's shelf. The other night I had this dream about him. He asked me to leave him there until spring. 'Wait until the first good solid sunny day,' he said. 'Then crack open a bottle of green death, dump me in. I'll toast my own passage.'"

"He's haunting you," Corrine said. "*Chindee.*"

"In the spring I'll haul his ashes off to Canyon del Muerto. He always enjoyed going to Chinlé. He just didn't much care for doing any work once he got there."

"I'm so tired I can relate." Corrine's stew arrived. She pushed it around the bowl with her fork creating a little well in the center, then she laid the fork down on her napkin. "Dog says you promised him a camping trip. I expect you to clear things like that with me before you go getting him all worked up."

"If I give you a hundred dollars, will you *try* to call him Walter?"

Corrine held out her hand for the money.

Junior emptied his wallet.

"This is only sixty-five dollars."

"I'm good for the rest of it. I told him we can't go camping until spring or summer. Thought maybe by then you might not hate the idea so much."

"So you really are planning to stick around that long."

Junior picked up Corrine's fork and speared a tasty chunk of mutton on the tines. He dipped it in the gravy and held the bite out to her. Sauce pooled downward, forming a tear that threatened to drip. Corrine made a face, but after awhile took it in her mouth, chewed, and swallowed. "It's kind of hard to be a father long distance."

"Staying at that motel without room service must be getting pretty old."

"It's not so bad. I'm getting me a great soap collection. Every day, rain or shine, they leave me a new bar. Camay brand. Easy on the skin. Might never have to buy soap again."

Corrine signaled the waitress for a refill on her Coke. "We're running low on your stock. I heard Aaron Scholder is looking for a roommate. Unless you plan on setting up a studio in your motel room."

Junior paused a minute. "You're going to wreck your kidneys drinking that brown sugar water, Corrine. How about a cup of chamomile tea? It's great for settling the nerves. Once your nerves settle down, you can develop an appetite for something more nourishing than potato chips."

"Coke and chips have served me just fine all these years. I don't need a lecture from somebody who lived off room service and takes all his meals in restaurants." She unfolded her napkin, twisted it into a cone shape and tucked it next to her bowl. "You and I both know why you're sticking around. It has very little to do with Dog—sorry, Walter. Don't try to hide it, Junior."

"Never said I was."

"We get one halfway decent white schoolteacher, and you make it your personal goal to drive him down the highway? He leaves, you'll break the boy's heart."

"I like the man," he said. "I'm here for Walter, so why on earth would I go after hurting his teacher?"

Corrine shook her head. "I don't know Chloe that well, but Oscar seems to think she's all right. Intuition tells me her heart's the kind that once broken, don't mend."

In the fading winter light, Corrine looked as old as her auntie, who had slowly succumbed to diabetes, helping things along with alcohol. Junior was about to bring up the subject of genetic links, the importance of regular exercise, having her insulin levels tested, and to once again put in his two cents' regarding diet, but Corrine had cared for the woman all her growing-up years, she didn't need to hear that sad refrain spill out of the mouth of a man whose father drank his dinner. "Walter can probably get along without a dad, but not a mom. I wish you'd start taking care of yourself, Corrine."

She forced a smile. "You pick him up from school, I can make it home an hour earlier."

He took her hand and gave it a squeeze. "You're the mother of my child. All you had to do was ask."

Junior stopped at the pawn case on his way out. The clerk had all the jewelry out, and was in the process of separating and cataloging the bracelets. She'd polished each item and now spritzed the glass with Windex. When Junior was a kid, examining the pieces in this case felt akin to studying the masters in a museum. These guys knew how to keep the designs simple, showcase the stones. Nowadays, the craft seemed dependent on the silver's ability to fancydance, shake a tail feather, detract from the poor quality stone available.

"That ring over there. What's the Indian-to-Indian price for it?"

The clerk scurried off with the ring in hand to get Oscar to figure it. Corrine was deep into negotiations with the magazine people regarding their layouts. The jewelry, the jewelry. So much silver in this one room he could hear the echoes of tools grinding, polishing, smell the lost wax burning away from one-of-a-kind molds. He felt the ghost of sweat gathering between his shoulder blades on those nights when he was one with the silver and didn't want to let go of how good working felt. A real father set up a proper workshop and invited his son in, spent long afternoons and early mornings on weekends revealing the secrets of his trade. A real artist answered Sami Gee's telephone messages, which, when turned face down in a stack, made their own kind of recycled notepad. All he needed to do was cruise some Scottsdale galleries, strike the profile and he'd be thick with orders. Take the first step. Execute the old style. People would buy. The stock was low. But whenever he let his mind approach the subject, it was as if he encountered a castle wall. There didn't seem to be any drawbridge to lift, or chink in the mortar wherein he might carve entrance. If the desire had dried up entirely, from now on, that was how it would be, this burned-out dead spot in his heart, this cultivated black hole. He considered the energy he was expending on wanting Chloe and wondered, briefly, if it might consist of redirected jewelry passion. It made him ashamed to admit it, but just the idea of having her seemed compelling enough to risk jettisoning his craft. What was art besides a pose one struck? He was tired of inlaid spiny oyster shell, the way it flaked when he tried to coax it into interesting shapes. Decent turquoise in workable sizes was almost impossible to locate, and nobody liked the imported stuff, which seemed crazy, since it all came from the same earth. But that was what had caught his eye about the ring. It was a damn good stone.

"Oscar says you can have it for one fifty, but not to tell Corrine. Wrap it up?"

Junior slid it onto his left pinkie finger, where it fit precisely. "I'll wear it." He looked for bills in his wallet and thanks to Corrine, had to resort to the credit card. He wandered over to Oscar, who sat behind the counter with a soldering gun. "Thanks for the square deal."

"I'm curious, Mr. Big-pants Jeweler. What you plan on doing with that ring?"

"For now," Junior wiggled his little finger and glanced down, admiring the stone, "wear it. Nice chunk of Lander, however. Begs to be reset."

"Won't get no argument from me. Certain people have had an eye on it for some time."

"Certain people?"

"Well, one in particular."

"I'm getting the idea this particular certain person is someone I know."

Oscar soldered a broken hinge back onto a heavy concho belt, waited for his work to cool, then handed it over to Junior to inspect.

"Hoo, you always had the touch for fixing things. You're the man. You're talking about Chloe, *enit*?"

Oscar pushed his glasses up his nose. "She tried it on a bunch of times. It fit her ring finger."

"Why didn't she buy it?"

"Price scared her off. I got the feeling she don't ask for stuff like other women. Can't do it. That's a rare thing among women."

Junior thumbed the band from underneath. "I guess."

Oscar set down his equipment and faced his friend. "They was doing pretty good before you came along. Don't mess up their life just to scratch the itch, you know?"

Junior studied the stone a while, its speckled blue surface featuring the slightest dent, like an egg with a slight blemish. "Itches go away. This goes deeper."

Oscar sighed and picked up his soldering gun. "Buddy, you can get along without, I heartily recommend avoiding the tangle."

Junior pulled up to the curb outside the mortuary, looking at the reflection of his red car in the window, the engine idling. Plain gold letters announced the serious business of laying the dead to rest. All he had to do was walk in and tell them his name, claim the ashes, drive a couple hours, throw them over the edge. Then he was done with Jimmy Whitebear forever. Instead he gunned the engine and drove across town to the elementary school. School wasn't out for a half hour. There was time to see his horse.

Sally lipped his bare fingers, nickering softly, delivering horse kisses so sweet and tender it only made things worse.

"Hey, Sally. You craving a foal this spring? You miss Chloe, don't you. I guess that makes two of us."

The mare butted her massive head against his chest, rubbing her winter coat, complex with its own itches, against the fringe of his jacket.

Junior kissed her muzzle, inhaling deeply. "Spring," he promised. "We'll ride again. After that, let's start looking for a boyfriend for you."

Inside the classroom children were working quietly in groups, four of them clustered around the aquarium, several in a circle of desks, and still others in the rear of the classroom, using primary colors to paint on butcher paper tacked to easels. Hank had two kids in chairs at his desk, where the subject seemed to be spelling. Dog was one of them. He sat in the tiny chair, looking down at his hands. Hank said, "Another way to look at it is you got two right, Dog. Come on, lift up that handsome chin. One way or another, these words still have to get spelled."

Chuey Alberto poked Hank's arm. "Hey. What for we got to spell this crap when most the time we spend is talking?"

"Or if you be an artist," Dog offered eagerly. "Artist don't got to spell nothing except his name."

Hank looked up at Junior, who had unobtrusively entered the classroom and now stood behind the boys. He nodded acknowledgment, then focused his attention back on his charges. "Someday you boys might need to write a very important letter," Hank said. "Or want to write down a story for your kids. You might have the kind of job that depends on your spelling words right, or costly mistakes will be made. Spelling's hard work, I know. I can't spell very many words in your language. Why don't you practice writing down these five words that you missed. Three times each ought to be enough. I'll come back and check on you in a few minutes."

The boys' dark heads bent to their task, and Hank came over to Junior. They watched two girls painting at the easel. Hank said, "We don't have any budget at all for art. I've had to dilute the tempera so much they might as well be painting with watercolors."

"You don't need to apologize to me."

"Yes, I do. This isn't the level of teaching I'm capable of offering. There are days it makes me ashamed. Today happens to be one of them."

Junior retrieved a brush one of the children dropped and

exclaimed over her broad strokes on the paper. "A lot of energy going on with the yellow in there. Keep up the good work."

"Volunteers are always welcome."

"Why don't I buy you some art supplies?"

"I'm sure the children would be grateful." Hank glanced up at the clock. "Already time to get them in their seats and cut them loose."

"I'll stand in the back here. Don't let me rush you."

At Hank's request they quickly sponged up spills and put away supplies. The girls sat in their seats with folded hands atop desks and the boys, bowing to the unspoken rules of masculinity, settled for sitting somewhat quietly. Hank stood in front of the world map, and together they watched the clock. As soon as the minute hand ticked over to three, everyone rose quietly and lined up. He walked them out the door, and Junior caught his son by the shoulder.

"Hey, Walter. Today's our day. On the way home, I thought we'd stop for some fries. Your favorite, right?"

Dog's smile was cautious. "Can I ask Chuey to come along?"

"Sure."

Dog ran to catch up with the boy, and Junior watched as his son received an instantaneous rebuff. Chuey went off laughing with his friends. Junior's heart cleaved for the boy.

Dog's lower lip trembled, but he managed to say, "Had to go to his grandmother's."

Junior patted his back. "Another time he'll come. You'll see. Let's go. You're going to have to help me eat the fries. I need serious help, Walter. Then how about we pick up some groceries, surprise your mom by starting dinner?"

"I don't know cooking."

"All the famous chefs are men. I'll teach you."

"Okay." Dog stuck the tie on his jacket hood in his mouth. They drove onto Main, the radio blaring KTNN, giving the Mormons and the picture takers a blast of words nobody had bothered to spell at all until white people decided they needed a dictionary.

Even on this cold day, the lure of the open road was palpable.

After stopping at the bank for cash, Junior gunned the engine and Dog cheered.

"Junior? Can we drive all the way to Phoenix?"

"Some time, sure. Just not today."

"Why not today?"

"Your mom wouldn't have any reason to eat dinner if her boy didn't come home."

"She never eats the dinner. Just me and Oscar do."

"You think she's feeling okay?"

"Maybe. She says Coke settles her nerves and not to bother her."

They ordered the fries and stood waiting in line. "Coke's not real good for you, Walter. It's okay once in awhile, but the best thing for a man is water. Six glasses a day at least. Lots of good, clean water. The same holds true for—"

"Can I have a quarter for the video game?"

Junior handed him one. That will teach me to lecture to an eight-year-old, he thought. He pictured the streams that ran through Canyon del Muerto. They would be frozen now, little more than icy ribbons, glinting silver with promise. But come spring, water would course down from the Chuska Mountains, torrential at first, almost angrily fingering their way through the sandy soil. Given all that had happened in the canyon, the water had every right to feel acrimonious. For three seasons the streams would flow steadily, just as they had over the past fifty million years, cutting their truths deep into the sheer-walled canyon, into land as unfathomable as Jimmy Whitebear's heart.

18

The little girl outside the drugstore looked nine, maybe ten years old, and God alone knew what possessed her to sit in thirty-degree weather, clutching a cardboard box. It was early Sunday morning, the day Kit would fly home, but there were hours yet until they had to leave for the airport. Kids this age were home watching cartoons or trying to gather enough of the thin snow in their hands to put together a halfway decent snowman. "Excuse me?" she said, aiming her words in Chloe's general direction.

Chloe didn't need Hank to give her a mythic example on leaving well enough alone. A year ago, when they were still getting to know each other, when life seemed manageable, occasionally even simple, she'd been curious to learn he taught mythology at the community college. From folklore to legends to crazy old sayings even she herself used, Hank knew the meanings behind them and more. *Pandora's box*, she'd asked him once. *What's the deal there? Sexual innuendo, like pretty much any story to do with women?* At first he gave her the short answer. *Basically it's death and rebirth, with complications.* News flash. And now that she gave it some thought, she could almost recall the particulars—something about the box having originally been a vase for storing honey.

That's right, in the blink of a tired translator's eye the womblike vase filled with blessings had transformed into a box of curses unleashed upon the world because of woman's curiosity. The only good that had come of that was hope, lying at the bottom of the chest like a consolation prize. No wonder those male scholars had so much to write about.

She knew she should avoid eye contact, ignore the child like the cookie-pushing Girl Scout she probably was, run in the store, get her medicine refilled, and drive straight home. But someday Reed could be this wide-eyed, shabbily dressed white kid with a mission so important it kept her outdoors on a cold winter morning.

"What are you selling?"

The girl reached her mittened hands inside the box and brought out a puppy. "One left."

"Oh," Chloe said. "I was expecting Thin Mints."

Big brown eyes blinked at her. "He's free."

"Nothing's free. I've already got a dog."

Her eyes clouded over. "I've got to find him a home or my dad says he'll have to drown it. Don't you know anybody who could use a dog?"

Oh, damn, damn, and ten miles down the road *past* damn. Motherhood had tipped her over from feeling fiercely protective of her own canine to wanting to save them all. In Indian country everyone seemed to believe the animal world took care of itself. Animals that didn't get flattened on the highway survived, but was survival all they deserved? Did every horse have to ride out the winter with barrel-stave ribs? Was the best folks could do for their dogs was to let them run the streets, dig through trash in an effort to fill their bellies? Domestication was man's responsibility; it wasn't as if a person could untie the bond of ownership when a dog got old, bit a mailman, or, left unspayed, gave birth. Chloe didn't have the *dinero* to buy every single homeless pooch a bone. Drowning—it made her so angry she wanted to hold this kid's father's head underwater in the stock tank, let his world grow dim at the edges, hear him choke on the last of his hope. Then she'd yank him up by the hair and ask what he thought of his prairie solution.

"Let me take a look at him."

The kid held the pup out for inspection.

Chloe removed her glove and eased her hand under his abdomen, feeling for the telltale bloat that indicated parasites. A hard, round, warm belly pushed against the ribs that met her fingers. The little guy shivered with all his might, and Chloe knew however better or worse his siblings had fared, she was holding the runt of the litter. Girls this age had good reason to favor the pup most likely to be drowned. They were beginning to realize, as Kit recently had illustrated to her, just what lay in store for them as members of the second sex. Pup probably needed a hundred dollars' worth of veterinary attention. At home in California her buddy Gabe Hubbard could have taken care of it *gratis*. Here, vet care took real money. She tucked the puppy inside her jacket and zipped it to her chin. "You can relax. He's got a home now."

The girl stood there mute.

"Here's a dollar. Go buy yourself a chocolate bar. That's all I can spare. I have to buy medicine. And dog food."

She clutched the money and ran off, leaving the box behind.

Wearily Chloe picked up the box and took it to her truck. Inside the store she cradled the puppy as she walked down the baby aisle, wondering if Reed had bottles decorated with cartoon characters, she might experience happier nights. She picked up a small bag of puppy chow. Baby food and estrogen: Witness the basic elements of my life, the cow and the caretaker. The clerk handed her the prescription. What would happen, she wondered, if she swallowed the entire bottle all at once? Would it deliver her a gush of motherly instinct so she could take better care of Reed, properly counsel Kit? Tell the truth? Walk away from Junior? Bring up a dog who didn't on principle innately distrust men? Would it make her read the letter from her own—*say it*—mother? It sure enough wouldn't convince Iris of anything. Poor Iris. How long would she last?

When his mother died, Hank would fall apart. Chloe couldn't help with that. Not even Reed could help. Oh, the hell with everything. Poor *all* of us, including this pup.

In the truck, she set the puppy into the cardboard box, tore open the kibble and offered a few pieces. "We're a one-dog kind of household, little guy. But I think I know somebody who could give you a home."

She drove to the motel, knocked at the door she knew was his. After waiting a reasonable amount of time, she used her laminated California driver's license to jimmy the simple lock and let herself in.

Junior was a belly sleeper. He had one arm flung over the edge of the queen-size mattress. Either he didn't move around much or he'd only just gotten to bed, because the sheets were still neatly tucked. The bed pillows were stacked on the only chair in the room, their covers crisp, white, and obviously unused. Chloe set them on the table. She pushed the chair over to the bed, then let the puppy loose in the sheets and sat down. At once it began making those compelling little grunts and whines nature, in order to assure adoption, purposely encodes onto puppy DNA.

Husky mixed with shepherd? He was a little large and skinny for that. Too small-boned for a malamute. The little brown face had black markings on the muzzle. His eyes were peculiar in color, or perhaps it wasn't the color at all but the piercing way he stared out of them. His tail couldn't have been any bigger around than her little finger, and it had a definite crook, as if it might have gotten broken during the birth process. The tail wagged madly now that he'd discovered Junior's hand. He began nipping and licking the long, tapered fingers. She noticed Junior removed all his jewelry to sleep. He hadn't the night at the Pony Soldier. Here on the dresser were his rings, his bracelets, the intricately tooled watch. Part of her was dying to go try it all on, to see how it felt to carry around all that weight of his own making. If she did, and he woke up, he would look at her hands and make all kinds of crazy assumptions.

Junior's hands were the first part of him to awaken. The long fingers began stroking the dog, attempting to soothe him long before his brain embarked on the quest to understand what new companion shared his bed. That meant he'd had a lot of women. Chloe'd bet money if someone held a gun to his head, Junior couldn't recall all their names. His scorecard had to top the hundred mark, easily. Calluses all over his equipment. Probably one of those guys who had to exercise the steed daily or eternally question his manhood. Junior pulled the pup close, and for a moment it snuggled up to his heat, but the crackle of sheets and intriguing shapes beneath them offered so many opportunities to pounce and wrestle that the dog wriggled away. Chloe reached out to keep the pup from leaping off the bed. Junior caught her wrist.

"Hmmm." His voice was husky with sleep. "I like this far better than my usual wake-up calls."

"I'm so glad you feel that way. In fact, I brought you a present."

He turned over. The pup nipped at her shirttail, and she directed him back to Junior. His long hair was loose from its braids, spread across his shoulders like streaming black water. He pushed himself up to a sitting position and squinted at the dog.

"There's wolf in that pup."

"I thought that was a fable, crossing wolves with dogs."

"Nope." He yawned. "It's a dumb idea, people wanting to possess something that wild, but they pull crap like this all the time. Breed something that can't make it in either world. There's massive appeal, particularly to fools who can't tolerate differences in their own species. Yeah, look at his eyes, Chloe, his conformation. Won't be easy to train. I don't suppose you brought me any coffee?"

"Sorry. The kid giving him away said her dad would drown him if she didn't find a home."

Junior sighed. "Hit me with some good news first thing in the morning."

"It's a *male* dog, Junior. Hannah'd go nuts. I'd take him if I could."

He reached forward and rubbed the little pup's ears between his thumbs. The sheets slid down to his belly. Chloe tried not to look at the nearly hairless skin, the sculpted angle of hipbone pressing taut against sheet. He pulled the covers up to his shoulders and studied her face.

"This here is all very coincidental. I was dreaming about you before you came in."

"Junior, you'd recite the Lord's Prayer backwards if you thought it might me get in that bed."

"I don't lie. You're the one who does that."

She bristled. "I fudge now and again. But only when absolutely necessary."

He looked at her gravely. "Be that as it may, in my dream, you weren't scared to look at my body. I think we were outside, dancing maybe. You like dancing? I bet you're good at it."

"Hold on a second." She reached into her purse and took out the bottle of estrogen pills, slid one into her mouth, and swallowed it dry. "Wait about thirty minutes before you tell me anything else."

He took the pill bottle from her hands, read the label, and set the bottle down on his bedside table, a serviceable wood-grained plastic creation that held an equally utilitarian lamp. They watched the puppy sniffing around the covers and chuckled as he attacked Junior's fingers, then flattened his ears and crouched at the sound of their laughter. "Uh-oh. Looks like somebody's wondering where to take a leak."

Chloe grabbed the dog and took him outside on the motel's porch. It was cold enough that the pup shuddered as he did his business. When she turned to go back into the room, Junior stood in the doorway, halfway dressed, the fly of his jeans partially done up, his belt hanging open, the buckle glinting in the winter sunlight.

She held the puppy up between them. "Give him a name."

"Chloe."

"Come on, Junior, a proper name. Lucky, Rex, Paddlefoot—"

"Chloe."

She looked away. "Junior, you and me have to be smart enough animals that we recognize how dangerous this is and walk away. We've got kids."

"We have wonderful kids. They could grow up like brother and sister."

He ran his fingers up and down her arms, cupped one hand under her breast, and she felt the milk in her—Reed's breakfast—rise, surface, and cause her flesh to ache. She shut her eyes. "I have to go."

"Where?"

"Home, that's where. I have to go home."

"Look me in the eyes, Chloe. If being with Hank's truly your home, you go on then. You got no business being here if that's how things are."

"Okay. I will. It is. Goddammit, will you stop saying crap like that?"

"Hey, you're the one who picked my lock. Maybe you should remember that before you start cussing me."

"Just take the damn dog. Please."

"Okay." He accepted the dog, and she backed away. Bare-chested, no shoes, he stood in the doorway looking at her while she stumbled into her truck.

"Nice wheels," he called out. "A classic. Careful of the ice."

She stalled the engine twice, swore until her breath fogged the windshield, then managed to drive away. In her rearview mirror, she saw Junior lift the pup to his cheek. The little dog squirmed frantically in an effort to get closer. Junior held his little paw up and made him wave in her direction.

That's what you wanted, she chided herself. *To give a dog a home. Let the rest of it go. Here's the deal: Turn the corner and don't look back. You're not even allowed to think about it.*

She and Hank drove Kit to the airport in Flagstaff and stood warming themselves next to the fireplace, waiting for the shuttle to land.

Hank said, "You remember how to get to the other plane in Phoenix?"

Kit scowled. "Hank, I got here, didn't I? All I have to do is basically the same thing backwards."

He jiggled Reed in his arms. "We know that, Kit. We just want you to be careful."

Kit's eyes filled with tears. Chloe took her by the arm and walked her away, closer to the windows. "You promised me you'd go to a support group when you get home."

Kit looked away. "What if I don't?"

"Well, Lita and I haven't had a heart-to-heart in a long time."

"Chloe! You wouldn't."

"Go on, try to bluff me. You know you'll lose. You may be a princess, but I am the queen. Admit it."

"You're the queen. The uncle, whatever. There. Are you happy?"

"No, not really. But the longer I live, the more I suspect happiness isn't what we're supposed to feel except on a few rare occasions. Look. Here comes your plane." The tiny twin-engine taxied into its slot on the tarmac.

Kit picked up her duffel bag, then dropped it. "God, it looks so small. I bet only ten people can fit on that plane. There's way more than ten people standing around here. Maybe they overbooked. Lita says sometimes they give you money if you give up your seat. Does that look like ice on the wings to you?"

"Kit, the pilot wants to get to Phoenix just as much as you do. You have to return to real life sooner or later. Now give me a hug, kiss Reed, and tell Hank you'll miss him. Then get your butt home to California. Do some schoolwork. Make the honor roll. Ride horses."

Kit flung her arms around Chloe's shoulders, and Chloe had to take a step back to keep her balance. She allowed the girl to weep her necessary tears for several long minutes. To onlookers, she imagined the scene came off like any other sorrowful good-bye, but thanks to halfway-decent horses, shitty mothers and the kind of pain only men could deliver, she and Kit would always be tight. Now, however, there was a shadowy side to the closeness that bound them. They could know each other until they were decrepit old ladies, and the dark sisterhood would always be present, part of their connective tissue.

"You behave, too," Kit whispered. "And you know what I mean." She hugged Hank and covered Reed's little face in kisses. She stood there holding the baby until the announcement came for all passengers to be on board. "I don't want to give her back. It's like I'm leaving my sister."

"Your sister will be here come summer vacation, Kit. Smelly diapers and screaming fits and teething pains, too. She'll need you then just as much." Hank put his arm around Chloe, and they stood watching the plane taxi down the runway.

She felt him tuck Reed up close to his chest. "I can take her for a while if you're tired."

"No, I've got her. You should rest whenever you can, Chloe. You lift her too much, and you'll end up with adhesions."

"It's been forever since my surgery. I feel genuinely healed up. I'm even starting to dream about riding horses."

"So long as dreaming's all you're doing."

"I *will* ride again, Hank."

He was quiet a minute. "I'm aware of that. I'm also aware of the toll your riding's taken on all of us."

Chloe knew she'd never stop paying for it. Maybe in twenty years he'd forgive her. Maybe not. Out the windows she saw the plane lift, tuck its landing gear and rake across the sky. The counter clerk who'd taken passengers' tickets opened the terminal door and came back inside, trailing a pine smell as strong and bracing in the chilly air as aftershave. In a few hours Kit would shed the jacket, turn up her radio, call somebody on the phone, begin laying out school clothes for the next day. Tonight Chloe and Hank were embarking on family life. No troubled houseguests, no more waiting for chances to be alone. Just the two of them and, Reed willing, one sleeping baby. They'd drive home, have supper, and then Hank would turn to her, touch her in that unmistakable way, wanting to make love because that was one sure way of cementing themselves back to each other.

She ran a finger down Reed's sleeping face. "You, my daughter, are looking awful damn cute for a screaming demon. What we've got to do is find a way to tire you out so you'll sleep through the night. What's it going to take? Baby aerobics?" She looked at Hank, who was watching her intently. "As long as we're in town, think maybe there's time to look for a real crib?"

"I think that's a brilliant idea."

"Well, I guess everyone gets to shine once in her lifetime."

As she was setting the table for supper, Hank fetched a bottle of wine down from the cupboard. He held it up for Chloe's inspection.

She squinted at the gold-embossed numbers. "Wasn't that a great year for horsewomen out to wreck normal men's lives?"

"It certainly was." He dropped the corkscrew and gave her a half grin as he picked it up. "A little wine's supposed to be good for nursing mothers. I—"

She pointed a fork at him. "Jesus, Hank, don't tell me. You read that in a book."

"A magazine, actually."

"Pour away, not that I need any help lactating." She held out her empty coffee mug. They were just about to sit down to deli food they'd shuttled home from Flagstaff. Now he was fussing with the tape player. A gust of early Van Morrison filled the small room. "*Moondance* and red wine," Chloe said. "Is this a formula for seducing the mother of your child or what?"

"I'd walk down Main Street naked if I thought that would yield better results."

"Yeah, but then you'd risk frostbite on your equipment."

"Can't have that."

She swallowed a mouthful of wine and felt the familiar sting hit the backs of her knees. "Whew. Better get some of that food in me. Being good all those months, I've lost my chops for booze."

Across the room Reed lay in her secondhand crib, which was painted somebody's idea of a sunny yellow. With the addition of a little black pinstriping, it could have passed for a taxi. "Don't you wonder what other babies slept there?" Hank asked.

Chloe thought of Rhonda in the hospital, nursing her son with milk derived from a diet of junk food. She wondered what name he'd eventually answer to, and if he'd settle into having a crazy mother or spend his life trying to outrun her. "To tell you the truth, it reminds me of foster care. On a daily basis, which bed you got to call your own was a crapshoot."

Hank opened his mouth to say something, then shut it.

"But it's a real nice crib," Chloe said. "Sturdy. Safe, affordable. All the things we need." She reached across the table and patted his hand. "Stop trying to impress me, and eat your dinner."

They emptied the cartons one by one, listening to the crackle of wood shifting in the stove. Hank cleared the table, took the trash out, fed the horse a coffee can of grain, threw a flattened Coke can for Hannah to fetch. Chloe woke Reed and gave her a cat-bath with a warm washcloth, wasted the better part of an hour feeding her, pulling her booties up high, playing with her, and making faces, making sure she was one tired baby with no reason at all to complain. For once Reed happily complied. Chloe kissed her sweet-smelling head and smoothed her dark hair. "I know what you're up to," she whispered. "Tilting the evening in your father's favor. It's always going to be like this, isn't it? The two of you in cahoots, making sure there's no place for me to hide." She wondered if Junior had taken the puppy to his son's house, if Corrine had made the dog a nest of blankets with a ticking alarm clock to remind him of his mother's heartbeat.

The back door clicked open and shut. "Here, I'll take her." Hank reached for his daughter. He rocked her to sleep while Chloe sat on the couch observing them. He placed the baby in the crib, and they stood quietly looking down as Reed settled into sleep. "What a good baby."

"Tonight, anyway."

Hank looked down at the floor. He rubbed his face, a gesture he couldn't seem to stop doing now that he'd dispensed with the beard and was shaving every morning. Hannah was parked so close to the stove Chloe worried she might catch fire. Van Morrison had long

ago signed off with *Glad Tidings*, and the wine had done its duty
blurring the edges. "Well, I see definite improvement." He couldn't
seem to locate his voice to speak or his feet to take the next step.

Chloe reached one hand up to his chin and tilted it down to her
face. "So. Ready for bed?"

"It's a little embarrassing how ready I am."

She laughed. "It's not like we haven't seen each other naked."

"I know. Things just feel so awkward."

"If it makes you feel any better, I'm nervous, too. All day I'm
wondering how in God's name we're supposed to fool around
when she might hear us, when she might be laying there with a
pin stuck in her side. Is this how it's always going to be? Part of me
can never stop listening?" She tapped her chest. "Right here, it's
like I've grown a third ear."

"I feel the same way. Maybe the trick is to take that as a given."

They walked down the hall together. Chloe sat down on the bed
and took off her shoes. A brief sulfur odor sparked through the air
as Hank lit the beeswax candle stubs on the dresser. He joined her
on the blankets and they lay back against the pillows, watching
shadows flicker across the walls. He reached for her hand, interlac-
ing their fingers, tracing the textures in her skin. In her mind's eye
Chloe flashed on Junior's hands petting the puppy while he looked
at her. She turned over, put her arms around Hank, kissed him like
she meant it and issued a stern command to the rest of her body to
catch up. "How's it feel having no basketball between us?"

"Like old times."

"Old times as in California?"

"Yes."

"It was a crazy, wild winter. I think we set records."

He stroked her hair. "I missed being inside you. This light makes
your skin glow. I wish I knew how to paint. The way you look is
worth learning how."

She plucked at her sweatshirt, spotted and grubby from the
baby. "Reality check, buddy. This ensemble would make a painting
only you'd buy."

"Oh, I don't know if that's true. I can think of a few other individuals who might be interested."

He kissed her forehead, began forging a trail down her body, unbuttoning and discarding clothing as he made his way. Every new increment of exposure made her shiver; every touch of his fingers loosened her up until, so long as she didn't think of Junior, she felt they'd arrived pretty much in the same place they'd been a year earlier, that first night in her cabin.

"Remember our first time together?" Chloe whispered into his neck. "Hannah barked you up a tree. The owl outside the window scaring you half to death?"

"The luckiest night of my life."

"Many would disagree."

"Time to forget all of that."

This night, at this time, beyond a yearling colt growing spoiled on handouts and hibernating prairie dogs, who knew what wild thing was waiting in their future? Hank placed his hand on her bare thigh. Automatically her legs opened. When he entered her, there was a sharp, unexpected jolt that caused her to cry out.

He pulled back, cupping his hand against her cheek. "Did I hurt you?"

She kissed his neck, murmured no, but she was lying. Everything hurt, just a little. She was different inside. Letting somebody in changed everything. She ran through her prayer of rational thinking: *This is Hank, not that awful cowboy. This man's the father of your baby. He loves you, he's solid. He'll stay, if you let him.* But in truth it wasn't about any of that, it was more the realization that she had served her time in safe confinement, and now her body was no longer hers alone. She had to be vulnerable for Hank, in order to allow him in. She had to remain defensive to keep Junior out. *For God's sake, just be here*, she commanded herself. *Drink in all this wonderful sensation the way you used to. Listen to the sound of nerves firing, doing their job. Breathe with him. Let it be about that and nothing else.* She felt herself begin to fall away, taking the first easy strokes toward swimming in the collective pool that announced *yes, of course, this was exactly what you both needed, and it was all so simple, patiently waiting for you. You forgot, that's all.* She felt him begin to move in earnest, desperate to work out all that unspoken worry that troubled them, kept them separate. Those tears she felt brimming in her eyes were hormone-related. *Hank wants to love you; now you're letting him.* And at once she remembered she'd left her pills on Junior's bedside table. Her heart fluttered, and the shocky feel of her blood rising made her mouth go numb. She had to take several deep breaths, and even fully oxygenated, the shame remained.

Hank misunderstood. "You like this?" he murmured, and the pride in his voice tore her heart in half as if the muscle was made of paper.

Throughout, Reed stayed quiet. Afterwards, as they felt the echoes of pleasure grow more and more distant, and settled under covers, Hank drew her close, his bare legs flung over hers, his toes rubbing up and down her ankles, prolonging contact. Reed didn't make a sound. "Hey," Hank said. "You kept your socks on. No fair."

"It's winter. My feet were cold."

He spooned his body against hers, his hand lightly clasping her breast. "They don't have to be cold." He kissed the back of her head. "I'll always be here to warm them."

Was there anything about this day that wasn't fraught with double meanings? She lay awake listening to Hank's even breathing, to the silence down the hallway where Reed slept, to Hannah's occasional shuffling as she settled herself on the floor. Somehow she had to get to sleep. Tomorrow she'd be on her own with her daughter.

Who the Hell Knows What the Date Is

Whoever you are,

Right off, I have to be honest. It wasn't me at all who looked for you, but a well-meaning friend too young and romantic to know any better. But as long as you wrote, I have got me more than a few questions I'd like answered.

Why did you give me away? Was I such an inconve-
nience that you had to be quit of me? I have a baby of
my own. They don't cost that much, except for doctor
visits. After you left me at the home, did you ever wonder how I was doing? If I was lonely? I looked for you in
the face of every woman who walked through those
doors. For a long time I was sure you'd come back. But
we both know that's horseshit.

I try to imagine being held by you, feeling that feeling
of instantly belonging. My whole childhood, and even
now, I guess I never stopped wishing something like this
would happen. But then I think of Hank having to deal
with his mother and how you might turn out to be ten
times worse than Iris and I want to run screaming across
the prairie. Just stand there and scream. You have no
idea how bad I wish I could forget the nights I laid in
one strange bed or another praying you'd come back,
the next morning or the next or the one after that. Idiot
social workers with real homes and families would say
Now Chloe, the good Lord never gives you more than
you can handle and up I'd rear, spit in their faces, get
sent someplace new and worse.

Whatever your name is, listen. The past truly dogs me.
It's my biggest flaw, and it has plenty of company. On
days like today, thanks to my friend, now so does your
letter, and I haven't even read it! Maybe some rocks are
just better off left unturned.

Jesus, what I wouldn't give for three solid hours of
sunshine and no goddamn wind blowing down my neck.
Guess my blood isn't thick enough for this kind of winter.
Maybe I'm catching that SAD disease after all.

If you're my mother, fine, start acting like one. Tell me
how to make a screaming baby settle down and take the
goddamn nap she needs when she's bound and determined to stay awake and miserable. With horses you

wean them and farm them out until they're a little more
grown up. I'd go to jail if I said that out loud. I graduated
high school with a C average. I live with a smart guy, but
so far none of it's rubbed off on me. That is about the
extent of my education.

Sincerely,
Chloe Morgan

Chloe read over the pages, then tore them up and threw the
pieces in the trash can.

Part 3

Canyon de Chelly

19

"This is not about anything other than me needing to get some sun," Chloe explained. "Otherwise I'm going to lose my mind."

"Where were you planning to go?"

She bit her thumbnail. "I was sort of thinking California. I'd like to see Hugh Nichols. According to Kit he hasn't gotten any better. And to save money, I thought maybe I could stay with Kit. I'd sure like to take Reed to meet everybody."

Hank thought long and hard before answering. "That's too long a trip for Reed. She's still too tiny. What if she got sick?"

"I'd take her to the doctor."

He shook his head no. "I'll pick up one of those sun lamps next time I'm in Flagstaff. All you really need is more light. Spring will be here before you know it."

"Maybe it was a stupid idea." She wandered outside and down to the horse.

Hank hadn't missed the slump in Chloe's shoulders. Logically he understood what she was proposing was no different than anyone else in town. The season had stretched on long past its turn, and cabin fever was epidemic. Reed wouldn't perish seven hours in the car; she'd probably sleep through most of the drive. But California? All that sun and familiarity was almost more dangerous than Junior Whitebear. He could no more let them go than he could explain the real reasons behind his decision.

He held on to his daughter and watched as Chloe stood at the edge of the corral he'd built, one gloved hand on the horse's neck, the other on the fence, holding on for dear life.

Back in September it had hardly mattered that his classroom's shoestring budget was knotted and fraying; Hank felt sure he could work with it. He went home each evening a happy man, slept well, and looked forward to the discoveries of the following day. Now, seven months later, he was grateful to lock the door behind him. Reed got him through the day. His daughter's growing awareness of the world was what mattered, not fighting for reams of paper or participating in those bitter lunchtime debates with Walker and MacNeal about "the Indian problem." Home: On a good night he made love to Chloe, fell asleep in her arms with only an hour of silent fretting. What he and Chloe had was a paper-thin promise, capable of blowing away in a strong wind. His mother's illness worsened, and he knew she wouldn't make it to summer. Every couple of weekends he forked over $150 he couldn't afford and flew home so he could hold her hand, witness her dwindling, and try to motivate his father into behaving like an adult. Steadfast and dependable, Hank put himself through the paces like one of Chloe's old lesson horses. Was there another, more appropriate route? Today, at the tail end of March, it seemed that even his hindsight was jeering him.

Technically the season was spring. Which probably explained last night's ice storm, and the latest pileup on the highway near the Trading Post. Three cars. Hank had heard the awful noise, come outdoors, and seen the flames from the cabin, known that people had died. All it took was a little patch of ice, a moment of inattention and in the time it took to snap your fingers, families were dismissed. Now he stood in the back of his schoolroom, watching his students bent over their desks. With straightened-out paper clips and dulled safety pins, they were scratching out designs on the rocks they'd collected in and around the schoolyard. Thanks to Junior Whitebear's generosity, there was more than enough paint and brushes, but very little paper, and Hank wasn't about to call the man up and ask for anything more. He didn't possess enough voice to read the children another story. They needed math, spelling, and recess, and he could deliver those subjects with chalk and blackboard, but they also needed art, so they were making do with the rocks, and the story was spreading. Ken Walker found this project to be the apex of amusement. Hank was fairly certain it was Walker who'd left the hardened cow chip atop his mail in the teachers' lounge along with a taped note reading: "Scratch something pretty on this." Hank opted to leave the cow excrement right where it was. If any of the teachers had a problem with the ensuing odor, let them deal with it.

When he went home to the empty cabin this evening, his voice would be thready, a whisper. It happened every night Chloe was gone. The bizarre, probably hysterical laryngitis healed itself when she returned to the cabin. Hank was furious she'd left and terrified she wouldn't return. If the phone rang, he let it ring, then wondered if some emergency-room doctor had been trying to get hold of him, needed his permission to save Reed's life. Crazy thinking, but he couldn't talk himself calm. The first time she had simply left a note, effectively dismissing his protests against their leaving, hers and the baby's.

You're suffocating me. I have to go sit in the sun.

And she'd left the telephone number of a motel in Phoenix, which he called at once, chagrined at hearing her voice, and handled badly. Three weeks later she made noises about going back, claiming the sun and warmth were better than any doctor's prescription. If that was so, why did it seem like Junior's Cherokee always disappeared around the same time as her truck? *You're not taking Reed,* he'd countered. *She's my baby, too. She deserves stability, even if no one else around here is getting any.*

And the look Chloe gave him cut to his marrow. She handed the baby over and said, *I was planning on nursing her for a year like you wanted me to, but if it means that much to you, I'll start weaning her right this second.*

"Haven't seen your dad come by to pick you up lately," Hank rasped in his scratchy voice to Dog Johnson, who was bending over his creation, shielding it from view. The other children often copied his ideas, and this bewildering flattery caused Dog to behave protectively.

"Had to go to Phoenix," Dog offered. "Mom got sick, or I would've got to go with him."

"Tell your mom to call if she needs anything, and to get well soon, okay?" In a whisper Hank complimented the boy on his art-work and moved along. Here was math at your most basic level. Chloe plus Junior equals trouble. He'd practically driven her to the man with his need to control her every move. *You really think it's a good idea to start training that horse while there's ice on the ground? Doesn't drinking caffeinated coffee affect your milk? Should the baby still be taking two naps during the day?* Jesus, who did he think he was, the universal authority on her life?

"Look here, Mr. Hank," Jolene Kee said, waving him over to her desk. "See how I make a scene on my rock like you ask me to. Couple of Kokopelli guys. Nice, huh?"

She held up her flat piece of sandstone and grinned. Two flute players and what was either a dog or a horse standing between them were incised into the rock's surface. Overhead three clouds rained down, the clouds and rain as stylized as sandpainting, yet the stroke trembled, its childlike rendering alluring.

"That's beautiful, Jolene. Be sure you use the marking pen to put your name on the back. If you want to do another, there's time before the bell."

The little girl nodded, reaching for a new piece of stone. Last September she wouldn't even make eye contact with him. In a few months she'd graduate to fourth grade, into the jaws of those dinosaur upper-grade instructors. Mrs. MacNeal would remind Jolene that her world had edges, that her skin color and tribal affiliation rendered the surface Hank had tried to round out to stretch beyond northern Arizona flat and unwelcoming. Jolene would learn to be shy all over again. She'd tune out and mark time. Could he fail the girl just to throw a wrench in what seemed inevitable?

Hank, we've got to do something with the finished pieces, Louise Begay, the classroom aide, kept saying. They had more than a hundred rocks now, collecting dust on the back counter. Patiently Louise took a dustcloth to each one. He wished he had an answer for her, but all he could do was keep handing them out and trying to wrap his mind around the empty crib, the empty side of the bed, the utter silence that was transforming his heart into a stone.

At his desk Hank halfheartedly began filling out roll sheets. He looked up. Dog Johnson had been standing there, waiting for him to notice. Setting down his pen, he looked into the face of the son of the man who was slowly stealing the woman he loved. "Walter, you look like you have something on your mind."

"Mr. Hank, I ask Uncle Oscar could we maybe sell them rocks in the Trading Post, and he say why not put a tag on all them, maybe a tourist like one for paperweight or something."

The boy delivered his words in such a rush that Hank knew he'd been rehearsing the speech for quite some time. He smiled. "Sell them? I never thought of that."

The boy's relief was palpable. "Sure! Dollar a rock, why not sell all them hundred rocks? We could be richest third grade of all Arizona."

"What would we do with the money?"

"Buy paper like we need. Big box of sixty-four colored Crayolas. Or the library, some new books like from that store in Flagstaff where my dad took me. Maybe, if it don't cost too much, we could get a couple of beanbag chairs to read in at that library." He blushed. "Maybe."

"Those are pretty big ideas." Hank reached over and tousled his hair. Dog was a great kid, and someday he'd be a truly decent man. Since his father had entered the picture, he'd quit caring about the other children's teasing, so they began to admire him, which he seemed to tolerate with a modicum of suspicion, which in turn magically allowed him entrance into their circle. "Let's talk this over with the class, Walter. Whatever we do, we have to agree as a group." He stood up and, lacking the authority of voice, clapped his hands. When everyone looked his way, he whispered, "Will everyone please give Walter their attention? He has something important he wants to share."

The Chevy truck was once again parked out by the barn when he came home that Friday. The old battered emblem of Chloe's independence looked as if it had spent a lifetime of eccentricity only to discover this small town was its homeland. Hank parked the Honda alongside it. His heart raced, and he did his best to walk at a normal pace up the steps and into the cabin. She sat in the rocker, a sullen Madonna, nursing Reed.

She looked up, neither smiling nor frowning, which he assumed meant he was still *numero uno* on her shit list. "Hank."

He managed to rasp out, "Chloe."

"If you're sick, you probably shouldn't kiss the baby."

"I'm not sick."

"Well, you sound like hell."

In a whisper he pleaded his case. "It's stress. That's all. I bought some throat spray. I don't have a fever. It doesn't even hurt." Which was a lie. Every word he uttered, not to mention the act of swallowing, made him feel as if he was choking. "Did you have a nice time away?"

Tight-lipped, she answered, "Okay."

"Was it warm in Prescott?"

She sighed. "Yes, Hank. I walked in all the antique stores. I sat in the goddamn sun in the town square and got a little sunburn. I saw one movie, *Tombstone*, which started out pretty good, but I don't know how it ended since Reed started screaming and I had to leave the theater. Want to see my ticket stub?"

"No." In the kitchen, he started clearing away the dirty dishes.

"Hank, that's my mess. I'll clean it up when I finish with the baby."

"If that's the way you want to play it." He let the silverware clatter in the sink and dried his hands on a paper towel, grabbed his Pendleton, and went out the back door. Thanks to the recent storm, the newly exposed prairie grass was yellow and brittle. Evidence of the colt's shedding was everywhere; fist-size puffs of brown hair littered the corral. Apparently Thunder had spent his day rubbing his ass up against the barn. Now he had hairy sides and a back end like a chimp. Hank wondered how it was Chloe could insist she was ready to begin training while so ardently ignoring issues such as basic grooming. He took down a shedding blade, halter, and hoof pick, then went to work.

With every pass of the blade, winter hair fell away. Without thinking twice about how he might not tolerate it, Hank picked the horse's hooves clean. The yearling had come a long way since summer, when Chloe had mentioned dosing him with sedative as insurance to surviving this very process. When Hank had first met Chloe, all this horse business had seemed so mystical. Equine communication sounded like a gift one was born with or else could only admire from a distance. A great deal of horse training, it seemed, involved a calm demeanor, patience, and the passage of time, during which one behaved with consistency or got kicked in the head. Were relationships really all that different? He mucked out the arena, spread a clean bed of shavings in the barn stall, and gathered up scattered wires from hay bales and used them to reinforce weakened areas on the fence. Then, for a long time, he sat on the pile of hay bales holding his hammer, wondering how in Christ his life had gotten to this spot. When the sun had gone down to the point that he could no longer clearly see his hands, he hung up the tool and went back into the cabin.

The smell of simmering onions made his mouth water. There

was freshly sliced bread on a plate—the mothers of the students at Ganado Elementary embarrassed him so with this kindness—and an unwrapped stick of butter, soft to the touch. He lifted the pot lid, looked inside and took a deep breath: chili. He gave the beans a quick stir. She couldn't hate him if she had cooked for him. And chopped fresh peppers, too, taking the trouble to set them into a small, unfamiliar dish. It was cowboy china, glazed tan, patterned with brands and steer heads. Possibly antique; with that thing it was hard to discern. Hank scrubbed his hands and set the table for two. If she'd already eaten, he could just as easily put the clean silverware back in the drawer. Across the room Reed was wide awake, kicking her legs, looking up at the mobile of sheep the nicer of his fellow teachers had bought him as a baby present.

"Hello, Sweetie," he whispered. "Your old man sure missed you. Your mother forgot to pack your favorite toy." He picked up the stuffed horse. Reed's big brown eyes tracked the toy's movement as he drew it along the crib's edge. He noticed the silver rattle peeking out from her blanket, and as he rolled it in his fingers he frowned. He'd never understood just how this piece of Junior's work had come into their lives. When the cup was given, he'd been standing right there, but the rattle seemed to have preceded it, like some kind of omen. During one of Hank's trips to Iris, perhaps Junior had come visiting, brought the rattle along with whatever else was on his agenda. He set it down at the foot of the crib, kissed his thumb, then like he was pasting a gold star there for good behavior, touched it to Reed's forehead.

Chloe came down the hall, brushing her hair. She stopped mid-stroke as their eyes met. "There's dinner."

"I saw. Thanks."

"Jalapeños—I don't know. Hot stuff always makes my throat feel better."

"I'll give it a try."

They sat down and cleaned their bowls. *Fueling our engines*, Hank thought, tearing off a chunk of bread to swipe around his bowl.

That's all we're doing. The telephone rang. He gestured. "You mind getting that?"

Chloe scraped her chair on the floor. "Hello? Of course, he's here. Where else would he be? Mr. Oliver, please give my best wishes to your wife, I'm—" Hank saw her wince, then gather her resolve. "I understand. I'll get him for you now." She let the receiver drop. It thumped against the wall as she fled down the hallway.

Hank looked after her, then reluctantly picked up the phone. "Dad?"

"Henry, you need to do something about that girl. This is not a viable situation."

"What would you suggest?"

"For starters, a course in etiquette might help. What in hell's wrong with your voice?"

"Laryngitis. How's Mom tonight?"

"Not good. Not good at all. She won't eat."

"Did you call the doctor?"

"Of course I called the doctor. He's no help. He even went so far as to suggest this was normal. Can you imagine? Not eating, he calls—"

"How about the hospice people?"

"You know how I feel about strangers. I want you to come home, Henry. I can't do this alone."

"I'll be there next weekend, Dad, just like I promised. I can't miss any more work. I'm overdrawn on personal leave. I could get fired."

"Henry, you're not listening to me."

The silence emanating from the hallway was more than Hank could bear. "Listen, Dad, I have to go. I'll see you in a week. If you get into trouble, call the phone numbers on the list I left you. Give Mom my love. Good-bye."

Chloe lay facedown on their bed, clean, unfolded laundry all around her. When Hank came into the room she sat up and began pairing socks. He pulled a pair of red Woolriches out of her grasp and tossed them back into the pile. Hands in her lap, she stared somewhere over his shoulder, her expression stony, only the tears glittering at the corners of her eyes giving her away.

"Just because I have an asshole for a father doesn't mean I don't love you."

She lifted one shoulder, shrugged.

"Wow. I must really be in the doghouse if I don't even rate both shoulders."

One corner of her mouth lifted slightly.

He cleared his throat. "Not a great day for anyone. Want to throw a couple of beers at it?"

"One of us has to stay sober. The baby."

"Okay, then. We can flip a coin."

"Heads I win, Hank. Tails I win too."

She reached into his pocket and without really thinking, Hank clasped her hand there, so near his penis he immediately became hard. He couldn't let go. He pulled Chloe closer and closer until there was no question at all this was not about beer or winning a toss of the coin. He sat down on the bed and kissed her neck, pulled her shirt out of her jeans, ran his hands up her breasts and breathed her scent in so deeply that his head went dizzy. The word "please" went unspoken, resonating in the silence.

She bent her head forward, and her hair fell into her face. Hank waited for her to look up at him. "You really think rolling around on the bed will change anything?"

"It might make us remember better times. Come on, let's at least try."

He pulled her down to the floor. Among sweet-smelling clothes and abandoned boots, Hank felt absurdly thankful that she was willing to take him to this place. He didn't care to hear her reasons; mutual use was all right by him. After several awkward attempts at finding a compatible rhythm, Chloe settled astride him, moving in those long, slow postings that reduced him to her animal half, a style of making love that was both sensible and pure Chloe and left him shaking. Being inside her again made his eyes wash over with a kind of startling blindness. He took hold of her hipbones, which, as pregnancy fat disappeared, emerged sharper, more obvious. The eager equestrian muscles ached for a task to tone them. She tilted her body forward so that her breasts grazed his chest and he felt her determination to feel good begin to overtake her anger. That was the moment he nearly always lost his control, when he felt her reach out and grab onto her own pleasure. She came so easily the sensations slid out of her, loose and lubricating, and tipped him over into his own brief remedy. Out of breath, Chloe laid her face down on his chest and twirled a finger around the hairs circling his left nipple. The small gesture of tenderness made his groin spasm once more and he couldn't help but cry out.

She laughed. "Not bad for a guy who's lost his voice."

He whispered, "Chili medicine."

Chloe sat up and stretched, twisting her torso toward the bed, looking for something. Hank studied her back, the terrible scar from her accident, the pale, smooth skin he loved to touch. She had strong, muscled shoulders, yet an elegant neck. Her skin was milky white from being covered up all winter. Nowhere could he detect any evidence of sunburn. Christ.

She groped around the floor into their discarded clothing, coming out of his pockets with a quarter, which she pressed into his hand. "This is your tip. You made me so happy just now I might even pour your beer in a glass," she said merrily. "Would you like that?"

"Baby, I'll take it any way you serve it up."

Somehow the governor had wrangled the deal without the environmentalists going into apoplexy. On Monday the flooding of the Grand Canyon would commence. The upshot of the reasoning was that floods were natural occurrences in rivers, and prior to the Glen Canyon Dam, the annual "scour-and-fill" of snowmelt had accomplished just that. A regulated deluge would, in effect, redistribute sand above the waterline, improve habitats for animals by flushing out the non-native fish, and, perhaps the only apparent monetary incentive, better the camping sites for river rafters. The scientific community was for it, and Secretary Babbitt was holding a press conference along his travel route from the dam, where he'd open the hollow-jet tube on down to Lees Ferry. In between, someone from the geological services would inject dye into the river to study flow velocity. It was a good thing, an ecological thing; hosanna, it was almost natural. For all Hank cared, they could flood the damn state. He'd come across a scrap of a letter written in Chloe's hand. What he'd read gutted him, like one of those fish that as a result of the flood path would enjoy a brief, improved habitat. In the end he'd still end up some larger prey's dinner.

I try to imagine being held by you, feeling that feeling of instant belonging. My whole childhood, and even now, I guess I never stopped wishing something like this would happen. But then I think of Hank. . . .

They were discarded words on a half page of notebook paper, scribbled through, a fragment of some larger whole. To confront Chloe was to make real that which he feared the most, yet to do nothing meant the slow disintegration of all he trusted. All he could do was tuck the paper away into his wallet, rock the baby, teach his class, and wait to see what happened. If all went as planned, the water would rinse the canyon clean of the destructive sediment.

On the morning of the flooding, he drove to the Trading Post to help Walter set up the display for the rocks. News vans and onlookers nearly filled the parking lot. Every table in the restaurant was full, and a long line of those waiting for seats perused the store aisles. Whatever its long-term effects, this flooding was good for business. Hank nodded hello to Corrine, who was showing a squash-blossom necklace to a pair of women wearing cameras sporting huge lenses. They wore press passes, badges that allowed them past the cordoned-off areas. One of the women was plain, in blue jeans and a navy blazer; the other was stylishly dressed, wearing one of those decorated black cowboy chapeaus Oscar called a "Santa Fe bitch hat." Hank approached the empty shelf cleared for the rocks, but didn't see Walter anywhere. He didn't have all day, so he began setting up the display without him.

The children had fashioned a poster and decorated it with Polaroids. The pictures had come out a little dark, but they communicated the basic idea of a pathetic school library and how the process of selling rocks might serendipitously come to fill it with books. Hank had his doubts, but the children were so eager he had to try. Louise Begay had typed out a history of the project on her home computer. The cardboard box holding the rocks bore a sign, too, penned in Walter's unmistakably artistic script:

PETROGLYPHS FOR SALE!
Handmade by Mr. Henry Oliver's third grade class at Ganado Elem. Only $3–$7 for a one-of-a-kind, mysterious and keepsake rock.

Louise's history, composed entirely by the children, read:

> There isn't much to do here in the summer, and we kids like to read! So we need to earn money and buy books for our library which doesn't have a lot. Every time you buy one of our rocks, we earn $$$ toward a book or a magazine subscription, all our own! Mr. Oliver says we get to choose every book and *Off the Beaten Path* in Flagstaff will give us a discount. All of the profits go for the *books*, not candy or anything else. Please buy a rock if you can, and help a kid read a book. Thank you!

It was signed by all twenty of his students:

Ivana Yellowhair	*Robynn Cameron*	*Tanya Blackwater*
Gary Yazzie	*Benjamin Begay*	*Clyde Lopez*
Anna Ortiz	*Mickey Spottedhorse*	*Rainy Desbar*
Tuck Manygoats	*Malinda Pasqual*	*Brian Martinez*

Chuey (the great!) Alberto   *Nelbert Begay, Jr.*   *Philberta Hobson*

Gilbert Bellymule   *Belva Small*   *Juanita Littlebird*

Jolene Kee   *Walter Johnson*

Their names, their names. Signed so proudly, so hopefully. Hank sat down in the aisle, holding on to two of his favorite rocks. One was Tanya's, thicker than most, a chunk none of the kids had chosen. Shaking it near her ear like a seashell, Tanya said, "I hear a story in this rock," and proceeded to draw her own version of the humpbacked Kokopelli, a cadre of four bearing curly Cootie-game feelers beneath a sun that was a simple spiral. The other rock was Robby's, a small boulder, really, a true boy's rock. It was loaded up with suns, moons, stars, and a parade of animals.

"You'd have better luck with sales if your sign had clearer photographs," a voice informed him.

Hank looked up to see one of the woman reporters studying the poster. It was the one he'd dismissed as plain, but up close he could easily recognize the error of his judgment. She was about his age, with honey-colored hair reaching halfway down her back. Her Leica looked old and expensive. "One of the kids' moms had a Polaroid. In education you learn to accept freebies." He extended his hand to shake hers, then noticed he was still holding the rock. He set it in the box. "Sorry. Hank Oliver."

"Sara. Sara Donaldson. *New York Times.*"

"New York? I'm impressed."

"Well, you're the first one to be. The guy behind the counter just asked me if that meant I got to watch *Seinfeld* two hours earlier than he did."

Hank looked over to see Oscar watching them. He waved and turned back to Sara. "Is that the guy?"

"The very one. Here I call myself a career journalist, and all it takes is one question to make me doubt my worth."

It felt so good to laugh with a woman. "Are you here to do a story on the canyon?"

"Yep. After I eat some breakfast. That is, if I can ever land a table. I've been waiting forty minutes. I think I'm ninetieth on the list."

"I have some pull with the restaurant people. It's a perk when you're a local. Let's go see if we can cut in line."

"Nice talk for a teacher. Don't you practice what you preach?"

"On the important stuff. Come on, they make great coffee here. All you reporters live on coffee, don't you? Pardon me if that's a cliché."

"It's not. But thanks for being sensitive enough to ask."

"You're welcome, Sara."

They drank coffee and, at Hank's suggestion, ordered Navajo tacos. The puffy frybread tortillas were hanging off the edges of the plates, and the spicy bean topping was bubbly with cheese, chopped tomatoes, and onion. The reporter found them intriguing enough to take notes between bites. She quizzed Hank about his class, about life in the slow lane, and insisted on picking up the bill. "I can write this off. Let me pay you back for sneaking me in."

"If you insist."

"I do." At the cash register, she turned to him and said, "You know, Hank, I can fly out tomorrow as planned, or I could fly out the next day."

Hank twisted the toothpick dispenser, which was fully stocked with mint-flavored picks. The cool feel of the wood against the corner of his mouth was bracing. He wanted to tell Sara about Reed and about Chloe, to ask somebody objective what he should do regarding the note in his wallet. He wanted to take her back to her hotel room, lose himself in what for an hour might feel simple and refreshingly uncomplicated, and even better, had no future. It sounded like maybe she wanted that, too. "Take the later plane."

She smiled. "Just so we have no misunderstanding, can you explain the subtext of what you just said?"

He grinned stupidly and touched her arm. "I'm not sure I know."

She sighed, and her brown eyes regarded him wisely. "Yes, you do. You'd love for me to meet your class. But tomorrow's Sunday."

"With a few phone calls, I could round them up, arrange for them to come here."

She pocketed her change. "I don't know, Hank. I have a lot of writing to do. This piece has to be modemed over for Monday's edition."

"These kids will break your heart, Sara. They have mine. They'll spend their entire lives here, and they'll be happy enough not knowing a bona-fide reporter from one of the biggest newspapers in America. But if they do get to meet you—"

"Stop it," she said, holding up her hand. "I've already survived one Jewish mother. What the hell, maybe I'll take some decent pictures for you." She leaned over and kissed his cheek.

It felt wonderful. He looked down at the floor. "Thanks. This means a lot. I don't know, meeting you, this nice thing happening, it feels like maybe my shitty luck might be turning."

"You have shitty luck?"

"Lately."

"Hank, that's hard to imagine. Someone as decent as you should be smiled upon by the gods." They walked into the Trading Post and stopped at the pawn case. Oscar came over to open the lock so Sara could try on rings. He nodded to Hank and stood there while the conversation continued. Sara said, "I don't suppose you have a twin brother who's single?"

"Sorry, I'm an only child."

She laughed. "Now that's bad luck, and it's all mine. Maybe you've hit a bad patch with your life. Just remember: If things don't improve, well, you have my card. I bet I could come up with a few ways to make you feel better." She motioned to Oscar, pointing to three of the rings. "I've got a tab at the front register. The squash blossom's mine, too. Can you add these in for me?"

"We'll get someone to wrap 'em right up."

Hank noticed how bare the case looked. He also noticed that Chloe's favorite ring was missing. "Oscar, what became of that ring with the dark blue stone?"

"Somebody bought it. Don't pay to wait when you see something you like. You should buy it or marry it, *enit*?" He dropped Sara's rings on the counter and hurried away.

Sara touched Hank's sleeve. "Tomorrow then?"

"Yes." Hank said good-bye to the reporter and braved his way through the crowds of curious onlokkers. All this fuss over what would have happened on its own, had nobody built a dam in the first place.

20

Junior's current state of mind—which he felt bordered on insanity—came about innocently enough, starting with a call from Sami Gee, who was enjoying a golfing holiday down in Scottsdale and wanted Junior to meet him at the Biltmore. *Come now, doesn't a wee sojourn in warm weather sound refreshing?* Wind blowing down his neck as he inspected the pup's latest damage to Aaron's yard—a den large enough to seat three adults—and Junior'd had to agree. A respite from the chilly north might just provide everyone with perspective.

When he was certain Hank was at work, Junior telephoned Chloe. She answered the phone, and he said, "Hoping for a miracle."

"That's good," she said. "Everyone should hold on to hope. What's going on?"

"Not too much. I have to head down to Phoenix. Come with me."

"Not a good idea."

"Then meet me halfway, in Sedona. A late-afternoon picnic. You always get hungry around four o'clock."

"So does Reed."

"Bring that sweet baby along. I don't get to see her as often as I'd like."

"Junior, you know I can't be gone that long."

"Meet me at three, then. Schnebly Hill Road near the lookout. Just show up if you can. If not, well, I'll enjoy the view without you." He hung up glumly, cursing himself for asking.

The valet boys at the Biltmore dressed like safari hunters, in tan Bermudas, short-sleeved jackets, and pith helmets with the little ventilation grommets. They were immaculate young men, probably college students, in the job for the tips. All this unremitting sun and not a single Skin in the bunch, Junior noticed. If they lacked the sense to sunscreen up, twenty years down the line this job would come back to haunt them. One motored the grimy Cherokee out of sight, and toting the wolf-hybrid pup, Junior made his way through the lobby, admiring the Frank Lloyd Wright designs present in murals, stained glass, every stick of furniture—indeed, the very columns that made up the building's structure. He kept his sunglasses and fancy jacket on, and as he walked past the guests and staff, heads turned in that subtle way of gawking only people with manners can pull off. Taking any kind of animal besides a stuffed jackalope into a regular hotel never would have flown, but here attitude coupled with skin color seemed to work a kind of magic. Only the rich and famous could afford the Biltmore during high season, and experience had proved that eccentricity was condoned, even encouraged, among the wealthy.

Sami Gee waited in the bar. When he caught sight of the wild dog in its beaded harness, he began chuckling and shaking his head. Pulling out a barstool for Junior, he gestured with one elegantly manicured hand around the cool, dark, expansive room. Junior tried to make out what the old man was pointing at. The Biltmore was not your typical luxury hotel. The design elements alone placed it in its own category. He passed a harpist dressed in a black velvet gown who plucked a moody Pachelbel canon from her strings. On a Mission-style banquet table sat a massive silver urn beaded with sweat, and alongside waited countless crystal goblets. Little trays of lemon wedges and sugar cubes were available to tart or sweeten up drinks, and an overflowing tray of baby vegetables so precious they could not be ignored would temporarily sate any heat-dulled appetite. With such choreographed ambience, who cared what time it was? An hour after lunch? Midnight? This was how southern Arizona laid out its high tea: constant, iced, soothed by music, an antidote to the glorious, endless sun.

The alchemy worked on Sam. "Every time I come into this bar," he said, "I get the distinct impression something wonderful is about to happen."

Junior's agent was in his sixties now and had traveled nearly the entire globe. He represented an eclectic gathering of artists and actors, plus a novelist who was making him wealthy with film options and a world-famous playwright who wasn't earning squat but expected Sam at his beck and call anyway. Junior snapped the leash onto his dog's harness. "Does it generally pan out for you?"

Sam spit an ice cube back into his scotch and petted the dog, who seemed content to receive the attention. "Infrequently."

"Well, pardon me for saying so, but that sounds kind of pathetic, Sam."

"My boy, we're not staring down the odds in Vegas. That's hardly my point by any stretch of the imagination. Remaining in the moment when all things are possible, that's what I'm talking about. That singular, divine, possibility-filled moment."

The bartender appeared before them. "I'll have a Coke," Junior said. "Maybe that way one of us will make sense."

"Diet, sir?"

"Whatever's handy."

"And for your companion?" The barkeep indicated his dog.

Junior smiled. "I believe his current beverage of choice would be water."

"Certainly, sir."

The barkeep returned shortly with the soda and a plastic water bottle bearing the distinctive Biltmore logo. He cracked the cap and, with a flourish, poured half its contents into a white china bowl. Little no-name stared briefly into the bowl, then eyed the cut-glass dish of nuts set alongside it. Junior gave his lead a tug. "None of that."

Sami Gee laid his arm across Junior's shoulders. "Well?"

"Well what?"

"The silver. I've been patient."

"Like I told you, Sam, I've been working on matters closer to home."

"I know what you told me, and now I want to hear the truth."

His agent wanted to hear Junior's enthusiastic description of designs that were burning through his fingers. He expected Junior's talk about burnout to prove nothing more than artistic complaint. He longed to feel the smooth metal in his fingers, to imagine what he could best place where, and to know for how much the pieces would sell. That kind of work kept his heart beating. Junior sensed all of that and said, "After you and me are done, I'm going to see these two women who run a wolf preserve northwest of here. This dog's half wolf and fully nuts. He steals everything unless I'm wearing it. Opens cupboards, digs dens the size of a basketball court, takes apart the furniture. I can't leave him alone long enough to take a dump on my own. If I'm ever going to work again, I need a little advice."

"Perhaps you could leave the animal with these women, make a donation, and be quit of the problem."

Junior thought of what Chloe might say about that. "Not an option. I'm signed on for the whole enchilada. Not sure about hybrids, but I heard wolves have a fifteen-year life-span."

"Perhaps that will prove to be rumor." Sam mulled things over for a few moments. "On the positive side, this animal could benefit your image, Junior. We'll get some Avedon-ish head shots of the two of you, redesign your publicity kit, capitalize on the 'wildness' aspect, the ladies will swoon, and your sales will skyrocket. That is, if we have anything to sell. The galleries are starting to sound a little restless. Unless I give them something to nibble on, they're going to stop calling."

Later on, Junior wouldn't know why he'd said what he did. The words just seemed to slide out of his mouth. "I've been thinking of trying some sandcasting. All this fancy shit bores me silly. Tiny little shards, so many colors, it makes my eyes ache just to look at it, you know?"

"Sandcasting's where it all began, correct? With that fellow Crybaby Something or Other?"

"Crying Smith. He wasn't the first, but everybody remembers his name."

"Well, then. I called that close enough for jazz. I'm with you, Junior. Really I am. What have you got to show me? Wax casts? Photos? Drawings?"

"I can show you a wild dog that's finally learned to sit."

His agent signaled to the bartender for a refill. He was drinking the oldest scotch in the house. "Does this reticence to commit have to do with your father's passing?"

"Of course not."

"These things do affect us, Junior. Did you have a service, put some closure on the situation?"

Junior shook his head. "Still haven't picked up his ashes."

"Why not?"

"I'll get to it when the time is right. Jimmy ain't going any-where."

"Is it about the boy, Junior?"

"Walter? We're getting along great. I almost brought him along today, but his mother wasn't quite ready for an overnight that involved skipping school. Next time for sure. He's a great kid, Sam, and what an artist. Too soon to tell where he'll focus his energy, but he's definitely got the curse. I've been staying out at this friend of mine's place, a painter, and when Walter comes for the week-end, he spends half his time going through Aaron's sketchpads. He's mad for those oil-based pastel crayons—"

Junior looked up to see Sam's eyes widening in an all-too-familiar expression. He opened his mouth to speak, but as soon as Junior pointed a finger, he shut it tight.

"Buddy, I know what you're thinking. Father and son, now wouldn't that make for an even greater publicity stunt than the freakin' wolf-dog? He's not even nine years old, Sam. The kid is going to grow up normal. If he wants to pump gas for a living, that'll be what he does. Hey, you want to get on my good side? Buy my dog here a BLT. He's eyeing those nuts like they're horse-meat."

"Sure." Sam smiled, swirling the ice in his drink. "But first let me ask you something, Junior. Why is it such a crime that I want to make you rich?"

"Because what I do's not about money, it just happens to bring some in."

"Some? Some? His holiness on rollerblades, Junior. I could quote from your schedule of earnings if you like."

"Hey, I know how much I made last year. And I know how much I paid the goddamn government."

"Which is a superlative situation to find one's self in, Junior. Much preferable to scrambling. I'm not prohibiting you from taking whatever time you need to get going again. Just remember, I need to keep myself in greens fees and decent booze."

"Your wallet might stay fatter if you roomed at the Motel Six."

The man snorted. "Motel Six would neither serve your wild bow-wow his repast nor would it come remotely close to making me feel that good things are within the realm of possibility. Mind this, my friend. I have chosen a lifestyle from which I shall not be budged."

And then just outside of Cordes Junction, as he was driving along, balancing the map in his lap, attempting to keep the pup in line while ruminating over Chloe Morgan, who had sunk her teeth into his heart, who held the market on toughness and unavailability, who said she *might* meet him later today at the lookout point, "might" being the operative word, he blew a tire on a long, lonely stretch of rutted road. His kidneys, sore from bouncing over rocks, were grateful for the break. He cracked the window, tied no-name's leash to the interior door handle, and set about changing the tire.

Can't call this simple lust, he chided himself as grit blew down his collar, sandblasting his neck. *If I wanted to, I could sleep with some other woman, say that airline girl in Phoenix, but I know what'd happen. I'd close my eyes, and she would be Chloe under me. I'd be substituting that girl's body for the one I don't get to call my own.* He remembered his mother and father, how they'd get to loving on each other sometimes in the kitchen, say, if she fixed him mutton stew and biscuits. Jimmy's way of saying thanks was to take her down to the bedroom for an hour. Sometimes, when the joy of sex overflowed the shabby rooms, he could hear them. The sounds of his parents making love always reassured him. That was because the flip side was his father's drunken rages, or the long walks his mother took Junior on to escape the yelling, the fists that might come flying their way. He wondered if maybe all his screwing around in the past was linked to that childish idea of keeping danger distant—if that was why he'd left Corrine. Would Walter be as messed up at thirty-eight? Would his son believe that the only women worth love and respect worked eighty hours a week and lived on junk food? That fathers came into the picture only to drift out, like poor television reception? Corrine still loved him. He could tell if he asked, she would find space for him. She'd alter her life and take him on whatever terms he offered. But the bottom line was he didn't love her, and pretending he did could not be sustained.

Junior scraped his knuckles raw hammering the lug nuts loose. Whoever'd owned this car before him had been lucky to go this long on such cheap tires. He'd have to get some new ones, quick. The pup scrabbled at the window, anxious to be with him, so every now and then Junior lifted his raw hand up for the dog to sniff. He finished changing the tire and sat on the ground, weary, grit everywhere, even between his teeth. Arizona had its stretches of ugly, and this road had just been inducted into Junior's personal top ten.

Truth always seemed to slap his face in such vapid places. His heart beat out its lonely rhythm: *Face up. Corrine was a practice run. You are in love for real this time. That's all your problem is. The mighty redskin has fallen like the old carved-up tree he truly is.* For the first time in his life, the situation appeared simple, straightforward, and its outcome entirely unworkable. Chloe didn't want her picture taken so she could parlay their alliance into a modeling career. She didn't want a signed piece of jewelry to flaunt as a memento of one night's passion. She didn't even want him. She wasn't happy, she was *satisfied* with her unmarried but live-together status, nursing little Reed and waiting for warm-enough weather so she could start in training the colt. *I can't leave now,* Junior said to himself. *I can't miss that. Her taming that horse will be something to behold.*

Thinking of her was like unleashing some wild virus in his blood. Try as he might, he couldn't stop the mental pictures. He imagined her astride the colt, bareback, at the lope, her strong legs holding her fast, moving fearlessly, fluidly, at one with the animal. Or the two of them riding alongside each other on Sally and the colt, taking cinder-laden trails through the pine forest. He knew how dark and quiet those trails could be. The kinds of looks you traded in thick, congested silence. What you could say without exchanging a word. He envisioned her seated at one of those rough-hewn tables at the steak house out by swampy old Lake Mary, where eating red meat was akin to worship. Chloe'd tear into a barely cooked ten-ounce and laugh at how good it felt to be hungry, how satisfying it was to feed that emptiness. Then he allowed himself to remember the taste of her kisses, that night in the motel room, and when he did he swore he could savor the exact essence of her on his tongue, that unmistakable tang he craved. When he discarded all the rationalizations, he could admit his intentions had truly been wicked, but in his defense, at least he hadn't acted on them. At the very moment of her surrender, Junior had seen the wisdom of holding back, and kept himself in check, dammit, and if that was all it ended up being, that one night of kissing and stroking and this full-blown yearning chained like a yoke around the heart, he'd truly lose his grip on the world.

He fingered the Lander's ring on his pinkie and wondered again how best to set the stone. In silver or gold? In platinum, surrounded by old-timey baguette diamonds, pried from some junky piece of estate jewelry? He'd occasionally played around with gold, and it was costly, but if you decided to set something in platinum, it had best be eternal. If Sam heard him talking like this, he'd cheer and lift his glass. Junior blinked hard, but the picture didn't go away, and he knew that sooner or later he'd have to get back to work in order to afford the vision.

The wolf lady and her friend owned twenty-two acres, wisely purchased ten years before the Californians invaded and claimed Arizona as a vacation spot. They lived in a log house surrounded by twenty chain-link enclosures and one rickety outhouse that worked well enough, it seemed, as Junior scooped lime into the pit. With Paolo Soleri's Arcosanti the only nearby draw, and in its own way exquisitely weird, two women and thirty-six wolves weren't likely to interest or bother anyone.

Anne had moved to the ranch in the eighties, she said, "sick to death of LA." She had one of those intriguingly weathered faces, high-set cheekbones, and kinky silver hair that reached halfway down her back. She looked to be anywhere from in her early forties to fifty-something, no facelift, but a natural attractiveness still resided there. "In another life," she explained, "I was an actress. To sum it up, I prefer the company of wolves to sharks." She led him through the compound to where her partner, Teresa, was at work in a small studio off-building, painting a likeness of a wolf on illustration board. She was using egg tempera, dipping her brush quickly, as the medium was at best fickle and brief.

"Not easy stuff to work with," Junior commented.

She smiled, then raised her arm to show off one of his bracelets. "Recognize this?"

"Sure." He'd made it three years ago, when he was enamored of sugilite. The grape-colored stone was inlaid with thin strips of coral and lapis, and all of that set off one small but fine chunk of spider-web turquoise. "My purple phase."

"This bracelet was the last thing I charged on my VISA before I left my cheating son-of-a-bitch husband. Figured for all that marriage cost me, he owed me one beautiful souvenir."

The cost issue always put Junior on the defensive. "A lot of hours went into that bracelet. It's signed. My agent would say you made a wise investment."

Teresa set down her brush. "And the card company I broker to wants to pay me a measly hundred bucks for the rights to this painting. Good thing we artists like what we do, huh?"

He gave her a noncommittal shrug. If she liked it, he didn't want to disillusion her.

"Your pup's part timberwolf, by the way. No more than half, though, possibly less. We have two of those crosses, one's three-quarters wolf. I can show you the differences when we take the tour. One got shot by a rancher who said he wouldn't allow anything on his land that he couldn't take out with a shotgun. We're awfully glad he had such a poor aim. The other we bartered for when we heard the owner was using construction rebar to teach the dog 'manners.' You'll have to leave your little guy in the quarantine pen on the other side of the house while we take you around. Vet care's expensive."

"Sounds reasonable."

They walked among the pens, which housed anywhere from two to six wolves each. The women explained they'd sunk the wire mesh six feet down and stretched it across the ceilings, that when a wolf could dig, he would, and that they'd witnessed them jumping eight feet up in the air from a sitting position. It was clear the wolves were thrilled to see their women off-schedule. Anne leaned her head back and howled, which incited an eerie canine chorus. The hair on Junior's head lifted at the keening sound. "Communication," Teresa explained, laughing at his stricken expression. "You hang with another species long enough, you learn the basic language."

Following the tour they checked on no-name, who was content to work the bone they'd given him, then they went inside the log house. The women showed him the rooms, decorated sparsely with secondhand furniture. Anne's bedroom was last. Atop the patchwork quilt on her king-size bed, five wolf hybrids rested, sprawled over assorted cow bones and well-attended rope-chew toys. "Come on over," she said. "Meet my house wolves."

They eyed Junior suspiciously but rolled over for Anne.

"This is Girdwood, and this here's Nome. Nome lost her eye before we rescued her. The white one I call Anchorage, and he's the trickster of the bunch, very sneaky. Such a handsome fellow, but not entirely to be trusted. I don't mean to have favorites, but what can I say? He stole my heart. And that's Sitka and little Skagway, both from the same litter."

"You must really dig Alaska."

"I visited there prepipeline. It made an impression."

"How do you keep on top of them? I mean, they outnumber you."

"At all times you must remain the alpha animal," she advised, "and risk looking utterly stupid whenever necessary. If you're charged, immediately tackle your dog and wrestle it to the ground. For God's sake don't hit; a wolf will submit once you get him down. Don't think, But he outweighs me, and don't ignore behavior you're not willing to tolerate. Keep the order intact and be consistent."

"What about destructiveness? I mean, he took my friend Aaron's sofa apart."

"He was curious as to what was inside, that's all. Wolves are highly intelligent."

"Does that mean he'll want to take me apart someday, too?"

"Not if you socialize him properly."

Teresa brewed them yerba buena tea and laid out a snack of fruit, nuts, and cheese. They sat at the kitchen table talking, and as

Junior set down his napkin he noted that there wasn't a single edge of the table that wasn't marked with teeth imprints.

"A wolf helps you simplify your life," Anne said. "In return, and I don't intend this romantically, you live with spirit and mystery."

"Plus a lot of wrecked furniture."

"That, too. But maybe you didn't need all that furniture."

"Something to think about."

Teresa added, "You'll never be lonely."

Particularly in the john, Junior thought. "What if I couldn't care for him? Could I give him away, or would I have to leave him at a place like this?"

The two women exchanged somber looks. "Your wolf-dog would mourn terribly if you gave him to anyone. He's bonded with you. He can't survive on his own. He doesn't know how to hunt, and he isn't socialized with other wolves. Dogs will never accept him. If you released him anywhere in this state, he'd either be run over or shot. An animal shelter will euthanize him immediately; after all, to them this is a wild animal. Chances are another owner would come up against the same struggles you encountered."

"Wow. Guess I didn't know what I was getting into."

Teresa added, "It's serious stuff. We'll take him for you. But we ask that you never come back, not even to visit. It's too confusing for the animal."

"They become attached, just like humans," Anne said. Then, as if she felt compelled to remind him, she said it again. "They grieve."

So he and no-name got back on Highway 17 and headed north, committed to whatever adventure they were in, together. Forty miles later, Junior spotted the turnoff for Schnebly Hill Road, and decisively set his blinker. Tunnel vision was required to skirt Sedona's New Age advertisements for "authentic" sweat-lodge experiences, crystal readings, and so forth. He deserved a reward, and time spent with Chloe was certainly that. It might only be the view from the cliffside of what seemed like a miniature Grand

Canyon, the occasional comically formed butte, and a glimpse of the clean, rushing gorge under the cypress, juniper, and pines. Well, if so, he'd still come out on the good side of things.

Only careful drivers could manage the high, winding ride up unpaved road to the cliffs of the Mogollon Rim. On its new tire, the Cherokee seemed up to the task. Junior drove the twisting road slowly, filling himself up with the nearly painful splendor of it, keeping a sharp eye out for Pink Jeep tours and the occasional hikers, which could appear out of anywhere. Here he wouldn't have minded stopping to change a flat tire. Any excuse was a good one, if you were waylaid in the presence of the earth's most eloquent prayers. Chloe wasn't coming; she knew better than to tempt herself. He was about to pull over and take a walk, when he came up behind the Chevy truck ahead of him, the old California plates calling out like a beacon.

He followed her for awhile, heart pounding at her bravery. Well, those New Agers insisted Sedona had the power. Maybe this was proof of it. He flashed his high beams twice. As she casually stuck her arm out the window for a hand signal, he could tell she'd been aware of his presence the whole time. He followed her to the lookout point. He shut down the engine, cracked the windows, and told the wolf-pup to behave himself.

She hiked ahead of him to the ledge, then sat down in the dirt, the pines casting shadows over her shoulders. Reed was awake in her arms, beaming her smile toward Junior, her tiny fingers tangled in her mother's yellow hair. Chloe spread out her jacket and laid the baby down. "Find a hobby, Junior."

"I have one. Hanging with a girl who can't stand my face."

"How about jewelry making? I heard there's big bucks in that."

"No kidding. I'll give that serious thought. Can't be too difficult compared to what I've been doing." He patted the ground, the pine needles under his fingers long gone to dusty mulch. "Come on over here, Chloe."

"Give me one good reason why I should."

"So I won't pull a muscle reaching all that way to kiss you. You don't want me to get a hernia, do you?"

"As a matter of fact, that's exactly what I want. You with a big, fat, total-body hernia that lands you in a hospital far, far away from wherever I am."

"All you're doing's getting me hot. You could read me ingredients off the side of a cereal box and set me on fire. Come on, baby, have a little mercy on old Junior. He misses you something awful. Hasn't he been following all your rules, staying away?"

"No. He shows up wherever I go."

"In your dreams?"

"Unfortunately."

"That means something."

"Probably trouble." Reed cooed, and they both looked down at her. Chloe said, "Last week I drove all the way to Tucson, then I chickened out. I'm such a coward."

It wasn't a word he would have ascribed to her. "Chickened out from doing what?"

"It isn't the first time. I did it two weeks ago, too."

"I'm listening."

She sighed, leaned her head back to look at the sky, revealing the neck he'd covered with kisses that night in the motel. Where her collarbone arced away from her body, leaving that wonderful dip at the base of her neck, there must have been a bundle of nerves, because when he'd kissed her there, her body had come off the mattress and fitted into his own, as if they had really been making love, not just teasing themselves into a fever playing at it.

"It's all Kit's fault."

"What did she do?"

"Meant well. That's Kit's long suit. Forget it, it's a really long story. Boils down to, I got this letter. It has to be my mother; the pieces all fit. I have her address. I thought maybe I could drive by and just look."

"I don't think you can ever have too much family. Of course, this advice's coming from a father who's just now getting to know his son."

Chloe frowned. "It's like turning over some big rock, Junior. Scorpions live under rocks. Whole families of them."

"Or you could be shining a light on something that only needed a little attention in order to grow into something wonderful. How are you going to know if you don't look it square in the eye?" He scooted himself closer. Reed was now between them. He put his hands on Chloe's shoulders, so near that hollow of skin in her neck he shivered a little. "Hey, I decided something today. Something important I want to tell you."

"Spare me, okay? I've got enough problems."

He shook his head, disgusted. "You think I give a damn, Chloe? I'm only saying this for me. Pure selfishness. I love you. I've said those words a bunch of times, yeah, but this time my heart's saying them with me. I want you to come away with me. Maybe we should get married. Never wanted that before, but seems like I want it now. We belong together."

"What about what Hank wants?" Her brown eyes filled up with tears. Slowly they overflowed, and with his printless fingertips, Junior smoothed each one into the skin of her cheeks. Then he pressed his mouth against the invisible salt trails left behind and kissed them clean. He covered her closed eyes with his lips, tracing his tongue over the globe of eyeball beneath the quivering lids. He kissed her nose, her chin, stopped himself at her neck, and left her mouth entirely unexplored. When he broke away, she opened her eyes and looked at him, startled, perhaps, that he'd stopped.

She blew out a breath. "You can't know how hard this is for me."

He tasted bitter laughter and exploded. "Well, that's a freakin' insensitive comment coming out of your mouth! You want to discuss difficult? Thanks to you, I got a wolf-dog back there probably tearing up the interior of my new Jeep because he wants to know how the damn thing's constructed. Thanks to you, here in my chest I got a heart so sore from wanting you there's mornings I wake up wondering if I'm having a myocardial event. And thanks to you and only you, little *amá*, there's this other matter of what it feels like to sport an erection for three solid months with no relief. I mean, that's arguably the least of my difficulties, but let me tell you, it's not pleasant."

"So fuck somebody else! I've seen how Corrine looks at you. She'd take you to bed. So would a million other—"

He took hold of her chin firmly. "I don't want Corrine! I don't want nobody except you. You let me kiss you, you show up at the motel, what am I supposed to think except you want that too? Jesus, Chloe, make up your mind."

He plucked Reed from the jacket and stood up. Walking to the cliff's edge, he saw the afternoon light filter through the trees and paint the red rocks scarlet. It was a color he sometimes witnessed in select pieces of coral, a red straight from God's own palette. The rock seemed to be covered with shimmering light, bathing itself in the shafts of waning radiance. Reed's little hand shot up into the air, as if with her limited coordination she was trying to capture a shard of that light for herself. Junior began to smile, and he laughed out loud, feeling his voice echo across the chasm. He took hold of her tiny hands and kissed them, whooping with the simple joy of this child's trying to touch the light, at how reasonable wanting all the magic things in life seemed to her. Reed lived in Sami Gee's moment, twenty-four hours a day. He hefted her body higher in his arms, matching her beauty to that of the canyon. Her whole body was washed in the falling-away sun.

Then, surprisingly, he felt Chloe's touch against his shoulder. This acquiescence flattered him, excited him, scared the holy crap out of him. He turned and they cradled the baby between their bodies and kissed, as long and hungry as two people ever could when separated by a four-month-old baby.

Junior followed her truck until they were within a mile of the Trading Post. There she made her left turn, and he kept going straight, to Aaron's. The small hole in the passenger's seat, courtesy of no-name's intelligence factored with curiosity, seemed like a small price to pay for the afternoon. Holding Chloe in his arms, hearing her say that just for one night they'd think of themselves, not Hank, that she'd find a way, that she'd go away with him, Junior could live with a rip in the fabric of the universe. *I feel like I'm going insane,* he'd told her. *No part of this is sane,* she'd replied. He nodded, agreeing; he'd have said anything to keep her there a minute longer. Hearing the yes in her voice, he wanted to take her back to Aaron's, make love to her all night. Name that bed or any other space they could call their own.

Then, at their cars, he'd almost blown the whole thing asking when.

You have to let me say when the time's right or forget it, she'd cautioned. *I won't hurt Hank, not while his mom's in such a bad way. I might be a faithless bitch, but I'm not cruel. I won't go ripping his heart out just because you and me have got hot pants.*

If only hot pants were all it was. Back at Aaron's he took the wolf-dog for a long walk, hoping to tire him out. He studied the night sky and felt the cool air chilling his skin. The constellations were so bright, so steadfast, little silver promises of constancy in the universe. Junior relived every moment of the day, savoring the images and feelings. He watched falling stars streak across the sky and calculated which formations he could recognize and which were probably just airplane lights. Then an idea struck him, and he hurried the dog inside to begin unpacking the boxes he'd had shipped out from Massachusetts.

All night he set up his equipment, arranging things, making sure his tools were sequential, each within easy reach. When he was satisfied that it made a working environment, he began to sketch out his drawings, to make plans for the silver.

21

Every day since she'd made that promise in Sedona, Chloe was up before dawn, frying eggs over easy, the way Hank liked them, filling a Thermos with coffee for him to take to school, throwing herself into whatever chore might possibly untangle that knot of guilt beneath her heart. Hannah and Reed didn't mind that their afternoon walks were fueled by Chloe's agonizing indecision. Fresh air and exercise almost made up for the mandatory grooming sessions that followed each trek. In a burst of household ambition, Chloe went so far as to strip the kitchen's tiny linoleum floor and give it a gleaming coat of wax. She found a great buy on tile down in Flagstaff, and had the bathroom Hank wouldn't let her work on when she was pregnant ready for grout before he arrived home. Domestic activity met with Hank's surprise and approval. Chloe did her best to try to make him happy, including waiting until he'd driven off to school before she started in working with the horse.

No matter what the weather—and in April they'd seen it all, from freak snowstorms to days so warm she took her shirt off and stood in the sun wearing only her boots, jeans, and bra—Thunder suffered from an unrelenting case of spring fever. The arena wasn't big enough for the kind of ideas the colt dreamed up. Some days the fence could barely contain him. Chloe wondered if this indicated he had natural potential as a jumper. Be patient, and horses generally revealed their inclinations, which was how she liked to approach training. His mother had come off the track in Caliente, and her half of the gene pool was evident in his lust for speed. On the longe line, he ran long, slow circles, his elegant muscles rippling, a sight so reminiscent of her lost Absalom that it made her throat close up. She knew Thunder would never be that one-of-a-kind horse, but he was better than no horse at all. Just before a rain Chloe could count on his explosive fits of bucking, sometimes lasting as long as an hour. However, as soon as the first drops began falling, he became docile and reasonable, not minding at all that he was getting wet.

Today, looking out the kitchen window, she saw the idiot horse had got it into his mind to rear. His well-trimmed hooves pawed the air in front of him, like an equine attempt at the *macarena*. Half of her heart sent him a big *olé*. All that power tucked into the youthful body, the joy of being able to announce it. The antics appeared playful enough to the uneducated eye. Thunder was simply a rear-engine animal discovering that depending on how he threw his weight around yielded amazing results, but rearing was one of the few lines she drew with horses. She tugged a sweatshirt over Reed's head and strapped her into her stroller, parking it twenty feet from the arena. No matter what Hank thought, she could keep an eye on the baby while she taught the colt some manners.

Boosting herself up on the fence, she took the bullwhip in hand. Snapped properly, it made a noise as loud as a firecracker. Thunder had no one-on-one experience with whips, but instinct made him pin his ears. He circled Chloe a few times, curious, then broke into an extended trot. Now and then, he'd rodeo to a halt, change directions, those gorgeous muscles snapping under the chestnut coat. But he wasn't about to give up his new trick just because she held that scary stick in her hand. He was bent on convincing her that rearing was his God-given right. Every time the horse leaned back, began the telltale settling on his haunches, she gave the whip a crack against the fence. The lash landed nowhere near the horse, but it sang as it reverberated in the metal gate, humming an unmistakable warning. After six tries at rearing up, and six cracks of the leather, Thunder broke out in a nervous lather. *What the hell?* he seemed to be asking the gods. *I learn a wonderful new trick that makes me feel like I can kick the ass out of the universe, and* she *decides that's wrong?*

"Give it up," Chloe said evenly. "You can be my horse, eat delicious hay, and drink fresh water every day of your life, or you can rear your wicked heart out all the way to the auction block. Ralston Purina's got a going operation down there in Flagstaff. Dog chow or quiet horse, it's your pick. I'll be here when you've made up your mind."

Thunder shook his large head, never taking his eyes off the whip. After a ten-minute standoff, he wandered casually over to the water trough and dipped his muzzle for a long, slow drink. Chloe sat motionless, the whip across her knees. Had she won that easily? Reed cooed excitedly from her stroller.

Chloe turned her face to study her daughter. "You're finding this all very entertaining, aren't you, young lady? You probably have your silver cup bet on the horse. News flash. You don't know your mother."

In reply Reed cut loose with a smattering of delightful baby noises. If anything, the olive cast to her skin at birth had deepened. Her brown eyes were a deep shade of sable, her dark hair thick and straight. She looked just ethnic enough so that in public, after people remarked on the pretty baby, they spent far too long looking at Reed's parents, wondering about gene pools. Hank, who didn't like anybody to feel uncomfortable, was given to saying things like, "We think she looks like herself," but Chloe knew where that dark coloring might have come from: her side of the family. Sometimes she could hardly look at her daughter without being reminded that she lacked the courage to seek the answers. Even Junior said to check things out. But why the hell should she, when life ran smooth otherwise? Why rock a floating boat? The baby had a schedule. Reed seemed to be adjusting to the bottle, nursing only in the evenings. Chloe looked forward to Reed's grins, her increasing attempts at laughter. It was as if seeing the same old mother every morning constituted the highlight of her daughter's day.

Hannah wandered into the barn as Chloe stowed the bullwhip among the tack. She gave her dog a pat. Hannah was more active now that warmer weather had arrived. The northern Arizona winter hadn't been so kind to her aging bones. Because she'd come to Chloe full grown, abandoned, her age and background were uncertain. The stiffness in her rear quarters could be arthritis; she could be that old. What she wouldn't be able to hack was too many winters like this one. Chloe threw the white shepherd a hoof trimming and watched her retreat to the fenceline to work on it. Then she brought out the horse blanket she'd bought from the Navajo last summer. After shaking out the dust, she walked into the arena, allowed the colt to sniff it all over, then began rubbing its coarse weave all over his body.

She remembered that rainy night when she'd helped Gabe Hubbard move aside the dead mare's guts to give Thunder his only chance. She had rubbed the horse dry, using slow, circular strokes, just like this. It was a miracle they'd been able to save the colt, who didn't have a clue that Chloe was responsible for his having a life, and maybe in the long run that didn't matter, but one fact remained: Thunder was an orphan horse, and the potential for vices would always be with him. Without enough to keep him busy, he'd become a cribber, a biter, the shifty kind of animal that would allow no human being to develop a bond. He needed a job to do, to be kept exercised, and to end each day feeling sweet exhaustion clear down to his heart. Softly at first, then with larger gestures, murmuring that it was all right whenever he got to snorting and blowing, she laid the blanket across his back. An hour later Reed was fast asleep and the colt was wearing not only the blanket, but a bareback pad as well, the girth fastened only one notch away from where Chloe wanted it to be. She laid her body across his back and let him get used to her weight. At once, he took a few steps forward. Forward, that was real progress. She took hold of his halter, led him around the arena, then out onto the prairie where they walked and explored and he tasted new grasses until she could tell he was worn out with all the new sensations. Chloe led him back into the arena, untacked him, and threw him a flake of hay. He was so tired he took a halfhearted mouthful and began to doze, his back against the fence, security he knew and understood. Tomorrow she would try it all over again. In a few days, if all was proceeding, she'd try getting up on his back, just for a moment, then lavish him with praise and thin slivers of apple. Praise and acceptance: A horse couldn't get enough of those in the training stages. Neither, she guessed, could a baby.

Chloe pushed Reed's stroller up the bumpy stretch of cinder path and sat with her sleeping daughter on the back porch. She had given Junior her word, but just this once, was it a crime to go back on a promise? It was the moral thing to do. Face it, there was never going to be a "right time" to cheat on Hank. The man kept her too yoked for comfort, but he worked like a draft horse. He deserved nothing less than hot suppers and adoration at the end of every day. He was such a decent, loving father in a world full of deserters and deadbeats. These feelings she had for Junior weren't true love, they were that word Ann Landers was fond of throwing around: "infatuation." Sure, that's what it was. Besides, as much as she might feel electricity down to her toes when Junior kissed her, her heart quietly owed Hank the same amount. This whole situation was crazy—imagining you could love two men at the same time—who could manage that? A good question for Ann might be: How on earth did shit like this happen? Love ought to boil down to a choice: This one will last, that one won't. At night Chloe got into bed next to Hank, lost herself in his arms, then fell asleep and dreamed about Junior Whitebear. She heard his voice calling to her so clearly in her dreams that she woke up expecting to see that dark hair spread across the pillow next to hers.

Reed awoke and started to cry. She flailed her arms and scrunched up her pretty face, sucking in a breath like it might be her last. When she exhaled in a scream, Chloe's heart felt like it was cracking down the middle.

"What's the problem here, little girl? You're not wet. Did your mother let you get too much sun?" She unstrapped the stroller's restraints and cuddled her daughter in her arms. "Shh, don't cry. You haven't got anything to be sad about. The sun is shining, and there's a whole lifetime ahead of you for picking the wrong man and feeling real sorrow. Tell you what, we'll go inside and have a bath. A bath always makes a girl feel better."

In the kitchen sink, she watched her daughter pat the water's surface, amused by soapsuds. Chloe lathered Reed's slippery little body, which was plumping up now that she was trying some solid foods. Reed was growing out of infancy into the mysterious future of her own life. Chloe powdered her, dressed her in the little red sleep suit she'd bought at the Wal-Mart in Flag, tucked her feet into mismatched booties. Red would always be a good color on Reed. She wasn't Gerber pretty, but her brown eyes were deep and soulful, her gaze sometimes so piercing it was unnerving to look up and find her watching you. Hank said that kind of scrutiny proved she was a searcher, that she would become a scientist, but Chloe knew Reed watched people for reasons that had squat to do with book smart. Deep in her genes, same as her mother's, she was afraid of being abandoned. For the millionth time since her birth, Chloe got mad all over again that the Olivers hadn't wanted to see her badly enough to overcome their uptightness. They didn't approve of Hank's choice in women, so what was the big deal about them not being married, and what in hell did that have to do with their son having a child? Well, those questions were neither here nor there, and it was getting on time to start dinner. She let Reed entertain herself in her crib, shaking her rattle and drooling on her stuffed toys, and set about making a pan of cornbread and some enchiladas. She put the pans into the stove, then spread a blanket on the floor in front of the woodstove. Hannah stood guard duty while Chloe played with the baby until Hank walked in.

He stopped in the doorway, smiling. "Hey. There are my girls."

"Hey yourself. Come kiss your daughter quick while she's all clean and happy. Be glad you weren't here a couple hours ago. What lungs. What temper. If we thought Kit was bad as a teenager, I think we're in for a rude surprise."

Hank's expression seemed forced, and Chloe's heart began to pound uncomfortably. "I figured this day was too good to be true. Did you get fired? Wreck the car? Did some asshole country start a new war?"

"My father called me at work."

"Oh, no. Your mom? Did she die?"

"Not yet, but she's in the hospital. They're saying it's only a matter of days. So I really have to go. To California. Tonight."

She got to her knees. "Of course you do. I'll help you get your suitcase packed."

He bent down and placed a hand on her shoulder. "I want my mother to meet Reed. Even if she thinks she doesn't want to. I just think she should. Whether it means anything to her is beside the point. It means that much to me."

"You mean, take Reed with you?"

Hank nodded.

"Okay. I'll get all our stuff packed, and you go grab a bite of dinner. Then we'll drive straight to the airport. We can just leave the car in the lot. Or do you think we should call Oscar, ask him to drop us off? Somebody needs to look after Hannah, not to mention feed Thunder."

Hank took the baby from her arms. He looked down at the floor for a moment, then into her face. "I've thought about this a lot. I'm going to take Reed by myself."

"Oh." Chloe stepped back and looked out the window. The horse was staring up at the house. Hannah, who had fled out the dog door as soon as the tension surfaced, was digging a hole. *There's a place I could fall in*, Chloe thought, *make everybody happy.*

"My father's a wreck, Chloe. One minute he's drunk and raving, the next he cusses me like the cancer is my fault. He's likely to take his grief out on whatever unsuspecting target's put in front of him."

"Well, I think I'm fairly tough. But if you want me to stay behind, I'll stay."

"It's for the best."

She had been shut out of the Olivers' lives from day one, and when they didn't embrace the birth of their grandchild the hurt had seemed almost too large to bear. *Jesus, get a grip here, Chloe, why should you expect anything different now? He's an Oliver, too. Blood sticks with blood.* Quickly, she swiped at her eyes and steadied her voice. "I have a bunch of breast milk in the freezer. Let me pack it in that small cooler for you to take along."

"You're okay with this?"

"Sure." Blindly, she pulled bottles from the cupboard, took down the box of rice cereal they'd begun trying, mentally calculating how many diapers he'd need. "We'd better get a move on. Did you call the airline?"

She turned to look at him, and he nodded mutely. In his arms, Reed looked like one of those babies from a Third World country who get adopted by wealthy, infertile couples.

She sat on the couch hugging a throw pillow, her enchiladas uneaten and dried out in front of her. The cabin was full of its usual creaks and odd drafty spaces, but it had never before seemed lonely. Now, when she looked at Reed's empty crib, panic rose in her chest. She didn't trust airplanes. What if something happened to them, or Hank decided to stay in California? Nonsense, he'd take wonderful care of Reed. He knew how to make her stop crying better than Chloe did. Nevertheless, here she sat, alone and expendable. She wandered outdoors, stopping a few feet from the house. In the utter dark, she listened to the sound of the horse moving around the corral. She felt Hannah's head come up under her hand. Animals sensed restlessness; they knew. Chloe stayed up all night, waiting for Hank to call, all the same figuring he wouldn't. Hank would wait until the morning, some hour he deemed reasonable, and even then, he'd give her only as much information as he thought she could handle.

"We're here," he said wearily when the phone rang at eight-thirty. "I'm just about to leave for the hospital."

"Reed sleep okay? Did you give her a bottle? The plane ride didn't bother her ears?"

"She's a champ. I probably won't call you tonight, unless there's anything to report."

After they hung up, Chloe loaded Hannah into the Chevy truck and drove to the Post for breakfast. There was a letter from Kit in the P.O. box, but she didn't think she could handle high school drama until she had some coffee under her belt. She took a table by the window in the restaurant, held out her mug, ordered cinnamon toast, then sat ignoring everything, staring at nothing, feeling as gutted as a deer. Oscar Johnson came up and pulled out a chair.

"*Ya hey*. You're looking more strung out than me. One of them legendary nights with the wee screamer?"

"Not this time, Oscar. She's with Dad in California. Just me and the animals for a couple of days. You want this toast?"

Oscar reached for a piece, looked at the cinnamon, then spread jam over the top. "Got to drown out the taste of cinnamon."

Chloe smiled. "Is that the trick? Listen, I know why I'm here, but the store doesn't open until ten. Is Corrine organizing another one of those shows where tourists descend and buy out the cases?"

He shook his head no. "I was supposed to bring Dog along. But he woke up with a fever, Corrine's home tending him, which means I get to run the Post for the day. Nothing difficult better happen. Corrine's got all the ambition in this family."

"Just give them your tough-guy face."

Oscar pulled a pose, and Chloe said, "A little more sneer if you can manage it. Poor Dog. Hope he's feeling better soon."

"It's just the flu. We all pay for the change of seasons." Oscar leaned back so the waitress could pour him a mug of coffee. He stirred cream in it and tapped the spoon against the edge of the cup. He listened while Chloe explained about Hank's mother. "You should take yourself a holiday down south, Chloe. Go lay by a motel pool. A chance like this might never come round again."

"Hell, I'd need a dog sitter and a horse tender to do that."

"I'll do it. Any one of them parents at the school would do it too. All you got to do is ask."

"Stop tempting me." She sipped her coffee and was about to call the waitress back over, order a real breakfast, now that she had developed some appetite, when Junior walked in the restaurant. He nodded at her, then began walking over to the table.

"Let me guess: That's who Dog was meeting."

"They was planning a camping trip."

"It's the middle of the school week."

"Traveling's educational. Hey, Junior."

"Oscar. Seen my partner in crime anywhere?"

"Yeah, home in his sickbed begging for Popsicles. Corrine sent me to tell you. Nothing serious, sore throat, little fever, but she nixed the camping. Sorry."

Junior looked away, disappointed. "Thanks for letting me know."

"Sure. Well, I got to go count out registers," Oscar said. "Hope they balance. Anything over ten fingers, I get nervous. Chloe, you want to give me a key so I can let myself in over to your place?"

"I'll drop it by. If I decide to go."

Oscar wrapped the toast in a napkin, took it with him.

Junior held onto the back of the chair Oscar had vacated. "Going to see your mother for real this time?"

"Thinking about it."

"Where's my Reed?"

"With her father. Hank's mom's real bad. He wanted to take her to meet her grandmother before she died."

Junior squinted. "The only thing missing from that family portrait is Mama. Why?"

Chloe shrugged. "Oh, you know. Trailer-park trash versus the royal family. Put enough time and distance between us, they're hoping I'll fade away. Don't blame Hank. He wanted to protect me from flaming arrows, that's all."

"Ain't the way I would have done it."

"I know. Everything would be simple and wonderful and positively enchanting if you were handling it."

"You're all alone out there?"

She pointed a finger. "Whitebear, do not push me. You promised."

He sat down, moved Oscar's coffee aside and unfolded his hands on the tabletop. Chloe noticed they were grimy, the fingertips black, the nails clipped short.

Junior saw her staring and held up his hands. "The bane of working silver is the stuff gets ground into your skin. Scrubbed them raw this morning, though you'd never know it."

"I wasn't staring."

"Yes, you were."

"Okay, I was. Have me arrested. How's your dog?"

"Me and Aaron built him a pen. I needed some time alone, and that pen was the only way I could get it."

Chloe picked up the menu. Her hands were trembling from lack of sleep. She couldn't make any sense of the words printed on the slick card so she set it back down. "Where were you and Dog headed? It's awful cold to camp."

"Chinlé. We were planning on picking up my father's ashes, taking them over to the canyon. Jimmy liked it there. I thought maybe that was where he wanted to end up."

"Are you still going to do it?"

"I've put it off so long that guy at the funeral home started charging me rent. I'd be ashamed to back out now."

She took a deep breath, trying to drive the air down to the bottom of her lungs. "Tell me about this canyon."

"*The* canyon, Chloe. Most beautiful place I know."

"How long a drive is it? Can you go there and back in a day?"

Junior picked up a spoon and stared at it, then set it down. "You could. But then you'd miss watching the sun rise over the rocks, the cottonwood leaves shimmering in the morning wind, not to mention a fine dinner at the Thunderbird Lodge cafeteria."

"Stop with the tour book, Junior. I'm coming with you."

He took a quick gulp of Oscar's coffee and made a face.

"Oh, for Christ's sake, pick up your jaw and let's go before I remember I have any good sense left."

Oscar accepted her house key with nothing more than a sober glance. He maneuvered a reluctant Hannah behind the counter and snapped her lead onto his chair.

Chloe petted her dog good-bye. "One night, girl. Oscar'll take good care of you."

Junior stopped in the grocery and bought bottled water, bread and cheese, green apples, strips of jerky. While they were standing at the register, Chloe threw several candy bars in the mix.

"If we're going to hell," she said, "why not do it in a big way?"

"The only hell that's likely to result from this feast is a trip to the dentist." Junior paid the bill, and they got into his Cherokee. The motor caught on the second try, and they drove into Tuba to pick up Jimmy Whitebear's ashes. Chloe waited in the car while Junior ran inside the mortuary. He returned with a plain cardboard box and a large manila envelope.

"What's that?"

"This," Junior set the box on the floor of the Jeep, "is Jimmy." He opened the envelope and quickly scanned the papers inside. "This other stuff looks like his death certificate, some bullshit about his effects. Probably nobody knew what to do with eight million empty wine bottles. I'll deal with it later." He threw the envelope on the backseat and pulled away from the curb and began driving.

They stopped once, at Chloe's request, while two horses wandered across the highway in search of forage on the other side. They were tame enough for Chloe to get close enough to offer them apples, but not interested enough to partake. Junior sat in the car, laughing at her. He leaned his head out the window. "Those horses were doing just fine without your handouts."

"The hell they were. I'm sure they haven't had their vaccines."

"Chloe, come on over here. Scoot up close to me. You have to get the city ideas out of your mind if you're going to make it in Arizona. This is another way of life going on here. It ain't California."

"That doesn't mean I have to like it. Can I drive your car?"

"Why don't you try to enjoy the scenery?"

She snapped her seat belt and wriggled uncomfortably. "I'm not a scenery type of person. I'm more a drive-the-car kind."

"Too bad, so am I. Sit back and eat that apple, why don't you?"

"I'm not going to eat this. It's got horse slobber all over it."

"Jesus, then eat the other one. Do *something*. You're driving me to distraction."

She stuck out her tongue, but Junior was busy watching the road and missed it. Chloe recognized the turn off for Second Mesa, where she'd been when she was first in labor with Reed. She took hold of one of Junior's braids.

"Tell me what kind of jewelry you're working on."

He lifted one hand from the wheel and touched her face. "It's a pin, a brooch, whatever they call the larger ones. Got the idea for it the night we came back from Sedona."

"That still doesn't tell me what it looks like."

"I'm working. That's all I'm going to tell you."

She dropped the braid. "You're awfully stingy today."

"It's been so long I had an idea of any worth, I've got a right to feel superstitious."

"Superstitious?"

He nodded. "Artistic types are allowed."

He was making her mad, being secretive. "I came along, and now you won't talk to me."

"I'll talk to you. Pick another subject."

"What is it with men? Can't we just talk? Spontaneously? Or are your tongues only good for sticking in women's ears?"

He gave her a look. "You want to turn back?"

"Yes. No. I don't know. I'm tired. I didn't sleep last night."

"So take a nap."

"I might shut my eyes. Just for a minute." She leaned against his shoulder, then thought better of it and chose the door. Her last thoughts were that somebody, close by, very softly, was laughing.

The town of Chinlé did little to impress Chloe. It was industrial in appearance, with huge storage towers for grain or gas, maybe both. She rubbed her eyes, yawned, and decided it looked like a long-drawn-out truck stop, a place where somebody might waitress her whole life away with very little excitement beyond car wrecks and daily specials. But that didn't mean anything. Cameron, Arizona, wore the same outfit, and look what had happened to her there. There were no signs advertising Junior's beloved canyon, just a four-lane blacktop, roadside diners, and too many gray buildings. Maybe it would turn out to be a little ravine he felt sentimental over from childhood. She scanned the horizon but didn't see mountains.

"You slept through everything worth sleeping through."

"Good." She'd make the best of it and go back home tomorrow, wait for Hank and Reed to return. Junior stopped at a light, put on his blinker, and they turned right. Suddenly there were groves of cottonwoods, late-afternoon sun hitting the leaves at an angle that caused them to dance, and a feeling rose up her chest that felt like dozens of trapped birds struggling to get out.

The Thunderbird Lodge was just ahead of them, funky, south-western architecture, and a directional sign pointing to a camp-ground, which was empty. There was a huge green four-wheel drive parked out front of the Trading Post and Lodge, with enough empty seats to take a tourist group on a trek into the canyon.

"All right," she finally said. "I've been patient. Where is it? This famous canyon."

"Not far. When we go into the Post, I'll show you on a map."

She stretched her arms and felt the chill in the air. It smelled like snow. A yellow stray dog came running up to her, and she fed him some beef jerky. Junior sighed.

"Lecture me," she said, "and I'll make you find a market and buy up all their dog chow."

"I'm not saying a word." He opened the door to the Trading Post, and walked to the window where they sold the various canyon tours. "I need me a tour into Canyon del Muerto," he announced. "You ladies got one of those?"

The woman behind the counter put her hand to her mouth. "Lettie!" she called out. "Oh, my God, Lettie. Look who's here. It's Jimmy's boy." Two old women came around the counter and began to fuss over Junior.

Chloe stood watching, astonished that two crinkled old Navajo ladies found Junior Whitebear's arrival reason enough to weep. She wondered if leafing through a brochure was enough, or if maybe she should go outside and wait in the car.

He put his arms around the old women and looked at Chloe. "These are my aunties," he said. "Lettie, Dawn, meet Chloe."

They giggled and smiled, and Lettie gave her a hug, too, but Dawn was shy and held on to Junior's arm speaking softly in Navajo. Chloe looked to Junior for translation.

"The horseback tours aren't fully operational yet," he explained. "But we can take the Jeep trip in as far as Antelope House Overlook, then pick up horses. That sound all right by you?"

"Are they decent horses?"

"I'll ask if they've had their vaccines."

"Very funny."

He laid down some money, and Dawn pushed it away. Junior walked around the other side of the counter, opened the cash register, and put the money inside before giving her a kiss on the forehead. He waved Chloe into the gift shop. "You want to take a look around? This place isn't as big as Cameron, but it's got its own charm."

Tony Hillerman books abounded, their glossy paperback covers featuring all manner of Indian designs. Sweatshirts in every size were folded onto shelves, and everywhere she turned there was pottery, animal fetishes, sandpaintings, rugs, and so much silver it was almost blinding. Chloe wondered how it would feel to be able to say yes to all those things, just to open your arms to what you liked and start filling them up. How a life surrounded by beautiful objects made by real artists might change a person's soul. The glass case nearest the register held an assortment of Junior Whitebear's jewelry, more designs than Chloe had ever seen at the Cameron Post. A part of her wanted to ask to look at everything, but she was afraid his aunts would think her some disposable one-night stand, and who could tell, that might not prove to be far from the truth. Junior was deep in conversation, so Chloe wandered through the store. In the back of the first room, she stopped at the collection of burden baskets, which hung from the ceiling. Chloe stood on her tiptoes, examining them. Woven with varying sizes of reed, they were strung along the edges with rawhide. They featured long, dangling threads of leather with metal wrapped into cone shapes on the ends, like bells minus the clappers. When she brushed her fingers against them, they clattered pleasantly. She admired one particular basket with three different colors woven into it. If, as the name suggested, they were for unloading one's burdens, they didn't make them in big enough sizes to be of any practical use. Junior's shy aunt came over with a long pole and pulled the basket down, handed it to her.

"Take."

"I can't," she said, noticing the price tag, $180.00. "It's beautiful, but I can't afford it."

The aunt pressed the basket into her hands. "Junior my favorite nephew. You can have basket."

Chloe held onto it, afraid. The small, wizened woman possessed a kind of power, an authority. She looked pleased when Chloe kept the basket, then hurried back to the small crowd of people that had gathered around her nephew. For such a small town, word spread fast.

Among the T-shirts and sweatshirts, Chloe fingered a pair of baby moccasins. They were nothing special, mass-produced with the requisite beading, but they were within her budget. She wondered if Reed would tolerate anything that fancy, or given her independent temperament, kick them off.

Junior came up behind her and took her arm. "We got to have dinner at the cafeteria or break these ladies' hearts. Then, I promise, we can go to our room."

"The sign out front said the lodge was full up. What makes you so sure we can get a room?"

He gestured toward the building. "They keep a room for me here, Chloe. In the older part of the lodge."

"I guess you rate."

"It's an Indian thing. Don't worry about it. Come eat a hot supper with my aunties and hear about what a rotten little boy I was."

The booths were ordinary overstuffed red vinyl, the same type as in the diner she had worked in back in California. If she didn't look up at the walls—which were covered with incredible weavings, rugs priced in the thousands of dollars, intricately beaded purses that looked as if they belonged in a museum, buffalo skulls bleached white, decorated with chips of turquoise, and all manner of baskets, large and small, including an entire case devoted to miniature horsehair braided baskets—the restaurant could be called ordinary, too. There was hardly time to appreciate it all as the aunties rushed her through the food line. They loaded up her tray with squash stew and three kinds of bread. Dawn urged her to have two desserts.

"Cake and pie," she suggested. "Ice cream good on both."

Chloe laughed nervously. "I feel like I'm being fattened for sacrifice."

Junior replied, "You are," and kissed her cheek, which made the ladies titter, and him squeeze her knee under the table.

Long after the food was eaten, they lingered over coffee, during which time the conversation began in English, then when someone was having trouble locating a word, switched fluidly to Navajo. Junior seemed to be in his element, fussed over by women who hung on his every syllable, but he wasn't merely reveling in adoration. It was as if he needed these women to approve of him, required that connection. Chloe realized she was privy to a side of him he generally kept hidden. He hugged his aunts at the restaurant door while Chloe fed her scraps to a couple more stray dogs. The ladies waved goodnight, walking across the parking lot while she and Junior headed in the opposite direction. Junior led Chloe down a gravel pathway under a lamp spilling yellow light. A few hardy moths danced in the incandescence. In front of a small cottage, independent of the lodge, he stopped her.

"Kiss me."

His mouth was soft and yielding. This kiss took nothing but the moment for granted. Chloe laid her head against his jacket and listened to his heart beat slow and purposeful inside his chest. He handed Chloe the key to the door. "You open it."

Inside there was one cozy room containing a couch, a small knotty pine armoire, and a television set. There was a double bed in a lodgepole-pine bedframe, with a worn Pendleton blanket woven in a chevron design covering the mattress. Clean sheets were folded on top; they'd have to make up the bed. The bathroom to the right of the bed was tiny, with a utilitarian shower, toilet, and an old pedestal sink complete with a dripping tap. A wrapped bar of soap sat on the edge of the porcelain. A window looked out on a huge old cottonwood tree that seemed to have stood there forever. The tree had a presence, as if maybe its roots reached clear down to the center of the earth, to the earth's secret core. It had stood here a long time, listening to people fall in love, fall out of love, make love, argue, cope with their lives. You didn't have to be Indian to understand that love grew at the center of that tree. Chloe let the curtain drop and walked back into the common room.

Junior was holding the burden basket in his hands, looking at the tag. "Velma Padilla made this."

"Let me guess, you know her, too?"

"I think I must have met her once. Probably one of Lettie's bingo buddies. It's a real nice basket. It's the one I would have chosen."

"Did you see the price tag? I felt horrible accepting it."

"They wouldn't have given it if they couldn't afford to."

"I hope that's true." Chloe ran her fingers through her hair. "Junior? Now that we're here, I have a question."

Junior came to her, holding the basket in front of him, looking for all the world like an altar boy bearing the collection plate. "Put all your questions in here tonight and forget about them. This is where I've imagined taking you since the day we met. This room."

"Hearing that's not exactly helping me relax."

"The air's thin up here, Chloe. Lie down and before you know it, you sleep like you're dead."

She took the burden basket from his hands and set it on top of the TV set, hoping Mrs. Padilla wouldn't mind her so casually abandoning her fine handiwork. Standing in front of Junior, she willed only pure sensation to flow through her body, ordered guilt and good sense to take a hike, for this moment to exist in and of itself. That was the only way what was going to happen could happen. To Junior, these walls held enough history that they mattered, the way driving past the house where you grew up mattered to people who'd experienced that luxury. Here was where he'd imagined making love to her. The moment his hands had caught hold of Reed the day she was born, she had become a part of Junior's history. They were connected. This night, and whatever it held, would be a onetime thing, would never come again, whether they deliberately walked away from it or followed it into a future. Making love with Junior could be as simple as friction of the flesh or it could change the courses of three lives. He wouldn't make things easy on her by taking charge, by throwing her down on the bed and acting macho. He respected her wishes enough to let her make this choice. Hank had been like that, too, and the recognition that two such men in the world existed and wanted her posed some disconcerting thoughts. Maybe there was nothing left to do except surrender to the moment. How many times had Chloe imagined how Junior's hands would feel on her breasts, cupped under her buttocks, his fingers tracing along the sides of her flanks, where the shivers ran so deep she could feel the echo in her stomach, in her throat, between her legs. Tacitly she understood Junior would take his sweet time discovering all that, placing his hands carefully there, and elsewhere, and likely come up with a few surprises of his own. The idea of all that yearning and fulfillment made her shake. *Is this how I was conceived?* she wondered, *A moment like this? When things made so little sense but my mother wanted it bad enough to wreck her whole life anyway? Maybe if I'd had a real mother, I'd have the* huevos *to walk away. Maybe I would have learned my own worth. But I didn't, I don't, and goddammit, I want this.*

"Enough procrastinating," she told him. "Make me a fallen woman."

"Soon as you get on over there and make the bed."

"Me? I get to do it?"

"Yes, you."

"And you're not going to help."

"Not right now," he said.

"That's pretty sexist."

"Call it whatever you want to. Later, I'll help you unmake it. Right now, I'm just going to watch and enjoy the show."

22

Junior pulled Chloe against him, feeling the heat of their bodies transfer warmth to the chilly sheets. The wind whistled across the parking lot. The night was full of voices: late-arriving travelers, a nocturnal bird's cry, his own memories. Chloe was in his arms. Outside this room that old cottonwood tree he'd tried to climb as a boy was busy growing its spring leaves. When he was young and believed anything was possible, its branches seemed spindly. Every time he managed to grab hold of one, he fell smack on his scrawny butt. Now, like the tree from which his mother had swung, the branches were too high for him to grasp. He thought about how the desire to hide in trees had left him, and he'd outgrown the notion that it was the other tree's fault his mother hadn't survived. But neither concern had prevented this tree's blood from coursing through the massive trunk, down those same, elusive branches. Chloe's mouth moved against his neck. His senses were so on edge he could almost hear the tree striving to shape its heart-leaves. Wonderful old tree, he thought, survivor. Be here for whoever next sleeps in this room. Wait for those lovers who've only just been born. Hundreds of years after what this woman and I are about to do is long forgotten, it won't matter that tonight two people behaved selfishly. You'll be rooted there, a rational old standing piece of timber that belongs to nobody but the earth.

He ran his fingers down Chloe's face, stopping at her mouth. With the tip of his index finger, he gently pressed between her lips until she let him in to explore. He traced this damp finger down her cheeks, across the bridge of her nose, over her eyelids. Then he palmed her throat, that racehorse neck of hers, which he enjoyed watching her defiantly thrust forward when she was trying to drive home some point she herself didn't quite believe. He lightly stroked her breasts, admiring the way each fit into his cupped hand. Touching her called forth past summers, chasing after playful dogs, catching horses that didn't want to be ridden, running for the utter joy of having legs. He wondered if that was because her blood, charging through her veins and various tissues announcing pleasure to the animal self that was her body, now belonged to him. He traced the angry scar across her soft belly. There was a sense of emptiness there, sorrow that throbbed behind the doctor's stitching. He wouldn't have given up delivering Reed for anything, but he was relieved that he hadn't become a doctor. Some women pretended that losing their childbearing ability didn't trouble them. When it came to that subject, these days too many women were downright men in skirts. The time Junior had asked Chloe, she'd responded, *Reed's healthy; I'm grateful. One baby's way more than I ever thought I'd have.* Which Junior understood to be a lie, only one of many her body had been telling for years. Honesty opened you to pain. Chloe'd already had too much experience in that corner, and here he was in bed with her, making her take step one of what was sure to add to her list.

He slid his fingers lower, glancing against her pubic hair, dipping into the hot cleft of skin beneath, trailing the dampness that met his fingers onto her thighs. He wanted desperately to enter her. She was more than ready for him to be inside. The obstacle was his unwillingness to sacrifice all this *before*. Doing so would take them both that much closer to the *after*. With both hands, he encircled her body, reaching around her buttocks, holding on, lifting her body to his. It was almost as if she became one entire taut, arching muscle of need. This discovery left him a little in awe, encountering the breadth of her desire for their coming together, the necessary abandon required for her to admit those feelings, her dismissal of the consequences, and—oh, man—he was sure there would be consequences.

Junior knew a million different ways to show a woman a good time. But that wasn't what tonight was about. They were on holy ground here. He held her close for a long while, observing the pull of desire, listening to her quick, soft breaths, exploring how it felt to behold all that yearning. When Chloe grabbed hold of his penis, trying to hurry things along, he laughed and gently removed her hand, kissing her fist until each finger opened. As much as he enjoyed the feel of her encircling him, her directness, he was not about to let it happen that way. Even when her face contorted with longing, her cries of pleasure dwindled to whimpers and rose in pitch to outright pleas for him to enter her, he held her back. He took hold of her wrists and kissed each one hard, moving down her hands, taking her fingers one by one into his mouth. With his tongue, he attended every knuckle, traced each working-girl callus. Fairness was his intention, not to favor any one part of her body over another. He wanted Chloe to believe he cherished the soles of her feet as much as being allowed inside her. And that worked for about five minutes more, until he realized he was starting to forget why she had feet and the throbbing aches of his own center obsessed him. It was a lie to continue so halfheartedly, so he stopped altogether, and at once she sat upright in bed.

"You're torturing me, dammit. Either get down to business or I'll take care of myself."

He shushed her, lowered her back to the mattress, kissed her face, her neck, the arch of each foot with exquisite, prolonged tenderness, pressed his mouth onto every part of her body his fingers had explored. Then he said a silent prayer of thanks, slipped his middle finger and forefingers, the same two fingers he'd used the night he delivered her daughter, inside her. He felt for the nerve root bundle that he understood was the source of a woman's deepest pleasure. He listened to her skin and membranes and muscles with his fingertips. The same way that Babbitt had ordered open the floodgates into the Grand Canyon, a man could make a woman come, with a torrential force that washed away whatever didn't belong. But only if she gave herself over to the process willingly. He wanted to take Chloe to those same floodgates, to show her that her pleasure mattered more to him than his own, that he considered it a sacred undertaking. Slowly, he began to move his fingers. She resisted at first, then, in time, began to float with the rise and ebb of her feelings. It took awhile, but they were in no hurry, and he helped her find her way. When he felt her on the precipice of falling away, he clasped his entire hand close around her, held her close and listened to her surprise as the blinding sensations hovered, then began to flutter the way a hawk's wings trembled as he held himself in midair before striking, then with one sharp war cry, swiftly took down targeted prey. Junior heard Chloe cry out in pleasure and in loss. He held her in his arms, letting her revel in her feelings. When all the sighing slowed down, she yawned, breathing out the words, "I love you."

He laughed. "You love these two fingers, anyway. We'll see about the rest of me."

Now that she was acquiescent, that he had named her his, he withdrew his hand and took hold of her shoulders. He slid his body over hers and entered her easily, and set about making himself happy.

"If you don't wake up, we'll miss our ride."

"For Christ's sake, Junior. I'm not asleep. You're not asleep. Nobody got any sleep."

"What can I say? We had a busy night. Get your clothes on. All of them."

"Why all of them?"

He gave her bare butt a playful slap. "It'll be cold down there. Layer your things. You can always take something off if you get too warm."

"I'm not good with cold. I'm better with blankets and snuggling. Come here and I'll show you."

He looked down at her, sloe-eyed and convincing in the tousled clutch of sheets. Her blond hair was so wild and tangled it would take half an hour to work out the knots. "Later."

"You're no fun," she grumbled.

He sat on the edge of the bed and kissed her a few times, slid his hand under the sheets and touched the now familiar places that made her sigh.

"Well, maybe you're a *little* fun."

He handed her clothes over to her, the jeans over from where they lay on the floor, the bra from under the pillow, and after five minutes of searching, the plain cotton panties that had somehow ended up in the pocket of his beaded jacket. She stood before him, cranky but fully clothed.

It was freezing out front of the lodge. To acknowledge that it was snowing was to invite a storm, but light flakes were definitely falling. Junior could tell Chloe was having second thoughts about the canyon trek. Particularly now that the jolly tourist group who had signed up for the Jeep tour were emerging from the cafeteria. They were clad in matching turquoise jackets with white lettering. Some kind of group-rate thing, he figured. Armed with cameras and sightseers' determination, they were far too happy for this early on such a fragile morning. He knew Chloe would just as soon spend the day feeding stray dogs. If the seniors started singing camp songs, she'd freak. He spoke a little Navajo with the guide, Jared Tuchawena, cousin of somebody who'd known Jimmy a long time ago but didn't remember Jimmy ever having a son. He said it was okay; they could ride in the cab with him.

"I got all sidetracked after the war," Jared explained. "Only been back in Chinlé about ten years now."

"That's about the time I left," Junior said.

"And you?" the guide asked Chloe. "Your first time to the canyon?"

She nodded. "Total newcomer."

Jared delivered his spiel, explained that, yes, there were two bathroom stops along the way, then warned everyone to hold on to their seats. He maneuvered the Jeep down into the canyon, four-wheeling along the sandy washes, fishtailing in and out of the streambeds, giving the tourists their money's worth. At the first bend of the road, he stopped and cut the motor to give some background on the route they would be traveling. Junior and Chloe remained seated in the cab as he pulled a hand-loomed rug from beneath the seat.

He stood on the truck's running board and delivered his spiel. "This here genuine Navajo Yeibichei rug, *na'aki*, ladies and gentleman, priced far below Trading Post cost. Yei dancers are healing spirits. Great souvenir of your trip to Canyon de Chelly. Instant heirloom. My auntie work a whole year on this rug.

"Well, maybe three months," he confided as he handed it to Chloe back inside the cab when there were no takers. Three young girls appeared from behind a waiting pickup truck, hoping to sell necklaces fashioned of dyed corn kernels. The tourists bought several, and the girls ran back to their mother in the red pickup, fists full of dollar bills, grinning.

Watching them, Chloe said, "Don't those girls look happy?"

"It's not so hard to be happy," Junior answered her.

"What's hard," Jared offered, "is selling a rug to a bunch of *bilagáana* bargain hunters."

He drove on. Junior held onto the backpack inside which he'd placed the box of Jimmy's ashes. With each passing mile, he could feel himself becoming lighter.

Jared said, "Your horses are just up ahead, with my cousin's nephew, Billy. If you don't mind, I'll drop you here. It's about time for me to have another go at unloading this rug."

"Thanks, Jared."

The guide shook his hand and smiled. "Have yourselves a nice ride."

"We'll do our best."

Junior spotted the ponies and the young man waving to him. The boy handed the reins over and rode off on his own horse, a flashy Appaloosa who still wore his winter coat. Their rental horses were true Indian ponies, mixed in heritage, mouse brown, strictly for transport. Chloe took an instant liking to the smaller of the two and went over every inch of his tack, adjusting buckles.

"Everything meet with your approval?" Junior asked her. "Or do we need to send out for fancy replacements?"

She stuck out her tongue and tried to hoist herself into the stirrups. "Ow. Well, that's not going to work. Give me a leg up."

Junior came up behind her, placing his hands on her buttocks. "Don't tell me the ace horsewoman is losing her chops?"

"No, she isn't, thank you very much. I think I pulled about a jillion muscles last night, that's all. Which is your fault. Can I get some help or just attitude?"

He gave her a boost. "Sore muscles to remember me by. Guess that's better than nothing."

Her face clouded over. "Goddamn you, Whitebear."

"I was just making a stupid joke."

"Stupid's about the right word for it."

"Forget I said anything."

She was quiet for a few minutes. "You know, neither one of us had a wink of sleep, I'm so sore from fucking I can hardly sit this horse. We haven't eaten breakfast, and nobody's said word one about what's going to happen when we finish this ride."

Junior stopped, waited until Chloe was even alongside him, then leaned across his horse and kissed her mouth. He reached inside her jacket and fondled her breasts. "Here's all I know. When I touch you, nothing else matters. For right now, I'm going with that." He pressed a finger to her lips before she could say anything. "Let's deliver Jimmy and enjoy the canyon. Later on, we'll eat and figure everything out, talk until we lose our voices. Right now all we need to do is head over this way, ride a couple miles, unload this burden, pray a little. There's time for everything, Chloe. Trust me."

"I trust you."

"Then there's no problem."

"It's me I don't trust."

He sighed. "*Awéé'*, you have more horse sense in your little finger than anyone I know. Your heart knows what it wants to do. You left your worries in the basket and that's where they belong. No more talking. Just ride with me."

With his heel, Junior nudged his horse forward. They kept to a trot, their jacket collars pulled upright against the morning air. The canyon walls were high and sheltering, ocher and brick red, streaked dark in places with oxides that marked the various ages of the earth and the blood that had been shed here. Junior adjusted the heavy backpack. He looked forward to feeling it slack against his back on the return ride. The sun filled the canyon slowly, reaching down the walls and glancing off rocks.

"Navajos weren't the only tribe to wander this canyon," he told Chloe. "Utes, refugees from the neighboring Pueblos, came and went. Everybody borrowed from each other's ways. It all contributed to the *Dinéh* culture. If it wasn't for the Spaniards, who knows when we would have acquired horses? But horses were a high price to pay."

"For what?"

Junior pointed out various pictographs decorating the rocks. In the center of a group of the riders was the outline of a tall man, a white cross decorating his dark cape. "Massacre," Junior said. "Bows and arrows might have been a fair fight, but Lieutenant Antonio Narbona brought rifles in. He harvested the ears of some eighty-four warriors. He wasn't after saving souls or procuring slaves, he just wanted to do a little sport hunting. The People took refuge in caves, behind the ledges, like that one, there, far up on the cliff. You can see the marks where the soldiers' bullets ricocheted off the rock walls. Plucked them off like they were ground squirrels. Oscar would tell you this place is *chindee*, haunted."

"Do you believe that?"

"I know that the sadness I feel here comes from prehistoric loss. If it had been Kit Carson carrying out the army's orders in 1863, there might have been a little less bloodshed. At least Redshirt had some respect for the People, having traded with them. Not Narbona. And General Carleton only had a score to settle."

"So your people lost the war?"

"You can't really call systematic decimation of some farmers and their families a war, Chloe. When the daily kill got too small to be satisfying to the army, they marched whoever was left to Fort Sumner, instilled them at Bosque Redondo. It took the army four long years to admit that resettling the Navajo into a land totally unlike their own wasn't going to pan out. So they signed a treaty, let us come back. Precious little of what's in the treaty matters when the government decides there's something of worth on reservation land."

Chloe reached out and touched a branch of a cottonwood. "It's so beautiful here. Hearing what you're saying, the stuff that never makes it into the history books, I wonder how you can stand to associate with anyone who isn't Indian."

"You forget I'm not full blood. Lots of people feel the way you're describing. That's part of what AIM was about. Where I lived in Massachusetts was Indian land, once. There isn't any place you can walk in the U.S. that doesn't fit that description. The Indian part of me alternates between feeling conquered and murderous, but the white part of me, my mother's blood, can't quite rest easy there."

"I don't see why not."

He shook his head. "It's a tribal thing. It's tribal, and I'll never be part of that."

Just past the Mummy Cave Overlook, Junior stopped his horse and dismounted. He motioned for Chloe to take his reins, and then he slipped the backpack off his shoulders. He opened the box that held Jimmy's ashes, so much grainy dust. Even pulverized, bone contained substance. He ran his fingers through the matter, amazed at how pale was the color of the bones of that dark-

skinned man who had made a religion out of beating his wife and
terrorizing his only child. By handfuls he scattered the ashes into
the wind. When the box was nearly empty, he spat into his palms,
poured the remainder of the ash into his hands, slapped his caked
palms against the red rock, pressing hard, leaving imprints. It was
nowhere near as vivid or enduring as the signature handprints left
by the Anasazi, but it constituted a kind of prayer. He bent his head
and said some words. The marks would stay for a little while,
Jimmy Whitebear's final upraised hands, never again to land on
human flesh.

On the return ride they stopped by a streambed and Junior washed
his hands. "I can't believe how this stuff is sticking to me," he said,
rubbing sand into his palms, trying to scrub away the ashes.

Chloe peeled the wrapper back from her candy bar and took a
bite. "Junior, what kind of man was your father?"

He sat back on his heels, trailing his fingers through the chilly
water, squinting up at the steep canyon walls. "A drunk, a good
card player. Friendly to strangers. The ladies liked him well enough
so that he hardly ever slept alone."

Chloe poked him with the toe of her boot. "What kind of *father*
was he?"

"*Amá*, don't go there."

"Come on, Junior. We drove all this way so you could spread his
earthly remains in this canyon. You prayed. I watched your face
while you were saying the words. You looked like somebody hit
you. Is it taboo to talk about?"

"The *Dinéh* say so."

"Couldn't your white side tell me a little bit about him?"

Junior touched his bracelet, turning it on his thick wrist. Not his
best work, but the silver glinted in the sunlight, and he recalled
every step of making the piece, of finishing it early one winter
morning, then getting up to look outside and seeing Jimmy
Whitebear sprawled in the snow, unconscious. Junior had slipped

on his boots and dragged his father inside, got him out of his wet clothes and into warm blankets. Then he lit out for Corrine's. Honoring your elders was one thing, but he hadn't wanted to be anywhere near when the bear awoke. Later he and Corrine had argued over something. When he returned home, Jimmy had completely leveled his workshop. Overturned anything that wasn't nailed down. Stomped all his finished pieces to junk. It had taken Junior the better part of a week to get it all back in some kind of order. He couldn't look at the bracelet without remembering that.

Chloe had taken off her jacket and unbuttoned her shirt halfway, pulled it wide open at the shoulders. One of her bra straps showed. She arched her neck, welcoming the sun on her body while she waited for his answer. She looked so beautiful that he didn't want to speak. "Jimmy had a sickness inside him, I think. Something that burned like a coal fire. For a long time I hated him."

"Why?"

"The beatings, the drunks, take your pick. I still can't fathom or forgive what he did to my mother. But the older I get the more I see how scared and messed up he was. All he knew was booze and fists. Meanness. I think the lesson is for me to always be there for Dog, no matter what he decides to do with his life."

"Why in hell would he beat you? Were you stealing cars? Doing drugs, what?"

"Let's just say I enjoyed my share of trouble. Mostly I think he beat me because I was there to beat."

Chloe folded the wrapper back over the candy bar and set it down on the backpack.

"You've been crying hungry since last night. Where's your appetite?"

"Gone forever."

"I don't believe that."

"Between your father and thinking about those mothers and their babies being marched out of here, mourning perfectly decent husbands and fathers, how am I supposed to sit here scarfing choco-late? That letter from my mother was postmarked Tucson, Junior, pretty damn close to Mexico. Take a look at my daughter's skin. Do the math. Maybe somewhere back there, I'm *related* to those soldiers, Junior, just like your family goes back to these people."

"That's a long way back, Chloe. Don't go Catholic on me."

"It's not. And it's just as horrible now as it was then. All my life I've belonged to nobody, had no history except what I chose to make up. Now I get to feel shitty for the sins of my stinking ancestors. Someday you'll probably want to throw me off a cliff like that ear-hunting asshole Narbona."

Junior smiled. "There's a legend, and probably it's true, that he went after a Navajo woman who was hiding in one of the ledges, jeering at him, and he found her, fought with her, and they both fell off the cliff together. The cliff's name is *ah tah ho do nilly*, 'two fell off.' I don't want to throw you off the rocks, Chloe. I just want to love you."

"Sometimes I freak that I might be a terrible mother to Reed no matter how hard I try. I mean, I had nobody to show me how to love her, and the stuff that happened to me happened. Isn't child abuse supposed to be some sort of chain reaction, some unavoidable—"

Junior put his hand over her mouth. "Are you going to let me love you?"

He took his hand away. Her mouth trembled. "I think my heart's a lot like this canyon, Junior. There's been so many battles fought in here. It's weary, untrustworthy. Divided in affections."

"Seems like a generous heart to me. Room in there for red-haired teenagers, the most beautiful little baby girl I ever held in my hands, every stray dog that walks the earth. You just keep tucking in people and animals and somehow they all fit."

"Right, and now I'm supposed to fit a long-lost mother in there, too?"

"Why not? And maybe a half-breed jeweler?"

Chloe leaned against his shoulder. "I want to. Reed fits. Kit fits. I wish you could have met the juvenile felons I taught riding back home, these huge black and Mexican gang boys. They fit so easily.

And so many horses. Check this out: A year and a half ago, I was working my way out of major debt, trying to live a regular life, and wham, along comes this professor and somehow I end up in this beautiful, sad canyon in love with two men at the same time. Go figure."

Junior frowned. "Spider Rock looks like one good wind tearing through the canyon should be able to blow the whole thing down, but it's still standing. These petrogylphs predate the scientists' carbon tests. Corn and peaches grow here on very little water. Creeks that run to rivers in the winter go bone dry in the summer, and somehow the people who got forced from their home keep coming back. I have a son who forgives me for not knowing him the first eight years of his life. I'm raising a wolf-dog. All of a sudden the silver is talking to me again, and I did nothing to deserve that. You just spent the night with me. Magic. After that, don't you think anything's possible?"

"Junior."

"What?"

"If I know any one thing about being a mother, it's that you can't behave selfishly one hundred percent of the time. Sooner or later, you have to put the child's needs first."

Her words made his heart feel as ancient as the canyon, as if a soldier's gun pressed against the organ, ordering it to keep on walking despite its exhaustion, its penetrating thirst. He took off his beaded jacket and laid it down on the soft sand, smoothing its fringe. "Then make love with me," he whispered. "Right here, out in the open. Nobody's looking except maybe a few ravens. One more time, Chloe, so I'll know I didn't imagine you."

She looked at him a long time. "You want too much."

"Only your heart and your daughter."

Chloe began pulling her clothes off, angrily yanking at buttons. "Us falling into each other's lives has to be some kind of cosmic joke, that's what it is. Jesus, what a mess. We'll make love like there's no tomorrow, but what about when the sun comes up?"

"Then we'll get dressed. We'll try to bear up. All my life I've been doing that, Chloe. I'm a fucking expert."

There were tears in her eyes, too. When he could bear to open his own, Junior looked over her shoulder, checking to make sure the horses hadn't strayed too far. Every rock, reed, and ruin was blurred, doubled. Where there were two horses there now stood four, two of everything, including themselves. If magic really did exist, why weren't there separate lives available, ample space, another point in time where one half of Chloe's heart could grow into another whole, make each man happy, grow old alongside him, from morning coffee to their final goodnights? In his mind's eye he saw Reed growing into a strong young woman, skipping between her two fathers like their lives were nothing more complicated than a series of stones one balanced upon to cross a river. Maybe, if he was lucky, he might walk away with that much.

Despite her attempts not to, Chloe started to cry on the drive home. Junior offered to pull over, get her a drink, but she shook her head no, told him to keep driving. They continued on that way, her biting back sobs and him feeling useless and responsible until the last thirty miles or so from town, when he watched Chloe start to pull herself together. She scrubbed her face with the back of her hand, she ran her fingers through her hair. She reached over and touched him with such tenderness that he wanted to scream. She asked him what was wrong.

Junior found it difficult to string the words together. He patted her knee. "Nothing."

By her expression, he could tell she misunderstood, thought he was shutting her down.

"I can tell something's bothering you."

"I'm thinking, all right?"

"Tell me what about."

He shook his head.

Five miles later she tried again. "I picked up a letter from Kit just before we left town. I haven't read it yet. Want to hear it?"

"Why not."

"Look at that. There's two letters in here. Well, I'll read the first one and look at the other one later.

> "Dear Chloe,
>   "Here's the deal. I did everything you asked me to do so please don't say anything to Lita or my dad, promise? I got a pregnancy test, negative. I got that HIV test, also negative, but the lady said I have to get another one in six months just to be sure even though I'm probably totally one hundred percent fine since we used the rubber, that groady green thing I will never, ever forget! And I went to the group thing and I wasn't the youngest idiot there, I wasn't even the first girl to go to bed with some dork because she thought it would solve all her problems. It's like, an epidemic or something, girls believing that fucking will make a guy love you! Sorry, I know you hate it when I cuss, but I mean, really, what's the correct vocabulary word? Screwing? Is that any better? *Intercourse*, I don't know, somehow that sounds even dirtier than just saying fucking which is probably what everyone calls it in secret."

Chloe laughed. "Score one point for the redhead."
"Yeah, I guess we could all take a lesson there," Junior said.

> "I get now why you wanted to sleep with Junior but I am so glad you didn't! Hank needs you, Chloe. What a geek he was when you first met him. It's like you single-handedly gave him a life while Junior—"

Chloe stopped reading. "Never mind. This was a dumb idea."
"Finish it."
"Junior, you're already upset. You don't need the ramblings of a romantic teenager on top of—"
"Finish the damn letter, will you?"

Chloe looked at him. "If you want me to.

"Junior could have anybody, even somebody famous and beautiful, like that Isabella Rosselini chick.

"Now it's your turn to deal with stuff. I've put your mom's letter in here. I hope you read it. Go see her, Chloe. Find out. In the words of somebody I know and trust, 'It's not going to get manageable until you do.'

"Love forever and ever,
Kit"

"P.S. Tell Reed I miss, miss, miss her! Hannah, too. Have you broke Thunder to saddle yet? You promised you'd wait for me. Don't forget. High school still sucks, but oh well, only three more years! If you see Junior, tell him I will always think he is the handsomest Indian in the whole entire world."

She stopped reading. "Oh, my God."

Junior said, "She's right, especially about that last part."

Chloe folded the letter back into the envelope. She leaned over and kissed Junior's cheek. "Yes, she is. You are one studly hunk in buckskin. I just wish you'd tell me what's on your mind."

"Sorry. It's personal."

"And what happened last night wasn't?"

He gripped the steering wheel tightly. "Chloe. Can you maybe give me some space here?"

"I can give you all the space you want."

Now she was really pissed. What was he supposed to do? Being called handsome was small consolation when you were not going to end up with the prize. In the parking lot of the Post, he cut the engine and looked down at his deeply pigmented hands. A fine trace of ash lined the creases of his palms. More than anything he wanted a shower and to scrub that away, even if in the process it took his skin off. Chloe scooted over next to him. He felt her arm graze his, as painful as nettles. It was unbearable to have her so near when he knew she was going home to Hank.

"We'll work this out," she said. "Some way or another. Some miracle will come to us."

"Or not."

She took his hand. "Junior, let's just give things a day to settle. I'll meet you here tomorrow, for lunch. We'll talk. I love you."

He nodded. Sure, right. Maybe someday world peace would be number one on everyone's agenda. Chloe got out of his car and walked to her truck, her limp pronounced from the strenuous ride into the canyon. She held the letter from Kit in her hand. He watched her drive off and sat alone in the Jeep for a long time, nursing his sore heart. Well, he needed gas or he wasn't going to make it home to Aaron's. He pulled into the Chevron station and set the pump. Leaning against the car, he noticed the manila envelope lying in the backseat. He opened the door and reached for it. It was something to do while the gas pump ticked off its gallons.

Jimmy's death certificate said he had died of exposure; the secondary cause of death was listed as liver disease. A bank account with a passbook was there, with a seven-hundred-dollar balance. It surprised Junior no end, as he'd never known the man to hold onto a nickel when he could unload it in a liquor store. He'd give that money to Ganado Elementary, let them establish an art supply budget. Then in a small white envelope at the bottom of the packet, he found something entirely unexpected: his own birth certificate. The embossed seal was barely discernible to his fingers. It was as if over the years, somebody had rubbed the paper over and over while they gave its contents considerable thought.

Long ago the problem of lacking proper birth registration had been resolved when Junior's mother had produced his baptismal records, his tribal registration, and in a story he'd often found amusing, recounted Jimmy having to claim his only child while standing before a Flagstaff judge. Junior had forgotten about the birth certificate. His passport and driver's license served for identification. Never having expected to encounter the piece of paper, he now inspected it eagerly.

CERTIFICATE OF LIVE BIRTH
State file #15136

THIS CHILD: *Walter James*

RESIDENCE OF MOTHER: *Phoenix, Arizona*

MAIDEN NAME OF MOTHER: *Veronica Louise O'Reilly*

MOTHER'S RACE: *White*

FATHER OF CHILD: *Manuel Hector Lopez*

FATHER'S RACE: *Mexican*

BIRTHPLACE: *Sonora, B.C.*

USUAL OCCUPATION: *Laborer*

KIND OF BUSINESS OR INDUSTRY: *Agricultural*

There had to be some kind of mix-up. This kind of thing happened all the time with Indians. But why had he never heard that his mother had lived in Phoenix? And the birthdate was his own, May 29. Jimmy Whitebear was his father; he'd sworn to the fact in a courtroom. But if James Walter Whitebear wasn't his father, then maybe Junior wasn't half-blood Navajo at all.

The car behind him politely honked. He removed the pump from the Cherokee's tank, question after question tumbling forth into his brain. Where did he get to call home—the place where he'd grown up, fought his battles of acceptance, or was all that suddenly dismissed? Would his aunties turn their backs to him? Or did he have living relatives he'd never met? What did that make his son? Definitely more of an Indian than his father. And—he couldn't say it out loud. He could hardly bear to think it—what did it mean for his jewelry?

Junior set the envelope on the passenger seat, paid for his gas, and pulled out of the lot. He felt his heart turn upside down and shake itself empty, like the crematorium box minus the ashes of a man who he now understood had a perfectly good reason for hating him. Had his mother's sadness come from holding in her secret while her husband beat her child? How had she made the move from a Mexican laborer to Jimmy Whitebear? Did she consider the reservation a step up, or had she been so desperate for security she was willing to sacrifice herself and her son?

He drove blindly into town, stopped at the Navajo barber's and sat thumbing through a two-year-old *Newsweek*. All the stories of impending doom seemed as pertinent and hopeless as the day they were first published. When it came his turn for the chair, he sat down. The barber took hold of the ends of his long braids. "What are you after, brother? Trim the ends?"

"Cut them off," he told the man. "Make me look like everybody else."

23

The Greeks appropriated all the credit, but it was the Oriental sages who articulated the concepts of reincarnation, the four ages of man, that whole business of the dreamless sleep. Yet when you boiled down all the myths and stories, the emergent soup made things clear and simple: Only matriarchal religions came to grips with death.

Hank stood at his mother's hospital bedside, holding his daughter, tears scoring his face. From time to time, he reached down and stroked his mother's hand. The doctors and nurses were boating down the river of denial here; nobody he asked would affix the word "terminal" to her condition. Which was absurd. It hardly took a medical degree to ascertain Iris was dying. He wanted her to look peaceful, but the truth was that thanks to the morphine, she appeared remote, uninvolved with the business at hand. Most women saw old age as the end of things, but it was a time to be respected, to be heard, as vital as any earlier beauty. Women had two doors before them, the start and the finish, while men could visualize only the way out. *That's because women give birth,* he thought. *The door for entering this spinning, daft planet never leaves them, it's there inside, even if they lose a baby, or when the ability no longer exists. So wouldn't it logically follow that death signals a graceful passage into the company of the departed?* He thought of his sister, Annie, dead nearly as many years as he had been alive. *Mother, wherever you go, I hope there are temple bells and violets in bloom. She's waiting for you, so go whenever you're ready.*

He carried Reed into the lounge so he could feed her a bottle. She nestled her sleepy head against his chest and squeezed his index finger. When Chloe fed her, Reed held onto a hank of her mother's hair as if this thin tether bound them. Chloe always laughed, but Hank understood how Reed felt. Caring for her these past few days, he was overcome with love for his dusky-skinned daughter. All the male poets took a stab at explaining women at one time or another—Yeats with his spiraling gyres was on the right track. Whether one was caught up in loving a woman or losing one, the path was twisted and dangerous. Nervous little orations executed in tidy meter were nice stuff, but when it came down to your mother's deathbed, what could a son do but stand there, weak-kneed, acknowledging the utter futility of being allowed on the planet with women in the first place?

Hank thanked God he'd had a daughter, because there was no way on earth he could possibly have explained all this to a son. The simple fact that Reed's life stretched out so far ahead of his own humbled him. Raising her was what mattered, not whether he dented any of the world's larger problems by where he taught school. He could make it through his mother dying because he had Reed to hang onto. And Chloe.

But the last six times he'd called, there'd been no answer at the cabin. The phone rang on and as he listened, he pictured her in his mind's eye, riding the green colt without her helmet, cupping a cigarette in her palm, standing at the fence Hank had built with his own hands and turning her face to speak to someone, and that someone always turned out to be Junior Whitebear. Hank figured the odds were pretty high that she was sleeping with the jeweler.

Hadn't he practically turned the sheets down for them? Shit, maybe that was for the best, giving Chloe the wide-open opportunity to explore this preoccupation of hers. Force the issue to crisis. Hank felt ashamed to admit it, but there was an infinitesimal part of him titillated by the idea of the two of them together that charged the atmosphere. If he gave his mind free rein, however, that arousal quickly sank lower in his gut, settled in, and renamed itself terror. Suppose she decided the Indian jeweler was the man to make her happy, the one to marry. She could do that. Jesus, how could she? Corrine had raised Dog on her own; she said the man was off in Europe half the time. Plenty of men fathered a child, shook off their dicks, and walked away, but Junior had come back, made himself a part of the boy's life. Dog adored him. During that colicky period where Reed was making them all nuts, only Junior knew the secret to make her stop crying. It was pretty damn hard to top a man who was unafraid of singing to another man's baby, who behaved as if there were nothing he'd like better than to have a hand in helping your daughter grow up. Which was to say nothing of the horse element, their connection there. *I may be able to ride*, Hank thought, *but I'll never get to where those two are on that score*. Christ, if it came down to custody, Hank could lose them both. If he hadn't left Chloe behind, hadn't continually forced the idea of marriage, hadn't been so goddamn controlling, he might have a wedding ring on his finger instead of a dangling pacifier.

"Da," Reed chirped at him.

They were random vocalizations. All the books said so. Six months was too young for predictable verbalization, but whether it was coincidence or effort, hearing her he was a grateful man. "Yes, that's right, I'm your dad," he said, gathering the bag of diapers in the crook of his elbow. "Let's take a break from all this, you and me."

He took Reed across the street to McDonald's, ordered himself a hamburger. There were plenty of families to observe. Burger joints probably sold more food than grocery stores. He could pick out the divorced dads awkwardly trying to make up for things by indulging in Happy Meals, placating their weekend children with movie tie-in toys. Hank tried to imagine forging any kind of relationship with Reed on a part-time basis. He thought of Jack Dodge, his old attorney, and how the man transformed into a shark in a suit the moment you cut him a check. The larger percentage of his caseload involved divorce and financial arbitration. He was a local phone call away, and attorneys were sworn to uphold the confidentiality of their clients, even if the discussion at hand was of a mere speculative nature. Dodge would say, *Possession is nine-tenths of the law, and you, my lad, cradle the bird in your hand.*

Hank threw his uneaten hamburger into the trash and extricated Reed from the high chair. He drove back to his parents' condo, bracing himself, but his father wasn't there. Maybe he was at the hospital. After the look his father gave Reed upon their arrival, each had made it a point to give the other a wide berth. Hank bathed Reed and rocked her to sleep. Without trying to reach Chloe again, he went to bed.

In the morning, when he returned to the hospital, his father was at the nurse's station.

"She passed away at six this morning," the nurse said.

"Excuse me? Why didn't I get a call? I asked specifically—"

"Your father said we should let you sleep."

Hank was furious. The man always insisted on writing his scripts. Now he couldn't say a proper good-bye. That privilege had been denied him by a man who didn't deserve the honor.

"Mr. Oliver?"

Both men turned to the nurse. "Yes?"

She came around the desk and extended her arms for the baby. "I'd be glad to hold your daughter if you and your father would like to spend a few moments alone with your mother."

"Well, Dad?" Hank asked. "Think we can get through this without fighting?"

Henry set down the pen and papers.

They embraced. Hank felt the slight shaking in the old man's shoulders give way to that rarest of events: male emotion. A nurse pushed an old woman in a wheelchair down the corridor, her plastic IV bottle swinging from its metal arm. The nurse holding Reed had her transfixed by dangling a set of car keys. Outside it was a typical Southern California day, suffused with sunlight. Hank patted his father's shoulder. "Let's go," he said softly, and his father nodded.

Iris lay still on what had been her last earthly bed. Someone had thoughtfully removed her IVs. Her silver hair was loose against the pillow, and her lips were slightly parted. Henry sat down in the chair and took her hand. Hank took a long look at the two of them, trying to recall every good deed his parents had done. His father had read him *Treasure Island,* and his mother, when called upon, would energetically act out the voice of the parrot. He laughed to himself, remembering. He hoped that during all those vacations he had spent with his grandmother in Arizona, these two had enjoyed some kind of holiday from it all. How hard it must have been to drum up enthusiasm for one child when you had lost your first. Someday he would sit Reed down and explain that absolutely it wasn't fair, but it was a fact that grief caused people to do the strangest things. How in periods of profound sorrow, it sometimes made perfect sense to give up the most prolonged and sustaining happiness. That people clung to what they knew how to do, even if it hurt, because sometimes the fear of opening one's heart to further pain was paralyzing. Maybe Reed would comprehend a glimmer of the grandmother who was afraid to allow her last five months to be penetrated by the hope of this child continuing on without her. Maybe he would, too. Or not, and together they would find some way to shoulder the ache. For himself he looked harder, more selfishly, indulging a heart that could only cave in on itself now that something so fundamental and basic was ended. He kissed his mother good-bye on the lips, then left the room so his father could be alone with his wife.

The following day he booked his flight. Henry insisted he was fine, that there was nothing more he needed Hank to do here. Iris had stipulated cremation in her will, no funeral, asked that her ashes be distributed near the cabin, which made sense to Hank, since that was where she had scattered Annie's. Hank told his father, "There's no hurry. Give a call when you're ready. You can come out here, or if you'd rather, send them along and I can do it myself."

"I'll think about it."

"Well, then." Hank picked up their luggage and headed to the rental car.

His father followed him out the door. "Son? Can you spare me a moment?"

Hank set the luggage down, hoisted Reed on his hip. "Sure, Dad."

Henry senior reached into his pocket and handed over a passbook.

"What is this?"

"It was your mother's doing. I found it in with her things."

Hank thumbed open the blue cover. The balance was in the mid five figures, and the account had been issued in the name of Reed Morgan Oliver, with Hank Oliver listed as beneficiary. He shut the passbook and held it in his fingers. "I appreciate the gesture, Dad. It's lamentable our best communication always seems to be conducted through institutions. I hope we can work on changing that."

Henry looked away. "You'd better get along or you'll get stuck in traffic. Who knows? Maybe the next time you visit, they'll have converted El Toro into a commercial flight operation."

They made their connections, flew north in unremarkable weather, and now he was breathing Flagstaff's pine-scented air and strapping Reed into her car seat in the back of the Honda, its windows dusty from sitting in the long-term parking lot.

Hank drove north, passing the Big Tree swap meet, Mary's Café, the Horsemen's Lodge, the fledgling bait shops again starting to do a decent business now that fishing weather was upon them. There was the saloon Hannah had run away to. It was miraculous she hadn't been killed crossing the highway. He no longer experienced a sense of heart-stopping awe at the sight of the San Francisco peaks, or rage at the red rock being quarried out of hillsides in order to pave the roads. Things were the way they were, and that was all there was to it. Everything that had happened here had earned him the right to own those mountains. Likewise, he was part of the problem when it came to the road resurfacing. Coconino was his county. He was no longer a newcomer, but he wasn't so arrogant as to assume he would ever be called a local. His grandmother had given him a gift: Hank Oliver was a little boy who had returned to the place he loved as a child in order to grow into a man.

In Cameron he stopped at the post office to pick up the mail—in case Chloe hadn't had time to check it, he told himself, but he knew that was a stall tactic, delaying until the last possible moment the return to the cabin that might be empty. Their box was stuffed. Letter for Chloe from Kit, utility bills, circulars, that free paper with all the singles ads that suddenly didn't seem so amusing. From the bunch he extracted an envelope addressed to him. The return address was Pima Community College down in Tucson, which meant nothing. He'd continued sending out CVs, applying to anything remotely related to his old position, only to receive in abundance tellingly thin envelopes all saying no. *Hardly paid to waste the stamps*, he thought. He tucked it into his pocket to feel bad about later.

The usual smattering of tourist cars filled the lot of the Trading Post, as well as a couple of news vans. More Grand Canyon flooding business? Hank wondered as technicians lugged cables across the lot into the building. Please, let this be about artwork, not accidents, he prayed. Oscar Johnson came out the front door with a FedEx box in his hands, and Hank whistled to get his attention, then waved. Oscar set the box down and motioned with both hands for Hank to hurry over. Regretting his enthusiasm, Hank lifted Reed out of her car seat. He wasn't up to polite chatter when so much weighed on his mind, but Oscar was a good friend, and for a friend he could muster a smile.

"Hank, you the man," Oscar said excitedly. "Can't say you got excellent timing because these reporter dudes been camped out here two days annoying the crap out of Corrine, but there'll be dancing aplenty once I drag your butt inside. Come on, you got to get your picture took."

"I'm in the dark as to why anyone needs my photograph, Oscar, not to mention kind of tired. Can we do whatever this is another time?"

Oscar shook his head, grinning. "You didn't hear, did you?"

"I guess not."

"Hank, that New York time-zone girl did some story on your class, man. The deal with the rocks, you know?" He slapped his shoulder. "Freakin' *New York Times*, it's a newspaper. The phone's been ringing off the hook. Everybody in America wants to buy a 'Mysterious and Keepsake' rock to raise money for the library. Letters coming every day. They send checks. I ain't shitting you, man, they gonna want pictures. Now come on, let's go. I want to watch you smile for the camera."

"Really?"

"*Enit*, man."

Hank let himself be led inside. He could sense without actually knowing that here came the moment, the one that would return to him over and over in his life, hovering on the edge of dreams, intervening in stressful times when his faith wavered, this moment would step in to sustain him when Reed left home for college and he wasn't sure how he was going to let her go without falling apart himself. Its message was simple: The effort put forth in trying to do a good thing mattered a hell of a lot more than its aftermath, but sometimes, once or even twice if you were lucky, what you'd struggled for panned out, and even got noticed. He walked into the Post and heard the rush of voices, blinked at the flashing cameras, saw Walter "Dog" Johnson, former geek, son of the errant Junior

Whitebear, beam excitedly as he demonstrated the correct etching technique, then elbow Chuey Alberto, who was making faces for the camera, out of the way, notice him and stop and point. Like riding a horse in bad weather, when the wind and rain assault the back of your neck, things came about, and what had been cold and chased him was now as invigorating as clean rain against his face. The rush of energy directed itself Hank's way as Dog said, "That's him."

Chuey added, "Best *bilagáana* teacher in the whole of Ganado El, third grade. *My* teacher."

"*Our* teacher," Dog corrected him, and for a few seconds there it seemed that a fistfight might be in the making. If it happened, Hank was laying his money down on Dog Johnson.

There were questions to be answered, requests for interviews; checks and donations to be counted, acknowledged with thank-you letters; everyone speaking at once. Hank stood in the middle of it all remembering something his grandmother had once told him, when his terrarium full of precious lizards had bought the proverbial farm. *For everything you lose, for all that hurts, there is something equally important waiting to take its place.* Hank understood she was telling the truth, and he prayed that Ganado Elementary wouldn't gain its library if it meant he had to lose Chloe Morgan.

He saw her bags packed, sitting on the floor, waiting. She was on the phone.

"Why did you have to come back?" she was saying. "Why now, when I finally don't need you?"

He stood just out of her line of vision, listening to his worst fears being realized. Then her tack changed.

"I know. I want to see you, too," she was saying. "I want to belong to you. I'm just afraid. You'll have to be patient with me. There's a lot of things we need to work through."

Well, it wasn't unexpected. They were adults here, and if they put Reed first, somehow they would manage to get through this.

He stepped into the living room and stood before her. In his heart he knew Chloe was talking to Junior, finalizing plans. She had just been waiting to catch the baby and then she would be gone. Chloe's cheeks flushed the same way they colored after making love. She was barefoot. Under her sweatshirt she wasn't wearing any bra; her nipples were erect and poking at the fabric. Any other time he would have pressed his palm there, just gone ahead and claimed the pleasure. He didn't think he could force enough air into his lungs to speak. Surprised, caught off balance, she gestured to the receiver and motioned for him to wait. What else was he supposed to do?

Chloe swiped the tears from her eyes and looked at Reed and smiled. "You don't just have a daughter, Belle, you've got a grand-daughter, too. Listen, I'm going to have to call you back. Hank's home, and we need to talk."

She hung up the phone and made her way across the room a little unsteadily, scooping Reed out of his arms. "Look at you, you big girl. How on earth did you grow so much in only five days? Did you miss me? I sure missed you."

Hank arm's were empty, and the feeling was frightening. His head still spun from the encounter with the news crews. He shut his eyes and felt his mouth fill with salt. All he could tell for certain was that the room was filled with the distinct odor of horses.

Outside, Hannah was whining, scratching at the door, barking for attention. Chloe danced across the room holding her daughter, chattering in baby talk. With one hand she pulled the rocking chair away from the dog door, and Hannah came rushing in.

"I had to shut her out, Hank, she was driving me crazy."

Hank figured who in hell needed a dog around when you're try-ing to conduct a passionate liaison? *Had they done it in his very bed, for God's sake? Who was Belle?* "Why is that?"

"Because I was talking to my mother," Chloe said. "It's only our second conversation, and well, sometimes things get a little emo-tional, and I raise my voice, and you know how much Hannah likes me getting upset."

"Belle is your mother?"

Chloe nodded. She set Reed down on the couch and handed her the silver rattle. "As stories go, this is a long one. But it can keep while you come on over here and tell me everything that happened. I don't want you to leave anything out."

He set his luggage down next to hers, more uncertain now than ever, afraid to ask whether she was coming or going. In the kitchen he poured himself a glass of water and forced himself to drink it down. His throat felt sore again; he could feel his voice retreating. "My mother died the day before yesterday," he said. What else was there? "She opened a bank account for Reed a long time ago. Like a college fund. Do those suitcases mean you're leaving me for Junior Whitebear?"

Chloe looked up from their daughter. Her brown, guileless eyes regarded him with honesty and soreness. "Why on earth would you ask me that?"

The confession was unnecessary. Just by looking, Hank knew she had slept with him, and that somehow the act had cost her dearly. He knew it as well as he knew his own broken heart. He sighed. "I understand why you did it, Chloe, but I sure wish you hadn't."

"Hank, listen," she started to say, but he interrupted her.

"No, you listen to me. I've given this a lot of thought. The only way things will work is if you do what's right for you. Don't pity me, and don't lie. The only thing I ask is that you don't cut Reed out of my life. I'm telling you, Chloe, that I could not bear." He set the water glass down. "If it comes down to it, I'll fight you both for her. I swear I will."

She laughed, and the sound of it was jagged, bitter in her throat. "Well, isn't that just you and me all over the map? Hitch the cart before the horse, and dog-cuss the animal for not moving fast enough. Cut directly through the preliminaries. Sleep together on the first date, have a baby before we can decide to get married."

"It was never me having trouble with that last part."

"I know. I never intended to lie to you, Hank. I meant to tell you right away. I haven't got a clue what's going to happen. All I know is I love you, I'm here, and there isn't anywhere else I want to be at the moment, except maybe down in Patagonia visiting my mother, which is where I was planning to go when you got back."

"You love me?"

"Of course I do."

"You never said it before."

"I have trouble with words—it's one of my biggest failings. But you have to know I always meant it. I have a *mother*, Hank. Like you, I want her to meet Reed. She raises *horses*, can you beat that? I have a whole set of uncles and cousins, and they *want* to meet me, they're excited to meet me." She stopped a moment. "But I won't go anyplace while you need me here. I can go there any-time. Come tell me everything that happened. Lay down here on the couch next to me and I'll rub your shoulders. Or I can fix you something to eat if you're hungry. God knows we've got plenty of bread."

He knelt down by the couch and took hold of her, his hands roughly encircling her upper arms, holding on hard enough to leave bruises.

"Or we can put this baby to bed and shuffle down the hallway, if that's what you need."

"Of course that's what I need." He began to cry, pressing his face against her loose breasts. He could hear her heart beating. He inhaled the horse sweat and essence of woman beneath it. Her hair grew damp on the ends from his tears. He cried until he had poured out all the suspicion and anger and sorrow, just let it all spill out of himself and onto her.

Chloe stroked his hair away from his forehead and kissed his cheeks, cradling him to her breasts. "Belle's waited thirty-odd years, she can wait a few days longer."

"And Junior?" he managed. "How long can he wait?"

He felt her stiffen. "Well," she said, sighing. "You'd have to ask him that, and Junior's gone. He took off."

"Forever?"

"He told Corrine he'd be in touch in a month or so, to pick Dog up for the summer."

"I'm sorry."

"Don't be. I'm guessing he'll survive. We all will, somehow or other, if we can forgive each other. Right now Reed is looking awful damn sleepy to me. Doesn't she look tired to you?"

Hank looked up. Mouthing the end of the silver rattle, the baby regarded them both solemnly. "I don't know how much good I can be to you in the bedroom."

"Does that really matter, when you know how good I can be to you?"

She was right about that. Trouble was, Chloe's kind of magic was so rare as to be addicting, and such powerful stuff worked on more than one man. Nevertheless he let her take him to their bed, surrendered himself, beholden to whatever she had left to give him, believed her when she said again, "I love you," and he gratefully wrapped the words around his heart like an almighty bandage.

There are myths, and then there are miracles, Hank thought, watching the tail lights on the horse trailer ignite as Chloe braked to make the careful turn off the gravel onto the unpaved road. *You awaken one day dreading having to drive to work in the rain, and this wild horse goddess charges into your life, covered in blood, baring her breasts, dismantling any notion of armor you thought you possessed. So begins the quest. Up a tree, outside a courtroom, stranded on the edge of a past civilization. And just when you think you've beheaded every dragon, survived the cold, dark belly of the whale, she delivers you a daughter, a most wonderful headstrong daughter who looks nothing like you and possesses—if such a thing is possible—even more will than her mother. Soldier that you are, you adapt your battle plans. You cling to this vision of raising her right, life settling down to a reasonable roar, the two of you growing old together, getting comfortable in squeaky rockers on a country porch, then along comes a handsome Indian and the* New York Times *and a long-lost mother, and you realize you've behaved like the perfect fool: The quest never ended, the* journey never ends. *You were simply set off course by a temporary siren call that rewrote your itinerary. You spent your money in an all-too-comfortable port, and now it's time to put your back into work again. So how do you do that when you know perfectly well the only thing you can do is let her go? Well, I guess you believe in your heart there's enough purchase there for her, the horse and the dog to come back to. And maybe there is Reed, bending easily between you both, braiding your lives together like the weave on a basket.*

The truck and trailer were out of his sight now, the airborne dust from the tires still suspended in small clouds, taking its time settling back to earth. Hank walked around back of the cabin and shut the gate on the empty corral, fastening it to the fence post. He'd built this fence with his own two hands, and it was a steady, decent effort that would easily go several more winters.

Always the larger question persisted: Would there be a red Jeep Cherokee meeting her at the confluence of the highways, eager to shadow her down the state? For reasons he couldn't explain, Hank doubted it. He put his hands inside his jacket and felt the envelope from Tucson against his fingers. Maybe the best thing to do right now was crack open a beer, reread his letter, savor the offer one more time before he called to accept it. He would never forget the honor of being a third-grade teacher, and it would be difficult to leave the children, but in truth they were ready to move on without him. The academic world had invited him back. He would get chalk dust under his fingernails and learn how to play hardball with a new administration, but he would be in a college classroom, doing what he loved. He could feel the phantom imprint of Chloe's body against his own, last night, this morning, less than half an hour ago. He had gripped her flank so hard he'd left a handprint, five fingers and the edge of his palm, marking her like an Appaloosa. He loved her that much. The sweetness and the impermanence of lovemaking turned him inside out; he was grateful for all of it.

The last few days, anyway, it seemed Hank Oliver was very much in demand. He walked up the slight incline toward the cabin, his boots leaving only the vaguest impressions in the silky cinder pathway.

Part 4

Cameron, Arizona
Twenty Years Later

24

It's late November, but nobody's explained that to the town of Phoenix. Outside the Heard Museum the honeysuckle bushes buzz with bees, and an endless stream of tourists files into the courtyard. Often I stop here, the halfway mark on my way north to Cameron. Sometimes the only thing to do is return to the place you swore you were done with in order to comprehend its role in your future. Hopefully, by the time I get to the cabin, things will make sense and I'll know what to do.

I hand the clerk my pass, and like she thinks I brought it along to steal something, she insists on checking my backpack. The treasures here are so plentiful and varied they wouldn't even fit into God's knapsack. Baskets, clay pots, paintings, photographs, the few remaining beaded ceremonial dresses that don't decorate hotel lobbies or western airport terminals. Arizonans may deserve the reputation of conservative politics, but no one can say we underestimate the importance of art.

My father was the first one to take me here. Pour him a few beers, and Hank likes nothing better than to wax nostalgic about our expeditions. *The Fred Harvey railway exhibit, do you remember, Reed? Daddy, I was what, two?* But the kachina room made an impression. It gave me nightmares, until over and over again, Junior explained the stories surrounding each doll. And I was impressed with the Edward Curtis photo gallery, the portraits of defeated-looking chiefs posing in the crosshairs of the white man's camera. *Daddy?* I asked. *Where's Junior's picture?*

Poor Hank. But the man I think of as my second father (for lack of a specific term we call him my godfather) looks just as desolate as those conquered warriors. *Someday his picture will probably be here,* Daddy answered, and he was right. The Junior Whitebear collection has been on permanent loan since I was a teenager.

I've come to see the ring the Famous One is famous for. It's the Lander stone, and it once belonged to my mother. By birthright I could lay a claim to it, I suppose, but that reminds me of those spooky stories of the Hope diamond, guaranteed unhappiness. I carry a letter granting me permission to handle the pieces. Today I want to study the ring and think about the only story I've ever been denied: How my parents, all three of them, met, fell in love, and rather than working that out in a conventional way—one man loving one woman—decided the solution was to share a child between them.

There are three different stories, three versions, all lies, and every one of those lies, in its own way, is true. Some nights it's almost as if I can feel each of them depending on me, the daughter they love, to make sense of their messed-up lives, and then I feel terrible, because things have gotten a little more complicated than their old news. If I do what I think I'm going to, the flames won't just fan up, there will be wildfire in the dry brush, everywhere I step.

Reed, you walked at nine months, probably trying to get away from me, ha! No more sense to you than God gave a rabbit, but there you were, standing on your hind legs, streaking barefoot across the prairie, looking for trouble. Says Mama.

I remember you used to pat my beard and lay your cheek so carefully against my own, saying in your small voice, Everything be all right, Daddy, *and I always wondered if you were trying to reassure me or making a statement.* Daddy.

Atsi', *my daughter. Right away I could tell you and me were connected for life. I cut the cord, and it was like you unhooked from Chloe and latched on to me. Maybe I'm not the father who made you, Reed, but I'm the one you chose on your own,* enit? Junior, who I visited every month, as if they had worked out some bizarre custody arrangement. Hank drove me north on the excuse of having to tend to library business, or to see to our cabin. In the parking lot of the Cameron Outpost he'd kiss me good-bye, and there were Junior's arms, waiting to catch me. Since I didn't know any better, I thought nothing of having two fathers.

As I walk the staircase to the second floor of the museum, I'm thinking they kind of made up for Mama, who was at best prickly. We tried to forge a bond, but Junior and Hank nourished me in a way that she tried but never mastered. Growing up, all my friends were petrified of their fathers. Seeing the welts from their whippings astonished me. I thought guys like that got arrested. The two men who raised me allowed their children to grow into adults armed with consciences. Whenever I screwed up, one or the other sat me down and said, *Think about how this will affect your life ten years down the line. How what you did will impact on the world. If you can live with it, fine. If you can't, let's do something about it.*

How was I to know that wasn't normal? These precious men I took for granted. In my studies I've learned that the evolution of the species proceeds slowly and arduously, and nine out of ten mutations are destined to fail. Yet my fathers seem to have apprehended the larger clues. In my house we didn't need thirty-four states to ratify an amendment saying that women deserved equality. If I do one good, scientific thing for the world, it should be to have these men cloned and distributed, and pray that their tribes increase.

The same woman is always behind the special collections desk. Her name is Norma, and she has really ugly glasses connected to a beautifully beaded chain. Norma loves being in charge of the Junior Whitebear collection. She smiles when she sees me.

"Home for Thanksgiving, Reed?"

"On my way. College keeps me so busy I forget there are holidays until I look up and notice everyone's gone."

"I saw a spread on your father's new work last month in *Lapidary*. Stunning. Will you see him over the holiday?"

Norma can't help but ask any more than such a question would pierce Daddy's heart. I'm a genetic throwback to my maternal grandfather, who was Mexican, with skin so dark he caused Gran's father to chase them off the ranch when she turned up pregnant. This led to Mama being put up for adoption, a whole lot of sorrow, and me getting stuck with a face that looks nothing like Hank Oliver. In fact, I look so much like Junior Whitebear that everyone wants to believe I'm his blood. Him being so handsome, the stories behind the jewelry he made for Mama, people get caught up in what she calls the "soap opera" of his life. It makes Junior laugh, and Daddy's a good sport about it, but it bothers me that he sometimes gets lost in the shuffle. "Sure," I tell Norma. "I see Hank nearly every weekend. But if you mean Junior, not this year. I think he's in Asia."

Junior's no more in Asia than I'm standing on the moon, but I'm not about to reveal to anyone that he lives year-round in Chinlé, within walking distance of the most beautiful canyon in the world. Canyon de Chelly is our special place, and I don't want that violated. The Famous One insists that living close to the canyon is good for his heart. He lives in a two-room cabin heated by a wood stove. I tease him and call that kind of thinking his hair-shirt philosophy. His oversized mailbox bears the generic name of J. White. Though it's human nature to ache to spill them, there are some secrets you can keep. A long time ago, everyone made an agreement that no matter how the rumors flew, they'd keep silent. It was unspoken but assumed that their children would do the same. But lately I'm discovering that kept secrets never stop burning. There's a hole in my heart I feel widening. Pretty soon it won't be able to contain all I've discovered. Everything will fall out, and we'll have no choice but to deal with it.

With the opportunity for gossip gone, Norma lets the subject of Junior drop. She answers the phone and shuffles her deskful of papers, and I stand there waiting patiently for the keys. Mama gets distracted like that when she senses that a mare's going to drop her baby. During foaling season, the world could be on fire and you simply cannot get through to my mother. She paces around the house, puts dirty dishes into the cupboard and I have to repeat whatever I say to her twice. Finally she goes off to sleep in the barn. Daddy checks on her, but even he knows better than trying to talk her into coming inside to bed. And when she's called away to somebody else's ranch, until she returns it's Daddy who does the pacing.

This one time she'd been gone a week, supposedly tending some rich guy's broodmares, but I knew where she was. It was as if she could only last so long, then like one of her prize mares descended from old Sally Ride, she'd jump the fence and go to Junior. She'd stay away from us for as long as it took to run her heart good and tired, and return home armed with gifts that were supposed to fool us into believing her absence was due to some ardent shopping gene. All during my teenage years I hated her for doing that. If she said my hair looked pretty long, I cut it two inches from my skull. When I took six firsts in English Equitation classes and saw her applauding in the bleachers I traded every bit of my tack for a Western barrel-racing saddle. My father took the more practical approach, and had her truck painted red. Mama took one look at the Apache and said all that paint would have to be sanded off; Chevy never issued that year truck in red. Daddy didn't bat an eye, and the color has faded very little over the years. It was a long time before she pulled an overnighter again, but eventually she resumed her pattern. Even Gran said it was nuts to try to stop her, that planets never vary in their orbit, even if it means they'll get bombarded by meteors.

Tonight, while twilight scribbles that orange crayon across the winter sky, Norma will be sitting at home, petting some old tabby cat. She'll haul out her Junior Whitebear fantasy and imagine herself in the position my mother will always be in. She'll think: *Lucky Chloe*, while the truth is that a muse that can move the artist to genius lives her life like a unicorn on a chain. My mother loved two men, and gave up half her heart in the process.

Next month I'll turn twenty-one. I want to go to medical school; I've got the grades. Discovering the art that lives inside the body, and ways to coax it into a state of balance, thrills me. But I'm in love with a man, a painter, and it's a love so dangerous and all-encompassing I can't imagine ever balancing it with something as consuming as medical school. I know what the practical thing is to do and I know what I secretly desire, and they are not even remotely the same pathways.

You've got smarts and a family that loves you. You can be anything you want. Brain surgeon pays a lot better than barmaid. Says Mama.

There's all the time in the world for you, Reed. Maybe you should spend the summer in Europe, expose yourself to other cultures. Daddy's always talking up travel.

Whatever you do, be careful of love, Reed. Don't take it too lightly. Once your heart gets locked up it never finds its final destination. Aunt Kit, who ought to know after two colossally bad marriages. Following her latest divorce, she moved in permanently with Gran, and took over some of the harder chores on the ranch. *This is where I belong,* she told me, *within the confines of my adopted tribe. When it comes to men, I have terrific luck with horses.*

For reasons that will become obvious, I can't tell Junior, who took care of Corrine the whole time her diabetes was out of control, who didn't have to stay with her when she died, but did anyway, right until she took her last breath. Dog said that long ago, his father made him a promise. Junior keeps his promises.

"Reed, honey. I'm sorry that took me so long."

Norma hangs up the phone and unlocks the drawer of a waist-high flat file and oh! my heart feels sore to look. On one hand, it is only a drawer lined with purple velvet, filled with odd pieces of silver someone has shaped into decorations for the body. I can name the properties of precious metals. I know the temperature it takes to melt silver, over a thousand degrees. I can even go so far as to call this art, but I have to acknowledge that what we have here are the products of a man's broken heart. Spiny oyster, spiderweb turquoise, tumbled stones so common they once sold in bins inside gas stations along old Route 66. Now they're so scarce they have become icons of the past, which always, always looks simpler than the present. Of course, to someone whose whole childhood held three adults' lives together, that idea smells like bullshit. The past is complicated and mysterious, and adults speak less of the truth than children. We who want to know are reduced to studying the clues they've left behind: photographs, letters, jewelry.

The year I was fourteen, I came across some of my mother's clothing in his cabin. Junior had always kept things like that hidden from me, but the faded flannel shirt, the blue jeans worn to the color of surf, and a fairly new bra, size 34B, were real. I held them in my hand and railed, *You're fifty-two years old, for God's sake, hasn't this gone on long enough?*

At great expense he explained to me how the year I was born he learned that his blood had betrayed him, that he had to reinvent a self he could live with. That if it wasn't for loving my mother, he couldn't have made it through that year. He took me by the wrists and pulled me into his workroom, stood me in front of the silver and said, *All this is the byproduct of your mother's love. She sustains me, keeps my heart beating, even if we only get to be together every couple of months. It's like the wax that is lost in the casting of a ring, Reed. Together Chloe and I make something that can't become real until it burns away. What's born is larger than two people going to bed. We made a choice. Your father understands that. Someday you will, too.*

But I was so angry. I just wanted them to behave. At fourteen you know it all, and you can't wait to explain this to the people you love. Make life all tidy, give it identifiable corners. Still, I understood what a secret it was for Junior to carry. We avoided each other a few days, then we rode horses down into the canyon, and the sheer rock walls made me speak up. *I love you*, I said, *no matter what the hell kind of blood you come from. We're all enrolled members of the tribe of human beings. Yes*, he answered, *but eventually you will learn that not even love patches every hole.*

Whatever my mother did for him, Junior Whitebear's breaking down to his simplest self led to this ring. Scholars in the art world call the Lander piece *The Phoenix*. The silver shines the way it must have the day he finished it. As radiant as sun rising from the ashes of the previous evening. There's a story that if you slip your finger into this ring, your life will change so fundamentally that you can never go back to where you stood before. I pick it up, the cold metal warming quickly to the heat of my body temperature. The heavy ring is formed of two wings, one of them proudly tucked against the arc, the other one obviously broken, folding its sore feathers as best it can. In between the wings nests that slate-blue piece of turquoise, cradled like a precious egg. I slip it on my finger and the metal seems to grow hot. But this is a fraction of the heat he had to employ to make it, and that heat is but a microscopic portion of what he must have felt—still feels—for my mother, and oh, what I feel is too hot and huge for a girl of twenty to fully comprehend. That speckled, webbed, dusky blue stone settles in my heart. Now, the next time it rains, that color will rise in my throat like a plug of lead. I'll get a crying fit, and Mama will say, "It's your period, isn't it?" Never knowing how close she is to the truth. I slip the ring off, return it to its velvet bed, slide the noiseless drawer shut. Wanting to possess what was intended for someone else is behaving like a crow, anxious to steal what might perk up her drab nest. If there's going to be a nest, I'll have to decorate it in my own way. Besides, that ring doesn't have to be on my mother's finger to bind us together. I wave good-bye to Norma and think to myself, someday I should really tell her about those glasses.

Walking down the museum stairs, heading back toward my car, I check my watch and calculate the amount of daylight left. If Mama knew what I was contemplating, she would suggest we go for a twenty-mile ride, or get out hammers and say between the two of us, there's no good reason we can't mend a mile of new fence before supper. Or she'd pick up the phone and warn the folks at Paul Bond's we were on our way, our wallets loaded: Lay out the ostrich skin and the patent leather, my baby needs new boots. After all her antics failed to move me, she'd send me in to talk to Daddy and go off in her precious truck to sulk.

And Daddy would patiently remind me that at age two, I was praised for every step I took, while my mother was left at a children's home to basically rot. That her skittishness and distance have a logical evolution. That maybe I didn't get a PTA mother and he didn't get a faculty wife, but we both got something pretty wonderful anyway. *I accept her for what she is,* he'd tell me. *I lose myself in loving the part of her she feels safe enough to give me. Forgive everything else, because you never know when you might find yourself in a similar position.* And that if what I'm planning to do is what I need to do to be happy, then so be it; here he and Junior would be in perfect agreement.

I stop to look at the Curtis photo, *Cañón de Chelly,* those seven people on horseback, one dog alongside them as they make their way into or out of the canyon, it's hard to tell. Over the years it's occurred to me there's room for everyone in this picture: Mama, Daddy, Junior, Me, Dog, Uncle Oscar and Auntie Kit. Only Corrine is missing; but it's like she chose to work that day, not like she's dead. Mama's old dog Hannah is along for the ride, or it could be Harmony, Junior's wolf-dog. Whoever those people are, that ride happened once, and to me it's become a symbol. I lie awake at night and think: If only it could happen that way again.

I aim my car north, toward the higher elevations, toward home. The love songs on the radio start to repeat themselves, so I shut it off. The closer I get to the cabin, the more silence feels mandatory. Here I am, driving the same roads my mother took when she came to my father, pregnant with me. We have more than this route in common: We both love horses more than ourselves, we cuss too much, but thankfully the men in our lives manage to find that charming. We are headstrong and blunt, and our hearts take no prisoners. She's as fair as I am dark, and in profile we look more like sisters than mother and daughter.

I pull the car around behind the corral my father built and park. There's the barn where Thunder, my mother's stud horse, used to live. He's retired; some of his colts have offspring of their own. This seems like such a small place to me now. I get out of the car and stand facing the winter prairie, and find myself dressed inadequately and shivering. Here I am again, in the first place I ever called home.

There's no snow yet, but in the wind I can feel it coming. Northern Arizona's November skies are bright but cold. Soon it will be dusk, my favorite time of day. For years, whenever my father was on summer break from teaching, we came here. I learned to ride along the cinder trails, where if you fell, the ground beneath was forgiving. With my bare hands I caught horned toads and watched the females, wide as dinner plates, give birth to babies no longer than the tip of my little finger. I was five years old when Hannah died, and here is where she's buried. Aunt Kit dug the hole with that old chipped shovel, and Mama just stood there leaning against the fence, stone-faced and inconsolable. Across this same prairie, I rode piggyback on Dog Johnson's shoulders while he showed me where to look for pot sherds and arrowheads. From the fence rail I argued with him that I was so old enough to rope cattle while he practiced for team-roping competitions. Then the summer I turned twelve Daddy rented the place to Dog on a permanent basis, and we didn't come here anymore. I spent summers with Gran.

She taught me to shoe horses, irrigate abscesses, and when the calls came, to pull foals alongside my mother. On her mantel my grandmother has this picture of Mama on an old Shetland pony. It was taken back in the days when photographers shot and developed black-and-white film, then colored in the picture with paints to personalize it. This was so far before computers it's hard to imagine. It always startles me, since he painted Mama with blue eyes and like mine, hers are brown. Around her neck there's this ragged red bandanna. She can't be more than two, but you can tell by the way she holds the reins she knows she's headed for a rough time. Gran says she keeps it there to remind her of what she lost by not following her own heart. She tells me if I look closely, I can see all the reasons my mother is a difficult person right there in the photograph.

My grandmother gets up before sunrise every day of her life to make bread. She stands at the counter and kneads dough into a grainy, round loaf like it is her holy occupation. Her reputation for raising even-tempered, healthy horses is renowned. Even in her seventies she has these old mooning cowboys sniffing around. They show up, hat in hand, stammering about the weather, complimenting her latest batch of colts. They're praying she'll agree to let them buy her supper, but any one of them would give up his teeth if she'd marry him. She told me if I get married she won't wear a skirt to my wedding, so don't invite her if there's a dress code. But if she pulls on her cleanest blue jeans, and ties her long, silver hair back with a blue ribbon, I'll know that means something. Gran's no great beauty, but there's a presence about her that makes even young men trip over their own feet. When I tell her she's pretty, she laughs. *Nieta,* she says. *Women are supposed to get old; wrinkles are part of the deal. If God wanted us to look like underwear models he'd have outfitted us with permanent tanks of estrogen.* Her hands are wider and rougher than either of my fathers'.

Last month, on the sly, I drove down to Three Sisters and told her my problem. She listened as I explained how none of the alternatives I'd come up with were satisfying. I could take the easy way out, and no one but my own sore heart would be the wiser. But I wasn't sure if I believed in that. Yet if I did what my heart was telling me to do—*whew!* Gran took me outside under Patagonia's night sky lit up like one of Junior's pins and told me:

Chachita, whatever decision you make has to be your own. How else you going to live with it? Make sure you can, Reed, because at crossroads like these, regrets can dog you forever. Believe it or not, your mother under-stands this. It's my fault she's the way she is, you know. She's only doing what she thinks is best for her heart. Rather than judge her for that, try looking inside your own and listening to what it's telling you.

Okay. The truth of it is, I have always loved Dog Johnson, in one way or another, and a year ago, we decided to stop pretending that our "brotherly" love hadn't grown legs, turned romantic. For the last eight months we've been racing up and down the interstate on weekends to each other, seeking out secret places to make love without the specter of our parents' entanglement dismissing our courage. And though we knew better and took steps to prevent it, now I'm going to have his baby, though there are pills just for the asking to make that go away. After the shock of it left me, I thought, *Whoa.* Gran, Mama, and now me—it's starting to seem like this kind of thing runs in my family. But the baby's only a small part of what's happening, and when I stop and think about it, really, the baby is the easy part. When Dog and I announce we're getting married, sooner or later Daddy, Mama, and Junior will end up in the same room, and all this thwarted passion and phony denial will be thrust into the fray. Dog says, *What the hell, none of 'em's ever had a moment's peace over it anyhow, so maybe we're doing them a favor.* Dog's probably right.

I hear the back door to the cabin creak open and close, and feel his arms come up over my shoulders, blocking the wind. He presses his face against my neck. I would know these strong hands anywhere. I turn around to face him. Norma gasps whenever she sees him; he looks so much like his father. His sweatshirt is covered with paint. He's so distracted when he's at the easel. I touch a stripe of vivid purple. It's wet, which means the back of my jacket is ruined. He says something to me, but I am so lost in trying to understand the story of my parents, in coming to recognize my part in all of this, in finally hearing Gran's words, that I don't catch it. Maybe my mother really had no choice but to love both men the best she could. Maybe I know nothing at all about the subject except that I need this man as much as I need to breathe.

"Nila," Dog says again.

It's up to me.

I throw myself into his arms and we kiss, two mixed-blood survivors, the baby I'm growing still a secret between us. Gran knows; she's probably knitting booties. Eventually she'll spill to Aunt Kit, who will get all territorial and talk Mama into forgiving me, and Daddy and Junior will both probably stand there and cry, because there are certainly worse things their children could have done than love each other and make a baby.

Dog presses a paint-stained hand against my belly, and there's enough pigment embedded in his fingers that it leaves a faint, hand-shaped mark. Now at least my blouse matches my jacket. I think, *Is it crazy of me to imagine my parents' story unfolding this way? Isn't this is how love happens? Stepping blindly into a future woven together of many threads larger than what we feel with our fingers?* It's the one continuous, ever-changing basket nobody owns save those who are holding on to its edges. Maybe love can be thwarted, but it makes its presence known, in other, more telling ways.

Dog takes my chin in his hands, and with his eyes he's asking me for reassurance. *Reed, are you sure can we do this?* And I look back into his eyes to answer, *Yes, of course,* because somewhere, buried deep in my genes and his, there has to be courage enough, just once, to follow along with what life bestows upon you.

Besides, I say to the baby growing inside me, *you're already here, aren't you? Between us, in the first place you'll ever call home. And it's winter, nearly dusk, which will become your favorite time of day, and if you listen closely, you can hear it, the sound of your parents' hearts beating, so fast, believing all it takes to sustain you is their love. . . .*